CAT'S EYES

ISBN: 978-1-7336587-1-3

Contents

Prologue

Well, apparently I've done it again. I've made the Council of Five and more than a few other vampires extremely nervous. To be honest, I do take a certain amount of satisfaction, if not downright glee, in that. I know, I know, I'm horrible!

Amon's not exactly pleased that I've written this book about our, um, well, 'life' isn't really the correct word, but existence sounds so clinical, and exploits is just too 'superhero'. Vampires are, by their very nature, a secretive lot and they guard the truth of their existence jealously. So, I walk the razor's edge. No big deal. I've done it before. Oh sure, I've changed names to protect the innocent. I've rearranged details to cloak verifiable facts. My beloved Warrior has read what you're about to read, and though some colorful French expletives did escape his lips, he has approved it.

I'm Catherine Alexander-Blair du Montjean and I am Vampire. There, I said it! And yes, it still feels weird to say it, type it, and even think it. My mate is Master Vampire Amon du Montjean, and yes, that feels weird too. Our world is one of exotic, mysterious beings and abilities, and machinations that would make Machiavelli's heart swell with pride. I've found that things are rarely as they appear in this world and are usually much more than I imagine. So I'm learning the ropes, I guess. At least, I'm still kickin', if not alive. One would think that being dead, more precisely undead, would be easy, a proverbial 'walk in the park'. It's not! On the other hand, a simple gesture instinctively offered can bring incredible rewards. Who knew, right?

It's been a few years since I became Vampire and, I must admit, it's not been an easy adjustment to make. Conforming does not come naturally to me and the rules and laws vampires are governed by do not sit well with me. Oh, I grasp why it's dangerous to be too forthright when it comes to sharing stories, but then again, that just makes the challenge all the more fun!

My beloved mate is, even now, observing me with hunger in those magnificent blood red eyes of his.

'*Stop that!*' Peering over the top of my glasses I shoot him a look of warning. '*I'm busy.*'

The slightest hint of a smile plays along his lips.

'*Stop it! I'm working!*' Our telepathic communication makes speech unnecessary.

Opening his mouth slightly, he slowly runs the tip of his tongue along those oh so sharp teeth.

'Don't stop!'

That's it! His hunger has stirred my own. My concentration's shattered. Please read on. I've something to attend.

Chapter 1

Lightning split the night sky and the wind whipped my hair into my face as I stepped out the back door of Lamey's Night Club. Humidity and heat in the air spoke of a tempestuous night ahead. Now that I was alone, I could safely remove my dark glasses and let my eyes adjust to the night. Having white irises was, I had discovered, very inconvenient and even though I covered them with green or brown contacts the white was so intense that they remained unnatural looking, which is why I usually wore glasses in public.

The crowd had been great, I had to admit, considering it was not only Thursday night, but also less than a week since New Year's Eve. The other members of 'Unseelie', the band I'd joined upon my return to performing, had already scattered to the wind. Duncan and Josh, drummer and bass, respectively, were currently enjoying of the perks of being handsome, hot, and talented, and had left escorting two tipsy, starry-eyed, adoring fans. Susan, second lead singer and guitarist, had a toddler and a babysitter awaiting her return home so she'd left the club while the rest of us were still putting our things away and watching the employees turn up the house lights to clean the place. Boone, lead singer and guitarist, and John, keyboardist, had loaded the band's gear into the van, enjoyed a complimentary drink at the bar, and then departed. They shared an apartment on the north side of Beaumont so they had some miles to turn before they could sleep.

Tucking my violin beneath my arm, I fished my keys out of the front pocket of my jeans as I made my way across the vapor light splattered parking lot. As I reached my Miata and pressed the "unlock" button on my keychain, I paused to look back at the club. A few employees' vehicles were most all that was left of the crowd of cars that had filled the yellow striped tarmac. Thunder rolling overhead and wind swirling around couldn't distract me from recalling another night club, another parking lot, and another lifetime that had led me here. It had been a very similar place, a dark lot with circles of light from overhead vapors, in which I'd been assaulted and left for dead. Nearly four years had passed since Sin, Master Vampire whom I eventually came to know as Amon, had rescued me and saved my life. Only the fact that he'd made me Vampire and his mate enabled me to return to my love of performing in small venues such as Lamey's. I was now, he admitted begrudgingly, somewhat able to defend myself, and though I still missed my first band, 'Hunter's Moon', I was enjoying 'Unseelie' tremendously. Shaking foolish thoughts from my head, I opened the car door, tossed my stage clothes bag in, and slipped into the driver's seat. I placed my violin case gently in the passenger's seat and strapped it into the special harness my beloved Amon had specially designed and created for me. There had been simply no safe place for my instrument to ride, given the way I drive, apparently I'd inherited my grandmother's lead foot and couldn't help but drive fast and hard, and I had often complained of it slewing this way and that around the seat and floorboard. My mate had grown tired of listening to me whine about my lack of storage in the Miata and had taken care of the matter as only he would.

As I started the engine and eased into reverse, I flipped on the headlights. Though I had no need of them, it was technically illegal to drive at night without, so I had to put my glasses back on to tone down the glare of the lights. As I turned left out of the parking lot and headed down the street, I started to turn on the radio.

Cat, my beloved! Are you on your way home?

Use the cell phone, Amon. That's why we got them!

Slamming down my mental shields I smiled and waited patiently for my cell phone to ring. Though Amon preferred to stay in contact via this strange telepathy we shared, it provided him with a bit too much access to my mind. I was much more comfortable using a cell phone as my thoughts were just as likely to get me into trouble as my words or deeds.

The cell phone did at last ring its annoyingly cheerful tune and I laughed out loud because I knew that Amon had to go fishing around his desk for the number. I was trying to keep him humble.

"Hello," I chirped as the lights on my cell phone nearly blinded me.

"Cat, why do you insist on this" he paused in frustration, "contraption?"

"I just like it when you call me," I laughed. "I am on my way home, so why'd you call? What's up?" Even though my mental shields were secure and our conversation was filtered through these compact devices, I could feel his energy running across my cheek and down my arm. It was a lover's caress that I knew so well and cherished, but I was tired and knew that I could be easily distracted so I ignored the sensations and focused on his words.

"You have received an urgent call from your agent, of whom I still do not entirely approve. It seems he is intent on reaching you immediately and you are to return his call at once. Would you like the number?"

"Tell me that you didn't talk to Doug yourself," I cringed at the mental image.

"Of course not, Little One," he replied succinctly, then added, "Lily took the call and gave me the message to give to you. As unaccustomed as I am to being your secretary, it seemed little exertion on my part to inform you of the matter, as I had planned on checking on your whereabouts at any rate."

Lily was Amon's maid and the closest thing I had to a gal pal, though she was not entirely informed of the 'unnatural' aspects of the life Amon and I, as well as many others at the Montjean estate and in our social circles, led. As such, she made a very handy liaison for those issues I still dealt with in the mortal world. I was relieved that it was she who had spoken with my agent.

"Hold on while I find a place to pull over," I mumbled, dropped the phone and wheeled into an empty church parking lot. "Hang on baby, I dropped the phone and I'm getting a pen and paper!" Squealing the brakes, I slammed the gearshift into park and took my foot off the pedal. Fishing through the depths of my bag, I found a pen and the back of a date book the bank had given me. I retrieved the open phone from the floor and put it back to my ear. "Go ahead, shoot," I nodded as if he could see me from the other end of the line.

As Amon recited the number I wondered what my agent wanted with me. It had been roughly two years since I published anything. In fact, I hadn't written or even thought much about writing since that time. Perhaps my book had gone into its second publishing, I laughed aloud at the thought.

"Cat, what is it?" Amon asked with audible concern, "What is amusing?"

"Nothing Amon, just a silly notion. I do still get those occasionally, you know?"

"Indeed," he sighed, "I am well aware of your notions. Please beloved, make your call and then hurry home. There is unrest in the air and it is not just the approaching storm."

"Yes, well, this weather's got nothing on me," I laughed. "I'll be there ASAP." I hung up knowing how my use of acronyms annoyed him.

Cat, you need to feed. I can feel your energy ebbing as I do my own when I have not fed.

Amon, get out of my head. I told you that I'll be there as soon as possible. I'm fine!

You are not fine, Passion. You grow weak even as you protest your strength. Make haste, the night is waning!

Smacking my forehead with the palm of my hand, I chastised myself for dropping my mental shields again. Maybe it was the distraction of the call or maybe Amon was right, maybe I was getting weak. My vampire metabolism wasn't wholly the same as Amon's due to my powers as a witch and possibly due to having been mortal such a short time ago, and I was still learning all the subtleties of its demands.

Punching the numbers into the keypad of my cell phone, I was nearly blinded by the glowing numbers and squinted to make sure the number was the one Amon had given me. So focused on the phone was I that when someone knocked on the driver's side window of my car I yelped and almost dropped the darned thing. In fact, I nearly leapt out of my seat. With the glare from the phone still in my eyes and the sheen of the rain that had just begun on the glass I could make out only the vague outline of a person. Rolling down the window a bit I smiled at the stranger.

"Can I help you?" I had to practically yell over the sound of the wind and increasing rain.

"You can't park here," a shrill female voice informed me and I saw her bony fingers pointing at the church across the parking lot. "This is Church property. You can't park here!"

I actually heard the capitalization when she said Church. '*Another fruitcake zealot,*' I thought, then shushed the notion.

"I'm not parking, Ma'am," I smiled as sweetly as possible into the darkness. "I only pulled in here to make a phone call, an emergency phone call, and then I'll be on my way. I didn't mean to trespass."

The woman seemed to consider my words for a moment as she pulled the hood of her rain slicker forward to protect her face. As she moved nearer the car, I felt an energy radiating from her that was at once heat and also icy cold. Her pungent odor wafted to me as I involuntarily drew back and grimaced. When she leaned over into the open window I could see her face clearly for the first time and what I saw made me lurch backwards in my seat. The notion that I might be able to just reach the handgun that I kept beneath the seat danced quickly through my mind but I froze rather than attempt the maneuver.

"You make your call then," she hissed, "and you go."

With that she turned and shambled away, the image of her horribly deformed and distorted face forever burned into my memory. After a few moments of composing myself, I checked the numbers on my cell phone once more then hit the "call" button. After two rings the phone was answered.

"Titan Literary Agency, Mr. Donahue's office," a female voice informed me.

"Yes, this is Cat Alexander-Blair returning Mr. Donahue's call," I replied. "I'm sorry for the hour, but I just got the message and was told it was urgent that I get back to him."

"Yes, Ms. Blair, Mr. Donahue's been expecting your call. I'll connect you."

The service operator was so fast that I didn't have the opportunity to correct her mistakenly calling me Ms. Blair. I was Ms. Alexander-Blair and Amon even wanted me to go by Montjean, his surname, though I wasn't yet ready for that. I wondered if Donahue was actually in his office or if the operator was putting the call through to his comfy high rise condominium in Dallas.

"Cat," Doug Donahue's booming voice filled my ear, "I'm so glad you got back to me so fast. I have wonderful news. Are you sitting down?"

"Doug," I sighed at his exuberance, "I'm in my car. I have no choice but to be sitting down. What's the news?"

"There has been some unusual interest in your book lately," he gushed. "In fact, so much that it's been suggested that you write another. A certain publishing house is offering a huge advance and a sweet contract deal. Baby, you can be rich!"

"Wait a minute, Donahue," I shook my head and rubbed my brow, as if that would clear things up, "what kind of unusual interest? And what kind of book am I supposed to be writing?"

"Sales have suddenly picked up across the entire country. This publisher wants another vampire story," he practically giggled. "They'd like a sequel to "Cat's Tale". Don't you love the idea?"

"Doug, I don't know," I sighed. "I don't know if I have any desire to write another book."

"Oh come on, Cat, I know you do," he pleaded. "It can be a 'further exploits' type thing. You know, your fans would love to learn what becomes of your heroine and her vampire friends."

That statement hit a clinker in my head and I had to interrupt him.

"Donahue, let me think about this okay? I don't care what kind of deal I'm being offered. I didn't write "Cat's Tale" just for the money and that wouldn't be reason enough for me to write another. Let me sleep on the idea, okay? It's very late, in fact it's so late it's early, and I've got to be getting home. How about I think about it and let you know in a day or two?"

"Twenty-four hours, Cat," he interjected. "That's all the time you have to make up your mind. I don't know why, but that's all you're being given."

"Being given?" I chuckled at the phrase. "Who is this publisher or what's the name of the publishing house?

And where do they get off giving me, or any author, twenty-four hours to accept a contract to write a book?"

"Don't shoot me, Kitten," Doug teased, "I'm only the messenger. The publishing house is called Dark Hours and I guess they can make whatever offers and demands they choose at this point. They contacted me, which as you know is nearly unheard of in this business."

"Dark Hours?" I grimaced as I tried to write the name onto the back of the date book using the sculpted surface of the dashboard for support. "I've never heard of them. And you know I hate it when you call me Kitten, Donahue!"

"I've never actually had any authors published through Dark Hours," I could almost hear a shrug in his voice, "but a couple of other agents in the firm have and they tell me that the house is a dream to work with. They treat their authors like royalty, have an excellent marketing department, everything's top of the line."

"Why me, Doug?" I could barely get the question out over the din of alarm bells going off in my mind.

"I was told that though they normally specialize in non-fiction and reference material they're looking to expand into the fiction market," he explained, "and they're looking for authors with some experience to groom into…"

"Cash cows?" I rudely finished his sentence then laughed at the notion of me being groomed for anything.

"Sorry Cat," he chuckled, clearly indicating that he was not sorry at all. "Again, don't shoot the messenger!"

"Fine," I said in exasperation, "I'll call you back within twenty-four hours with my answer. Good night, Donahue,"

Snapping the phone off, I tossed it into the bag and relaxed back in the seat. It made no sense that I was only being given such a short time to accept the publisher's offer. Who had ever heard of such a deadline, practically an ultimatum? Rubbing my brow, I took a deep calming breath and had one hand on the ignition when another rap on the window made me scream in alarm.

Again, a shadowy figure stood beside the driver's side door, but this time there was something familiar about the form. Rolling down the window and letting the rain in once more I squinted into the wind.

"Winter, what are you doing here?" I smiled in spite of myself. Just seeing his beautifully formed face, that long curly blond hair, and those golden eyes of his, always made me smile, whether I wanted to or not.

"His Lordship sent me to fetch you," he answered as he bent down to peer into the car. "He wants you home now."

"Winter, you're getting soaked, and getting me wet too," I complained. "Get in the car now." I leaned across the passenger seat and lifted the door handle while releasing the straps that held my violin in place. As my current friend and former protector, Winter was also one of my creatures, as I had been given dominion over the owls and his shapeshifting form was a snowy owl. Amon seemed to still consider Winter my body guard, though I didn't feel I had any need of protection, and often had him following me or collecting me. It had been one of those annoying habits of my mate's that I could not seem to break and right now it was making me seethe.

As Winter folded himself into the tiny passenger seat, I handed him my violin case to hold. If his legs hadn't been so long he could have held it across his lap, but his knees were nearly up to his chin in the tiny vehicle so he had to improvise. He held the case upright on the floor between his booted feet and steadied it with his calves. Wiping the rain from his face, he grinned and turned to face me.

"Cat, seriously, His Lordship wants you home," he explained. "We should fly."

"Winter, I've told you before," I retorted, "I've never flown with you and I'm certainly not going to do so for the first time in this weather." Flying with a vampire, I had discovered, could be a wonderfully freeing and exciting thing, but it could also be uncomfortable and very disconcerting. I had only ever flown with Amon and once with his guard and pack member, Chimaera. The journey with Chimaera had made me wary of flying with just anyone. And though theoretically, now that I was vampire myself, I should be capable of flying solo, I had never attempted it and had no plans to do so. I wasn't ready to embrace that aspect of being, well, undead.

"You're a weather witch, you could move the storm or disperse it, chère," Winter suggested.

"You know I don't like to do that unless it's unavoidable," I reminded him. "It isn't fair to people who have no control over the weather. And besides, I fail to see that this situation would warrant such a feat."

His golden eyes radiant with that hyper beauty of vampire, Winter looked at me with a sober expression. His flaxen tresses, I noticed, were nearly dry already. Another perk of being supernatural, the elements did not affect him as they do mere mortals.

"Something strange is going on, 'tite souer," he sighed. "I don't know what but something's up. His Lordship is being called to a meeting with…" his nose wrinkled comically and he grimaced. "What is that smell in this car?" He covered his nose with his hand.

"Oh that," I laughed. "A rancid little old lady nearly called the cops on me for parking in the church parking lot. When I rolled down the window to see what she wanted, her stench kind of swam right out of the night and into my car." Though I expected him to join me in my little joke, he only looked at me and rolled down his window.

"Cat, for Goddess sake," he gasped into the fresh air for affect. Though capable of detecting scent, he had no real need to breathe, "Did you not realize that is the smell of corruption? That odor is not human. Didn't you realize that?" He looked at me incredulously.

"Um, well, no," I admitted. "I really hadn't thought about it. I was intent on making my phone call so I could get home. The old lady left so I didn't think anything more about her."

"Tell me, Cat," he took my left hand in his and looked at it closely, even lovingly, "did your Healing Hand tingle or burn? Did it react in any way?"

"Well," I thought back over the incident, "no, now that you mention it, it didn't and that was strange because she was horribly disfigured. My hand should have made me want to heal her, shouldn't it?" Having been gifted by the Goddesses and Gods with the ability to cure sickness, mend bone, and heal flesh, I had learned that whenever I was around such afflictions my Healing Hand ached to serve, physically burned to do its thing. The fact that it hadn't so much as tingled should have set off alarms in my mind, but I'd been so distracted.

"Cat," Winter shook his head in something like exasperation, "whatever it was that confronted you and smelled like this, it was not human. And the fact that your hand didn't stir would seem to mean to me, at least, that it never had been human. I don't like this, something is not right. We really need to get back to estate. His Lordship will want to know of this immediately."

"Fine," I nodded, "put on your seatbelt. We're going home."

Starting the car, I was throwing the gearshift into reverse before Winter could launch a protest. He scrambled to get into his seatbelt, though being vampire and immortal, a car wreck would not be the end for him were I to drive my car up a pole. However, he worried about me constantly and habitually, and I knew I'd be getting an earful all the way back home. Lamey's was on the outskirts of the West End of Houston and since the estate was close to Lake Charles, Louisiana, it would take some time to get home. In fact, thanks to the delays, it would be very near sunrise when we returned, but I was not going to leave my car and my violin behind. I stamped down hard on the accelerator and shot out of the parking lot and up the street. The exit ramp to the interstate lay just a few blocks ahead.

"Cat, what…" Winter started before I held up my hand to quiet him.

"Winter, it's after 3 am, it's raining, the lights are killing my eyes, and I need to concentrate on the road for a few minutes so," I warned him, "please save it. Whatever you need to say can wait for a little bit, at least until I get us on the straight-away." Glancing at the beautiful vamp in the near darkness of the car interior, I could see that I'd hurt his feelings. It was not the first time I'd been too brusque or used the wrong word and ended up wounding or insulting a vampire. For all their power and powers, they were, for the most part, a fairly emotionally sensitive group, which was something I often forgot.

Chapter 2

We took the wide loop of the on-ramp nearly on two wheels then I kicked the accelerator down till the speedometer read 85 mph. There was too much water on the pavement to use the cruise control so I made my foot comfortable on the gas pedal, leaned back in the seat, and sighed.

"Okay, Winter," I began, as I glanced briefly at his silent form beside me, "now you can go ahead and tell me what you started to back there in the parking lot. What were you saying about Amon?"

"His Lordship received a call from Thammuz," Winter said simply, and though I expected further explanation, he seemed reluctant to offer any. I drew in a sharp breath and it caught in my throat. Thammuz was the head honcho of the Council of Five, a body of vampire jurisprudence. The Council acted as judge, jury, and executioner for any member of the vampire community who broke their laws or risked the secrecy of their existence. So far, what interaction I'd endured with the Council had left me feeling victimized and vulnerable, neither sensation I greatly appreciated.

"So what are the Council of Goons up to now?" I snarled into the glow of the dashboard lights.

"My Lady, you should not refer to them that way," Winter spoke in a hushed tone. "You are now vampire and subject to their rule."

"Winter," I sighed in exasperation, "is the car bugged?"

"Of course not," he replied in obvious confusion. "Why would you ask?

"Are the Council telepathic, can they read my mind, hear my thoughts?" I insisted.

"Not that I'm aware of," he answered defensively, "though you would likely know more of that than I would."

"Then how the devil would they ever know how I refer to them?" I shook my head in wonder, "And you know perfectly well that I was subject to their rules and their form of justice long before I became His Lordship's mate."

Silence ensued as we sped down the rain-slicked highway, reflective lane markers ticking away the miles in a glare of headlights and overhead vapor lights. Winter cleared his throat and turned to me, touching my hand hesitantly.

"Cat, My Lady, I'm sorry," he offered soberly. "I know full well what you've endured at the hands of the Council of Five. I didn't mean to remind you or to bring up painful memories. Forgive me."

"It's okay, Winter," I braced the steering wheel with my knees and patted the hand that held my right with my left. "You just can't expect me to be that respectful of people, or vampires for that matter, that have only ever doubted me or punished me harshly for minor infractions of protocol. In my head they are, and likely always will be, the Council of Goons."

In the early days of my relationship with Amon, then known as Sin, I made the embarrassing faux pas of trying to protect myself from a demon after having been instructed not to do so by his Lordship. The Council of Five had landed on me like a ton of bricks, not only because of my actions, but because they were fearful of my powers and felt I could not be trusted to keep their reality a secret. They had branded me with a "Mark of Penitence," a painful burn on my right shoulder that remained so until I admitted submission and penitence for my actions. It had never happened. I had healed the mark myself using the Healing Hand with which the Goddess Nemesis had blessed me.

"Well," Winter admitted, "I do not know what Thammuz was contacting his Lordship about, but it's generally a matter of great importance if he agrees to meet personally with someone. And he has requested a meeting tomorrow evening. I was not privy to the issue or those who would be in attendance at the meeting."

With that, he released me and I took the steering wheel back into my hands

"Damn," I hissed as I mentally thumbed through my memory files for any indiscretion or infraction that I might have unwittingly committed. I drew a blank. "Winter, what have I done now? You know that anytime the Council gets in my general vicinity, it's my fault."

"I'm not aware of you doing anything wrong, Cat," Winter smiled, his white fangs gleaming in the head-lights of an oncoming car.

"Thanks, sweetie," I smiled at his left handed attempt at encouragement. "You always know just what to say to make me feel better."

Turning my attention back to the road, I stamped down harder on the accelerator and pushed to speedom-eter to 95mph. The rain had nearly stopped, but standing water on the highway was sending plumes of white mist from the rear wheel wells into the air. Beyond the reach of Houston proper, the lights began to dwindle and the darkness became deeper and more natural. We sped on in silence, each deep in our own thoughts.

Just as we neared the Louisiana state line a sudden blur of feathers hit the hood of the car, at the lower edge of the windshield, and bounced off to the passenger side bumper. I slammed on the brakes and hydroplaned the car into a spin, fighting to control it and slow it at the same time. After what seemed like an eternity of slewing this way then that, I finally brought the car to a standstill and Winter looked at me with shock and surprise on his face.

"Winter, that was an owl," I started to unfasten my seatbelt, "and she might be hurt."

"Cat, wait," he demanded, peering into the darkness outside his window. "If it was one of your creatures risking itself like that, it was surely a warning of danger. You cannot go out there." Reaching across my middle, he held my door and would not let it go.

"Winter, that owl may be injured," I said sternly, "and my Healing Hand can save her, but only if you let me out of this car. I will be careful." Leaning over his extended arm, I managed to touch the butt of my Beretta Tomcat, stowed beneath the passenger seat, with the tip of my finger. It slipped down beside Winter's booted foot. He released the door handle and picked up the pistol. Sighing, he handed it to me and nodded, "Very well, but let me look around for a moment first?"

Nodding silently, I took the gun and checked the safety as well as the ammunition. It hadn't been used since I last practiced on the shooting range so the gun was clean and the clip full. Winter opened his car door and stepped out into the night. I waited for the count of ten then could stand it no longer and opened my door. There were no unusual sounds around us so I got out of the car and walked through the headlight beams to where the heap of disheveled feathers lay piled beside the white line of the emergency lane. I slipped the Tomcat into the waistband of my jeans at the small of my back. Crouching slowly over the crumpled form of the owl, I reached out with my right hand and gently touched a wing, discerning how the bird was actually positioned. My left palm began instantly to burn and tingle. As soon as I figured out where the owl's head was, I touched her shoulders and her chest with my Healing Hand. It warmed and glowed in the dark of the night highway. Lifting the bird carefully, I straightened and held her against my solar plexus. The Healing Hand continued to thrum and glow and the power in my Third Chakra answered the call and began to exude heat and healing energy. Though sticky, warm blood decorated the feathers of the majestic creature, her head came up with eyes alert and clear. She peered around as if in confusion, then looked up at me and closed her eyes in acknowledgement. I stroked her head and smoothed the feathers down her back and wings. Feeling her energy and strength return, I lifted her on my right hand.

"If your appearance is a warning, little one," I smiled, "I thank you. But in the future you should be more careful of how you deliver your messages."

Winter stood beside me looking carefully at the owl, now clasping the edge of my hand with her talons. The two seemed to be having an exchange of a sort. It was *Owlspeak*, I knew, a language of subtle movements and almost imperceptible sounds that only such creatures understood. I was given dominion over those creatures but I was not given their language.

"This is Oola," Winter took his eyes off the bird and looked at me. "She is not only owl, she is vampire. She asks permission to speak to you. I'm not sure you should allow it."

"Why not, Winter?" I looked at him in dismay, "She risked her life to get my attention. Okay, well maybe not her life, but injury at least."

"She is vampire," he replied tersely. "There is no obvious immediate danger. Why did she not simply approach you in the traditional and respectful manner? Why the dramatics?"

"Wait just a minute here, I'm not tracking," I shook my head. "She is owl and vampire, and she wants to speak with me? Why me? Unless it has something to do with my dominion over the owls, this makes no sense. Why not approach Amon?"

"I do not know why she needs to see you," he admitted, "but I am suspicious of her tactics. And if the matter does not have something to do with your creatures she is making a very grave mistake in approaching you before His Lordship."

Considering all the possibilities briefly, a thought occurred to me.

"Winter, I've only shapeshifted once," I looked into his golden eyes, "but it seemed like it took a long time. Well, maybe that was partly the pain, but it wasn't an instantaneous thing, right?"

"Generally it does take several minutes, sometimes even up to half an hour, depending on how practiced the creature shifting is and whether he or she is a Master Vampire," he nodded in agreement.

"We don't have the time for her to change back to talk to me right now," I reasoned aloud. "We're already running behind and will be lucky to be back at the estate before sunrise as it is."

"You're right, Cat," Winter shrugged, "and His Lordship is not going to be happy with either of us anyway. We shouldn't make the situation any worse than it already is."

"Oola," I petted the bird's head gently, "it's getting late and we must be getting home before sunrise. Come to the estate tomorrow after sunset and I shall see you. Meet me in the gardens behind the house. I'll be waiting on the veranda. I'll speak with you then, okay?"

With that, the beautiful golden owl gave a shriek and spread her wings to soar away into the night sky. I pulled the gun from my waistband and walked back to the car, thinking how lucky it was that no State Trooper happened by to offer assistance or investigate.

We both climbed back into the Miata, buckled up, and I revved the engine. Putting the car into gear, I floored it and headed down the highway into Louisiana as I handed the gun back to Winter. He slipped it back under his seat after reassuring himself that the safety was still engaged.

Pink was beginning to seep into the sky as we pulled into the long driveway leading up to the Montjean estate. Soft lights still burned in the arched windows and small black clouds hung over the steepled rooftop.

I pulled the Miata into the gatehouse and headed for the door, Winter close on my heels. The front door stood open and a familiar shadowed form stood in the light that spilled from within. Amon stood silhouetted by the light, cutting an imposing figure.

"Catherine," he spoke with a touch of venom in his voice, "I sent Winter to fetch you long ago. You were to return with him. Why did you not leave your car and obey my wishes?"

My mate was, as always, a vision of sensual beauty, a treat for the eyes. His long black hair lay loose about his shoulders and the one shock of silver at his left temple never failed to remind me of how he once looked. When first we'd met Amon's hair had been a glorious silver mane, only changed by the fulfillment of an ancient prophecy and consuming my Life's Blood. Now his lustrous raven hair framed his pale, well-chiseled, facial features. He wore a dress shirt of white silk and perfectly fitted tight black trousers. His wolf's head belt buckle shone in the light and drew my attention unerringly to one of his attributes that left me weak in the knees. Impossibly soft-looking black leather boots rose to barely touch his thighs. It was difficult standing up to such power and such beauty, but I was resolute.

"Amon, my beloved worrywart," I smiled trying to defuse the situation, "I didn't want to leave my instrument, it was storming, and I've never flown with Winter. There was, as you can clearly see, no problem with me driving home and I made it in plenty of time. See, not yet sunrise." Risking his wrath, I leaned forward and planted a kiss on his cheek. He growled and grabbed my wrists. I was going to have to reconsider my witchly and womanly charms apparently.

"Have I not taught you that your safety is my greatest concern," he glared blood red eyes at me, "and that my word is law?"

"Um," I wriggled, trying to loosen his grip on my arms, "yes, indeed, you certainly have. But you knew I was on my way home. All this fuss was unnecessary. I was safe, nothing happened."

"Witch, you do try my patience," he feigned exasperation, then smiled slightly. "I am relieved that you are home safely, but this is the last time that you shall fail to obey me, n'est-ce pas?" Leaning his face very close to mine, he took the glasses from my nose and peered at me intently. As was often the case, I found myself swamped by his power and the intensity of his love. My response caught in my throat and my skin tingled at his touch.

"Uh," I smiled weakly, trying to find the answer he wanted and not the one I would normally volunteer, "I'm, um…Amon, let me go!" Struggling to free myself, I laughed and squirmed in his arms.

"Ma chèri," he breathed in my ear, his lips very close to my throat, "we have been over this time and time again. You are precious to me. I am your sire, your master, and your mate. I seek only to keep you safe."

"Darling, I know that we've been over this," I grinned and looked down at his chest, tearing my gaze away from his eyes, "and I do try to obey you, gadz, how I hate that word, but I'm a witch and a woman, and I have a mind of my own. I should be allowed to use it. I'm not an idiot or a reckless child."

"You are my mate," he insisted, squeezing me a bit tighter, "and you are a unique creature. You are not merely vampire, nor are you simply a witch. You are vampire, witch, and one touched by the Divine. Your blood is unlike any ever known. My hunger for you cannot be sated and I shall always endeavor to protect you. You do not know your own worth."

"Fine," I sighed dramatically, "from now on, your word is the final word, your wish is my command, and whatever you say goes, even though I don't think I need protecting. Now, will you let me go?"

His blood red eyes regarded me carefully and I could feel his mind pushing against my mental shields. Bending over me, he kissed my neck and gently slid his teeth ever so slightly into the flesh of my throat. Erotic sensations ran up and down my spine and my body reacted to his despite my best efforts to remain aloof. He drew a small amount of my blood into his mouth and I sighed in delight. My mental shields crumbled without warning.

"So," he smiled wickedly, licking his lips, "still not contrite, are you, Little One? Once again, you were just telling me what I want to hear. Will you never learn?" With that he bent over and swept me up into his arms, licked my neck to seal the wounds his teeth had made, and carried me half kicking and screaming, half laughing and squirming, deeper into the mansion.

"So what's the deal?" I giggled as he strode purposefully past the parlor, the grand staircase and into the gloomy halls leading into the lower levels of the home. "Why did you send Winter anyway? What's going on with the Council of Goons?"

"Catherine," he sighed, "I have warned you about your tongue. One day it shall get you into more trouble than you know." He playfully swatted my behind.

"Yeah, yeah, fine," I replied, "but what's going on?"

"I do not yet fully know, my love," Amon answered as he continued to stroke one long hand down the back of my legs, "but Thammuz has called for a meeting tomorrow evening. It is likely some political issue, or perhaps someone committed a transgression of some sort. But when an issue such as this comes up, I want you home and safe in my protection. Whatever the case may be, it could bring about danger. Do you understand?"

"Amon, I'm a big girl, I can take care of myself," I whined. "Would you please put me down now?"

Just then we rounded the corner of the corridor and entered his coffin room two doors down. His gleaming black coffin lay open and inviting. Though I never thought to be comfortable with the concept, I had actually become quite accustomed to sleeping in repose in his arms.

Lowering me gently to my feet, Amon kissed me deeply, his lips opening mine, his tongue exploring my mouth. He drew me into himself and I melted against him, wrapping my arms around his waist. At length he released me and I stepped back from his embrace.

"Passion," he said in a voice an octave lower than normal. I knew it meant trouble.

"Amon," I responded in kind.

"You have blood on your shirt, but I can feel that you have not fed," he indicated the stain on the front of my tee shirt. "I sense you are weak, so how is it you are wearing blood?"

"Oh that," I smiled, relived that the issue was minor, "it's nothing. It's not human blood and it's certainly not mine." I turned to go get dressed to retire and was startled when Amon appeared suddenly before me, blocking my way.

"Cat," he insisted, "explain!"

"You know," I shook my head, "you really don't need a minute by minute account of my day. You don't have to know every tiny thing that happens to me. I'm more than capable of dealing with matters that are of my domain."

"So that is owl blood?" he raised an eyebrow at me.

"It is," I said succinctly, "and I handled the matter. It is of no concern of yours."

Even before the words fell out of my mouth, I knew I'd gone too far. But that's the tricky thing about words, once uttered they cannot be sucked back in. Before I could draw a breath to explain further, Amon caught me under the ribs in his strong right arm and lifted me from the floor. I could feel the anger coming off of him in waves, like a fevered heat.

"Passion, you go too far," he hissed and I felt the two-armed mark he had branded on my lower back flame to life. The pain caught me off guard and I cried out involuntarily. Tears of blood appeared in my eyes, staining my vision a ridiculous shade of scarlet. My vampire name, Passion, which Amon had bestowed upon me as my sire, was regrettably "girlie" and whenever Amon used it I knew things were serious.

"Amon, wait," I sobbed, "don't. Please let me explain." I kicked my legs uselessly against him, trying to wriggle away and lessen the pain. I knew that if he got carried away and gave me the third arm of the triangle of the brand that I would forever physically feel it when he was displeased. Our life together was not so idyllic that the prospect of being permanently debilitated by that pain would be out of the question.

As vampire I was immortal, but being a witch with unusual powers meant that I was not always subject to the physical laws that affected both humans and vampires alike. I felt pain perhaps more keenly than normal vampires, yes I realize 'normal vampires' should be an oxymoron, and suffering in perpetuity did not appeal to me. Being an independent thinking and acting woman, witch, and vampire often had me running afoul of my mate, sire, and, I could hardly bring myself to even think, master. It was not in my nature to conform or admit subservience to anyone, even if my very existence depended on it. I was trying to learn and to remember to at least act the part, but it was not coming easy. Only my love for Amon kept me trying to be something I knew darn well I was not.

"Please, Amon," I gasped, "don't do anything rash. You said you'd be more circumspect, remember? Just put me down and I'll explain."

I rose in his embrace as he stilled and composed himself, then sighing, he released me to the floor. Rubbing my middle where he'd held me, I turned to look into his eyes and plead my case.

"I should not have said that, I know," I held up my hand in surrender, "I was wrong, I admit it. It's just that this was an owl issue and I didn't think you'd be interested. It was nothing of importance, I'm sure. I'm meeting with her tomorrow evening. I've no idea what her problem is, but she wants to see me. That's all, I promise."

"And you know that only I decide what is and what is not my concern," he said sternly. "Where you are involved, beloved, I am always concerned."

"You're right again," I nodded. "I'm sorry. I just don't think this matter is important enough to finish this stupid mark of yours. Do you?"

"Stupid?" He gaped, his countenance stern, then broke into a smile, "You dare to call my mark stupid? Woman, will you never learn?" He caught me up in his embrace once more, but this time he put his mouth on mine and kissed me deeply. I laughed around his lips and dug my hands into his hair nearly up to my elbows.

"You know that I must punish you for this, do you not?" he grinned wickedly.

"Nope!" I shook my head emphatically, "I don't know that at all. I mean, after all, you are Master Vampire and can do whatever you want. You don't have to punish me if you don't want to. And you love me of course, so you really don't want to punish me, right?"

"Oh, you know I take no pleasure in disciplining you," he sighed. "This is for your own good. You simply must learn that actions have consequences. And here in our world those consequences may affect not only you but others as well. You would not want to bring about some innocent's destruction, would you?"

"Well, of course not," I started to admit, then looked into his eyes. Merriment just danced at the edges of his mouth and in the twinkle of his blood red eyes.

"You rat," I swatted at his chest. "You were teasing me. I may live to regret reintroducing the concept of humor to you."

"Oh do not worry, Little One," he smiled proudly as he put me down, "I will impose my punishment at my leisure. It will be exquisite, I promise."

Looking over my shoulder as I went to gather my clothes, I stopped and stared back at him, unsure if he was joking or not. His expression gave away nothing. I had learned that he generally did what he said and though I hoped he was teasing me about punishment, I now suspected I had some coming somehow.

Later, as I lay beside Amon in his coffin, my left thigh along his right and my right knee slung over his legs, it occurred to me that he had not mentioned that the blood on my shirt was not only owl, but vampire too. Normally, he would have spotted that in an instant. I wondered if he had not noticed or if there was some reason that he could not sense it. I also realized that I had inadvertently not mentioned that, and in a moment of disbelief, I recalled that I'd not told Amon of the old woman in the parking lot. If he somehow discovered this before I got the chance to tell him myself there would be a very dear cost to be paid, and it would be me who paid it. Slowly and quietly, I slid my mental shields into place so Amon could not read my thoughts. We had become telepathically linked even before I was made vampire and he had the annoying habit of reading my thoughts when I had no desire for him to know what was on my mind. He always said it was to check if I was thinking of him, what an ego, but I often suspected other motives.

Chapter 3

Suddenly I was awake with no idea why. Still curled against Amon's body, my ears were ringing with the echo of some unknown sound. Absently, I wondered why I had heard noise and my mate apparently had not. Unable to resist the temptation, I carefully disengaged myself from Amon's embrace, and as silently as possible, climbed out of the coffin. It would take too much time, I realized, to put on my protective and disguising contact lenses, so I grabbed my tiny dark glasses from the shelf as I tiptoed from the room. I was wearing silk pajama pants with the waistband rolled down on my hips. The camisole top I had on covered me sufficiently, but I wished I had time to change into something more substantial. Tight blue jeans and a snug white tee shirt brought out the tom boy in me and made me feel able to scrap with the best of them. Since that was not a possibility at the moment, I put the matter out of my mind and quietly made my way down the hallway, passing several closed doors until I came to one I knew well. As I opened the door, the smell of chlorine assaulted my nose and I smiled at the turquoise light of the indoor pool. Slipping inside quickly, I pulled the door closed behind me and ran across the cool tile, skirting the softly glowing rectangle of shimmering water. The underwater lights illuminated the natatorium just enough to see comfortably, as the heavy dark drapes that covered the wall and windows kept out all natural light. Pulling the curtains aside, I squinted in surprise to find the sun had not yet gone down and daylight still held dominion over the world beyond the manse. Thankful to have my glasses on, I unlocked the sliding glass door hidden by the curtains, and stepped out into the heat and humidity of the Louisiana late afternoon. Gnats and no-see-ums swarmed and separated as I passed through their insect clouds, grateful to no longer be affected by their annoying habits. Keeping to the shadows, I crept along the side of the building, ran across an open area, and then put my back to the wall of the carriage house. I stood quietly, trying to discern any unusual sounds or movements. Crickets chirruped in the high grass and a squirrel ran up the trunk of a tree beyond the driveway, but I heard nothing else. I opened my senses and could 'feel' nothing moving near me but I knew something was close. The air felt different, as if it had been disturbed by something's passing and had not yet settled again. Just as I was about to give up and go back inside, a hand appeared out of nowhere and clamped over my mouth. The arm that quickly wrapped around my middle hoisted me into the air then pulled me back against a warm body.

"Ssshhh..," an obviously masculine voice whispered, "don't move and don't scream."

I was suddenly released and turned quickly to find myself looking into the smoky brown eyes of Bear, one of Amon's daytime body guards. The look of surprise on his face was priceless.

"My Lady, Cat," he whispered desperately, "a thousand pardons. I didn't know it was you. What are you doing out here?"

He stood, bare-chested, in tight fitting jeans and a pair of comfortably worn boots, and seemed embarrassed to be so exposed in my presence. Bear was one hundred percent man of Native American and Creole descent, and truthfully, he was just too pretty for his own good. His long brown hair was straight and silky smooth, and his cheekbones high and well defined. He had a broad, genuinely open smile and shoulders as wide as the Mississippi, Lily, the maid, would say. Bear was ex-marine, so I was not surprised to see washboard abs above his narrow waist. Actually, I was rather enjoying the view when he bent down and looked me in the eye, well, through my glasses, anyway.

"Ma'am," he whispered again, "what are you doing here?"

"Oh," I grinned, knowing that despite being vampire I was still capable of blushing. It had certainly been a common enough occurrence when I'd been human. "Um, I heard a noise. It woke me so I came out to find out what it was."

"Yes, I heard it too," he nodded. "But you should have just called one of the guards. You shouldn't have come out here by yourself. His Lordship won't like it."

"What are you doing out here?" I countered, nodding at his shirtless chest.

He smiled almost sheepishly, "I was in the carriage house going over the vehicles for bugs and explosives. It tends to get dusty and oily doing that, so I took off my shirt. I'm sorry."

Being one of the few mortals that helped maintain the security of our vampire compound during the day when we were, or had been at one time, at our weakest, Bear was not completely informed as to the truth of the situation. He and Dodge were paid muscle and were trained to not ask questions. What they believed of us I did not know, but they were surely aware of our strange, mostly nocturnal, hours. Before I was made vampire, I had learned to recognize their "unnatural" beauty and could spot one on sight. Being in security and being trained to observe, I assumed that Bear and Dodge both had their own theories as to the eccentrics that lived here at the Montjean estate, but they knew not to mention them or speak of such matters. Silence was a large part of security and trust. Since Amon was always addressed as His Lordship and I was supposed to be addressed as My Lady, they, as well as Lily, and her brother Lucius, the stable hand, must have believed us some sort of royalty, though I'd never been told the story given them. Secretly, I'd always inwardly cringed when addressed so formally and often corrected them with a "Cat, please". After all, they'd known me as Cat before I became His Lordship's mate, so we could be more informal with one another.

Just then a noise rang out across the yard. It sounded like an arrow whistling through the air before solidly striking its target. Bear pinned me with a look of warning, "You stay here, Cat!" Then he was racing toward the origins of the sound.

I waited in the shadows of the carriage house for a few moments, considering how I might make my way to where the action was without getting into the sunlight. Bear suddenly came around the corner of the house with a black-cloaked blond woman in tow. She was struggling in his grasp and appeared to be most unhappy. Presumably this was an intruder and judging by the sound we'd just heard, she'd run afoul of one of the security trip wires. As Bear drew her nearer, I could see the vampire beauty in her perfectly proportioned features and the brilliance of her golden eyes. Her long, thick hair was the color of honey and hung in disheveled curls. She was not quite my height, but she had an air of litheness about her that made her seem taller than she actually was.

"Oola," I gaped, when at last all the pieces fit.

"You know this woman?" Bear looked at me skeptically as his captive continued to struggle away from him.

"She's a friend," I answered pointedly, looking the woman in the eye, "aren't you Oola?"

Though she refused to speak, she did calm down and stand still, then nodded when she felt Bear's eyes upon her.

"What should I do with her?" Bear asked, "His Lordship will want to know of the breach of security." A drop of sweat ran down his nearly hairless chest and mesmerized me for a moment, leaving me grateful for the protection of my tiny dark sunglasses. The silence hung heavily until I looked up at his face again and smiled innocently.

"You can report to His Lordship that it was an accidental breach. He's aware that my friend here was coming for a visit today, I told him last night. Knowing His Lordship, he probably knows of the breach already and is expecting that report right now, " I added as I took Oola's arm from him and proceeded to walk away with her as if we were indeed old chums. "Why don't you put your shirt on and go tell His Lordship that I'm entertaining my guest by the pool? I believe he has Council business to attend to this evening, so I'm sure he's stirring around here somewhere by now."

Leaving the strapping bodyguard somewhat stunned and not waiting for him to recover himself, I hustled Oola a bit more quickly across the lawn. Sliding the glass doors open quietly, I ushered her inside, then stepped in and closed the doors behind me. Breathing a sigh of relief, I looked at Oola and shook my head.

"I don't know what business you think you have with me," I began, "but it had better be darn good to have risked what you just did. I told you to come after sunset! You have no idea what a security breach here would have meant for you if I'd have not been there. How did you get onto estate grounds, anyway?"

The beautiful vampire pulled back the hood of her cloak and regarded me silently. I could see by the shadows shifting across her expression that she didn't know how to begin to explain her actions.

"I, um," she looked at her fingers as if looking there for an answer, "I flew over the wall, landed near some bushes and hid until I could shift back into this form."

"How long have you been on the grounds?" I marveled that she could avoid detection for so long.

"I don't know," she shrugged, "twenty minutes or so?"

Impressed at her ability to arrive as she did as well as how quickly she could shift forms, I could only shake my head to dispel the image of one of our human security guards coming upon her in mid-transformation.

"Come," I offered. "We might as well be comfortable. Would you like some refreshment?"

"No, thank you," she nodded succinctly.

We moved to the ornately designed wrought iron deck furniture that stood at the far end of the pool area. The mosaic scene of the sun and lush jungle vegetation on the wall lent an air of tropical relaxation to the entertainment area that was raised and surrounded by a low stone balustrade and coping. I took the chair on the right of the ornate table and indicated to Oola that she should take the one on the left. This, at least, offered me a view of all three doors and had my back to the wall, which is how I generally preferred things.

"So," I raised my eyebrows and nodded at Oola once she was seated, "you wanted to speak to me on some matter. I assume it has something to do with my dominion over the owls."

She looked at me steadily, as if summing me up, then finally sighed heavily.

"I have been sent to seek your protection," she said perfunctorily.

Many ideas ran through my mind at the utterance of that simple statement, but I could not seem to focus on a single issue.

"My protection…" was all I could manage to stutter.

Just then, before Oola could draw breath to reply, the far door opened and Winter stepped into the room almost hesitantly. I nodded at him and he came forward, thoughtfully carrying a mug of coffee for me. Even though I needed blood now to survive as vampire, I still enjoyed some of the more pleasant habits of my former life, and coffee was a big part of my past that I clung to in my new situation. Though eating was no longer a necessity for survival, I found I still could savor the taste of food and drink, I could still enjoy it and my body, unlike the bodies of some vampires, did not suffer any adverse effects. When I first became Amon's mate, when I first became a vampire, I'd thought eating, as I'd done when I was human, was an act of futility, something to be discarded and dismissed as a waste of time, but within a few months I'd realized I missed it. Eating and drinking had been a part of who I was, pieces of my humanity even, so I'd slowly and over time reintroduced it to my activities. I'd reclaimed my pleasure.

Thankfully accepting the cup of hot black caffeine, I smiled and introduced him to Oola. The air became electrically charged as the two beheld each other in this form for the first time.

"Oola, this is Winter, my bodyguard and friend," I offered, "and Winter this is Oola, whom you met last night."

"So I did," Winter smiled broadly. "My pleasure, Oola."

Oola bowed her head and then looked up at Winter, who, I realized with a start, was practically her twin. "I must apologize for my," she grinned mischievously, "rather grand entrance last night. I was desperate to get My Lady Passion's attention and it seemed worth the risk at the time."

"So this is a matter of some great importance?" Winter asked with obvious concern.

"Please, Winter," I moved over and offered my chair to him, "join us. Your input may be invaluable."

Looking at me doubtfully, he sat in the wrought iron chair between the other vampire and I then looked at me pointedly. I shrugged, then turned my attention back to Oola.

"Now, Oola," I started anew, "you were saying."

"Just that I, and others somewhat younger than myself, need your help and your protection," she said quickly, as if to release pent up anxiety.

Winter touched my hand and covered it with his own, as if I was to understand some meaning in the act. He turned to face me and his golden eyes glowed unnaturally. There was warning in those eyes.

"My Lady Passion, if I might be so bold," Oola continued undaunted, "might I ask that you remove your glasses so that I can see your eyes?"

Realizing that I'd not taken the time to put on my dark protective contact lenses, I suddenly suspected this was some sort of test of trust or at least Oola was asking for proof of my powers.

Winter nearly knocked over his chair, standing so abruptly. Waves of anger and power rolled off of him as he stood looking imperiously down at Oola.

"You do not come here, into His Lordship's home, insult him by going behind his back, ask protection of Her Ladyship, and then ask such a thing of her! This is unmitigated gall!"

"Forgive me," she stood and practically genuflected, "I mean no offense and no disrespect. It's just that, well, I have reason to be concerned. If my plight were only my own I wouldn't dare ask such a thing, but I am here representing others who are relying on me. I do not wish to fail them. "

"Okay," I stood and indicated that both Oola and Winter should take their seats, "that's enough. Winter, Oola, both of you just take a minute, please." Looking first at my dear sweet friend and protector, then at the mysterious female adjacent to him, I silenced them both with my hand, took a deep breath for affect, and took my seat once more. Sliding the dark glasses slightly down my nose, I peered at Oola with my naked eyes, irises as white as the driven snow. She flinched in surprise then recovered herself, lowering her gaze in a gesture of acknowledgement and thanks.

"So, if you seek protection," I began on a different tack, "why did you not seek it of my mate and Master Vampire of this region, Amon?"

"We," Oola stammered uncomfortably, "we are not subjects of Master Amon's. And frankly we were unsure of how he'd receive us."

"You are not from this region?" I asked, beginning to see some of the issues unfurling. Vampires, I had learned, were terribly territorial and there was a protocol involved in moving from one region to another, almost as if passports were required.

"No, My Lady," she smiled weakly, "those who now seek your protection are from the eastern seaboard."

"That would be the territory of the Master Vampire Sabre, right?" I grimaced at the thought. Amon had let me know early on that there was no love lost between himself and Sabre, whom he thought of as more of an annoyance than any real power.

"That is correct," Oola nodded. "Sabre is the sire of those who seek your help."

"I'm not tracking here," I shook my head and threw up my arms. "Why do you need my protection? Why can't your sire protect you?"

"That's a rather complicated story," the beautiful blonde sighed.

"Hey," I grinned, "I've got time. And if you really want my help, you'd better tell me the whole thing."

"Well…" she started and I yelped involuntarily.

Just at that moment the conversation with my agent the previous night popped into my mind and I jumped at the thought.

"Damn, scratch that! I don't have time," I hissed, as I recalled the deadline rapidly approaching. "Winter, I've got to, oh man, I don't know what to do. My agent gave me twenty-four hours to accept a book proposal, and that was last night before you came to me. I haven't even so much as considered what I should do and I haven't even had the chance to talk to Amon. And he's probably already off with the Council by now and the clock's ticking."

"What can I do, My Lady?" Winter offered, standing out of respect and sweet chivalry.

"Okay, I'll tell you what," I smiled, rubbing the pain that had suddenly appeared at my forehead, "Oola, you tell this whole story to Winter. He's owl and my closest, most trusted confidant. I'll go talk to His Lordship, if I can find him, and Winter, you catch up to me and fill me in when you can. Oola, I'll hear the whole story and give you my answer as soon as possible, okay?" The silent glances that passed between the two seemed to indicate that they were amenable to my idea. Downing the remainder of my rapidly cooling coffee, I put the mug down, mouthed a silent "thanks" to Winter, then left the two ridiculously matched blond vampires to their business.

Once I left the natatorium I opened my mind to the coffin room, only to find it empty as I'd expected. Quickly padding my bare feet on the cool marble floor, I made my way through the labyrinthine corridors, up the stairs, and around many corners until I reached the Sapphire room. This had been one of the first and most opulently appointed bedrooms I'd stayed in when I'd first arrived. Over time the décor had changed somewhat, but it still felt comforting and familiar. Grabbing a pair of jeans, loosely knitted white sweater, socks and undergarments, I headed for the bath to wash the remnants of Lamey's fragrance from my skin and hair. The too hot shower felt relaxing and invigorating as I shampooed and lathered soap across my skin. Once sufficiently clean and wrinkling to pruniness, I turned off the spray, squeezed the water from my hair and exited the shower. I toweled myself dry, wrapped another towel around my hair and set to dressing. After donning my bra and panties, slipping into my black jeans and pulling the sweater over my head, I combed the tangles out of my hair and grabbed the blow dryer from beneath the vanity. Bending over at the waist, I tossed my hair and blew it dry upside down. One of the unexpected benefits of becoming vampire was, I discovered, that my hair had taken on a measure of body and bounce that it had sadly lacked while I was human. I found that ridiculously ironic.

One quick toss with the hairbrush and I was set to go, the results, I laughed, mirroring those of a shampoo commercial. Grabbing a new package of disposable contact lenses, which I kept stored here and there as many far-sighted people do reading glasses, I stopped at the sink and patiently slipped them in. Seeing myself with brown eyes was always a shock, but it was better than others seeing my irises as the frosty white freak shows they were. It had even taken Amon quite a while to be able to look me in the eye without a start or a flinch.

Exiting the bathroom, I paused momentarily to perch on the edge of the huge, thickly mattressed bed long enough to put on my socks, then retrieved my boots from the closet and pulled them on.

As I left the bedroom, I listened to the sounds of the house while making my way down the corridors. I could neither hear nor sense any unusual activity and only the sound of my boot heels echoed on the marble floors. Unsure of where Amon's meeting was taking place, I thought his office a good place to look for him. When I put my hand on the ornately carved office door, I felt that my mate was not within, but pushed it open and stepped into the silence anyway. The beautifully decorated room was immaculate and every surface of rich wood finish gleamed in the soft light of the desk lamp. Amon's massive antique desk was the centerpiece of the office and its size and unique design demanded the appropriate attention. It had been at this very desk some few years ago that I had written my first book and I wondered if I was capable of sitting there writing another. A burgundy tufted leather sofa sprawled against the far wall before the rich brocade draperies that always kept the windows beneath covered.

Though Amon was not there, I knew that he had only recently left as my sensitive vampire nose could detect my lover's essence still lingering in the air. Sighing, I went behind the desk and sat down in his big leather chair. To my right, on a small table adjacent to the desk, sat a computer monitor, its screen dark and buttons unblinking. I considered turning it on and sending a message to Doug Donahue, but I wasn't really clear on what I was going to say, so what was the point? Then another thought occurred to me and I clicked the computer's ON button and waited while it purred to life. As soon as I could, I typed "Dark Hours Publishing" into the search bar and waited. The search engine offered Dark Hours Films, Dark Hours Haunted House, and the band, Dark Hours, but no Dark Hours Publishing. I was about to shut the computer down in frustration when I noticed the flashing 'did you mean Dark Ours Publishing?' prompt.

"Well," I murmured to myself, "maybe that's what I do mean!" Clicking on the suggested morsel, I quickly scanned the 'About Us' information. 'For more than a century Dark Ours Publishing has offered a wide variety of literature, both fiction and non-fiction and will continue to do so far into the future. Our authors are among the best in the world and our clientele are among the most discriminating in the industry. We invite you to enjoy our catalogues and our list of available e-books.'

"Boring," I huffed, then clicked on 'further information' to find 'Dark Ours Publishing, a member of The Chameleon Group, is a subsidiary of Enigma Enterprises'.

"How inscrutable can you get?" I laughed, "Might as well have called it "If Vee Tell You Da Name Vee Must Keel You Publishing"! Reluctantly I admitted that I was not likely to find any further information online so I turned off the computer and again considered calling my agent, but I was too frustrated.

Instead, I opened my mind to Amon's, hoping to get some idea of how things were going in his meeting with the Council. What I experienced when I did so, however, was nothing I'd ever felt before. A huge red cloud appeared before me and it roiled, becoming a vortex of tremendous power. I felt it pulling me in. In a panic, I grabbed blindly on the desk for something, anything I could find, to anchor myself against the turmoil. My right hand chanced upon what felt like a letter opener, and acting without conscious thought, I stabbed it down through the back of my left hand. The motion pinned me to the desk and the pain snapped me away from the vision of the churning red cloud. My mental shields slammed shut and the connection to that force was broken. Blinding pain assaulted me and I gasped at the sensation. A sound brought me back to myself and I realized that I'd screamed until my throat hurt. When my vision cleared, I found the sight of the letter opener protruding from the back of my left hand oddly disconcerting. Deep crimson-black blood was pooling around my fingers and beginning to make its way along the edge of the massive desk. I watched, oddly indifferent, as it drip, drip, dripped onto the hardwood floor.

Bishop, Amon's right hand vampire and something of the concierge of the estate, burst through the door and drew up short when he saw me. His brilliant blue eyes were wide in alarm as he looked from my face to my hand, to the blood on the floor, then back to my face.

"My Lady," he gasped, "what have you done?"

My thoughts were so unsettled, so chaotic, that I couldn't answer him. I could only regard him in mute recognition. When he moved toward the letter opener as if to remove it, I tried to stand then realized such action was unwise.

"No," I rasped and shook my head, "don't try to remove it yet. It may be the only thing keeping me here."

"What do you mean, Cat?" Bishop furrowed his brow as he continued to inspect my hand. His eyes held something of a mad fascination as he watched my blood flow and spill off the desk. Though vampires do not usually drink from one another, my being a witch and having been touched and blessed by the Goddess had apparently given my blood properties that other vampires still found appealing, though most had no idea why. Bishop licked his lips slightly, but I knew he'd not have actually tasted my blood even if I'd have offered. As Amon's mate I was strictly "hands off" and to taste my blood might very well mean destruction or permanent torture.

"I don't know," I coughed. "Something of a psychic vacuum tried to suck me into itself. This was the only thing I could think to do. And apparently, as you can see, it is working. I'm still here."

"I don't understand," he replied, "but if you don't take that thing out of your flesh you're going to continue to bleed. Your hand cannot heal with the blade still in it."

"I know," I sighed. "I'm just not quite ready to risk removing it. The vortex still feels too close. What are you doing here, by the way?" Looking up into those wondrous blue eyes, I couldn't help but smile. Bishop was rather an enigma to me, a friend I supposed, but not the confidant that Winter was and not the begrudged power and foil that Chimaera was. Those two I knew and I was comfortable with them. Bishop just never was clear in my mind, though his story was one of the first I'd learned when I'd arrived here at the estate.

"My Lady," he looked at me in disbelief, "I heard you scream!"

"You heard that?" I grinned, "I thought this room was soundproof."

"Cat, I wager that most of Louisiana and possibly part of Texas heard you," he smiled. "And it wasn't just your human voice I heard. I heard your leopard voice in that scream."

"Really?" I asked, wondering what that must have sounded like, "I've only ever shapeshifted the one time and that's been quite a while ago. How could I still have that part of her in me?" The memory of the discomfort rising to excruciating pain as my bones and sinews transformed from human to snow leopard remained fresh in my mind, and in fact, I knew I'd never forget the experience.

"Once you've transformed, you will always have your animal as a part of you and you will always be a part of her," he explained as he turned toward the far wall. A rustling sound then a heavier thud hit the window beneath the drapes. We both heard the noises at the same time. Looking at each other, Bishop and I froze waiting to understand or recognize the commotion. After a moment the high pitched, mournful cry of a wolf broke our trance. The first call was quickly answered by a chorus of additional howling and barking. The hoot of an owl just outside the window let me know that the first noise we'd heard was one of my creatures landing on the sill beyond.

"Your scream has called your creatures," Bishop nodded toward the windows, "and His Lordship's, who are sworn to protect you."

"Crap, Bishop," I sighed, "I can't deal with them right now. Just make them go away."

"I don't believe that they will leave until you assure them that all is well," he said, "and you cannot do that with your hand still pinned to the desktop."

"I'm a little unsure of pulling this thing out," I touched the end of the letter opener with my right hand. "If that vortex is still out there I don't think I can hold on against its pull. If Amon were here I'm sure he's strong enough to hold me, but I don't even know where he is."

"Do you not believe me strong enough to keep you from being pulled away?" Bishop looked at me almost sadly.

"I, uh," I stammered, "I hadn't really even considered it, Bishop."

"You think I'm weak?" he asked dejectedly.

"No, I didn't say that," I rushed to explain. "It's just that psychically I'm more connected to Amon, then Chimaera, then Winter. I've not had much experience with you on that plane. I don't doubt your strength, I've just not really tasted it, or tested it, if you like."

"I am strong enough to hold you, Cat," he said solemnly. "I would not suggest it if I did not know this to be true. I would not risk your wellbeing or His Lordship's displeasure if I were not certain."

What could I do? With reasoning such as that, I had no choice but to trust Bishop and take the chance that I might soon find myself being yanked out of this reality and into another. I let out a deep sigh and looked up to meet Bishop's eyes. Nodding silently, I steeled myself for whatever might happen.

Bishop approached the desk most reverently. He placed his left hand on my right hand and gave me a reassuring squeeze.

"This is your anchor," he said softly, but assuredly. "I will not fail you."

With that he grasped the handle of the letter opener with his right hand and pulled it first from the wood of the desktop then from the flesh of my hand. The sucking wet sound was sudden and only barely preceded the pain as my torn flesh met the air. Bishop squeezed my left hand and I was able to choke back another scream. Though tears of blood escaped my eyes, the pain was subsiding and there was no return of the vortex. I was beginning to feel better as the novelty of being free presented itself and I stood and held my left hand up before my face. Dark blood still coursed down my wrist and forearm, but the tissue seemed to be mending and the flow was slowing. I smiled at Bishop and was about to thank him when a force hit my solar plexus and lifted me off my feet. My right hand was torn from Bishop's grasp. The pain of my back slamming into the far wall was the last I felt as darkness took me.

Chapter 4

Dull, throbbing pain pulled me back into consciousness. My back hurt and my left hand felt heavy
and numb. The back of my head was tender, as well.
When I opened my eyes I saw Amon's face, very close
and full of concern. My emotions swirled involuntarily
at the mere sight of him.

"You had a meeting," I murmured, realizing that I
was still half-lying on the floor, half- propped against
the wall.

"I felt your pain," he answered softly, "so I ended
the meeting."

"Did you get your business taken care of?" I groaned
a bit as I struggled to sit upright. "Oh, man, that hurts."
Unsure of which body part to whine about first, I
merely grinned at Amon's wonderfully handsome face.
His long black hair was smooth, shining, and brushing
gently across the back of my right hand. I touched the
side of his face and he closed his eyes in a moment of
rapture. We had that effect on one another, for I still
felt like a feline curling myself around him whenever
he touched me.

"Passion, what happened?" he asked rather sternly.

"Bishop," I gasped, remembering the moment I became airborne, "is Bishop alright?" Looking past Amon's broad shoulders, I strained to get a better view of the office. Bishop stepped from behind the desk with his medical bag in his hands.

"My Lady," Bishop looked not at me but down at the floor, "I failed you. After promising your safety I failed you. Can you ever forgive me?"

"Wait a minute, Bishop," I hesitated briefly as I moved into a more comfortable position, "you didn't fail me. You anchored me from the vortex, which is just what you promised to do. Whatever force hit me after that, I assure you it was not that vortex. This was something else entirely."

Though he seemed dubious, at least he looked up and his eyes met mine. Sadness and hope seemed to be waging a war in his expression, as if neither could advance completely.

"I still should have been able to protect you," he sighed.

"Bishop, I'm not sure that anyone could have held me when that force hit," I admitted, glancing at Amon to see if I'd just committed a faux pas. Though technically I'd just as much as suggested the power might be more than even the Master Vampire could handle, he regarded me steadily and I met his gaze and held it. There had been no offense intended and he could feel the truth in my words.

"Cat," Amon touched my chin and turned my face to his, "again I will ask you. What happened?"

"Bishop didn't fill you in?" I looked first at my love, then up at Bishop, though it was an uncomfortable strain until Amon released me.

"There was no time, My Lady," Bishop spread his hands. "I just got back with my medical bag when His Lordship arrived and you woke up. There has been virtually no time for explanations."

Looking down at my left hand, which had been haphazardly wrapped in a towel, I sighed then looked back at Amon. He was not going to go away without sufficient explanation and I loathed the thought of going back over everything. There was also some risk to Bishop if I let it seem, however briefly, that he'd put me at risk. I often found myself walking on eggshells around my mate, as we saw things from greatly differing perspectives, and I couldn't always predict his reactions.

"Fine," I smiled and nodded at Bishop, "you see to this 'owie' and I'll explain what happened."

Gently, Amon hoisted me from the floor and cradled me in his arms, my back and head throbbing complaint at the change of position. He took three long strides and put me carefully down on the leather sofa, propping a pillow behind my head.

"Now, Catherine," Amon fairly purred as he stroked his long cool fingers down the side of my face, "you were saying?"

"I don't know exactly what happened, darling," I breathed deeply and leaned my cheek into his caress, "but I was here in your office and I opened my mind to you, well, I thought I'd opened my mind to you. There was this big cloud-like thing that started spinning and it tried to pull me in. I was blinded, but I found your letter opener and stabbed my hand to anchor myself to the desk and break the connection. It worked, but when Bishop tried to free me, another force slammed into me and ripped me away. I must have been tossed back against the wall, judging from how my back and the back of my head feels."

"Beloved," Amon said soberly as he lifted my swathed left hand, "I do not own a letter opener."

A moment of silence settled between us as I tried to digest this revelation.

"You must!" I insisted, not understanding his meaning. "It was right there on your desk. Without it I would have surely been pulled away from here."

"Listen to me, Catherine," he said pointedly, "I have no letter opener. Whatever you stabbed through your hand was not mine. Do you recall what happened to this letter opener?"

"Bishop removed it," I shook my head. "I didn't see it after that."

Unwrapping the sodden towel from my hand, Amon lifted it up before my eyes. The wound remained jagged and raw looking. The bleeding had stopped but the injury remained.

"This should have healed as soon as the metal was removed, right?" I marveled at the open wound.

"Yes, my love," he nodded grimly. "It should have healed and been nothing but a small scar, if even that, by now. The fact that it is still open and shows little sign of healing may mean some dark magic is involved."

"I should be able to fix it with my Healing Hand, shouldn't I?" I grinned at the thought, as using my Healing Hand always felt like such a rush.

"Beloved witch," Amon shook his head slowly, "that is your Healing Hand."

The weight of what he'd just said finally sank in and I looked up in confusion. Amon's blood red eyes were hidden behind contact lenses as dark as my own, but I could feel his emotions churning in those depths.

"What?" I nearly cried as an awful truth dawned on me, "I've skewered my Healing Hand? You think it won't heal and it won't work anymore? Was this some sort of trap that I walked right into? Amon, tell me! Is that what you think?"

"Precious, be calm," he replied, obviously avoiding my question as I teetered on the edge of hysteria. "I do not know what to think yet."

Momentary silence settled on the room.

"Your wolves!" I suddenly recognized the silence outside. "What happened to your wolves and my owls? We heard them outside."

"They departed as soon as I arrived," Amon responded. "Once I assured them that you and I were together and that all is well."

"Is all well?" A slight crack in my voice gave my emotions away. My mate looked at me without comment and I could feel his energy surrounding me. Whether it was an illusion or not, the sensation was wonderful and I sighed in relief.

"Bishop," Amon turned his eyes away from me reluctantly, "where is this letter opener?"

Pausing in his arranging his first aid supplies, Bishop turned and looked across the room.

"I left it on the desk when I rushed to get my bag," He nodded in that direction. "It should be there still."

Amon rose and crossed the room quickly. Silence rang out as he looked across the top of the desk then on the floor all around it.

"It is not here," he announced in clear frustration. "There is no letter opener here."

"It must be there," Bishop insisted and crossed the room to aid in the search. He pulled the big leather chair away from the desk and got down on his hands and knees to look beneath it. Again there was silence and I knew it meant trouble.

"I swear My Lord, it was right there on the desk blotter when I went for my medical bag," Bishop said adamantly.

Amon reached abruptly across the desk and yanked the phone from its base. He punched a series of buttons then spoke into the speaker on the desk.

"Bear, Dodge, wherever you are, seal the perimeter of the estate. We may have a trespasser and possible assailant on the grounds. Meet me in the foyer in two minutes," he commanded, then turned back to Bishop and me. "Bishop, see to Her Ladyship. I must make sure there is no one here. It could be that the letter opener disappeared of its own volition once its purpose was served, but it is possible too that someone came in here and took it away while you were out of the room, Bishop. You do realize that you left Catherine alone, unconscious, and unprotected do you not?"

"What else could he have done?" I started to protest.

"I do realize that I failed you, My Lord," Bishop said soberly. "I was torn between seeing to Her Ladyship's condition and waiting for assistance from Winter or someone else. I feared it would take too long for help to come so I went for my bag. I beg your forgiveness. I would never intentionally leave Her Ladyship unprotected."

Amon's eyes flashed in anger even behind his contact lenses and the electricity in the air became palpable.

"I will see to you later," Amon growled at Bishop, through clinched teeth, as he came and sat beside me on the edge of the couch. "Precious, rest here while I go meet with the security team. Bishop will see to your hand." Leaning carefully to avoid touching my hand, Amon placed his lips on mine and blessed me with a divinely hungry kiss. The power that ran through me when my mate kissed me was enough to stir my magick and take my breath away. I caressed the side of his face once more, already regretting the void I knew I'd feel as soon as he left the room. He stood reluctantly, nodded silently to Bishop, then left without making a sound.

Moments later Winter abruptly opened the door. He rushed in and took my right hand in his, then sat down beside me just as Amon had.

"Cat," he shook his head, "I can't let you out of my sight for one moment, can I? His Lordship just told me what happened. I'm to not leave your side."

As both vampire and body guard, Winter was one of the few supernatural beings I knew that carried physical weapons. He and I shared a love of handguns and he was teaching me the value of fine blades. And though there were certainly beings out there that a gun or knife wouldn't destroy, I was learning to take comfort in the knowledge that one or the other would surely drop an attacker, if only briefly, and give me the chance to flee. Though considered immortal, because technically we were already dead, we vampires could be destroyed or made to suffer horribly. Immortality, I had discovered, was not the free ride that I had expected. Immortal did not mean invulnerable, nor did it mean eternal.

Bishop cleared his throat and looked expectantly down at Winter. He had a cloth in one hand and a brown glass bottle of something in the other. Winter released my hand, stood up, and stepped out of the way. Bishop did not sit down, but took my hand, removed the towel, and began to clean my wound while standing bent over me. I looked past him to Winter.

"You have information for me?" I hissed as the pressure on my hand made the flesh sting. Bishop was being as careful as he could, but a through and through wound is exquisitely tender.

"I do," Winter nodded brightly, then shook his head again, "well, sort of, and you're probably not going to like it."

"I didn't expect to," I agreed.

Bishop paused in his ministrations to my wound and looked down at me.

"If you two don't mind," he smiled grimly, "I'd rather not be privy to anything His Lordship is currently unaware of. I'm facing some sort of discipline as it is and I'd prefer to face him with a clear conscience."

"Oh," I nodded, "I understand. Winter can wait with his story until you're finished."

"Thank you, My Lady," Bishop sighed in relief as he began binding my hand.

"I told you, Bishop, it's Cat when it's just us," I reminded him of my distaste of formality.

"Of course, Cat," he nodded, "and this is the best I can do for your hand at the moment. Hopefully it will heal, though perhaps at a slower rate than it normally would."

As he gathered his supplies back into his medical bag, Bishop kept his head down and his eyes averted. He simply nodded curtly as he left the room without further comment.

I gingerly swung my legs down from the couch and leaned back against the cushions, patting the seat beside mine for Winter to join me. The cool leather of the couch supported my aching back and eased the pain a bit.

"So," I said at last, "tell me Oola's story."

Pausing to adjust the shoulder holster on his back and move his handgun out of the way, Winter lowered himself onto the sofa and sighed dramatically. He was normally cheerful and buoyant, but he now seemed troubled. He appeared reluctant to begin the conversation, so I waited silently, just looking at him. He propped a booted ankle on his knee and began to examine the hem of his blue jeans.

"Come on Winter, spill it," I smiled and punched his arm.

He leaned back on the sofa and fixed me with a look that said this was not the time for levity. Shaking his head, his mane of golden curls spilling lightly, he sighed once more and said nothing. This was so unlike Winter. He was normally so forthright and forthcoming.

"Cat, I don't even know where to begin," he admitted, spreading his hands in a gesture of helplessness.

"Come on Winter," I demanded in exasperation, "you're killing me here with the suspense. Dish!"

"This is such a mess," he shook his head once more, "and I'm afraid I know how you're going to react and I can see trouble coming."

"Geesh, am I that predictable?" I laughed, trying to brighten his mood.

"Predictable? You?" he smiled at last and it was a genuine smile that lit the gold in his eyes.

"I'm going to have to know eventually," I added. "You might as well give it to me with both barrels."

"That's what I'm afraid of," he nodded and took a deep breath. "Okay, I'll tell you what Oola told me."

"Finally," I rolled my eyes and lifted my hands to the heavens, though the pain in my left hand reminded me that it wasn't a good idea.

"Oola's sire, Sabre, went missing," he stated then turned and looked directly at me. His expression seemed to impart a hidden meaning in his words.

"Yes, and…" I forced myself to be patient.

"The rumor is that he fell in love with a mortal," he continued hesitantly.

"So…" glancing sideways, I raised one eyebrow.

"She was a witch," he replied, looking me squarely in the eyes as if to impart some profound wisdom.

"A witch," I murmured, already not liking the implications. I was a witch when Amon, my mate, fell in love with me, though I had been unaware of it at the time. I was sensing an uneasy parallel arising.

"Yes, and word is she rejected him."

"So according to vampire rules, he had to either erase her memory of him and the whole vampire community or destroy her, right?" I offered my understanding of the situation.

"Well, he could have taken her and made her vampire against her wishes," Winter pointed out, "but he truly loved her, so the story goes, and couldn't do that. Nor could he kill her."

"So he tried to erase her memory?"

"Unsuccessfully, it seems," he nodded.

"So he was forced to kill her?" I asked, not liking where this story was going.

"Well, this particular witch was of an ancestral line of witches that stretched back centuries. As such she was very aware of the cycle of progression and would not deny her place in the evolution of her kind. She would not submit to becoming immortal and being removed from the wheel of life," Winter explained.

"So Sabre had to destroy her or face punishment," I reasoned.

"Yes," he replied, "but he did not. It seems that rather than risk being forced into immortality, she committed suicide."

"So, what's the problem?" I tried to grasp the issue. "The threat is gone, so what's the big deal? She's gone, the vampire community is safe once more. All's right with the world, right?"

Winter's silence left me confused. If the witch had destroyed herself, why was Oola petitioning me for protection and why was Sabre missing?

"All's not right with the world or Oola wouldn't have come here seeking help. What's the deal, Winter?" I insisted.

My beloved bodyguard and friend sat silently looking at his hands. It was obvious that he didn't want to continue the conversation. When he got in this mood, which luckily was seldom, getting information from him was like pulling teeth. It was one tooth at a time.

"It came to be known by the Council of Five that Sabre had failed to act in his capacity as Master Vampire. Sabre couldn't bring himself to destroy the witch or force her into this life. When his attempt at erasing her memory failed he should have acted immediately, but he didn't. The fact that she took her own life means nothing in vampire law. The Council sees only that he failed to eliminate the threat. He's being sought for possible punishment."

"Wait a minute," I held up my hand, my right hand. "Amon told me about this. Failure to act in such a matter could mean torture in perpetuity or destruction, right?" Suddenly I was proud of myself for having recalled that information. Vampire laws were so arbitrary and so confusing to me, I had a hard time making sense of them, let alone remembering them all.

"Indeed," Winter agreed then added, "destruction of the sire in question..."

"And of his entire line," I finished the line with a sigh of realization.

"So you see why Oola and those she represents came looking for your protection," he said soberly.

"But, wait a minute," I chewed the corner of my lip absent-mindedly while I considered the tidal wave of questions that rolled toward me. "I understand that Oola would come to me because I hold dominion over the owls, but why would she and those she represents not go to Amon? He's the one with authority around here. The Council of Five barely tolerates my existence and the vampire community would probably be relieved if I were to fall into a black hole!"

"If His Lordship knew you felt this way, he would likely be taking the Council to task one member at a time," Winter smiled sadly. "But you are not wrong, Oola should have gone to His Lordship first. It's a grave insult to have approached you as she did."

"So what am I supposed to do?" I heaved a sigh, "Not only am I to protect Oola and the others from the Council of Goobers, I also now have to protect her from Amon and this vampire stuffed-shirt sense of protocol."

"Oola does wish to speak to you personally, you know," he cocked his head to the side and looked pointedly at my injured hand. "Are you up to it?"

"I have no idea," I chuckled as I stiffly rose from the couch and touched the back of my head with my good hand. "I'll admit that I'm sore."

"She gave me this to give to you," he stood up, shoved his hand into the pocket of his jeans and pulled out a folded slip of pink paper.

"Great," I murmured as I opened the note and read *"My Lady, please meet me at the Bistro in Lake Charles tonight at your earliest convenience. I shall await you. Regards, Oola."*

"Alrighty then," I smiled, refolded the note, and stuck it in my pocket. "Time for me to change these clothes and get busy."

"Is there some way I can help you, Cat?" Winter stood aside as I hobbled slowly by him.

"No, Winter," I smiled. "I'm going to take a hot bath and then dress. I have business to attend."

"I'm not to leave your side, petite sœur!"

"Fine," I nodded, "then by all means, come along."
I laughed then checked my mental shields to make sure
my mate had no idea what was stirring in my mind. All
seemed well.

Moving slowly down the corridors, I cradled my
wounded hand in the crook of my right arm and thought
myself making good progress when my beloved body
guard scooped me up in his arms.

"Good grief, Cat," Winter shook his head in dismay,
"you are not as strong as you'd have everyone believe."

"I'm plenty strong," I insisted. "I'm just a bit wobbly.
The hot bath will fix me right up, I'm sure." Even as we
made our way down the long hallway I could feel the
muscles in my back and the back of my head beginning
to relax. Though becoming vampire had not left me
impervious to injury, my body was now, usually, capable of accelerated healing. Inwardly, I fumed at the fact
that my wounded hand had not spontaneously healed.
The notion that increased cellular regeneration might
be a necessary development to vampires due to their
penchant for fighting amongst themselves did cross my
mind, but I dismissed it as unlikely.

Winter carried me through the Sapphire room and
into the bathroom suite beyond. He placed me gently
on the edge of the bathtub and bowed before excusing
himself.

"I'll wait in the other room, if you like," he offered, "or do you need further assistance?"

"I'm fine, Winter," I responded, half-turning to reach the faucet and turn on the water. "I'll call you when I'm done. Just go relax, please."

As he left, I pulled off my boots and socks then stood up, removed my clothes, and stepped gingerly into the very warm water now filling the tub. Sighing, I lowered myself into the water and leaned back as I grabbed a folded wash cloth from the pile on a nearby shelf. I wet the cloth and placed it over my eyes, relaxing as the tub finished filling. Turning off the faucet, I leaned back once more and relaxed, going over all that had happened in my mind. I knew that it would be impossible for me to leave the estate if Amon was about when I needed to depart, so I could only hope that he had a meeting or some business to attend to elsewhere.

The water was cool when my eyes snapped open and I sat up in the tub. I'd no idea how long I'd been asleep, but physically I felt good. Neither my back nor the back of my head caused me pain nor even discomfort, and I sighed in relief as I pulled the plug on the tub, stood, and dried myself on a large, fluffy white towel. When I opened the bathroom door I found Winter leaning against the corner post of the four poster bed. His arms were crossed over his chest. He looked up at me suddenly, as if he'd been asleep on his feet and had just awakened.

"Thanks, Winter," I smiled as, wrapped in a towel, I went to the dresser to get undergarments, fresh jeans, and a top. "I'll get dressed then you can help me with this," I grabbed the Tomcat from the drawer along with my throwing blades and the forearm holsters.

"You think you'll need weapons?" He looked startled.

"Likely not," I admitted. "But I have the sense that there's much going on that we're unaware of and I'd rather be safe than sorry."

"Indeed," he nodded in agreement. "Shall I step out while you dress?"

"Not necessary," I responded, "and in fact, I may need your help as this hand is not worth much at the moment." I held my bandaged left hand up and tossed a pair of socks at the blond vamp. "Think you can get these on my feets?"

"I believe I can," he chuckled and caught them handily, pulling them apart and rolling down the top of one sock. "Please," he patted the edge of the bed, "have a seat."

With Winter's assistance, and a fair amount of patience, I managed to get into my clothes, donning dark jeans, a scarlet sleeveless t-shirt, black brocade fingertip length jacket and black boots. I dragged a brush through my mane and drew it back with a deep red velvet ribbon, then put my tiny dark glasses on my nose. Winter had helped me slip on the underarm holster for the gun and had strapped the blades onto my forearms before holding out the jacket so I could slip it up my arms. Pausing briefly before the full-length mirror, I slid the Tomcat into its holster then made sure that no weapon could be detected at a glance before nodding approval.

"Let's go," I brightened at the prospect of actually doing something.

"My Lady, Cat," Winter started, as I opened the door to step out into the hallway. Turning to look back at him while still moving forward, I ran almost face-first into the chest of my beloved Amon.

"Passion," he said soberly, "where are you going?"

"Amon, my darling," I offered him my sweetest smile, "what are you doing here?"

"Where would you have me be when my beloved is planning something ill-advised?"

"Ill-advised?" I parroted in mock confusion.

"You were planning to leave the estate," he raised one eyebrow and crossed his arms over his chest.

"Damn, Amon," I seethed, "I wish you would stop prying into my thoughts!"

"To be fair, it was not intentional," he offered. "Your plan to leave came to me clearly while you slept."

"I didn't sle…" I started to protest then realized that I had indeed fallen asleep in the bath tub. "Dang, how do I keep you out of my brain while I sleep?"

"You thoughts do not always come to me when you sleep, Cat," he smiled gently. "But I am happy that they did so in this case."

"Fine!" I grabbed my mate's hand and started pulling him down the hall, calling back over my shoulder, "Thank you Winter. I'll have no further need of you tonight so you can take the night off!"

Amon was dressed in a long gray silk shirt with tight black pants and knee-height boots. His hair was loose and he looked comfortable and relaxed. He looked delicious.

"You'll want to change your clothes since we are going out?" I offered as we passed one of his many wardrobe rooms.

"Naturally, my love," he replied. "I would not leave the grounds dressed thusly."

"You look great, by the way," I grinned, looking him up and down in obvious appreciation. "But I'll wait for you here."

"You would not like to assist me as I dress?" He purred and bent to gently kiss my lips.

"I'd enjoy nothing more," I whispered into his mouth then pulled away, "but we have no time right now. Later, my love."

"Very well," he nodded, inhaled resignedly, and turned to go into his room. "You will remain here!"

"Right here," I agreed with a laugh.

Chapter 5

The mild night embraced us as we stepped out onto the veranda. A gentle breeze carried the heady scents of gardenia, magnolia, and sweet olive as it danced through trees adorned with softly glowing lights. Amon, still clasping my hand, pulled me to a sudden stop and caught me in his embrace. Looking down, his eyes shining unnaturally in the darkness, the red-gold of his irises easily visible beneath dark contacts, he smiled enigmatically. There were, I hated to admit, still some expressions of his which I could not clearly read and such a smile only confused me. It held love, of course, and some small delight perhaps, but there was also something…almost cruel in the curl of his lips, the glow of those eyes. *'Well, it's not cruelty, exactly,'* I admonished myself, *'but maybe a look of smug satisfaction one wears when observing one's possession.'* The thought of being anyone's possession, even my beloved Master Vampire's, brought me no happiness and even raised my ire, so I quickly dismissed the thought and met his smile with my own.

"Our destination, my love," he murmured as he lowered his lips to my right ear.

"You mean you didn't glean that when you were poking around in my thoughts, uninvited and unannounced?"

"Passion," he raised his head and one eyebrow, "let us say my surprise at your intention to leave the estate tonight was sufficient to render all other information of small consequence."

Sighing, I shook my head with a grin, "And why would you be surprised?"

"Indeed," he nodded slightly, "I should not be surprised, and yet ever I am. By now one would think you would have learned how I think and what I expect of you in the way of obedience and your actions in general. Yet you insist on irresponsible behavior."

"Amon, my darling," I interrupted his reprimands, "light of my life, love of my eternity…"

"Yes?" His confusion was made obvious by the crease in his forehead.

"Lake Charles," I answered quietly, then added, "The Bistro."

"Ah," he paused then nodded succinctly, "very well."

Slipping my right arm around his neck forced me to stretch up on my tiptoes, and I gently tucked my wounded left hand inside his open coat as he tighten his arms around me. Nuzzling beneath his chin, I closed my eyes and drew my power up to meet his as we rose into the night. I'd discovered that it was much easier on my mind, not to mention my stomach, to keep my eyes physically closed when we flew, as sometimes the 'reverse x-ray' effect of what I saw made me nauseous. What should have been brightly lit, was now dark to my sight; what should have been dark was now clearly alight.

"You are armed, beloved?" Amon murmured as he moved one hand along the shape of the gun and holster secreted beneath my coat.

"I am," I replied, and said nothing further.

Covering the short distance very quickly, Amon brought us to earth in a wooden-fenced backlot behind a dry cleaning shop. A startled alley cat shrieked and bounded away between discarded cardboard boxes and barrels of plastic bags, but no one else witnessed our arrival. Once my feet were safely on the ground and my equilibrium returned, I patted Amon on the chest and made to step out of his embrace. He caught my hand and held it firmly, a serious look on his face.

"I shall accompany you," he announced.

"I had intended to speak with you about that," I replied, startled by his refusal to release me. "You see, the person I'm meeting is a bit timid and I'm afraid that if she sees you she may bolt."

"She knows you are my mate?"

"Of course she knows that, my love," I explained, "but like I said, she's kind of shy. And let's face it, you're a bit intimidating."

"Hear me now, witch," he spoke firmly, "you are not at your full strength, you have been wounded and still your Healing Hand has not mended. I shall not leave you until I am sure you are safe. I shall escort you into the Bistro, I shall meet this person who seeks your attention, and when I am fully comfortable that you are in no danger, I shall excuse myself to sit at some distance. You will have privacy for your meeting once I am sure it is safe."

At that, I knew there was no point in arguing the matter further. I had learned long ago that when it came to my safety, Amon was immovable. Though I didn't see the matter as one involving any danger, he did, and once he considered me in peril, no amount of persuasion on my part would change his mind. Reluctantly, I smiled and nodded my assent. At last, he let go of my hand and I captured his other hand quickly.

"Come, my love," I grinned as I pulled him around the refuse and toward the street, "if we're going to do this, let's do this."

Overhead vapors threw bright pools of pink light on the thoroughfare. Neon flashed from the windows of chic eateries and cheap bars alike. The changing traffic lights seemed to be trying to cheer the mostly empty streets. Few cars moved along Broad Street at this hour and even fewer people made their way along the wide, broken sidewalks. The lights inside the Bistro had been dimmed, as I knew they always were after 10pm, so the ambience was quiet and intimate. Votive candles burned on the table of each booth along the walls and on small square tables that occupied the center floor area. The kitchen and bar were straight back from the door and I had an inkling that Oola would be sitting in one of the booths nearest them. The Bistro was a funky place where we did not stand out wearing dark glasses late at night. The crowds that frequented it were 'artsy', bohemian, even somewhat hippie, but they were disinterested enough that Amon and I could both come in wearing dark spectacles and no one would even look up, let alone make a scene. Folk music wafted from invisible speakers as we made our way between the tables, peering at the occupants of each booth as we went. From several feet away, I spied Oola's blond hair in the last booth on the left and squeezed Amon's hand to gain his attention. He nodded understanding without comment.

"Oola," I smiled as I slid into the seat across the table from her, "I'm happy to see you. This is my mate, His Lordship Amon." I nodded at the towering vampire

87

standing silently beside the booth, his hand still holding mine. "Amon, my beloved, this is Oola."

Her already pale face blanched and her neck convulsed slightly as she struggled to swallow. Oola's expression was one of abject horror. For a moment she simply froze, taking in the sight of the Master Vampire, then her expression shifted and I could see she was considering the possibility of successful flight; not the aviary, winged flight, but all out 'feets don't fail me now' type flight. To her credit, and my considerable relief, the beautiful blond vampire held Amon's gaze briefly as he peered at her over the top of his dark glasses. She then demurred and lowered her eyes without comment, a customary greeting among vampires when one is introduced to a more powerful entity. Amon said simply, "Oola," and then turned to me. "I shall leave you to attend to your business." With that he nodded, almost imperceptibly, then strode across the room to take a seat at a booth near the front door and on the opposite wall. Unexpectedly, he slid onto the seat facing away from the door, apparently so he could keep an eye on Oola and me.

"So," I smiled and sat back in my seat, resting my right hand on the table, cradling my left hand on my lap, "you wanted to see me. Here I am."

"I did," she nodded, swallowed hard and pulled her hands from atop the table and into her lap. "First let me apologize for not telling Winter everything. I understand that he's your trusted bodyguard, but I don't know him. I couldn't risk trusting him."

"He's much more than just my bodyguard, Oola," I nodded in reply then looked up and smiled at the waitress who had materialized at the end of the table.

"We'll have two glasses of your best Merlot," I ordered without consulting Oola and the young waitress nodded silently before disappearing.

"I'm sorry," the blonde sighed, looking nervously across the room to where Amon sat. She chewed on her bottom lip for a moment before adding, "I'm just feeling a bit lost."

"So, let's not dwell on that," I interjected. "Tell me, why is it that Sabre is unable or unwilling to protect you and how it is that you know you're in need of protection?"

"Three of our number have already been destroyed in manners most gruesome," she answered succinctly, "and no one has been able to contact our sire."

"You have no telepathic or psychic link you can use?"

"Of course, many of us have such links to Lord Sabre, but when we try to access him there's simply nothing there. It's like reaching a dead end or a blank wall."

"And that would seem to indicate to you…" I prodded as gently as possible, though instead of responding Oola looked up and startled.

When Winter suddenly appeared at my elbow I nearly jumped out of my skin before recovering my wits to slide over so he could join us. Oola remained immobile and silent.

"I got the message that you wished me to join you," Winter smiled as he leaned back in the booth and rested his elbows on the edge of the table. "Good thing too, because I nearly missed it. Hope I'm not too late."

"Um, no," I smiled and went along with whatever charade he was playing, "you're just in time, though I wasn't sure you'd make it so I didn't order you a drink."

His golden eyes glowed unnaturally in the dim light of the votive and his teeth and white shirt adorned with gold buttons gleamed as he moved.

"That's quite all right, My Lady," he nodded, the golden curls near his face stirring ever so softly as he spoke, "I am here for you and Oola, I need no refreshment."

Wishing desperately that Oola would excuse herself and make for the Ladies Room so that I could find out what the devil my beloved yet unexpected friend was doing showing up in such a manner, I could only hope that I didn't say the wrong thing and reveal my confusion. Oola, for whatever reason, as my vision was now completely blocked by the back of the booth and Winter, kept glancing nervously either at the door or at Amon, who was undoubtedly watching us with equal interest.

"Actually, your timing's just right, Winter," I touched his hand as I changed the subject, "Oola was just telling me that Sabre's sirelings cannot reach him, either by traditional methods or those more especially of our nature. Any idea what that could mean?"

Winter neither stirred nor answered as he and Oola had locked eyes upon one another and either they were sharing '*Owlspeak*' or they were enjoying the challenge of a staring contest. Suddenly I felt like the odd man out at the table and was relieved when the waitress returned and placed the two glasses of wine on the table. When she asked what she could get Winter, he turned his attention from Oola, smiled and told her that he was fine for now. She half-curtseyed and spun away from the table, somewhat dazed by the glamour that was pouring off the two blond vampires.

"As I was saying," I picked up my glass and sipped the Merlot. "I could guess what this lack of access to one's sire might mean based on my limited experience as," I looked around and dropped my voice, "what I am, but it would only be a guess."

"Oola?" Winter stared across the table, his simple utterance of her name some sort of weapon, apparently. She glared back at him for a moment then her expression softened and she heaved a sigh then nodded. Either my beloved friend had broken her defenses or somehow at least had made clear to her that she'd have to drop her shields if she wanted or expected our help.

"Either he's intentionally blocking us," she admitted grimly, "or he's somehow unable to let us reach him, or to reach us. Either way, it's highly unusual and does not bode well."

"I think it's time you explained what's going on," I smiled, trying to be as patient as possible yet losing the battle quickly.

"All I know for sure is that a few months ago, Lord Sabre met a woman," Oola offered, pretending to sip her wine. "He told us that she was a witch and that they were very much in love. As time went on, we saw less and less of him. He would disappear for a few days, then longer. Now, we've been trying to make contact with him for many days and can't. In the meantime three of our number have been destroyed and, as you might imagine, we're feeling a bit vulnerable."

"So, how many of you are there?" I wondered aloud.

"As of now there are 270 of us, though until recently we numbered 273," Oola smiled sadly.

"Two hundred seventy!" My mind wobbled at Sabre siring that many vampires as my beloved Master Vampire, Amon, had transformed me and only me. Over time I had come to discover that those who swore fealty to him did so out of respect and gratitude, it was not that he had actually sired those who called him 'Lord'.

"In Lord Sabre's region there are over 800 of our kind," Oola explained, "but not all are owl, just the 270. The rest are pack or other species."

"Hold the phone, central," I held up my hand and drew in a deep breath. "As one who holds dominion over the owls, you already have my protection. However as vampire and actually being in His Lordship Amon's region, that is something else. Are you seeking protection for all of Sabre's sirelings or just the owls?"

"Other creatures of Sabre's making must find their own means of protection and self-preservation," she answered matter of factly. "I seek protection from you only for those of your domain. We will need your permission to move into the area."

"Ah," I sighed, wondering what possible absurd chain of command would be involved it garnering such permission. Yes, I had dominion over the owls, but the region was entirely Amon's and, though as his mate I enjoyed certain liberties that others would never attain,

I suspected this might be one giant knot of Christmas lights I was being asked to unsnarl.

"I'll speak to some other individuals whose specialty is finding," Winter hesitated, "difficult to find entities and see what they can discover as to what's happening with Lord Sabre. In the meantime, My Lady, you can attend to the details of this matter with the owls, if you'd allow me to serve you so."

"Yes, Winter," I grinned at his proper verbiage, "that would be lovely."

As I lifted my wineglass to take a sip of the fine Merlot, I noticed movement in my peripheral vision that should not have been there. Turning to look more closely, I discovered that what I'd taken for ornate paneling was actually silver surface shot through with veins of color. What I thought was marble was actually mirror and what I was seeing in the reflection brought me no joy. Across the room, a petite female with short dark hair and equally dark tight leather attire was standing at the end of Amon's table and it was quite clear that she was not his waitress. Turning away from the reflection on my left, I elbowed myself above the top of our booth to look for myself at what was happening at my beloved's table.

By merely glancing at the scene, I picked up pheromones that the leather clad Goth chick was spewing like Vesuvius spewed lava. Her energy was trying to coil itself around his power like a snake and though he was not encouraging her in any obvious way, he was not discouraging her either. Something powerful and ugly rose from deep inside me and suddenly my thoughts and intentions were clear.

"Excuse me, Winter," I nudged his elbow. "I need to visit the Ladies Room."

Without further explanation, I slid out of the booth behind my confused bodyguard and strode purposefully across the room.

Taking the brunette Goth firmly by the elbow, I pushed her away from Amon's table and toward the back of the bistro, speaking quietly and emphatically into her ear.

"There's an emergency with a friend of yours in the Ladies Room," I whispered, "and you're needed there now!"

Giving the surprised Goth no time to complain or argue, I shoved her past the bar and down the hallway into the restroom. Before she had a chance to look around and register that the place was actually free of any occupants, I turned her quickly and sank my teeth into her throat. She only struggled for a moment then went quiet, enraptured by the sensations that I'd once enjoyed. As I fed, I stole her memory of this event and any of seeing or speaking with Amon, though when I touched her mind where thoughts of him were stored, I found an energy that actually enriched and heated the blood I was drinking. '*Ah, the emotions and hormones of mortal youth*,' I thought as I finished feeding, licked the wounds to seal them, then pressed the fingers of my left hand on her throat. The Healing Hand thrummed and felt strange as it did so, but it did heal the marks on her throat completely. She shook her head as if to clear it and stared at me in confusion.

"What happened?" She whined, her thickly lined eyes widening in surprise as she took in my appearance, "Do I know you?"

"We've been chatting here for a few minutes about where you got that great outfit," I smiled and nodded encouragingly, "but you got dizzy for a moment and I had to catch you to keep you from falling. You do seem to be feeling better now, though."

Her ensemble, though perhaps a bit too cliché for my taste, was actually quite attractive on her. The purple lace blouse beneath her black leather bustier dramatically let her very pale skin peek through the weave and the neckline highlighted the upside down crucifix she wore around her neck. The long coat she wore over black leather pants just reached the top of her chunky-heeled combat boots. Her hairstyle, probably more punk than Goth, was a 'bob' with the bangs jagged and actual chunks removed to appear that her stylist was both armed and angry and she merely the victim of rage.

"Yeah," she touched her forehead as if seeking an injury then peered around at the restroom. "I think I'm okay."

"Maybe you should splash some water on your face, that should do the trick," I offered, pointing to the water-puddled but reasonably clean sinks on the adjacent wall.

"Um, yeah," she huffed and regained her composure, "well, thanks." It was clear that I was being dismissed so I took the opportunity to push a well-aimed spell at her as I left the Ladies Room. *'You will never approach or speak to His Lordship Amon again unless you are invited to do so. You will not recall any of this incident nor will you recall even seeing or speaking to me.'* As the door swung shut behind me, I straightened my jacket and made sure my lips were clean then made my way back to Amon's table.

"That was," he tried unsuccessfully to hide a smile, "interesting. I rather like seeing you jealous."

"Jealous," I gaped. "As if!"

"What did you do with the tiny morsel?" He pretended to look around and even past me. "I do hope nothing untoward befell her."

"Pffftttt! I was killing two birds with one stone, my love," I bent down and put my lips on his, breathing the taste of young Goth blood into his mouth. "I needed to feed and she needed to be taught a lesson."

"Mmmmm," he purred as I pulled away from him, "and what lesson would that be, ma chèri?"

"No one messes with my man," I leered then bent quickly and planted another quick kiss on his lips.

"So you were jealous," he chuckled in obvious delight.

"Hey, I didn't raise you from a pup only to have some little tartlet move in on my territory," I smiled and touched the curve of his cheek before returning to Oola and Winter at our booth.

"Raise me from a pup?" Amon snapped in confusion as I knew he would. "You will explain that remark later!"

"Of course," I called back over my shoulder, noting that I smelled vaguely of the cologne my meal must have been wearing.

Though my beloved teased me about jealousy, and though I had no doubt he was enjoying the notion, he had taught me how to choose the proper 'meal' shortly after I became vampire. That young male blood enhanced by passion was the most satisfying and powerful made complete sense, though it did take me some time to understand that though anger can be a passion, its flavor and resultant energy was not even close. The difference between the two, I'd come to realize, was that of a fire in the fireplace and an explosion. Both were technically fire, but the first was not only manageable but deeply satisfying, the second…just really bright, loud, and gone in an instant. A female's blood, stirred by lust, was not quite as rich as her male counterpart's, but it was still very satisfying, especially when taken from one so young. So, if it happened that feeding off the 'wanna-bee' scooted her fanny away from Amon succinctly, I reasoned, I was just doing her a favor because it was considered the height of bad manners, as well as extremely dangerous, to approach a Master Vampire unannounced or uninvited.

Winter stood politely to let me slide back into the booth, but I waved my hand dismissively.

"I'll sit over here with Oola," I announced and the blond vampire looked up in surprise. Not waiting for her to react, I sat down on the bench and slid in, resting my elbows on the table as I inspected my new, unob-structed, view of the door and Amon. My mate sat with his long legs outstretched beneath his table, one hand idly touching his wine glass, a wicked smile playing on his lips. He had donned a silver silk brocade vest over an exquisitely tailored black dress shirt and had pulled the top of his hair back and secured it with a braided silver cord. The choice of attire highlighted the flash of silver hair at his temple and the tiny dark glasses made him appear both eccentric and mysterious. He was well aware of the vision he made and the affect it had on me. Though my need to feed had been sufficiently satisfied, his power and appearance brought other needs to mind and I had to tear my eyes off of him to drag my attention back to the business at hand.

"My apologies," I grinned at Winter, offering him a wink. He merely shook his head almost imperceptibly. "So, Oola," I turned to address my new seat-mate, "you do understand that I'm going to have to discuss this matter with….I don't even know who I'm going to have to discuss it with, in fact. But ultimately, of course, if you and the other owls wish to move to this region I will have to take matters up with His Lordship Amon."

"Yes," she looked down at her hands, then looked up at me, "I understand. I hope that the tales of you I've heard are true and that you'll be able to help us."

"Once more, I've no idea of any tales you might have heard," I shrugged and reached across the table to retrieve my nearly-empty wineglass, "but I can assure you that I'll do everything I can."

"They're true," Winter laughed and looked from me to Oola, "trust me, they're true!"

Though I started to argue with him, Winter just looked pointedly at me, then glanced at Oola. Relief was written on her face. She relaxed against the upholstered bench back before taking a long sip of wine. I realized that he'd been re-assuring Oola in order to give her confidence in my power, but I hoped he'd not set her up for disappointment. The fact that I'd no real idea where to start or how to proceed with getting all of Sabre's owls under my protection, let alone how to approach my beloved Amon about how to get permission to get them relocated, certainly didn't boost my own confidence in my power. Giving Winter a knowing look, I emptied my wineglass then stood.

"If there's nothing else," I looked at Oola who was now smiling softly at Winter, "I'll take my leave of you. His Lordship awaits and I've much to do before the sun rises. Winter, why don't you stay with Oola, keep her company, and see that she makes it home safely?"

"Home safely," he murmured, then brightened. "Oh, of course. Yes, I'll stay here and keep her company. You know how to reach me if I'm needed or can be of service."

"You're of service right where you are," I patted his shoulder, squeezing slightly to make sure he was wearing his shoulder holster and side arm. "Enjoy your evening!"

My beloved Amon stood as I made my way across the room and he slipped his arm around my waist and kissed my cheek.

"Your business is complete," he spoke softly into the curve of my neck, his tongue slipping along my jugular vein, "and you are all mine now?"

"It is," I shuddered at the sensation, "and I am."

"Then come," he drew me forward, held the door of the Bistro open, and ushered me out into the night, "let us fly!" We strolled arm in arm, well, his arm around my shoulders, my arm around his waist, down the now dimly lit sidewalk. There were even fewer pedestrians about at this hour than there had been when we arrived and we were relieved not to meet any passers-by as we made our way to the dry cleaning shop. The hunger that had been assuaged by my feeding had been shifted to a hunger of another kind and I was anxious to be home and in Amon's embrace. Swallowing a lusty laugh, I took him by the hand and hurried him back into the vacant lot amongst the empty cardboard boxes and garbage bins.

"I'm ready if you are," I whispered hoarsely, my voice already growing thick from passionate thoughts. Slipping my arms around his neck, I buried my face in the collar of his cloak as he answered, "I am." My power rose and entwined itself with his as we soared through the night sky. My lips found the pulse at his throat and I secretly reveled in appreciation that he could make that happen for me. Breathing in his scent, I kissed his neck and released all thoughts and concerns save him and him alone. *'One hunger at a time, Cat,'* my inner voice chided me, *'one hunger at a time!'*

Chapter 6

Tree lights twinkled in the garden when we landed among the rose bushes and wisteria trellises. The windows of the mansion were still softly aglow. I knew that Lily and Lucius had gone home for the night, and with Winter out with Oola, that meant that Amon and I had the place to ourselves, if we didn't count Bishop and the guards that patrolled the grounds periodically. Though we'd often made passionate love in the garden, when Amon released me from his arms he did not linger for a kiss as I'd expected. Instead, he tilted his head slightly to one side, as if listening to something I couldn't hear, then silently slid his arm around my shoulders. Without a word he escorted me quickly to the wide flagstone veranda before the French doors that led into the Great Hall. To my surprise he then released me and started to go inside.

"Whoa there, peaches," I called out in confusion, "haven't you forgotten something?"

"I have forgotten nothing, beloved," he stopped, took two long strides back and stood before me, "but I must postpone that which I would find most agreeable at this moment."

"Wha..." I stammered.

"Thammuz awaits me inside," Amon explained and suddenly any hopes of passionate lovemaking crashed and burned. "It surprises me greatly that you did not perceive his presence the moment we arrived, Cat."

"Yeah well," I glared in annoyance that was only slightly exaggerated, "I had my mind on something else when we arrived and I suspect it would take more than a visit from the Grim Reaper to um, well, to distract me from it."

"Something," he grinned lasciviously, "that would be me?" He bent down and ran his tongue from the base of my throat up to the lobe of my left ear.

"Perhaps," I swatted him away gently, though my toes were still curled up in my boots, "but now that you mention it, I can sense Thammuz inside." I was being honest though I was amazed even as I said it because this was yet another new ability, not only sensing an entity, but also identifying its energy signature. Thammuz's felt like a brooding, humorless...rock!

"Grim Reaper?" Amon had started to walk inside then glanced back at me, "Pardon?"

"Never mind, my love," I shook my head and motioned him on with a brush of my hand. "You've business to attend and I have some things that need my attention too. I'll see you when your meeting's over?" Though in my mind Thammuz was about as lively and as much fun to be around as the Grim Reaper, I had no desire to stop and explain that to Amon. And the possibility that my attempt at humor might be slightly misunderstood was always about fifty/fifty; best to skim over the issue and keep moving.

"Of course, Passion," he bowed slightly and smartly, then turned and strode in through the French doors, leaving me alone in the darkness and not unhappy about it.

To my huge relief, either Amon had forgotten the message from Doug Donahue, or he'd at least not yet had the opportunity to query me about the matter. This gave me some time to further consider my options so I followed him through the French doors and turned on the lights in the Great Hall. The ornate chandeliers suddenly threw bright pools of warm light across the cool marble floor. Thammuz and Amon were greeting one another in the parlor just off the hall on my left so I made my way silently by, hoping not to disturb them or, better yet, not even be noticed. There were some abilities one gained eventually upon becoming vampire and cat-like stealth was one that I'd taken pains to master, as it often served me quite well. Making my way up the wide staircase, I moved quickly to the Sapphire room, considering a change of clothes along the way. Sleeveless tank and slouchy lounging pants seemed an appealing alternative to the constrictive garments and weapons I was wearing. Entering the softly lit bedroom, I started removing my boots as I hopped on one foot then the other to the dresser. I'd just bent over to open a drawer when something whizzed past my ear and lodged with a profound 'thunk' in the doorframe just beside me. Whirling, I searched behind me then all around the room looking for the assailant that had thrown the weapon, but found I was alone. I pulled the blade from the doorframe, turning it over and over in my hands. To my surprise, it was the letter opener that had been in Amon's office, earlier in the day, and the one with which I'd pinned my hand to the desk.

"So where did you come from, you wicked little thing?" I wondered aloud as I looked closely at it. Though I didn't actually expect it to answer me, images of a Disney animated blade suddenly opening its eyes and singing a jaunty answer to my question did cause me to hope. "Hmmm," I pondered aloud, "and what does your sudden appearance from out of nowhere mean?" The letter opener must have been regarding me silently or maybe communication with such items only worked in cartoons.

Moving into the bathroom, I turned on all the lights and inspected the object more closely. The handle appeared to be maybe four inches long and was white stone of some sort, though at a glance I couldn't tell what kind. The blade was black, probably five inches long, and elegantly narrow. When I ran my finger along the edge of the blade there was no sting from it cutting me, and I could tell by that touch that the blade, like the handle, was stone. No markings or carvings marred the smooth surfaces of the handle or the blade and only a small shiny ring separated the two. Squinting and moving it into various positions in the light, I realized that the separating ring was clear and possibly quartz crystal. Holding the thing at arm's length, I had to admit that it really was a lovely specimen of stone. I made a mental note to have it inspected if Amon was unable to tell me what stones were used in its creation.

"Alright then," I nodded at the letter opener, "I'm going to put you over here and change my clothes. Hopefully Amon's meeting won't take too long and I can have him look at you." Placing the thing carefully, if not reverently, upon the pristine coverlet atop the bed, I returned to the dresser and gathered my clothes. As I'd planned on returning to Amon's office to borrow a tablet of paper and some pencils to use in roughing out some manuscript ideas, I changed quickly and brushed my hair perfunctorily before tossing the brush in a basket on the bathroom counter. Removing the Tomcat and shoulder holster was easy, but though the throwing blade sheaths were designed to be put on and taken off with one hand, I always seemed to have difficulty, often resorting to colorful language and threats of the scissors. Pleasantly surprised that the hasps on the belted connections sprang open on the second try, I took the right sheath off with a sigh, then turned my attention to the left. Once free, I quickly removed my disposable contacts and tossed them in the tiny waste can, rubbing my eyes vigorously with a sense of relief. Making sure the bandage on my left hand was still clean and secure took only moments, as Bishop was a master at his craft. Snapping off the lights as I entered the bedroom, I placed the weapons in the top drawer of the dresser, then went directly to the bed to retrieve the letter opener. It was gone.

"Wait," I looked around, puzzled at what might have happened, "where did you go now, Wicked Little Thing?" That I suddenly realized I'd named the letter opener did little to make its disappearance easier to swallow. I knew before kneeling beside the bed and peering beneath it that I'd find nothing there, not so much as a missing sock or a lonely little dust bunny, and I was correct. The letter opener had neither leapt to the floor to scurry beneath the bed, nor had it tumbled end over end across the void between the bed and the nightstand to land gracefully beside the lamp that stood there. Wicked Little Thing had simply vanished. My sense of dread grew as I considered the possibilities of what that might mean.

Forcing myself to remain calm, I took one last look around the room, standing in silence as I used all my senses to search for something unusual or amiss. There was nothing. The room felt normal, quiet, and as cozy as it ever had. Stepping out into the corridor on bare feet, I padded quietly to Amon's office, considering what, as well as what not, to tell him of Wicked Little Thing. As soon as I'd found a legal-sized pad of paper and two pencils, I tucked them under my arm and hurried from the room, happy to be away from the scene of the vortex. Though part of me wanted to race to Amon and tell him every detail of what had happened, another part of me knew the value of selective disclosure. Nothing of this matter would bring him pleasure and I'd found when Amon was displeased I was often the recipient of his reaction. This was not always a bad thing, but was very often inconvenient and even restrictive to me. In the years we'd been together the eight-hundred year old vampire had softened considerably, especially toward me, but I was far from being able to predict his reactions in some matters. His perspective was simply that different from my own.

Before I was halfway down the wide stone staircase the sound of voices raised in anger reached me and drew me up short. I stopped and waited, though I was unsure for what. It was obvious that Amon and Thammuz were 'having words', but the acoustics in the Great Hall distorted the sound. Though I clearly understood that both were angry, I could not discern the matter of such discourse.

Eavesdropping was rude, I was well aware of this, but it was sometimes accidental or accidentally intentional and becoming vampire had done nothing to lessen my curiosity. Once the voices emanating from the parlor calmed to what seemed polite murmurs, I tiptoed the rest of the way down the stairs and stood silently outside the room.

"No action can be taken until further information is gathered, Thammuz," Amon spoke forcefully, "and this is a matter that demands much investigation. I shall not allow the destruction of so many of our kind unless circumstance clearly demands it. Send out as many investigators as you deem necessary, and when they have all reported their findings, we will then meet to determine a course of action."

"I agree, My Lord," Thammuz replied, and though I could not see him from my vantage point, I heard a nod follow his words. "But in the meantime it might be wise to curtail your mate's activities."

"I assure you that Catherine's activities are of no concern of the Council's," my champion responded and I couldn't help but smile.

"Given the number of owls who were sired by Sabre, it could be that he's in contact with her. It may be possible that he's reached out to her regarding those in his territory. Perhaps she's coop..." Thammuz was cut off mid-word.

"Silence!" Amon growled, "Speak no further of this. Sabre has not contacted my mate, nor is she in collusion with him. Were you not sitting head of the Council of Five I would have your throat for merely suggesting such a thing. Catherine is loyal to me and to vampires as well as protector of the owls."

"I mean no disrespect, My Lord," Thammuz's tone dropped, as did the volume of his voice, "but having a rogue vampire on the loose is serious business. Our very existence is at stake."

Inwardly, I giggled at Thammuz's choice of words, 'rogue vampire on the loose,' and the images the phrase brought to mind. But I dared not make a sound lest I give away my position.

"It has not been determined that Sabre has gone rogue," Amon's voice rose slightly as his patience with the Senior Councilman was clearly waning. "Come back to me when you have proof and facts. I allow no action until all is clearly understood. I will not give permission for Sabre and his entire line to be destroyed until and unless it is proven that there is no other recourse. Am I understood?"

At the mention of Sabre's destruction I cringed, but at the mention of the destruction of his entire line of sirelings the gasp that escaped me left me with no choice but to announce myself and approach the parlor.

"My Lord," I nodded formally to Amon, then bowed my head slightly in the direction of Thammuz, "I apologize for the interruption. I am loath to disturb you, but a matter which needs your attention has arisen." Speaking so formally did not come naturally to me and I sometimes felt the need to stifle a giggle lest I slide into my Queen Victoria voice and start referring to myself as 'we'.

Thammuz turned and bowed deeply, his white hair gleaming and catching the light as he moved. He always seemed to be dressed for either a funeral or a circus and I was never quite sure which. Always he wore a dark suit, crisp white shirt and, more often than not, a white tie. His appearance was fastidious, every detail clearly seen to and elegant, yet no amount of fashion could cover the energy that emanated from him. Thammuz was powerful and he was my enemy, though I'd never done anything to warrant that position. He distrusted me and it was only his loyalty and trust of Amon that forced him to tolerate my existence and my position.

"You have been injured, My Lady?" He raised his white eyebrows as he glanced pointedly at my bandaged hand.

"It's nothing," I gave him my best dismissive expression and slipped my hands behind my back. "If you two need more time to conclude your business I shall excuse myself."

"No, My Lady," Thammuz offered quickly and Amon added a succinct, "No," as he stepped forward and took me by the elbow. "Our business is finished," the white haired vampire continued, "and there is much to be done. I shall bid you both a good night."

Amon led me to the sofa, then turned and escorted Thammuz to the door. When he returned his expression was grim. He walked past me, picked up the fireplace poker and stoked the fire while I waited for him to speak. Finally he turned and regarded me, at length saying only, "Yes?"

"I am sorry to have interrupted you," I began in earnest, "but I couldn't help but overhear you and Thammuz arguing. I hope everything's okay?"

"Everything is fine, my love," he sighed and smiled weakly, "or it soon shall be. Now, tell me of this matter that has arisen." Sitting beside me on the sofa, he slid his hand along my shoulders, cradling me in his arm.

"The letter opener returned," I started then added, "or well, I should say it returned briefly before disappearing again."

"Indeed?" He peered at me closely, "Please explain."

"I was getting my clothes out of the dresser, was bent over a drawer, when the thing flew past me and lodged itself in the door frame. If someone threw it at me, they were invisible because I inspected the entire room and I was alone."

"Wait," he sat upright with a look of concern on that handsome face, "the letter opener was thrown at you? Someone is targeting you? Are you harmed?" He began cursorily inspecting me for injuries.

"I'm fine, Amon," I assured him. "Like I said...the letter opener went past me into the woodwork. I can't say for sure that I was targeted. If so the assailant wasn't a very good shot, but I suppose it's possible. What's more remarkable is that I had some time to look at the blade and it was beautiful. Then, of course, there's the fact that it disappeared as mysteriously as it reappeared."

"What can you tell me about the weapon?" He relaxed once more into the sofa, sliding his arm back around my shoulders.

As I described the letter opener to Amon his expression changed from one of polite interest to concern and then to alarm. His right eyebrow shot up at a severe angle and I could almost see his thoughts closing in on themselves. At length he drew a heavy sigh and rubbed his forehead with his right hand.

"That, my love," he spoke at last, "was no letter opener. It was an athame."

"Athame," I parroted, turning the word over in my mind. "As in a witch's knife?"

"Yes, witch's tool of power, actually. Surely you learned of it in your studies. You are a witch, after all."

"Yes, I learned of it," I nearly snapped, "but I've never had one, nor have I felt the need to get one. What's the significance of this thing showing up when and how it did?"

"It is not only how and when it showed up that concerns me, Passion," he explained, "but the description you just gave matches that of the athame that once belonged to Arathia."

At the mention of the name, my blood, had I been human and mortal, would have run cold. As it was, every fiber of my being grew taut.

"Arathia," I gasped. "But that's not possible, is it? She was a sorceress after being demoted from Goddess and you destroyed her years ago! Are you suggesting she's a ghost now or that she's found some way to return?"

"I suggest no such thing," he grimaced. "But it is possible that one or more of her followers has taken it upon themselves to act on her behalf."

"Still, what would be the purpose of such action?"

"That is what I intend to find out, my darling," he squeezed my shoulders and lifted me with him as he rose from the sofa, "and the sooner the better."

We stood before the fireplace and I watched the flames dancing merrily along the burning wood, my mind awhirl with memories of the sorceress who had made my life a messy Hell. The mental image of Amon putting his Hand of Destruction against her face, her countenance shifting from haughty anger to terror and finally to despair, then her subsequent disintegration played with uncanny clarity in my mind. I could still recall sweet relief at the realization that she would no longer be able to meddle in my life. Through her machinations I'd been robbed of my parents, the world in which I'd been raised and was comfortable, and the normal life span of a human woman. I'd not exactly danced with glee that she was dispatched as she was, but that's only because I'd had other issues to attend at the time. The mere thought of having to deal with anything remotely connected to her made me cringe deep inside, at least briefly, until it fanned the smoldering embers of anger that I'd dismissed at her demise.

"Come, Love, "Amon whispered in my ear, "let us rest. It has been an eventful night and you need your energy to heal."

"I am suddenly tired," I admitted, though thoughts of resting with him in his coffin brought thoughts of activities other than rest. The hunger that had been raised then denied reared its head again and it was all I could do to stifle a purr as I slid my arm around his waist, lifted myself to my toes, and placed my mouth on his. "Or maybe I'm not actually tired at all. Maybe I'm hungry."

"Mmmm," he growled deep in his throat, "your hunger is my delight." He swept me into his arms, face buried in the hair draped across my neck, and cradled me as one would a child. The trip to the coffin room was spent nuzzling, kissing, licking, even biting, but soon he was depositing me into the soft satin-lined box.

We made slow and passionate love repeatedly and when dawn came and we could sense the sun rising outside, Amon closed the lid on his coffin for us to rest. My left hand tingled and the muscles of my back clinched and then relaxed. A headache kept me awake briefly, then I slept.

In my dream I stood, draped in a gray cloak, surrounded by others of my kind on a rugged stretch of beach. Gentle mist blew in from the ocean tide, but we felt no discomfort as we watched the distant sun rise, cross the sky, and set. Over and over the sun made its journey as the days turned into nights then into days again. We stood silently and watched. I felt a deep connection with those who stood with me. I was safe, I was loved, and I was home. I knew that I'd been here before and lamented I'd not be allowed to stay. I heard Arathia's voice, though at first it was so distant that I could not clearly make out what she was saying. Dreading to see the sorceress my warrior had destroyed, I clinched my hands into fists and looked at the other gray-robed beings beside me. Suddenly they disappeared and I stood alone. A shadowy form appeared on the water and as it neared I recognized Arathia. Her cloak was shimmering black and as she approached she drew the hood of it back so I could clearly see her face. Piercing black eyes shone from beneath her sculpted brow and her ruby lips curled into a perfect smile.

"As my power was taken from me," she incanted, "so shall yours be taken from you. Cherish what you have now, child."

At that, a wave rose from behind to swallow her completely and it washed her away. I awoke with a gasp and a start.

"What is it, beloved?" Amon touched my arm and whispered into my ear, "Did you have a dream?"

"I did," I whispered in reply, "and I'm glad it's over."

"Would you like to tell me about it?"

"I don't even want to think about it," I admitted, kissing his shoulder before rolling over. "I don't want to think. I want to sleep."

Opening one bleary eye, I found myself staring at the accordion pleated lining of Amon's coffin. It was white, pristine, and instantly made me angry for no reason.

"Ugh," I groaned as I rolled over, opened both eyes, and stared at the ceiling.

"You are awake, beloved?" Amon inquired from across the room and I had no intentions of moving or looking in his direction. "Are you well?"

"I'm fine," I huffed.

"Has your dream left you in a foul mood?" His shadow fell across me and he touched my cheek with the back of his hand.

"What makes you think I'm in a foul mood?" I realized that he was right, my mood was less than cheerful. Sitting up, I stretched my arms above my head with a yawn, and turned to look at him. To my surprise he was immaculately groomed and exquisitely dressed. "Are you going out?"

"You have been groaning and growling in your sleep for some time," he answered. "And yes, I have meetings. I trust you shall remain here at the estate tonight."

"Wait," I scratched my head then rubbed the sleep from my eyes, "what day is it? Or what night is it?"

"Saturday, my love," he responded succinctly, bending over the coffin and planting a chaste kiss on my forehead.

"Darn," I heaved a sigh, realizing Lamey's had a southern rock band scheduled for the night's venue and that I'd be left to my own devices if Amon was busy elsewhere.

"Are you going to tell me the details of your dream, Cat?"

"Oh that," I scrabbled as gracefully from the coffin as I could and landed barefoot on the earthen floor. "I'm going to thank you for that dream, as I dreamed of Arathia. I'm sure it's because you mentioned her and the athame."

"Did you have a nightmare?" He looked deeply into my eyes.

For a moment I considered telling him everything about the dream but something made me hesitate.

"No nightmare, sweetie," I grinned and kissed his chin, smoothing the lapel of his black dinner jacket. "Just a silly dream and nothing more."

"I expect you shall stop dreaming soon," he touched my hand and nodded. "I am certain your dreams are but a remnant of your human life and in time you shall cease dreaming."

"I know," I smiled and moved away from him, intending to go to the Sapphire room to dress. "You've mentioned that before, but I'm in no hurry to stop dreaming, Amon. There has never been a time I've not dreamed and I suspect I'll miss it if I do stop dreaming."

"You are a unique creature, Catherine," he offered. "No one can say with certainty that you will cease to dream, it just seems likely that you may."

"So, will you be gone long?" I changed the subject as subtly as possible. "And where are these meetings?" I made quotation marks in the air with my fingers.

"No, precious," he took me into his arms, "I shall only be gone a short time. The meetings are in New Orleans, if you must know, and in the Vieaux Carré, to be exact. When I return you and I shall ride the forest, yes?"

"Oh yippee!" I chuckled, "You always slide into using French after your meetings in New Orleans. Makes me wonder who you're really meeting."

"I assure you there is no need for curiosity," he said matter of factly. "My meetings are regarding financial holdings and investments, take place in stuffy offices or sterile board rooms, and usually include stale coffee and brilliantly disinteresting men. They are, however, quite necessary. I much prefer riding the forest with you."

"Aw," I feigned my best coquettish expression, "you say the sweetest things."

"Stay safe, my love," he planted a kiss on my forehead.

"Enjoy your stale coffee," I grinned, though I couldn't help but feel I'd been dismissed.

Amon slipped diamond cuff links through the French cuffs of his shirt and straightened his jacket, before favoring me with a graceful bow. I blew him a kiss before taking my leave.

As I made my way upstairs, I replayed the details of the dream over and over in my mind. The appearance of the athame and its connection to Arathia hinted that something was stirring in the wind, and experience had taught me that was not a good thing. I knew that Amon was doing what he could to find out who or what had sent the vortex into his office and why. But the mention of the sorceress had set off all manner of alarm bells in my head, and the dream and her words did nothing to quiet them. As I pulled a pair of jeans and tee shirt from the bureau, I tried to recall all I'd known of the fallen Goddess and her subsequent existence as a sorceress. Amon had explained that she'd been a Goddess who developed a taste for blood sacrifice and she'd, well, she'd run amok. Her bloodlust had led to her own destruction, as eventually the other Gods and Goddesses had united and stripped her of much of her power. That she might have, at one time, had a following had not occurred to me, and that some of her followers might still be active gave me cause for concern.

"Surely, none of her followers know what became of her," I reasoned to myself as I rummaged in a drawer for a pair of socks. "I mean, if that were the case they'd have taken action before now, right?"

"Talking to yourself must mean something," Winter suggested as he stepped hesitantly into the Sapphire room.

"I'm sure it does," I nodded. "I'm just trying to figure things out, I guess."

"What's up, 'tite sœur?" He smiled as he handed me my boots.

"Arathia," I sighed, as I pulled the boots on.

"His Lordship destroyed her years ago," he replied. "How is it she's once more on your mind?"

"The letter opener I stabbed through my hand to keep from being sucked into the vortex," I grimaced, "was apparently her athame. It returned only to disappear again and I'm just trying to figure out what it could mean."

"I understand," Winter shrugged. "But, on another note, have you discussed Doug Donahue's offer with His Lordship?"

"No," I admitted, "I've not yet had time. But we're riding in the forest when he returns so I'm in hopes of discussing the matter with him then. And I'd like to pick his brains as to the situation with Sabre. I overheard Thammuz and Amon arguing about Sabre, but I came in too late to get the juicy details. I'm hoping that if he and I put our heads together we can straighten out much of this confusion."

"And where are you off to now?" He smiled, offering his hand to help me from the bed.

"Amon's office, I think." I responded. "I want to go over the place for evidence and use his computer. There must be some answers there."

"And Oola?" Winter asked, head cocked and eyebrow raised.

"One crisis at a time, Winter," I rolled my eyes and chuckled. "I can't do everything at once!"

Chapter 7

Warm, ambient light washed up the walls of Amon's office when I hit the switch near the door. The room was empty, clean, and silent. Though tastefully decorated, the office held nothing personal of my mate's; it could have belonged to anyone.

I pulled the big leather chair from beneath the desk and got down on my hands and knees to look for any evidence that might have been overlooked. The pool I'd bled onto the floor had been cleaned and the lustrous wood now showed no sign it had ever been stained. The desktop held a blotter, an antique banker's lamp with a green glass shade, an hourglass, and a phone charging on its base. Sighing as I resigned myself to the fact that I'd find no evidence or clues to point me to anything of value, I pulled the chair back up to the desk and sat down. I swiveled one way and then the other while I waited for the computer to cough up what I wanted. I typed "Arathia" into the search engine box and scrolled down the responses. Various sources offered standard mythos, but I did manage to find a few links I might investigate in hopes of finding further information. In the reflection of the monitor I saw Winter lean one hip on the doorframe to watch silently.

"Who would know more about Arathia when she was a Goddess?" I swiveled the chair around to look at my beloved bodyguard.

"You mean more than His Lordship?" Winter raised an eyebrow at me.

"Yes," I nodded, "more than His Lordship. Surely there are more details somewhere!"

"Perhaps the Council would have some information," he suggested.

"Hmmm...." I chewed the inside of my lip, "I'm not sure that the Council would be so inclined as to share information with me. I'm not on their 'favorites' list."

"Chimaera is a member," Winter observed. "Perhaps he could be of assistance."

"Again, I'm not on his 'favorites' list either," I laughed, "but maybe you could speak with him. Maybe he'd help you?"

"What possible reason could I have to be asking about Arathia?" He countered, "I mean, if Chimaera asks."

"You could tell him about the athame," I suggested, "and that you're looking into the matter in order to protect me."

"That might work," he rubbed his chin which was currently devoid of stubble. "All right, I'll contact

Chimaera and see what I can find out. Perhaps he can access Council information and we can go from there."

"Excellent!" I clapped, leapt from the chair, and planted a kiss on his cheek. "Now, as to the other crisis."

"Sabre," he sighed.

"And Oola," I nodded, "and those she's trying to protect by coming to me. Why does this feel like, I don't know, juggling chainsaws?"

"Because it is?" He grinned.

"You go, talk to Chimaera," I patted him on the chest. "I'll stay here and wait for Amon, maybe take a swim and clear my head."

"Are you sure?" He grabbed my hand and looked at me soberly, "You will stay here?"

"I will, I promise," I chuckled and pulled my hand free. "Go!"

As he turned and walked away, I considered my next move. Truly not the least bit interested in taking a swim, despite what I'd told Winter, I realized that the pool was actually calling to me. Meditation near the water might lead to insights about my dream, I decided, and as I had time on my hands I figured it was worth a try. After shutting down the computer, I paused at the door, hand on the light switch, and inspected the room. There were still no clues, no evidence to help me find answers.

Sighing in frustration, I turned off the lights and stepped out into the hallway, closing the door firmly behind me.

The scent of chlorine met me as I opened the door to the natatorium. I switched on the lights in the pool and put the room lights on 'dim'. The drapes on the far wall of windows were, as usual, drawn closed. The effect of the dim recessed ceiling lights, as well as the soft lights from beneath the water, offered a place of calm and contemplative silence. The soft purring of the automated filtering pumps were as quiet as to be mostly impercep-tible. I made my way to a wicker mat on the floor, lit a stick of frankincense incense as well as a votive candle, and assumed the lotus position. Taking a deep cleans-ing breath, I closed my eyes, touched thumbs to index fingers, and tried to relax. Though technically I had no real need to breathe, breath was necessary for speech and I found it helpful at times in dealing with emotions. Sometimes I found myself just doing it out of habit. One more deep breath and... I thought of Cheese Doodles, wondered why some cows were black and white, shoved a James Brown song out of my head, and opened my eyes. Straightening my spine and squaring my shoul-ders, I tried again. I took a deep breath, exhaled and inhaled once more. I listened to compressor of the air conditioner chugging away just outside. I inspected the inside of my eyelids. I wondered if a coffin with leopard print pleated lining would be thought gauche. The leopard print idea led me naturally to think of dangly bauble earrings and women who snapped their chewing gun.

"Too good to chant 'Om', are we?" a voice in my head taunted me.

"I don't know who or what you are," I responded in my mind, not wishing to disturb the silence of the room, "but you obviously don't know me if you think I could 'Om' to save my life!"

"I am Zador," came the voice once more and with it came the image of a gray haired, dark-skinned man attired in saffron robes.

"Zador," I responded silently, "and you're in my head...why?"

"Because you called me," the guru-looking entity replied succinctly.

"Um," I shrugged, "I'm pretty sure I didn't call you, and if I did it was certainly unintentional."

"I can help direct you to that which you seek," Zador offered.

"Again," I was overwhelmed with a sense of trepidation, "I'm gonna go with...no!" The notion of a cosmic tour guide was amusing, but also a little creepy.

"But, you called me," the being protested, "so I must be allowed to help!"

"No, I think not," I chuckled, envisioning the gray haired guru in his saffron robes leaping up and down like an angry gnome before disintegrating into dust, then dispersing as if poofed by a strong gust of wind.

Silence and darkness arrived with Zador's departure and I relaxed to think about the situation with Sabre and those of his sirelings seeking my protection. Oddly, the image of a coven of witches appeared in my mind's eye and for a moment I thought I'd fallen asleep and wandered into a dream. But, as I was still aware of my body, I knew this was not so and this was no dream. The coven seemed to be having a celebration of some sort, their deep green robes swirling and twisting in time with their movements as they danced in a circle around a brightly burning fire. Flickering flames created dancing shadows on the ground until one witch, ostensibly the High Priestess, rang a brass bell and all motion stopped. She raised her hands, tilted her face up to a moonlit sky, and began speaking or singing. I could hear nothing, but I had the sense that whatever she was saying or singing was important. As I watched, mesmerized, the witches' robes changed from green to burgundy then back. Then I realized it was not merely the robes that were changing, the witches were different too. Those in green robes were much shorter and I noticed no men among them, but those in burgundy robes were tall and I could tell

131

that many were men. It was as if one vision was super-imposing itself over another and it was not only confusing me, it was giving me a headache. Willing myself to shake off the energy, I clenched my hands into fists and opened my eyes. It was clear I was not going to receive further insights to any matters at hand, so I reluctantly rose and blew out the candle. The incense had long ago turned to ash.

Rubbing my forehead, I turned off the lights as I left the swimming pool room and paused in the hallway. There was so much to consider and so little information with which to do so; my frustration level was increasing by the minute. I quickly decided to put on my riding clothes and dawdle around with a legal pad and pen to see if I could come up with any ideas for another book. If nothing else, I could put Doug's issue to bed, I told myself as I made my way to the Sapphire room.

Replacing my comfy pajama pants with snug-fitting jeans and swapping my tank top for a bra and white blouse, I pulled on my socks and rummaged through the closet floor for my boots. Since it was night and we were not going out into public, I didn't bother putting on contacts and instead grabbed dark glasses from the night stand beside the bed. As I pulled a chestnut brown riding jacket from the closet I considered again the prospect of writing another book. Granted, Amon had shared a few stories with me about what happened between the various Master Vampires with their territorial issues, some personal and personality conflicts, the usual dramas, but I couldn't image I'd have enough to fill a book or how I might weave the tales together.

"That's it," I sighed in relief. "The answer is a resounding no! Dark Ours can take their offer, stuff it in a pipe, and smoke it!"

"Beloved?" Amon stood in the doorway with a puzzled look on his face.

"Yes, my love," I grinned as I slipped my arms into the sleeves of my jacket and straightened the collar and lapels.

"You were speaking with someone?" He looked around the room as he moved smoothly toward me. "I see no one here."

"Just talking to myself," I assured him with a peck on the cheek. "Are we ready to go riding?" Sliding my glasses into the inner breast pocket of the jacket I checked the room to see if I'd forgotten anything. It seemed I had not.

"Indeed," he offered. "I have instructed Lucius to saddle Belladonna and Abraxis. They await us even now." He bowed gracefully and moved to the doorway.

I never tired of looking at him. Tall, slim, and just delicious looking, his black hair was tied at the nape of his neck and the shock of silver at his left temple accented his blood red eyes, which he did not have hidden behind contact lenses. Being Master Vampire, and having had eight-hundred years or so of practice at it, he had the ability to simply escape notice and to take any memories of himself with him when he left if he chose to be acknowledged; this made his need for contacts considerably less than mine. The dark gray riding jacket he wore sported black patches on the elbows and black lapels. The crisp white shirt he wore beneath it was open at the throat affecting a relaxed, and very sexy, appearance. His black trousers accentuated his long slim legs and the black leather boots he wore were polished and covered his calves to his knees. I'd grown accustomed to the beauty of vampires, as it was a part of our hunting prowess, but I never grew accustomed to being mate to Amon.

"Let's go," I accepted the elbow he offered and slipped my arm through his.

The lights burned low as we made our way through the mansion, but there was no one in evidence.

"Where is Winter?" Amon asked as we walked down the wide stone stairway.

"I sent him on an errand," I responded. "Since I wasn't going anywhere I figured it would be safe to do so."

"You were here alone with only Bishop while I was away?" He paused and raised one eyebrow at me.

"I figured Bear and Dodge are on the property, aren't they?"

"They are," he nodded. "But I believe it is time I add more guards to the security team. This place is too large to have just one man to protect you."

"Whoa there," I pulled up short. "One man to protect me? Since when do I need protection? I'm perfectly capable of protecting myself, you know!"

"I agree that you are capable of protecting yourself," he began then paused, raised a single index finger, and continued, "to some degree. But you must realize that we have many enemies. I have many enemies. Some may not be vampire, they may be other creatures not susceptible to your powers or your arsenal of weapons."

"But…" I started to complain before he cut me off.

"You need not protest, Passion," he added, "as my mind is made up. This will be and you will accept it. If I assign twenty guards to your safety you will agree."

"But, Amon," I struggled to sound calm, logical, and not at all the petulant child I suddenly felt, "this estate is guarded forty ways from Sunday! It would take a Seal team a week to figure how to breach security here. I'm practically a prisoner as it is. I truly don't need more guards."

"Did you not hear me, Catherine?" He looked askance at me as we crossed the wide foyer and stepped through the French doors onto the stone patio.

'Again with the Catherine,' the voice in my head, well hidden behind the mental shield I was currently projecting, grumbled. Weighing my options to determine if further discussion and protest would serve any purpose, and not put me in the doghouse for the upcoming conversation I had planned, I offered Amon a grimace and nodded.

"I did hear you, Warrior," I slipped my hand up his lapel, around his neck, and pulled his mouth to mine. "I did hear you." Kissing him deeply, I hoped to finish the topic dramatically and turn his attention to the night, the horses, and the ride ahead.

"I will always keep you safe, Passion," he growled softly as he laid a line of gentle kisses up the side of my neck. In my boots, my toes curled and other muscles in my body clinched involuntarily at his touch. Though part of me cherished what my mate could do to me, another part didn't like it one little bit.

Suddenly wanting no further discussion, I pulled away from his embrace and grabbed his hand. Moving ahead of him down the path, through the gardens, and across the perfectly manicured lawn, I hurried to the stables. Abraxis, Amon's huge black Friesian stallion stood, saddled and ready, beside Belladonna, my chestnut Andalusian. I dropped my mate's hand and hurried to Bella, releasing her reins from the hitching post and pulling them back over her head. She snorted and pawed at the ground then calmed as I turned her by her bridle. I mounted and settled myself in the saddle, adjusting my hold on the reins. Amon mounted Abraxis and looked at me. With a nod, he nudged his horse forward and I followed suit. We made our way across the vast well-tended, neatly trimmed lawns, past an ornately carved fountain and through a hedge of lushly blooming azaleas. In the dark their colors would be indiscernible to others, but to us they appeared vivid crimson, pink, and white. When we reached the tall security gate, Amon drew Abraxis to a halt and punched his code into the keypad then waited until the red 'secure' light switched to green. He swung the gate open, we moved the horses through, and then he stopped to close the gate behind us. Ahead lay rolling fields fringed by tree lines and forests. All the acreage in the area belonged to the Montjean Estate, but only the estate proper was guarded and secure. It felt wonderful to breathe free air.

"Race you to the forest!" I called as I kicked Bella in the haunches and lowered myself over her neck. She whinnied and bolted forward, evidently as happy to be free as I felt. I laughed as Amon caught up with me and gave me a stern look of disapproval. Tickling me further, I faced forward and ignored him as Bella and I fairly flew over the fields. Though his Friesian was very large and very powerful, he was not as fast or as fleet of foot as Bella and she easily outdistanced him. When we reached the edge of the forest, I turned the horse and we waited for Amon, who drew Abraxis to a skidding halt a few feet from me.

"Why must you insist on doing that?" He frowned and patted Abraxis' neck to calm him.

"I don't know," I smiled. "I just do!"

"Shall we ride the forest or would you prefer to lead the horses until we reach better riding terrain?" He offered, "Before you answer, I know well that you have something on your mind you wish to discuss."

"Can't fool you, can I?" I shrugged.

"Was that your intention?"

"No," I sighed, "I wasn't intending to fool you, but I was waiting until we could go somewhere safer than the mansion to discuss it."

"Safer than the estate?" He paused and looked at me seriously, "This must be a matter of great importance."

"No, not really," I shook my head. "I just didn't want to risk being overheard or interrupted."

"You have piqued my interest, Cat," he admitted. "Come, follow me."

Without further comment he moved Abraxis ahead and led the way through the forest. The trail was very narrow with the trees moving in closely as if threatening to take it back. Conversation was impossible, so I relaxed and looked around, just enjoying the feel of the horse beneath me, the rhythm of her stride, and her careful steps behind Abraxis. We traveled in silence for some time until the trail opened into a clearing where Amon drew his horse to a halt and dismounted. I reined Bella in and swung myself down from the saddle. Amon took Bella's reins from me and led her and Abraxis across the clearing where he tethered them loosely to a couple of trees. A bird screeched overhead and a distant growl let us know that we were not entirely alone.

Before I could make comment, Amon drew me into his embrace and lowered his mouth to my ear.

"Come," he commanded as we rose quickly into the sky. With no time to prepare myself, I clutched awkwardly at him and held on for all I was worth. Even though I knew, in theory, that I was capable of such flight by myself, I'd never tried it. In fact, I felt no real desire to learn this flight business; it still felt strange and unnatural to me. Perhaps, deep down, I sought desperately to hold onto what vestiges of my humanity I could recall and functioning best with terra firma beneath my feet fell into that category.

I barely had time to close my eyes and hide my face in Amon's lapel before he was gently lowering us to land. When his booted feet touched the stone cliff he bent his knees to absorb the shock, but in doing so he suddenly put my feet on the ground too. I was unprepared, having had little time to steel myself, and my knees buckled beneath me. My mate caught me, of course, but I staggered back and my hand slipped from his grasp. I did a graceful little accidental curtsey then righted myself with a nervous laugh.

"Next time, please give me more notice before you fly off with me," I smiled. Looking around at the familiar aerie, Amon's favorite spot for contemplation and brooding, I gazed at the star-lit sky and took a head-clearing breath.

"You should be accustomed to such things after all this time, my darling," he responded, pulling me once more into his arms.

"Yes well," I sighed, "apparently I'm not."

"Very well," he nodded. "So what is it you wish to discuss? Is it the matter with Oola and your owls?"

"Well, yes," I started, then shook my head, "and no."

"Yes and no?" he chuckled softly.

"Yes," I admitted, "fine, you're right. That's one thing, but first I want to tell you about the phone call from my agent."

"Yes?" he pulled back and looked at me squarely.

"I was offered a lucrative contract to write another book, a sequel to the last one," I held my breath as silence responded. Daring to look up into Amon's blood red eyes, I could see his expression wavering between anger and reason. "And before you blow a gasket, I think I've decided to turn it down."

"It is good that you have decided against such action," he spoke carefully. "As you know, the Council did not approve of me allowing you to write your book and I am certain that their stance would not be otherwise regarding a sequel."

"You realize that alone makes me want to write another book, don't you?" I patted his chest and he grabbed my hand.

"Cat," he warned, "do not give the Council of Five reason to see you as enemy."

"They already do," I gasped, "and you know it very well. Were I not your mate, I'd likely be toast by now."

"But you are my mate," he insisted, "and you are vampire in your own right. You are now subject to their rules, as well as mine."

"You didn't have to add that last bit," I hissed and turned away, walking to the stone ledge that offered a reasonably comfortable perch. "On another note, I should tell you about a creepy, smelly lady I ran into in the church parking lot."

"You should, of course," he nodded. "Please, tell me."

"Well, a creepy, smelly lady knocked on my window in the church parking lot when I was taking your call and making my call to my agent," I began, unsure of how to continue.

"And…" he waited patiently.

"She was creepy, she smelled horrible, and she was disfigured, but my Healing Hand didn't as much as tingle," I explained. "Winter said she wasn't human and had never been."

"She spoke to you?" he asked.

"She did, but she said nothing of importance," I answered. "Just that I couldn't park there and that I needed to move on."

"That is all?" He gazed at me intently.

"Yes," I replayed the incident in my mind. "Yes, that's all!"

"It may have been a scout," he suggested, "sent to taste and test your power."

"And she just happened to be waiting for me in the parking lot of a church I'd never been to in the wee hours of the morning in a rainstorm?"

"You misunderstand," he paused then added. "If indeed it was a scout, it would have likely been following and tracking you for some time. It would appear when it did, where it did, and as it did when circumstances were right for it to complete its mission."

"To taste and test my power," I parroted.

"Indeed, Passion," he assured me, "if that is what it was."

"And if it wasn't a scout?"

"Alas," he lowered his eyes, "it could have been any number of creatures approaching you for any number of reasons."

"Okay…" I exhaled dramatically. "Well, that's helpful!"

"Rest assured that I will not cease searching until I learn the truth of this matter," he offered.

"I've no doubt, my love," I chuckled, "no doubt whatsoever. So there is one more matter we should discuss."

"And that would be," he raised one eyebrow, "what?"

"Sabre," I sighed.

"I cannot discuss that matter with you, Catherine," he spread his hands. "You are not a Council member."

"But I am Master of the Owls," I retorted, "or Mistress of the Owls, whatever, and some of Sabre's sirelings are looking to me."

"All I can tell you is that Sabre's whereabouts are unknown," Amon admitted.

"And the Council has no idea why?"

"I did not say that, Little One," he answered cryptically.

"But all you will tell me is that no one knows where he is," I pried.

"All I can tell you," he nodded. "And all I will tell you, yes."

"So, I'll have to find alternative means of finding out what's going on," I insisted.

"I would suggest you not do that," he warned. "Please remain as distant from this matter as is possible."

"So not gonna happen, baby," I chuckled and walked to where he stood. "But I do have another question."

"Ask, my love," he smiled softly.

"I woke up when Oola arrived on the estate," I broached the subject delicately, "but you didn't. Why is that? And how is it she was able to breach security and get onto the grounds without an alarm going up?"

"I assume that you woke because you heard her arrive," he answered simply, "and I did not because it was of no consequence to me. As to why there was no alarm? There was no security breach, darling."

"What do you mean, there was no breach?"

"Did you not invite your guest?" He cocked his head in question.

"Well, sure," I responded, the fog of confusion securely in place in my thoughts.

"When you invite someone to the estate you are, in essence, giving them permission, therefore there was no breach."

"So, even though she flew across the wall as owl and shifted back into human form on the grounds," I reasoned aloud, "she could have just walked through the gate and would have been…"

"Invisible to our human guards, yes," he finished my sentence.

There was some thought, some subject, some issue swirling deep in my mind like the beginnings of an itch, but it would not coalesce or rise to the surface so, in frustration, I turned my face up to my beloved. Smiling, I placed one hand on his chest and another around his neck. "Let's fly!"

"Our discussion is complete?" He looked at me curiously.

"It is for now, my love," I responded, and closed my eyes before hiding my face in his jacket.

"Very well," he murmured as we rose into the night.

In what felt like no time, we were touching down in the forest near where the horses stood tethered. Instantly, I knew that we were not alone. I froze as I sent my senses out in exploration.

"Amon," I whispered and turned away from him toward the east where an eerie light painted the woods. "There's someone over there."

"Trespassers," he growled, "on our land!"

"Wait," I cautioned him, "these are not just any trespassers. Come, my love!"

As quietly as possible, I led my mate toward the strange glow, fairly confident of its origins. When we reached the edge of a small clearing we could see several pillar candles burning merrily on the ground. Inside the circle the candles formed stood two young girls I judged to be in their early teens. They were chanting with their eyes closed and I could guess at what they were doing.

"Stay here, please," I murmured to Amon, "at least for a few moments. You'll know when to join me." With that I straightened my jacket and stepped purposefully into the clearing, slipping my dark glasses on as I walked.

The teens squealed at my appearance, then danced a panicked two-step, smacking one another repeatedly until I raised my hand.

"Wait, wait," I commanded, "calm down. I'm not going to hurt you!"

Though the duo stopped screaming and swatting one another, I could tell by their expressions that they were far from calm. I could read the 'fight or flight' reaction in their eyes, which were the size of dinner plates.

"Ladies, please," I held up my hand. "Let's just talk for a moment."

At that, the girl with blond hair pulled severely back in a ponytail released a barrage of expletives that would have made a sailor blush. Her companion, as dark as she was pale, stood blinking at the insults until she'd finally had enough.

"Carly Jo!" She smacked her foul-mouthed friend on the arm, "You hush that shit!"

"I told you this was a bad idea," Carly Jo whined. "You and your witchcraft nonsense. Lookin' for a witch to get you a spell for that no-good, lyin', cheatin' son of a…"

"I said shut up, Ho," the dark-skinned teen yelled. Her brunette tresses, bearing accents of plum clearly visible even in the scattered candlelight, were long and woven into thick, heavy braids. Her green eyes, high cheekbones, and long, slim nose were clear indication of her Creole roots.

"Ladies," I tried once more to bring about some semblance of order, "please, just tell me what you're doing here."

"Nene has a no account boyfriend and she dragged me into the woods here looking for the witch that's supposed to haunt the place so she could talk her into giving her a spell to hold on to him," Carly Jo explained rather succinctly.

"Are you the witch?" Nene stepped back slightly and regarded me with trepidation.

"Don't be stupid, Nene," Carly Jo laughed and gently swatted at her friend, "you can see this lady ain't no witch!"

"How do you know?" Nene snarled at her friend then turned back to me. "Are you the witch that haunts this forest?"

"Look at her," Carly Jo insisted. "Witches don't wear clothes like that, they wear them long capes and pointy shoes. In pictures they always have a broom or a staff with them. She's wearing jeans and a jacket! She's no witch!"

At that, Amon, having donned his own dark glasses, stepped from cover and walked to my side without a word. Both girls went silent at the sight of him.

"Wait, I know who you are," Nene's expression changed from one of hopeful anticipation to fear. "You're the folks that live over there in that big mansion, right?"

"We are," I nodded. "I'm Catherine and this is my husband."

"Pleased to meet you," Nene bowed her head slightly and Carly Jo stared at the tops of her shoes.

At that, I took my dark glasses off and looked the young woman in the eye. She gasped at the sight of my white eyes, then she was trapped in my gaze. I felt Amon do the same thing with Carly Jo and then both of the little birds were ours. Pulling the sleeve of Nene's hoodie up, I sank my teeth into the tender flesh of the crook of her elbow and fed. Her blood was hot, rich, and filled my mouth quickly. As young and excited as she was, her blood felt like rocket fuel to my system and I knew Amon was experiencing the same with his prey. Three deep draws on Nene's vein and I'd fed sufficiently, so I withdrew my teeth and licked the wounds to seal them. Pulling down her sleeve, I stepped back and waited for Amon to finish with Carly Jo. When we once more stood side by side, we both donned our glasses and I coughed loudly to break the girls' stupor.

Though at first I'd had some qualms about feeding on innocents, I had made an agreement with my beloved that whenever we found trespassers on the property, they would pay a fee for their audacity. We made sure that they'd not feel the loss of blood, nor would they remember the encounter, but my need to feed on human blood still did bother me. My mate had lost that need when we'd been transformed at Arathia's destruction and though we'd hoped that one day I might also lose the need, I had not.

149

"My love," I turned to Amon, "why don't you walk the horses back to the house and I'll catch up with you shortly?"

"I shall do no such thing," he responded, "however, I will walk them to the edge of the forest and wait there. Take your time, I await you." He nodded succinctly at the girls, raised one eyebrow at the circle of candles, and glanced at me as he turned to leave.

"I'll be along shortly," I offered, then turned back to Nene and Carly Jo. "So, you two came to the woods looking for a witch so you could get a spell for your boyfriend, Nene?"

"Yes'm," she admitted as she inspected the cuticles she nervously chewed. "His name is Gerald and I know he loves me, but there's this other girl, Shanika, and she's throwin' herself at him. She's tryin' to steal him away from me so I came looking for a spell."

"A spell to keep your boyfriend true to you," I sought clarification, "or one to keep this Shanika away from him?"

"I was thinkin' to turn Shanika into a toad or a weasel, or somethin'," she chuckled, "but I don't suppose that would work."

"Well," I chuckled, "long ago I was in a similar situation and I was fortunate enough to find a witch who taught me what I needed to know."

"Really?" Carly Jo looked at me suspiciously, "You had a cheatin' boyfriend?"

"Gerald ain't cheated," Nene insisted vehemently.

"Maybe not yet," Carly Jo chided.

"I don't know if the boy I was seeing actually cheated on me or not," I explained, "but maybe I was afraid he would so I went to the local witch for help."

"And she gave you a spell?" Nene asked, obviously hopeful.

"She did," I replied, "and it may be of some use to you, but you have to pay close attention and do it exactly as I tell you, otherwise it won't work."

"So, does that make you a witch?" Carly Jo queried.

"Would sharing this spell with you make you witches?" I countered.

"Well," the blonde shrugged, "I guess not. So you're not a witch?"

Ignoring the question, I bent down and picked up a small twig. Handing it to Nene, I told her soberly, "Take this twig home with you. Prop a picture of Gerald up behind a lit candle and prick a finger of your right hand, because you'll need a tiny drop of blood. Put this twig in the palm of your left hand, add a drop of your blood, then spit on it. Cover your left palm with your right and say 'Love of mine be, 'til I set you free,' three times. Put

151

the twig some place safe, blow out the candle, and thank the Goddess."

"What Goddess?" she whispered, eyes growing big with wonder.

"It doesn't matter," I shrugged. "Just picture a Goddess in your head."

"Then what?" Nene looked skeptically at the twig.

"Then nothing," I answered. "The spell is done. Gerald's yours, unless at some time in the future you find you're no longer interested in him, in which case you toss the twig into a fire or a river and set him free."

"Really?" Carly Jo now seemed as fascinated as her friend. "And this will work, it's real?"

"According to the witch who told me about it," I nodded emphatically. "But since the twig is from this forest, you must never return here. If you do, the spell will be broken."

"Ah," Nene nodded, "I understand. Thank you, Miss Catherine."

"Now, you should really clean up your circle and get home," I offered, "as it's getting very late."

"Yes'm," Nene bowed slightly, clutching the twig in her right hand. She went about the circle, blowing out each candle in turn, then stuffing them in a burlap bag that Carly Jo held open. As the pair turned to leave, Nene turned back to me once more, "Thank you again,

Miss Catherine, and by the way, that is one pretty man you married."

"I think so too, Nene," I laughed, grateful that Amon was out of ear-shot, "and you're welcome. Be safe getting home!"

As they made their way out of the woods, I heard Carly Jo say to Nene, "Did you notice her glasses? She wears sunglasses in the woods at night. Don't you think that's creepy?"

"Maybe they're special glasses," Nene offered, then subsequent conversation was lost in the distance. Their memories of our meeting would fade as they made their way out of the forest and they'd have none by the time they reached their homes.

Sighing heavily, I brushed my hands off on my jeans and made my way through the trees to the edge of the woods. Amon stood silently looking across the open fields.

"My love," I greeted him, touching his arm, then took Bella's reins from his hand.

"Was that wise, witch?" He caught me up in his arms and looked at me intently.

"What? Oh, you mean dealing with those girls?" I grinned and kissed his lips. "Yes, it was wise beyond all wisdom! Trust me, darling, they'll not trouble us again."

"I hope you are correct," he sighed, kissed my forehead, and returned me to the ground. "Come, precious, we should return to the mansion."

We let the horses set their own pace as we returned to the Montjean estate. Amon was silent, either deep in thought or listening to the night that surrounded us. As we neared the gate, he finally broke the silence.

"You gave teenage girls a spell of magic," he challenged. "This does not bode well."

"How do you know what I did?" I drew Bella up short and glared at Amon.

"I overheard your conversation," he admitted.

"You eavesdropped," I quipped.

"Catherine, my love," he explained calmly, "as you know, I have highly sensitive hearing. The forest was otherwise quiet and the girls' voices were high pitched in their excitement. I overheard."

"Well, the conversation was private, so you can just forget what you overheard," I suggested.

"I cannot forget, however I will hope, for your sake and mine, that nothing more comes of this situation," he replied.

"Meaning?" I paused.

"You are a witch, yes, but you are also vampire," he added, "and as you know the rules of conduct for a vampire is…let us say, stricter."

"I so am not going there," I fumed, as Amon opened the gate. "We fed, and the girls will have no memory that we ever met, eventually. That's about as much vampire rule as I can abide." Conveniently leaving out the spell instructions and the twig I'd given Nene as being proof they'd met someone or something, I raised my mental shields and would say nothing more. I nudged Bella through the gate and continued to the stable, intentionally ignoring my mate and any thoughts of the Council of Five.

Despite the wee hours of the morning, Lucius had been waiting to tend to the horses. I wondered if he was so dedicated to his job or just experiencing a lack of female companionship and hoped to busy himself.

Winter was waiting for us when Amon and I made our way through the French doors off the patio and into the Great Hall. He nodded politely to Amon and the two exchanged information regarding the security status as I went into the study to pour myself a glass of wine. The night was warm enough that no fire burned in the ornate hearth, but the room was aglow with candlelight. Once more, I was reminded of my words and actions with the teens in the forest and I could not find anywhere that I might have broken or even bent a vampire rule. Shaking off any doubts, I poured Merlot into a crystal goblet and made my way to the couch. Sighing deeply, I put my glass on the coffee table then removed my riding boots, pulling off my socks for good measure. I propped my bare feet on the arm of the couch and wiggled my toes as I took a sip of the rich, warming wine.

"Cat," Winter smiled, as he entered the study alone. "His Lordship had to make a call. He told me to tell you to relax and he'll be with you as soon as his business is complete."

"Sit," I returned his smile and raised my feet, offering him a seat on the end of the couch. "Tell me what you found out from Chimaera!"

"Right to business, huh?" He laughed and sat down. I returned my feet to the armrest, my calves suspended above Winter's lap. "Very well. Chimaera told me all that he knew, but whether or not that will be of any help, I have no idea."

"Spill it, Winter!" I nudged his thigh with my bare foot.

"Very well," he chuckled, "I'll spill it! Beyond what you already know about Arathia's having once been a Goddess and how she was, what would be the word? Demoted? Anyway, she had most of her powers taken away and was relegated to the status of Sorceress, as you know."

"Yes Winter, I know," I nudged him again. "Tell me what I don't know!"

"Wow," he teased. "I believe your mate is rubbing off on you!"

"Winter!" I growled and his face lit up before he broke out into hearty laughter.

"Okay, okay," he tried to sober, then laughed again before recovering himself. "As Sorceress she not only had her own cult, she had a group of seriously devout followers. It's estimated that her followers numbered as many as three hundred, possibly even more, but there was a core group numbering fifteen. Those core members are extremely powerful, and yes, they are dangerous."

"What do you mean, are powerful and are dangerous?"

"Remember how Arathia attempted to train you in the ways of magic and energy manipulation?" he asked.

"Sure," I responded, nodding before taking a sip of wine.

"These fifteen graduated her training," he offered, "and then went on to even more."

"Eish," I sighed, trying to wrap my mind around the thought of fifteen people with Arathia's powers and training being still loose in the world.

"Eish, indeed!" He nodded in agreement before answering.

"Anything else?" I asked.

"Not really," Winter admitted, "but Chimaera said he'd do some covert research and get back to me. I think asking about Arathia now and telling him that it was in regards to protecting you lit a serious fire beneath our dark friend."

"Good," I laughed at the visual of Chimaera with his pants afire. "By the way, did Chimaera happen to say what happened to Arathia's followers after she was destroyed?"

"He did not," my leonine guard and friend responded, "though perhaps that will be part of the information he uncovers in his search."

"It's odd that we heard nothing of these people before now," I thought aloud.

"It is," Winter agreed. "Perhaps you could contact your friend, the Goddess Nemesis, and ask what she knows about the situation. As Mistress of Owls, you surely still have access to Agamemnon. He could get a message to her that you wish to speak with her."

"No," I shook my head. "I'd much prefer to avoid the divine as much as possible. I don't always fare well when I'm playing in their sandbox."

"Playing in their sandbox?" He looked at me dubiously.

"Running with dogs so big?" I offered.

"Too big?" he chuckled.

"Trust me, Winter," I finished my wine and swung my legs around to plant my feet on the floor, "Amon is as big a dog as I have any desire to run with." Cringing at my own analogy and sentence structure, I shuddered at the thought that it might be a side effect of the adolescent blood upon which I'd just fed.

"Just a suggestion," Winter nodded and patted my knee, as he stood and stretched his arms over his head. "My shift to patrol the perimeter. I'll take my leave of you, My Lady!"

"Goodnight Winter," I stood and stretched as well, then returned my goblet to the bar before following him out of the study.

As I made my way across the Great Hall and up the wide stone stairs, I considered Winter's words. That anyone might suggest the Goddess Nemesis was my friend was enough to wobble my mind. The deity had been kind enough, I supposed, but I had no desire to contact her for information, as such an act might be seen as asking a favor. The possibility of being in debt to a Goddess made me very uneasy, so I dismissed the notion by the time I reached the second floor landing.

Boots in one hand, socks in the other, I padded barefoot and quietly down the marble-tiled corridor. As I turned a blind corner, an arm shot out of nowhere and grabbed me around the middle. I was quickly spun, footwear dropping suddenly, and pinned against the wall. Amon pulled my arms over my head and held my wrists against the wall.

"There you are," he breathed heavily against my neck and leaned his body against mine. "We have business to attend!"

"What business?" I wriggled beneath his weight and power.

"What business, indeed," he murmured as his lips found mine.

I slipped my tongue into his mouth, carefully running the tip along the edge of his fangs. He kissed me deeply and ravenously.

When he released my wrists I slid my left arm around his neck and my right hand behind his head, my fingers running through his hair. Though my need to feed on human blood had been sated, my hunger for Amon roared to life as his passion rose.

"You taste like wine," he whispered, "and teen."

"You taste like teen," I breathed, "and power."

"Come, my darling," he commanded as he grabbed my hand and pulled me into the Sapphire room. My boots and socks lay forgotten in the hallway.

"You realize that we smell of horses," I laughed as he pulled my riding jacket down my arms.

"Does the scent offend you?" He paused and looked at me before gently removing the little dark glasses from my nose. He'd removed his own glasses before coming to me, I realized, as I looked into his blood red eyes.

"Offend me?" I chuckled, "Not especially."

"The scent of witch, horse, and forest is intoxicating to me," he admitted, his voice thick and deep with lust.

"Silver-tongued devil," I teased before putting my mouth over his for a deep, luxurious kiss.

He swept me up into his arms and carried me to the bed, depositing me gently on the down-filled mattress covered with a silken comforter. I lay brazenly watching him remove his clothes and take the leather tie from his tresses, the sight mesmerizing to me. When he joined me on the bed, a deep growl rose from my throat as our animal energies were released and fought for dominance. Sex after feeding was always more primal, more wanton, and more liberating.

Chapter 8

Spent and a bit stiff from our physical exertions, I tiptoed from the bed where Amon lay sleeping. I pulled on a pair of gray stretchy cotton lounging pants, then slipped a white cotton camisole over my head, pulling it down over my middle and straightening the spaghetti straps. Though the room had no windows, I could feel the sun rising in the east, as I still felt its energy as anathema to me. Amon was able to walk about freely and unaffected during the daytime, but that was not an ability to which I'd been given access because of my overly sensitive eyes. The sun's rays didn't burn my skin, well, not much anyway, and I'd not poof into a pile of ashes as some vampires would, but they did cause me discomfort and, thanks to the white irises and silver pupils gifted me by the Goddess Nemesis, I was nearly blind in daylight. Glasses with the darkest of lenses only helped slightly.

Sliding beneath the comforter, I snuggled in beside my mate and rested my head on his shoulder. Before he made me vampire and his mate, he'd always made himself warm for me, for as human I'd found it most disconcerting to touch cold flesh. Once I'd been vampire for some time, I realized that such details no longer bothered me and told him that making himself warm for me was no longer necessary, but I found he often did so regardless. Putting my palm on his chest, I felt his skin was warm to the touch, though his chest did not rise and fall with his breath, as we don't breathe when we sleep. There were details regarding vampires that I found fascinating, and some I found disturbing, but I was not only vampire, I was witch, and both Amon and I had been gifted unusual powers by the deities.

I closed my eyes to sleep, knowing that when I awoke Amon would be gone from our bed. I would not awaken until near sunset and my mate would have been busy for hours attending his many business pursuits, as well as those of the vampire community.

Chanting drew my attention in my dream and I followed the sound through vaporous curtains and sheets of energies varying in color from violet to orange. At length I found myself in a grove of trees; it was night and the stars and distant firelight illuminated the scene. Witches in deep green hooded cloaks chanted and moved around the fire in a large circle. Within the circle and very near the fire stood a witch whose appearance was much more vivid than the others. She raised pale hands and pulled the hood of her cloak down, turning to look at me. She saw me. I felt that 'electric' connection when her eyes met mine, and she smiled in obvious relief.

"You came," she bowed slightly, "thank you, My Lady."

"Where am I?" I asked, still somewhat confused. It was obvious that I was dreaming, but the witch before me felt as if she were more than mere dream. "Why am I here?"

"This is my coven," she offered, indicating the cloaked individuals surrounding us. "Well, it used to be my coven. I am Thea, My Lady."

"I can't think with this chanting distracting me," I replied. "Can we move away from the circle?"

"I'm sorry," she looked down at the ground, "this is the only way I can reach you. I'm borrowing the energy of my coven. I'm afraid that if I step outside the circle you will not be able to see or hear me."

"I am not just a fellow witch," I offered, "and I'm willing to risk it. Will you trust me?"

"As you wish," she sighed softly. We both stepped outside the circle of chanting witches and immediately the noise lessened, but Thea did not disappear. She followed me into the quiet of the forest.

"There now," I stopped and turned to Thea, "I can still see you." And in fact, I could see her quite clearly. Her hair fell in chestnut waves about her shoulders and her eyes were deeper green than the cloak she wore. She had generous lips and a heart-shaped face. It was obvious that she was of Celtic ancestry.

"What a relief," she smiled. "I need your help, if I may be so bold."

"You are a witch," I observed, "and I take it you're no longer among the living?"

"I am not, you are correct," she agreed. "But that was my choice. The help I seek from you is for another. In fact, it's for someone I love. He needs your protection."

"Please, explain," I urged my ghostly companion.

"I was in love with this man," she smiled sweetly, her face rapt in the joy of memories. "But, I could not bear to remove myself from the wheel of life to remain with him, so I took my own life. Because of my actions, his existence is now in peril."

"I don't understand what you mean," I shook my head. "How would your suicide cause your lover to be in danger?"

"He is vampire," she uttered. Alarms went off in my head, part of me cringed, and I wanted very much to awaken and immediately.

"Sabre," I sighed as things began to fall into place.

"When he told me that he was a vampire I thought I could handle it," she explained, "but I didn't learn until later that either I had to become vampire to stay with him or I had to have all memories of him erased from my mind. I loved him too well and too deeply. I knew that it would be impossible to let go of all the memories."

"So you had no choice but to become vampire?" I reasoned.

"Or he would be forced to kill me and I could not let him do that. For him to exist with the guilt of having to destroy me...well, I just could not allow that. So, I took my own life so that I might remain on the wheel of life. I will be reborn, but Sabre's continued existence is not so assured."

"Wait," I paused to consider the ramifications of all she'd said, "you are no more. There is no risk to the vampire society so Sabre might be in danger because he didn't kill you?"

"I am not clear on that matter, myself" she admitted. "But I overheard him discussing things with someone on the telephone and it was clear that my actions did not clear him of retribution."

"So what is it you need of me?" I asked, though I wanted vehemently to know nothing of the situation.

"You are a sister witch," she bowed her head slightly, "and vampire. In fact, though you admit it to no one, I can see that you are Master Vampire. I know no one else to ask, so I've come to you. Will you investigate and do what you can to protect Sabre? I've tried to contact him but, as he doesn't sleep as you do, I cannot. If you find him will you tell him what I've told you? Tell him that I love him completely, but that it was not my fate or my time to leave the wheel of life. Will you do that, please?"

"How can I refuse?" I tried to smile gently rather than grimace. It seemed unkind to show my real reactions to my ghostly companion, though she had no idea what a difficult position she was putting me in. Oh, sure, I'd been between a rock and a hard place before, but I preferred it when I went there on my own and not on behalf of another.

"Thank you," she smiled in relief. Her radiance grew to the point that I had to shield my eyes until she turned away. I followed the line of her gaze to see a golden light in the distance. As it drew nearer, I spied fruit-laden trees and a river meandering between green banks scattered with wildflowers.

"The Summerlands," I marveled. "I never expected to see it."

"Yes," she turned back to me, a look of pity on her face, "it's come for me."

"Why can I see it?" I asked, suddenly intrigued at the possibilities. "Can I go with you?"

"You may come with me," she agreed, "but you cannot cross the river and you cannot stay long. Would you like to join me?"

"No," I confessed, keenly aware of how enchanting the place was and how it would likely break my heart to have to leave it. "It's beautiful and I am curious, but no. I will do what I can to help Sabre, you can rest assured of that."

"I shall indeed rest," she nodded and turned toward the growing scene of the Summerlands, "and I shall go now. Thank you, My Lady!"

"Farewell, Thea," I called out to her disappearing form then turned back to where the chanting witches still danced around the fire. As I neared the coven, their cloaks shimmered from green to ruby and some of the figures changed. The High Priestess that had been leading the assemblage grew taller and the hands that extended past the sleeves of her cloak became larger, stronger-looking, and clearly masculine. Frozen, I stood and watched as the High Priest in ruby began to turn toward me. I glimpsed the masculine profile as he turned and…

I sat bolt upright, suddenly awake and alert. It took a few moments for me to recover my scattered thoughts and realize that I was still safe and comfortable in the pristine canopy bed of the Sapphire room. Amon was nowhere to be seen, as I'd expected, and my senses told me sun was beginning to set.

"Interesting dream," I murmured as I crawled from beneath the comforter and touched my feet gingerly on the cool marble tiles of the floor. "Though it's amazing to me that I manage to get myself into trouble just sleeping!"

"Miss Cat," Lily bustled in with a tray of coffee and beignets. "Here's your coffee, and a little somethin' to eat. Mister Sin is in his office and he told me to tell you that he'd like to see you as soon as you're awake and moving."

"Thank you, Lily," I tiptoed to the white flokati rug before the mahogany high boy and began rifling through the drawers for something to wear. Pulling a black sleeveless t-shirt over my head, I went to the closet for a pair of jeans and raked the first pair I saw off the hanger. Shoving one foot then the other through the legs, I half-jumped, half-shimmied into the tight pants and tucked the shirt into the waist before securing the zipper and button. Opting to go barefoot, I closed the closet doors on my boots and grabbed my coffee mug and a beignet as I headed for the hallway.

"Great coffee, Lily," I raised my mug to her in a toast, "and awesome beignet, as always. I'll go see Mister Sin now, thanks!"

"You're welcome, Miss Cat," she smiled, her eyes shining.

"Lily," I paused, turning to the maid, "it's Sunday, isn't it?"

"Yes, ma'am, it is!"

"Are you leaving for church soon?" I knew the woman was a devoted member of the local Baptist church and that she seldom missed a service.

"Already been to Sunday services this morning," she smiled broadly at me, "but there's evenin' services and choir practice in a bit. I'll be leavin' soon. Lucius is gonna' drive me."

"Have a great time," I returned her smile and drew a sip of steaming coffee into my mouth before stepping into the hallway. Drinking hot coffee while walking was not my forte, I realized, and I had to stop from time to time to take a sip to avoid slopping the burning stuff all over me. Unlike living flesh, my skin wouldn't blister and peel from a burn, but it still smarted, I'd learned. Though I couldn't drink and walk, I could eat and walk, and I was savoring the beignet tremendously as I padded barefoot down the marble floored halls.

The door to Amon's office stood ajar, which instantly set off alarms in my head. Whether he was inside or not, his office door was always closed. The soft blue light on his computer blinked calmly on his desk, his phone rested in its charger. I could sense he'd been there recently, I could feel the echo of his energy, but Amon was nowhere to be found. Putting logic before my desire to panic, I crossed the room, went past his desk, and opened the nearly invisible door to the file and supply room. Clicking on the light with one slightly sugared finger, I took a quick look around, but knew the room was empty but for several file cabinets and three shelves of office supplies. Huffing my displeasure, I turned off the light and closed the door, turning once more to Amon's empty office.

"Amon!" I called to the silence and received the response I expected. Nothing.

"Why did you tell Lily you wanted to see me if you were going out?" I peered at the ceiling and spoke aloud to my love's absence, "Amon, where are you?"

Nothing in the room was out of place. There was no furniture overturned, no drapes were ripped from the windows, no mirrors broken, no vases shattered, but there was such a feeling of ….'wrongness' that I couldn't help but shudder.

"Fine," I sighed, "I guess I'll try another form of communication."

Closing my eyes, I took a moment to still myself and calm my thoughts. In my mind, I called my beloved and waited patiently for his response. When after a time it became clear that no answer was forthcoming I opened my eyes, took a seat in his office chair, and went in search of him with my spirit. Our telepathy was not working, I could not speak to him or hear him with my mind, but I had the ability to go to the Master Vampire with my energy, my soul. This had, at various times, proven most valuable and I'd eventually been informed that the 'gift' had been another bestowed upon me by the Goddess Nemesis, acting on behalf of a myriad of Gods and Goddesses. All I had to do was send my thoughts out to him and wait patiently. In time, I'd find myself, my spirit, drawn to him with little effort on my part, but that was not the case this time. Though I waited patiently, nothing happened. Not only could I not sense my mate, I was not being drawn to him. Nothing happened. I felt only a void, an absence of him. That he might have his thoughts guarded, his mind shielded, crossed my mind, but then I had to wonder what matter might cause such a reaction from my beloved. I'd become quite adept at shielding my mind, my thoughts, but if Amon did so, it was a rare thing or one I'd not noticed. Whenever I'd called or 'gone' to him in spirit, he'd been right there for me.

"Guess I might as well take care of one matter," I sighed, picked up the phone, and punched in the numbers from memory. Putting the phone to my ear, I listened as it rang across the miles. After two rings I was greeted with a click and the familiar "Titan Literary Agency, how may direct your call?" Giving the secretary my name, I asked for Donahue's extension and was briefly put on hold until he answered.

"Cat, what's the good word?" His voice could not hide his eagerness.

"I'm sorry, Doug," I began before he cut me off.

"Don't say another word," he interjected. "I've been authorized to give you another day to consider if you're tuning down the offer. The publisher contacted me earlier and they really want you to do this for them. They've given you more time to think about it. Isn't that great?"

"Great," I moaned, trying to make myself sound excited. As I'd dialed the phone I realized that I was actually relieved to be putting the matter to rest. Now that it was being thrown back in my lap for further consideration I found myself being torn once more. I'd already told Amon that I was refusing the offer and now here I was agreeing to consider it further.

"Fine," I heaved a sigh. "I'll think on the decision a bit more. I'll call you tomorrow then."

"Thanks, Cat," Donahue's relief was audible. It was clear that he thought the extra time would have me seeing the benefits of accepting the contract. I, on the other hand, was more concerned with the difficulties and possible complications. "Have a good evening, Ms. Alexander-Blair," he added with a chuckle.

"Eh?" I returned the laugh, "It's better than Kitten! Good night, Doug."

Ending the call, I put the phone back on its charger. Looking around the office, I was reminded of my reason for being there.

"Amon wanted me to meet him here, according to Lily," I reasoned aloud, "but he must have gotten called away or something. This is impossible!" I fumed, as I began to pace the office. "I've never been unable to reach him. Why would he shut me out?" Glancing once more around the room, scanning Amon's desk for a clue, I struggled to hold back the panic. Every nerve in my body was singing, the vampire blood stirring in my veins ran icy cold and anger simmered deep within me.

"Come on, Amon," I grimaced. "Where can you be?"

Clicking off the light, I slammed the office door closed behind me and stood in the silent hallway, considering what actions to take and in what order to take them. Twirling the now empty coffee mug on my right index finger, I idly licked the beignet sugar from the fingers of my left hand.

"Check the grounds and check with the other guards first," I released the seed of panic and shook the emotions off. "Let's be logical about things. We'll see if Dodge or

Bear has any idea where Amon is, and casually ask Lily if Sin mentioned if he had business elsewhere today."

Though I knew I was being calm and rational, a little voice in my head and in my heart was SCREAMING that this would never happen. Amon insisted on knowing where I was at every moment, so protective was he, and I'd had to practice to keep my mental shields up and him out of my thoughts. But, the moment I dropped my shields he was always right there. Instincts told me that something was wrong, though I had no choice but to follow the steps of logic and hope they'd lead to my beloved.

Sighing deeply with regret that I'd not donned footwear, I made my way back to the Sapphire room. I grabbed a pair of white anklets from the top drawer of the dresser then pulled my worn brown leather boots from the closet. Placing the empty mug on the nightstand, I perched on the edge of the bed to slip on my socks and pull up my boots. Though I considered strapping on my blades, I knew I didn't have the patience, so I just slipped the Tomcat into the waistband of my jeans at the small of my back and grabbed my empty mug. Pulling a denim shirt from its hanger, I slammed the closet door and rushed from the room. The clack-clack-clack of the heels of my boots on the marble floor sounded not only loud, but purposeful, and it spurred me on even more. As I reached the top of the grand stairway, I called out to the maid.

"Lily!" I paused only momentarily before descending the wide curve of steps, "Lily! Where are you?" I took a deep, cleansing breath, swallowed all the panic that tried to crawl up my throat and into my voice then called again lightly, "Lily!!!!"

Stepping into the Great Hall from the short hallway that led to the kitchen, the young woman wiped her hands on the white apron she wore tied around her waist, pushed a lock of dark, deeply curled hair out of her eyes and looked up at me.

"Whatcha need, Miss Cat?" She smiled, as her eyes fell on the empty coffee mug in my hand, "You ready for a refill?"

"Not just now, Lily, much as I'd love one," I made my way down the stairs and placed the mug in her hands. "I'm looking for Amon. He wasn't in his office when I got there. Any idea where he is?"

"Mister Sin said he wanted to talk to you," she shrugged. "I've been cleaning in the study and workin' in the kitchen. I ain't seen a soul come or go."

"That is odd," I considered. "And are you ever going to call him Amon?"

"Miss Cat, I've known that man as Mister Montjean or Mister Sin since I was just outta high school."

"I know, Lily," I laughed, "but you know it's okay to call him by his real name now, don't you?"

"Yes, Ma'am," she nodded, "but old habits die hard."

"They do indeed," I agreed and looked back up the stairs as if my beloved would magically appear there because I willed it so. "So, do you know where anyone else is here on the estate?"

"Lucius had to run into town for supplies earlier today, but he's supposed to be back by now," she offered. "And I saw Bear walking the grounds, but I don't know where Dodge is and I ain't seen Bishop or Winter today."

"Fine," I sighed. "I guess I'll go look around outside. If you see Amon, please tell him where I am."

"Yes, Ma'am," she agreed, "If I see him before I leave, I'll surely do that!"

Pulling the long sleeved denim shirt up my arms, I made my way across the

Great Hall and to the French doors that opened onto the flagstone veranda. The sun had set behind the gently sloping hills on the horizon, leaving only a tinge of pinky orange in the sky. Crickets had just started their night song and the solar lights that dotted the garden were just beginning to glow softly. A few peacocks meandered around the gardens, but they were the only things stirring, except for the insects that buzzed around my head.

I walked down the path toward the stables, then turned to the right toward the gatehouse. The long black ribbon of asphalt driveway wound through a stand of trees before reaching the ornate wrought iron gate with the massive stone columns on either side. There was always, twenty-four hours a day, seven days a week, someone on duty in the gatehouse, for when the perimeter was to be walked a second guard took over gatehouse duty so the first could stretch his legs. Looking at the top of the tall stonewall perimeter, I wondered about the open sky and if my mate had contrived some type of security that denied overhead access. Was there invisible razor wire atop the wall? Was there an electrical charge that raced along the ridge coping? Sure, Oola had arrived unchallenged and unseen by our human security guards, but that was because I'd invited her. What about other creatures who flew or leapt, or heavens, could teleport like a member of a Star Fleet landing party? What of them? I made a mental note to ask Amon how the estate was protected from otherworldly entities, since he'd brought up the fact that not all of our possible enemies were vampire.

As I rounded the curve of the drive I could see the gatehouse ahead and I recognized Dodge's back in the window. If he had guardhouse duty that meant Bear was still walking the premises. I approached the small stone structure and rapped on the window with my fist. Dodge turned quickly and stepped out, hand resting on the door knob.

"My Lady," he beamed and nodded, "what can I do for you?"

"Have you seen His Lordship?" I tried to act nonchalant.

"He's not come or gone since I've been on duty," he offered. "I've been here this afternoon since two."

"Ah," I heaved a sigh, "okay. Thanks Dodge!"

"Is there something wrong, Cat?" He let go of the door and took two steps toward me. "Is there anything I should know?"

"No, I don't suppose so," I grinned.

"Would you like me to use the security system and contact His Lordship for you," he offered. "It's only for emergencies, but if you like..."

"No," I waved him off, "that's not necessary. I'm sure I've just missed him somewhere. I was supposed to have a meeting with him and he's not where he said he'd be. It's not important, but it's given me an excuse to walk around the place and enjoy the evening air."

"Evening air," he smiled and wiped his forehead with the back of his hand. "You mean Louisiana humidity?" Smoothing his long brown hair back from his brow, he looked up into the darkening sky, as if searching for relief.

"Well, yes," I laughed, "there's that too! Goodnight, Dodge!"

"Have a good evening, My Lady," he called, then with a wave of one hand he disappeared back into the air conditioned gatehouse.

Walking back up the drive, I peered through the trees in search of Bear, but there was no sign of him. Darkness was claiming the land as the hour grew late. Lights burned in the windows of the stable so I knew Lucius had returned from getting supplies. As I neared the building I could see his dark green jeep parked near the double doors and I could hear its engine ticking as it cooled. He'd obviously just returned and would no doubt be leaving again soon to take Lily to church.

Though I considered stepping inside the stable and having Lucius saddle a horse for me, I knew that he'd go all 'protective guy' on me and insist on calling in someone to dog my steps so I did not. I stepped off the gravel drive and into the soft grass so the sound of my boots crunching on rocks would not alert him as I passed the building. I'd not been outside unattended or unescorted since Amon had brought me to the Montjean Estate and I was relishing the freedom and the chance to explore.

The tall stone wall that surrounded the grounds was solid and without a break through which one might view the surrounding countryside. Were it not for the occasional decorative lamp mounted near the top it would have created a very dark and formidable bulwark, though the stones themselves were pale. I knew that when Amon opened the gate in the wall with his code, the information was relayed to the guard house so the guard on duty would know which entry was being used and by whom. Unaware of Amon's code, and not having been given one of my own, I knew that I'd be unable to leave the grounds, but I could at least look around. Pausing briefly near a live oak tree, leaning against the trunk for support, I closed my eyes, centered myself, and tried once more to reach my beloved. Again, I ran into a silent void, an almost physical lack of him. That void hurt me, it ripped at something deep within me, and I vowed to not try to reach my love again. It would be up to him to contact me.

Sighing in frustration, I opened my eyes and pushed off the tree, squaring my shoulders and renewing my determination to get to the bottom of things. As I no longer needed their protection, I removed my dark glasses and tucked them into the breast pocket of my denim shirt as I moved along the stone perimeter. Here and there, along the edge of the property, vines and bushes climbed the wall, appearing as avant-garde shapes of deeper darkness in the shadows of the night. As I moved away from the wall to skirt what I took as merely a clump of bushes, I happened to glance into the shadows to find a door glowing almost as if lit by soft neon. The sight brought me up short and the thought of opening the door to find what lay beyond immediately presented itself. It didn't make sense that such a door would be here, hidden in the brush, and I wondered if it had been included in the security system. Pushing some vines and bushes aside, I moved closer to the door and looked for a keypad, which would be connected to the system, but there was none. The door itself was arched, wooden, and in obvious need of repair. Iron hinges were rough to my touch and rust stained my fingertips when I touched them. An equally rusty iron latch held the door closed and it gave a mighty squeal when I pushed it down to open the door. Just when I thought the door wouldn't open, and disappointment threatened to overtake me, the latch clicked, the resistance disappeared, and the door swung back a few inches. The clear and sure knowledge that Amon would have a conniption when I stepped off estate grounds rose in my mind and I realized that if there was any way possible, he'd appear or make contact with me to strongly suggest I not do so. Feeling lucky and grateful to have found the door,

I shoved against it with my shoulder and eventually it moved back far enough for me to squeeze through the gap.

Though I wasn't sure what to expect on the other side of the door, what I found disappointed me greatly. Only the dark rolling fields that surrounded the estate greeted me and I could just make out the tree line that lay beyond. Stars twinkled in the dark sky as they played hide and seek amongst the clouds. The moon was not visible but I knew it was up there somewhere behind the clouds and it was near first quarter phase. Laughing at my own foolishness, I realized that on some level I'd expected to find a mystical, magical landscape beyond the door and was disappointed that the mundane farm ground colored by night was all I'd found. Thinking to get a better perspective of the grounds, I made my way through the rough remnants of the previous season's harvest, wondering idly what it was I was tramping on.

The sound of movement drew my attention to my right, though the night was dark enough that even with my sensitive eyes I could see only rough ground. Idly, I wished for a flashlight, then realized that my sense of disappointment was not entirely due to the landscape but was also due to the fact that Amon had not come to keep me safely on protected grounds, nor had he screamed his displeasure in my mind. Suddenly I felt small and vulnerable and pulled the Tomcat out of my waistband. Grumbling silently that neither my owls nor Amon's wolves were anywhere in sight to be my protectors, I clicked safety off the Beretta and shifted into aiming position.

When the moon suddenly peeked out from beneath the clouds it lent enough illumination that I could see a low shadow moving parallel to my position several yards away. Silently I froze, waiting for whatever was sharing this field to come into my line of sight. The sound rippled toward the wall and I realized whatever it was, it was not coming at me. Relaxing slightly, I lowered the gun and then stopped short when the shadow of a canine, either wolf or large dog, appeared on the stone wall. The shadow froze too and I realized, in frustration, that the creature stood between me and my returning to the safety of the estate.

"Here doggie," I half-sang, half-whispered. "Nice doggie. Good puppy."

A soft, deep growl answered.

"Okay," I reasoned nervously, "so you're not a nice doggie. You're not a good puppy. How about you just go away and let me pass?"

The shadow on the wall shifted slightly, but the creature did not move.

Just as I considered releasing a shot into the air in hopes of startling the creature into fleeing, the shadow grew and then disappeared entirely. Though I could hear the beast moving through the empty field, I couldn't see where it had gone. Steeling myself, I rushed toward the door hoping it had moved away and had lost interest in me.

Gaining the door, I slipped through and slammed it securely closed behind me. Resting, leaning on the wooden door, I watched the stars in the sky for a moment.

"If my heart was still beating it would be hammering itself out of my chest," I chuckled to myself then straightened, returning the Tomcat to my waistband. "Well, that was an adventure and all it taught me is that Amon is beyond me. Wherever he is, he's out of my reach. Damn!"

Brushing invisible dust off the thighs of my jeans, I paused to decide if I should continue my walk along the perimeter of the estate or just return to the mansion. I knew my walk wasn't going to provide me any answers, but I was loath to return to the empty house.

"Empty of Amon, anyway," I clarified my thoughts verbally as I determined to continue my exploration of the grounds.

Keeping the wall to my right, I made my way around the mansion to the formal front porch and elaborately ornate grand entrance. Lights in the windows illuminated the wide stone walk and soaring columns. A porte-cochere lay adjacent to the mansion proper and the carriage house lay just beyond it. I was quickly running out of grounds to explore, I realized as I passed the azalea hedge that surrounded the gently gurgling fountain that was the centerpiece of the front lawn.

Motion in my peripheral vision drew my attention and with a start I recognized the shadow of the wolf or dog I thought I'd left on the other side of the door in the wall. To my dismay, it had apparently been tracking or stalking me, but at least now I had the lights of the mansion behind me. As I drew closer to the portico the creature followed and at last I was able to see it clearly. To my relief, I found it was just a dog. To my dismay, it would come no closer to me when I called it, nor would it take to its paws and flee when I tried to 'shew' it away. The dog, which I took to be a large black German shepherd, merely sat down and regarded me silently. Chuckling, I shook my head and resumed my walk.

"Fine," I spoke to the animal, "you do what you're gonna do and I'll do what I'm gonna do. I can't waste my night dealing with you."

The creature didn't answer, merely cocked its head to one side as if curious then rose to its feet and paced me.

Cutting through the porte-cochere to the back lawn, I crossed the manicured gardens to the wide flagstone patio. I slipped silently in through the French doors and turned to see the big black dog arranging itself into a comfortable position on the other side of the glass.

"Feel free to go elsewhere," I spoke to the dog as if it could not only hear me but understand me. "I'm going to go have a glass of wine."

Entering the study, where elegant black tapers burned in silver candlesticks, I made my way to the cart where a bottle of Cabernet had been decanted into an elegant clear crystal carafe. As I was pouring myself a glass, I turned to find Winter standing in the doorway with a perplexed look on his face.

"Cat," he started, paused, then continued, "um, why is there a big black dog sitting on the patio staring in at me?"

"Funny thing about that," I grinned. "I have no idea!"

"Are you just going to leave it there?"

"What do you suggest I do with it?" I countered, swirling the wine in its goblet and taking in the scent.

"Well," he offered, "have you checked to see if it has a collar? Perhaps it is a stray."

"Have you ever had a stray anything on this estate?" I waved my glass, "Could a stray even get onto the grounds?" Not about to admit that I'd found the door in the wall and had breached security by opening it and leaving the place, I reasoned as if entirely innocent, or so I hoped.

"Now that you mention it," he nodded, "I have not. The wall should have kept the animal out, unless it snuck in as the gate was open when Lucius returned."

"That must be it," I agreed, perhaps a bit too enthusiastically. "That must be where it came from. And no, I've not checked to see if it has a collar. I called for it to come to me but it wouldn't. So, it just sits there and stares."

"His Lordship did say he was going to be employing additional guards, didn't he?" Winter offered me a wry smile.

"Oh yippee skippy," I laughed. "That's what I need, a four-legged body guard with fleas and dog breath!" Sipping my wine, I cleared my throat and changed the subject.

"On another note, have you seen His Lordship?"

"I have not," he replied, "but I assume he is here, perhaps in his office?"

"Perhaps," I responded wistfully, not yet willing to admit that I knew he was not only not at home but beyond my reach. I wasn't sure how to approach the subject for I had the suspicion that if others knew what I knew, what I feared anyway, all Hell would break loose.

"If you like, I'll go check and see if the dog has a collar on so maybe we can find its home," Winter offered and I nodded in response. He disappeared and I heard the door open then the click, click, click of toenails on marble. Suddenly the big black dog stood in the doorway, tongue lolling, with what I swear was a big grin on its muzzle. It sauntered into the study, walked around in a tight circle twice and then stretched out on the rug in front of the couch. The beast promptly rested its head on its front paws, whuffled, and went to sleep.

"Winter!" I called, frozen with wineglass inches from my lips, afraid to move.

"My Lady," he answered, leaning on the doorjamb, crossing his arms over his chest, and grinning broadly.

"What's this?" I pointed at the sleeping beast.

"That is a dog, Cat," he laughed, eyes twinkling. "And by the way, she has no collar or any identification of any kind."

"Great," I sighed. "So what am I supposed to do with it?"

"I'd suggest you let her sleep," he crossed the room giving the dog a wide berth. Taking my wine glass, he helped himself to a sip of Cabernet. "And you might have Lily put some kind of food together for her. Oh, and you may want to think of a name for her, she is female."

"Winter!" I gasped in exasperation, "I can't have a dog!"

"Why not?" He countered, looking kindly at the sleeping canine.

"I, I..." I stammered, "I don't know. I just can't!"

"I'd suggest you already do, My Lady," he took another sip of wine then handed the goblet back to me.

Making my way around the rug, I took a seat on the couch, placed my wine glass on the jet black coffee table, and pulled off my boots. Withdrawing my little black glasses from the pocket of my shirt, I laid them next to my glass and rubbed my eyes. Though I wanted desperately to avoid the matter altogether, I knew I'd have to talk to Winter and the other guards about Amon's unexplained absence. Lifting my glass to my lips I drank deeply then looked at my beloved body guard.

"Winter, sit," I nodded to the couch cushion beside me. "I have something to tell you."

"This doesn't sound good," he regarded me guardedly.

"It's not," I struggled to hold back tears that erupted without warning. "Amon is gone!"

Moments of heavy silence ticked by. I looked Winter in the eye and he looked at me. The possibility that the Master Vampire of the South East sector of the country might be missing was simply too much to consider.

"What do you mean gone?" he raised one eyebrow as he finally broke the silence.

"I mean," I shrugged, spreading my hands, "he's gone. He's not here!"

"Wait, Cat," he commanded in a calm voice. "His Lordship comes and goes as he sees fit. If he is not here, he must have business to attend elsewhere!"

"He was gone when I woke up," I tried to speak as calmly and rationally as I could. "Lily told me that he wanted to see me in his office as soon as I was up and moving, so I went to see him and he wasn't there! He wasn't in his office!"

"Okay," Winter smiled encouragement. "So, he got called away to some emergency and didn't have a chance to contact you or leave a message. Surely this is not the first time it's happened?"

"I, I…" I stammered, my thoughts going back in time, "I don't know!" Alarm caused my voice to rise and I spoke louder than I'd intended.

At my outburst, the dog suddenly stood, hackles raised, and howled. The grating, guttural sound seemed to come from some depth in the beast and it brought me up short. Turning to face me, the animal's eyes seem to grow larger, darker, and more intense as if she was trying to tell me something, though I had no idea what it might be. The urge to call the dog Lassie and ask if

Amon was stranded down the well suddenly appeared fully formed in my mind and I couldn't help but laugh.

Winter looked at me as if I'd lost my mind, and understandably so.

The big black dog howled once more and in that sound, besides that of her previous strident vocalization, there was a tone similar to a woman's scream as well as an owl's screech. It was such a cacophony of noise that my hands went to my ears and I yelled at the top of my voice.

"Enough!" The volume of the dog's howl diminished and I repeated myself. "Enough already! Silence!"

Startled, the solid black German shepherd just blinked at me as if insulted. Suddenly, it turned around and bolted from the room with Winter and I leaping to our feet to give chase. The creature fled the study and raced up the wide stone stairs off the Great Hall, then disappeared around the corner. Running on marble in only my socks, I was unable to gain as much purchase and speed as Winter so I trailed him by several feet as we followed the dog upstairs. Finally, laughing and dismayed, we found the animal in the Sapphire room. She'd leapt up on the pristine white comforter atop the four-poster bed and made herself comfortable, lying there like a sphinx, daring us to challenge her.

"Anubis," Winter gestured grandly with his hand at the posing beast.

"What?" I grinned slightly as I pulled off my socks and stood with my bare feet on the cool marble floor.

"Well," he added, "maybe not THE Anubis, but she certainly does bear a resemblance, doesn't she?"

"Anubis," I murmured the name as if trying it on for size. "It's not a bad name, though it's not really a name for a female."

"She seems to have made herself at home," Winter offered.

"Apparently!" Agreeing I added, "And she doesn't look like the type to share the bed. Come, Winter. Let's go back downstairs. She obviously doesn't need us."

"Yes, My Lady," he nodded smartly.

Glancing back at the dog lying comfortably atop the bed, I shook my head and followed Winter back down the hallway, bare feet padding quietly on the stone floor, a sock in either hand.

Chapter 9

Two hours later, as midnight approached, I found myself once more in the study and alone. Winter had called Bear and Lucius up to the house and he'd put the security team on high alert, which he claimed Amon always did when he was away from the estate. The fact that the security team had not been notified, or put on alert, only added to my concern, but Winter seemed to take it in stride. Despite my wishes, he'd also contacted Chimaera, who was on his way to the mansion. Chimaera, though still technically a member of Amon's security staff, had been mostly busy elsewhere since he'd accepted a temporary seat on the Council of Five. This had worked out quite well for me, as he and I did not get along. I was not exactly looking forward to his return.

Resting my head on the arm of the leather couch, I had my knees drawn up and my bare feet resting on the cushions. Exhausted, more emotionally than physically, I closed my eyes and listened to the sound of the room, the soft ticking of the wall clock in the adjacent Great Hall, the gentle whooshing of the air conditioner. Though my body remained relaxed on the couch, I found myself standing near the coffee table, looking at the otherwise empty room. The black German shepherd appeared without actually arriving and for some reason this did not surprise or alarm me.

'What are you doing here?' I asked, fully expecting an answer.

'I could ask you the same question!' The dog retorted.

'You talk! You're a talking dog. How cool is that?' I couldn't help but chuckle in delight.

'Firstly, I am not a dog,' she lifted her muzzle and sniffed, *'and secondly, I don't talk. That would be ludicrous. And it is impolite to be amused.'*

'I am sorry,' I sobered and assumed a straight face. *'You look like a dog. If you're not a dog what are you?'*

'I am Siri,' the creature answered succinctly.

'What's a Siri?'

"Siri is what I am. It is my name,' the beast insisted. *'What are you called?'*

'I'm Cat,' I offered, bowing slightly to be polite.

'Strange name for a witch,' she observed.

'Is it?'

'Yes, it is!' She nodded.

'So how is it I can hear you if you can't talk?' I asked, curious as to how she'd explain things.

'*I cannot speak,*' she sighed. '*That does not mean I cannot communicate. Have you not noticed that my mouth is not moving?*'

'*Ah, now that you mention it, yes, I do see that.*'

'*I am not speaking and you are not hearing, yet we are communicating.*' Her ears rotated forward as she lowered her nose and looked at me with huge brown eyes.

'*All right, let's try this another way...why are you here?*'

'*Not to put too fine a point on things, but I am not, in fact, here. Nor are you, for that matter.*' Siri cocked her head and looked at the sofa, then glanced back at me with one raised eyebrow. '*See? Is that not your body there?*'

I regarded my prostrate form on the leather couch with an odd detachment.

'*So, is this a dream,*' I wondered aloud.

'*Do you often witness your body elsewhere when you dream?*' The animal queried as her image disappeared then reappeared a few feet nearer the bar. '*Do you have any beer back there?*'

'*You drink beer?*'

Siri just 'woofed' at me then offered me puppy eyes.

'*Has anyone ever told you that you can be extremely frustrating?*' I heaved a sigh.

'They have not, though I would not be at all surprised if some find me so,' she grinned, tongue lolling to one side of her mouth.

'So, why are we communicating?' I tried to come at the matter from another direction as I walked behind the bar to get a beer from the small refrigerator there.

'Ah, a better question,' she agreed, licking her muzzle in what I assumed was anticipation.

Just then a great white owl flew into the study and landed, wings flapping dramatically, on the bar before me. I knew it was Agamemnon, Nemesis's totem creature and intermediary between the physical world and other worlds. As I bowed to address the magnificent creature, the room filled with blinding white light. I knew that if I glanced toward the doors I would see Nemesis herself, in all her divine radiance.

"Oh, Helsa," I moaned as I started to look up…

"Damn," I gasped as I sat straight up on the couch, swinging my legs around and banging my knees on the coffee table before my feet reached the floor. "What a dream, or vision, or something," I mumbled as I rubbed my knees. Dread washed over me at what the appearance of Agamemnon meant, even if it was in a dream, and I sighed at having to deal once more with Deity. It was very cool to be in the presence of such powerful beings, but it tended to make me feel small, powerless, even like a pawn in some cosmic game. Nemesis had been gracious enough when she'd borrowed my body and left me, well, I wasn't really sure where she'd left me though it was out of my body. It was true that I'd been repaid for my kindness with incredible powers, but I couldn't help but feel out of my element when I was forced to deal with entities I'd not previously believed existed.

Standing, I stretched my arms over my head and yawned. Darkness still enveloped the sleeping world beyond the windows. It would be hours yet before the sun broke the horizon. The mansion was quiet. If Chimaera had arrived he'd gone off with Winter or was with the security staff or something. I had time on my hands and was unsure what to do with it. I'd been under close scrutiny since I'd arrived at the estate years ago and these moments of sudden freedom, as sought for as they were, felt unnatural, like I was suddenly in a freefall.

Taking my violin from its case in the cabinet against the wall, I rosined the bow and gently fingered the strings to check its tuning. Making minute adjustments, I rested the instrument on my shoulder, tucked my chin and drew the bow across the strings. The purity of the tone that issued from the beloved handcrafted violin never ceased to call forth tiny shivers of delight and I smiled despite myself. As it seemed the night was fine, if a bit warm, I made my way quietly out the French doors and sat down on the top of the steps that led down to the garden. The twinkling lights in the trees created a beautiful, almost magical, ambience and the water in the distant fountain gurgled a soft accompaniment as I began to play. Beginning with a sonata from Mozart, I worked my way through the classical pieces I used to warm up and exercise, then moved on to the more modern pieces I liked. Eventually I ran through my performance repertoire before letting the instrument go still. Silence reclaimed the night for a moment then I heard a gentle scratching behind me. Beyond the closed French doors the black German shepherd sat peering at me, one paw on the door near a pane of glass.

"Siri," I smiled and tucked my bow between the fingers of my left hand then stood and stretched once more. Carrying the violin gently, I made my way across the flagstone veranda and opened the door for the dog. She padded out onto the patio and sat down next to where I'd just been seated. "Shall we talk further?" I asked the beast who regarded me silently. "Perhaps not," I sighed, resuming my seat and daring to touch her head. Her tall, pointed ears twitched briefly, but she settled beneath my touch and did not growl or move away. The swishing of her long, furry tail across the flagstone indicated her pleasure and I scratched beneath her ear until she shook her head and snorted. We were just getting comfortable and, I like to think, getting to know one another when voices in the distance made Siri's ears perk up and her tail stopped wagging. A low growl rumbled deep in her chest. Though I had no idea why, I leapt to my feet, ran to the door and opened it so the dog could enter the mansion. I watched her cross the Great Hall and disappear up the wide stone stairs before returning to my spot on the veranda steps.

Feigning interest in a string on my violin, I looked up in mock surprise when Winter and Chimaera came through the garden and stopped before me.

"Chimaera," I nodded in greeting, "and Winter. Good evening to you both. I trust all is well?"

The two vampire body guards could not have looked any more opposite. Chimaera's hair was long, smooth, and black to the point of being almost blue. His pale blue eyes were beautiful, yet disconcerting. The goatee he usually sported was gone, so his face looked younger, but his eyes carried none of the merriment of youth. He wore black trousers and the tailored long sleeved white shirt beneath the black vest accented his narrow waist and broad shoulders. He was certainly a beautiful creature, yet he still aroused feelings of fear and anger in me. Winter, on the other hand, had a mane of curly blond hair and golden eyes. His skin appeared tanned across wide, high cheekbones, and his smile was genuine and inviting. His pale blue jeans rode low on his hips, and though I couldn't see them in the dim light of the veranda, I knew he wore brown leather boots that were scuffed and worn. His white sleeveless t-shirt showed off sculpted biceps and covered his washboard abs. He was the light to Chimaera's darkness and he stirred nothing but feelings of safety and trust in me.

Chimaera stepped forward and bowed slightly.

"My Lady," he nodded then stepped back. "I am, as ever, at your service."

"Thank you," I replied, making my way to my feet as gracefully as possible, careful to not bump my violin or its bow.

"My Lady," Winter took my right hand, kissed the back of it, and smiled at me. "I am yours."

"Winter," I struggled to keep a straight face amid such proper behavior, "is everything okay?"

"The estate is secure," Chimaera offered as he turned to Winter, "but perhaps it would be wise to go inside."

"He's right, Cat," Winter took a deep breath and nodded, "you should be inside."

"I'll go in," I responded, "if you'll tell me what's going on. You're both kind of creeping me out!"

"Inside, please," Chimaera extended his hand in a gesture that bordered on a command.

Winter led the way and bowed graciously as he opened the door. As I paused to acknowledge the gesture, Chimaera, who was close on my heels, put his hands on my shoulders to keep from bumping into me. In an instant I was blinded by a kaleidoscope of neon lights, deafened by a cacophony of bells, whistles, buzzers, canned music and voices raised in excitement and delight. The scents of women's perfume, men's cologne, deodorant, tobacco smoke, fried foods, and alcohol assaulted my nose, and the deluge of gamblers and partiers emotions threatened to knock me off my feet. Instinctively I took a step forward and the moment Chimaera's hands were no longer touching me I was back at the estate, stepping through one of the French doors into the Great Hall. I gasped and shook my head.

"You've been at a casino?" I turned to look at Chimaera, my surprise likely evident in my voice and my expression.

"I have," he shrugged, then looked at me more closely. "And you know this how exactly?"

"I, I…" answering his question would only lead to more questions, I realized as I stammered.

"Don't work any of your witchy ways on me, woman," he growled and I couldn't tell if he was in jest or in earnest.

"I did nothing," I gasped, chuckling nervously. "I have no idea what happened or how it happened, but it must have something to do with you touching me."

"That was entirely accidental, My Lady," he raised both hands in mock surrender.

"Yes, yes," I snapped, "I know that. But I've not experienced anything like this before. It was…surreal!"

"Let's discuss this further inside," Winter suggested and we agreed, entering the Great Hall. "Perhaps in here?" He gestured toward the game room opposite the study.

"You two go ahead," I smiled, lifting my violin, "while I put this away. I'll be there in a minute."

Winter opened his mouth to complain, then shrugged and went into the game room. Chimaera paused to look at me then turned and followed.

"Things are just weird," I thought as I went into the study and grabbed the empty violin case. Granted, considering we were vampires, that observation might be an understatement anyway, but even for us, for those of us at the Montjean estate, things were just weird. There were times when our existence bordered on the monotonous, peace overtook us and we became complacent, then other times intrigue suddenly inserted itself and there was no end to the chaos, shifts, changes, or challenges.

Placing the violin gently into its case and anchoring the bow, I put the lid down and snapped it securely. Almost sadly, I put it away, realizing how much fun I'd been having playing for myself on the veranda. For a moment I thought to blame Winter and Chimaera for ruining my fun, but in truth it wasn't their fault. They were doing what they were supposed to do, what they were actually paid to do, and if that happened to mess up my pleasure, well, I'd just have to get over it.

As I crossed the Great Hall, I could hear music playing in the game room and knew that Winter had fed the juke box. It was a ridiculous toy that Amon had bought me, thinking it would make me happy, and though I seldom used it, I did actually enjoy it and appreciated his thoughtfulness. It was full of classic rock from the 80's with a few newer hits sprinkled here and there across the neon bordered playlist. To my surprise, Charlie Daniels' "Devil Went Down to Georgia" was playing as I entered the room and I couldn't help but move to the beat.

The lights, set to come on via motion detection, had come up when the body guards had entered before me so the room was bright and beckoning. Clear white lights shone from the recessed lamps in the ceiling and from behind sculpted molding along the dark paneled walls. Silver pendant lamps cast wide pools of light from above the ornate pool table and smaller pendants illuminated the bar along the wall to the left. At the far end of the room a sleek gray stone fireplace took up most of the wall and hand carved panther statues of black stone stood sentry on either side. Chimaera was removing pool cues from the cabinet on the wall and Winter was racking the balls on the navy blue felt table.

"You're playing pool?" I stopped in my tracks, surprised that they'd be interested in entertaining themselves while I was intent on finding out what was going on.

"Why not?" Chimaera grinned. "Care to join us?"

"I can't believe…" shaking my head, I began when an ear-splitting howl came from somewhere upstairs.

"What the devil is that?" Chimaera propped the cues against the table and started toward the door.

"Siri," I gasped as I recognized the dog's howl. I bolted from the room ahead of both bodyguards and ran up the stone steps. Her howling echoed against the marble walls and floors, making it difficult to pinpoint precisely where the animal was, but I figured she was most likely back in the Sapphire room and headed there. To my surprise, when I reached it, the room was empty, the white bedspread sporting only an indentation where she'd been sleeping. Pausing to get a better idea of where the sound was coming from, I turned first left, then right, and could perceive a slight increase in the volume of her howls further down the hall. Only one other door along the hallway stood open and as I neared it I could tell Siri was within. It was Amon's bedroom, where soft lights from sconces lit the deep green walls, the shimmering gold in the wallpaper adding rich ambience to the room. Atop the bed, with its headboard of Dave the dragon, Amon's family crest, stood the great black German shepherd, her hackles up, ears laid back, and eyes focused intently on the far side of the room. At first I could not tell what the dog was alerting to, but when I crossed the threshold, I saw the shimmering energy near the wall. Looking much like a waterfall, or the waves of heat rising from a summer-hot tarmac, the manifestation was probably 6' wide and 6' tall. Moving gently beside the bed, I place my hand on Siri's back. She whimpered and lowered her haunches to sit, but she did not turn her head or acknowledge me. Suddenly the energy, or whatever it was, blinked out and was gone. Siri chuffed softly, turned, and licked my hand as Winter and Chimaera rushed into the room.

"What is it?" Winter gasped, his eyes searching the room frantically. "What's wrong?"

"You missed it," I grinned and glanced at the place near the wall where the shimmering had been. "It's gone now."

"What's gone?" Chimaera pushed further into the room, inspecting the corners, moving the drapes aside looking for something. "And what is that?" He cocked his head and raised one eyebrow at the dog perched atop Amon's bed.

"Didn't Winter tell you," I laughed. "This is my new bodyguard. This is Siri."   "His Lordship got you a dog?" He moved toward the dog, then paused to look at me, "Is she trained?"

"She's Siri," I responded, "and she's quite good at it. Beyond that, I have no idea if she's trained or not! She just arrived and took up residence. I've not spoken with Amon but I assume he got her for me. He did say he was he was hiring more bodyguards." At the mention of her name, the dog licked my hand once more, grinned as only a dog can grin, turned, and leapt off the bed. She paused near the door, wagged her tail enthusiastically, then turned and trotted down the hall.

"You named her Siri?" Winter asked as he escorted me from Amon's room.

"It just seemed to fit," I lied easily. In truth, I hated that her real name was the same as Apple's 'Speech Interpretation and Recognition Interface', she whose voice made me want to gnash my teeth. To my amusement, the black German shepherd did not lead us down the hallway to the stairs, but instead turned into the

Sapphire room. By the time we walked past the door she was walking circles on the bed, making a comfy place to sleep.

"Some bodyguard," I grinned at her.

"So what was the dog howling about?" Winter asked, slipping his arm through mine as we walked down the stairs.

"I'm not sure what it was," I shrugged and tried as best I could to describe to them both what I'd seen. "Keep in mind," I added, "that I only saw it for a moment or two before it was gone."

"Interesting," Chimaera observed. "But this is not the same thing that you witnessed in His Lordship's office, not the vortex?"

"Definitely not," I assured him. "This wasn't spinning, there was no pulling force, and it wasn't even circular."

Gaining the ground floor, as we crossed the Great Hall and were about to enter the game room, the lights flickered and lightning lit the night beyond the windows. Thunder rumbled just as the rain began pounding on the roof. Being a fairly 'new' nocturnal creature, I immediately looked around for candles in case the lights went out, before two realizations kicked into my mind. First, that the mansion had an automatic generator that would run everything until the electricity came back on and second, that I could not only see in the dark, but was more comfortable doing so. I wondered how many centuries it would take to wipe away my previously learned 'fear of the dark'. Once my eyes adjusted to the darkness I moved surely past the pool table and went behind the bar. From the wine cooler I withdrew a bottle of Chardonnay and a bottle of imported beer.

"Here," I handed Winter the wine, "please open this and pour me a glass. I've someone else to serve." Pulling the cap off the beer bottle in the gaping fanged mouth of a gargoyle opener, I took a small bowl from the stack behind the bar and emptied the beer into it. Moving toward the door, I whistled as loudly as I could then called, "Siri, beer!"

Almost immediately I could hear the clicking of toenails and padding of paws on the marble coming down the stairs and running across the floor. In the darkness, the black dog was nearly invisible, but when she began lapping the beer from the bowl where and what she was could be easily heard. The generator kicked in and the lights came back on.

"Dare I ask why you're giving the dog beer?" Winter queried as he sauntered across the room and handed me a glass of Chardonnay.

"I had a hunch," I grinned and patted the dog as she drank loudly, wagging her tail. "So tell me what you two were discussing before you came up to the house. I'd love to know why you were acting so weird."

"Weird?" Winter raised one eyebrow at me in mock surprise. "Whatever do you mean?"

"Knock it off, Winter," I rolled my eyes at his histrionics. "You know exactly what I mean. All that "let's go inside," and "we'd best be inside" business. What was that all about?"

"And you don't hear the storm raging, Cat?" Chimaera interjected, chuckling. "It's a fast moving front. Winter and I could hear distant rumbling thunder when he met me at the security gate."

"That's it? That's why you two were acting so odd?"

"I don't know that we were acting odd," Winter shrugged, "though we were discussing Council business, as well as His Lordship's absence."

"Did you find out where he is?" I asked perhaps a bit too excitedly.

"I did," Chimaera answered. "His Lordship had business to attend. Bishop drove him into New Orleans in the limo. If his business goes well he hopes to return to the estate before sunrise. If he's delayed he will contact us."

"Us?" I cocked my head, "What's this 'us' business? You've not lived on the estate since you became a Council member. Does this mean you've returned?"

"I have," he bowed slightly. "I am to be a Council member no longer, as my replacement has finally been found. He will be installed in ceremony soon and my responsibility to them will be done. I will be here once more."

"Ah," I nodded slowly, pausing to consider all the information I'd just received.

"Isn't it odd that finally, after all this time, the Council of Five has found your replacement?"

"Odd or not," Chimaera offered, "I am not unhappy at the notion of being free of Council duties and responsibilities. However, I feel a more important matter to discuss is how it is you knew I'd been at the casino."

"You touched me," I shrugged, "and I was there. I saw it all, smelled it, heard it, and felt it as if I were there."

"Have you ever experienced this ability before, Cat?" Winter paused in racking the balls and looked at me.

"I don't know," I chewed the inside of my lip absently. "If I have it wasn't exactly like this. Besides being in the casino, I could feel other entities there, I mean, other than human. There were four, I'm sure. Three male and one female and at least one of them was aware of my presence, though I broke the connection as soon as I realized that."

"You know what this means, don't you?" Chimaera grinned as he lifted his pool cue into position, leaned over the table, and took the first shot, breaking the rack.

"What does this mean?" I shook my head, trying to keep the sarcasm out of my voice.

"Experiment time," Winter laughed and chalked the tip of his cue as Chimaera took his second shot and missed.

"What kind of experiment?" I asked reluctantly.

"If you have new abilities we should determine if you're going to experience such things every time you touch someone or something, or if it's just certain people or things, or if certain conditions must exist in order for you to make use of them," Winter explained, sounding logical and entirely reasonable.

"And we'd do that how?" I wasn't clear where my beloved body guard was going with this line of thought, but I was pretty sure I didn't like it.

"Simple!" He made his shot, sank a solid, and leaned one hip against the table. "We replicate what happened, with Chimaera and then with me, and maybe we should even invite Lily in and use her too."

"Whoa there," I shook my head adamantly, "it's late and Lily's long gone. Lucius took her to church some time ago and he'll drop her off at home if he's needed back here. Let's just leave everyone else out of the experimenting for the time being." I took a cue down from the wall and chalked the tip. "We're not playing an actual game, are we?"

"Just sinking balls," Chimaera answered. "Go ahead!"

I took my shot, missed pathetically, and propped the cue against the wall before retrieving my wine glass.

"So, how do we do this experiment?" I looked from Winter to Chimaera before sipping the cold wine.

"We duplicate what happened as closely as we can, first," Chimaera answered and stepped behind me, resting his pool cue against the table after sinking a ball then missing his second shot. I'd no doubt he'd missed intentionally, as it was clear he was anxious and curious to experiment.

"Fine," I sighed. "Go ahead!"

The instant his hands touched my shoulders I was surrounded by candle light in a darkened room, soft music playing in the background. I could smell dragon's blood incense burning, and tasted red wine on my lips. A warm human female body moved beneath my hands and my hips. My teeth sank into her oh-so tender flesh, hot blood gushed into my mouth and an orgasm rocked my body. I gasped and leapt forward.

"You….you…" I was so startled, so shocked, and the experience left me quivering, unable to think or speak clearly.

"What, Cat?" Winter approached with concern on his face. "What did you experience?"

I could do nothing but gasp and point an accusing finger at Chimaera.

"I believe Her Ladyship here might like a cigarette, Winter," Chimaera grinned wickedly and actually winked at me.

"What do you mean?" Winter looked confused. "What happened Cat?"

Finally gathering my wits, I sneered at Chimaera, "Aren't you the clever one?"

"It was not intentional, I assure you," he insisted. "That memory just popped into my head. You must admit, it was a wonderful thing!"

"I admit nothing," I fumed as the rush I'd experience finally began to wane. Even if the experience had been a wonderful thing, and it was in some ways, I'd never give Chimaera the satisfaction of admitting it to him. "Suffice it to say that I now know what it is to be voyeur, Grand Frere," I glanced at Winter, hoping that I wasn't blushing.

"Voyeur," Chimaera raised an eyebrow, "or participant?"

"Let it go, Chimaera," I hissed at the vampire who was enjoying the situation a tad too much. "So now what?"

"Winter's turn," Chimaera nodded at his fellow bodyguard.

"Fine," I turned my back to Winter, "do your best!"

Again, the instant I felt Winter's hands on my shoulders I was transported, this time into a deep forest. I felt the warm, humid breeze on my skin. I could see the leaves and the trees, the rocks, and various creatures. I smelled fertile earth and distant cool water then felt dizzying weightlessness as I leapt from a branch into the night sky.

"Whoa," I gasped again as I jerked away from Winter's touch, "been hunting, have you?"

"Of course," he responded, a look of confusion on his face. "What did you experience?"

"Everything!" I replied then added, "Though I'm happy to have broken the connection before you caught your prey." Taking a deep drink from my wine goblet, I petted Siri as she came to me. "So what does this mean? Am I going to experience such things whenever anyone touches me? Will it work the same way in reverse? Will I experience the memories of those I touch or is it just those who touch me? Or is it only other vampires? This experiment creates more questions than it's answered!"

"If you really want to know, we could call Lucius up to the house," Chimaera smiled mischievously. "He's probably sleeping in the cottage next to the stables tonight."

"No," I responded adamantly, "absolutely not! Certainly not yet, anyway."

"Perhaps His Lordship should be in on any further experiments," Winter suggested and I smiled in relief.

"Yes," I brightened, somehow hoping Amon would have some explanation for the matter and some suggestion as to how I might control it. "No more experiments tonight. Let's just shoot pool."

"We could do one or two more experiments, which might put you at ease," Chimaera offered as he chalked his cue once more.

"And that would be…"

"You touch me," he suggested, "and then you touch Winter."

"So, we could determine if I am merely the recipient when being touched or if I can draw such things from those I intentionally touch?" I reasoned aloud.

"Precisely," he nodded.

"Fine, but not you," I glared at Chimaera. "I'll touch Winter first!" Resting my wine glass on the edge of the pool table, I sighed and offered my empty hands to my beloved bodyguard.

"As you wish," Winter bowed slightly and moved to stand before me. I took his hands in mine and closed my eyes. Nothing happened. I saw only the inside of my eyelids.

"Well, that's a bust!" I chuckled and started to step away when Winter caught my hand.

"Wait, Cat," he said softly, "let's try this." Taking my hands in his, he placed them on either side of his face and looked into my eyes. I focused on his beautiful golden eyes and stilled myself. Instantly I was in a silent room that smelled of flowers, dust, and a chemical scent I couldn't quite identify. Wall sconces cast circles of light up deep cherry paneled walls. Drapes of lush violet velvet covered the windows and folded wooden chairs were lined up on either side of a narrow aisle. A black wooden coffin stood at the head of the aisle and I could just make out the profile of a woman's face against the white satin lining. Moving slowly forward, I began to make out the details of the body, the simple black dress she wore, the subtle makeup that adorned her face, the tiny gold pin at her throat. Suddenly it came to me that I was viewing the body of Winter's mother, I felt his sorrow, though it was damped by time and distance. Pulling my hands away from his face, I opened my eyes and stepped back from him.

"Well," I sighed at the tingling in my palms, "that was interesting!"

"What did you experience, Cat?" Chimaera asked.

"Winter's memory," I answered succinctly. "At least one of Winter's memories."

Leaning near the blond maned vampire's ear, I whispered what I'd seen to Winter and he nodded, eyes wide in surprise.

"That is one of my memories," he admitted, "but it is not what I was thinking. Perhaps there is some art to this ability of yours. Your eyes changed too."

"What do you mean, my eyes changed?" I added, "And how could you tell if they did? I'm wearing my contact lenses."

"Beneath your lenses, something changed in your eyes," Winter explained. "I can't say precisely what happened, but something did. Perhaps you should remove your contacts before your next try."

"Willing to try me now?" Chimaera interjected with a grin. "I'll wait while you take out your contacts."

"One minute," I raised a finger, took a drink of wine, then put the glass back on the edge of the pool table. "Give me a few minutes and I'll be right back."

At that, I left the game room and made my way to the Sapphire room. In the drawer of the nightstand beside the bed I kept extra lens cases and extra contacts, some disposable, some not, as well as a few different pairs of dark glasses. Pulling an empty case out with a bottle of contact fluid, I went into the bathroom, flipped on the light, and removed my dark green lenses as quickly as I could. It felt great to let my eyes "breathe". Relieved, I put things away on my way out of the bedroom, and rushed back downstairs.

Chimaera and Winter were still shooting pool when I got back so I retrieved my glass and took a sip of wine.

Winter looked up from the felt-covered table and, though he tried to hide it, I could still see him startle when his eyes met mine.

"Shall we continue our experiment?" Chimaera offered, as he returned his pool stick to the rack on the wall.

"You needn't look so excited," I chided.

The raven-haired vampire was fairly beaming in anticipation and I feared he was about to pull another stunt to cause me embarrassment or worse. I knew quite well that he delighted in keeping me off-kilter. He stood before me, staring into my eyes before taking my hands and pressing them to his face. I found myself outside in the night, surrounded by fog. Billows of cool mist swirled around my knees, ebbed and flowed against and around me. Tombstones jutted out of the ground on either side of the path and Spanish moss dripped from tall, gnarled

219

trees. The swamp was apparently taking back the land upon which the cemetery was built and it was claiming the last evidence of those buried there. Upon a slight rise behind a broken and leaning wrought iron fence, far from the encroaching swamp, stood the mausoleum. I made my way there unerringly, swinging the ornate gate open, then pushing against the heavy stone door. Rusted hinges screamed in complaint, but with a little effort I opened the door. Into the darkness, broken only by one 'eternal flame' lamp which afforded almost no illumination, I stepped with an odd feeling of familiarity. Her crypt lay in the center of the stone mausoleum, her coffin securely inside. I stood by the ornately carved stone crypt for a moment, then pushed the lid aside, and touched her coffin with my hand. She stirred within her sleeping prison and I shuddered at the sensation. I could feel her hunger and it quickened my own.

Suddenly the French doors in the Great Hall banged open and closed. Startled, I turned to see Amon, Bishop, and another man standing in the doorway. Chimaera still had his hands around my wrists, though I was able to pull my palms away from his face to break the connection we'd shared.

"What is this?" Amon's voice boomed.

Chapter 10

Lightning flashed through the windows in the Great Hall, silhouetting Amon as if on cue. He was obviously surprised by what he was seeing, but I couldn't tell if it was anger in his voice or something else. As if waking from a dream, I shook my head and stepped away from Chimaera, pulling my hands from his.

"Amon," I sighed in profound relief, running to my mate and throwing myself into his arms. "I was so worried."

"There was no need to worry, my love," he embraced me tightly then let me go. He turned to Bishop, "Please, take Ulrich's things to his room." Bishop nodded smartly and picked up three good sized suitcases, disappearing into the depths of the ground floor labyrinthine halls.

"Ulrich," Amon addressed the man standing silently beside him, "this is my beloved mate, Her Ladyship Passion. She prefers Catherine or Cat."

The burly man stepped forward out of the shadows and extended his hand, "My Lady," he offered. There was so much of him to take in at one time that I was busy looking and almost failed to respond. With a start that I hoped he didn't notice, I put my hand in his and he dropped to one knee to kiss it politely. I couldn't help but look to Amon with a surprised expression.

"Catherine, my love," Amon continued the introduction, "this is Ulrich. He is to be your new mentor."

"Mentor," I murmured, startled and confused.

"It will be my honor to counsel you in your Craft and in any other way I'm able, Ma'am," Ulrich offered, rising from one knee. He was not only a big man; he was a powerful presence. His dark brown hair, streaked with silver and combed straight back from his forehead revealing a widow's peak, hung long and loose. Bushy eyebrows shaded exceptionally blue, deep-set eyes that shone with merriment and light. A neatly trimmed mustache gave way to his long beard which lay atop a broad and formidable looking chest. He had wide shoulders and thick arms; every aspect of him suggested muscle and force. He wore gray trousers and a natural colored tunic with a long draping pale blue vest over it. His garb did nothing to hide the fact that he was neither long nor lean. There was something about him that puzzled me. When his eyes finally met mine I realized…he was not a vampire! His eyes were bright with the shining life force of a mortal. I couldn't tear my eyes off him for a moment and then movement caught my eye. At first glance I thought there was a mouse peeking out from his beard, but when I looked again I realized it was coming out of the breast pocket of his vest.

"You have a mouse…" I stammered, not sure how to even say what I was thinking.

"Oh," Ulrich laughed, "Rufus is my familiar. He was told to behave and stay out of sight, but alas, a mouse is nothing if not curious! I do beg your pardon, Ma'am. I hope you are not offended."

"Not at all," I smiled in relief, as my new mentor lifted the fuzzy brown rodent from his pocket and placed it on his palm. The creature sat upright, wiped its ears with its tiny paws, then looked at me with bright black eyes and twitching nose. It bowed its head.

"Oh my," I laughed, "did he just bow?"

"I should hope so," Ulrich replied. "He knows his manners."

"I'm pleased to meet you, Rufus," I barely refrained from clapping in childish delight.

The mouse accepted a piece of biscuit Ulrich offered him, then scurried up the man's beard and disappeared back into his pocket.

I looked at Amon for further edification.

"Ulrich is a Witch Master," my beloved explained, "and I requested his assistance long ago when your previous training…"

"Nearly ended in my demise?" I chuckled.

"Indeed, my love," Amon admitted, "indeed. It is only now that he is free to train you, as he previously had other obligations to fulfill."

"Train me," I sighed, suddenly feeling that my mate was endeavoring to keep me busy or distracted from that which he thought might cause him grief. "So, he's a male witch? He's a warlock?"

"I'm a Witch Master, Ma'am, I train witches," Ulrich offered, "but I'm no warlock."

"Aren't male witches called warlocks?" I swallowed a chuckle when it became clear he was not going to join me in my amusement.

"That, My Lady," he replied soberly with a slight nod, "is for another time, as it is neither straight-forward nor simple and I am weary from my journey. Alas, my days and nights are not the same as yours, so I'll beg your indulgence as my system adjusts to your active hours."

"Of course," I smiled, embarrassed at my thoughtlessness. "I should have…"

At that moment, Siri padded out of the game room, burping indelicately, and trotted up to Ulrich, sitting before him. Ears laid back, she placed one paw gently on his leg and he bent to pet her without questioning if it was safe to do so.

"This is Siri," I smiled as Ulrich looked up from giving the dog the attention she was seeking.

"And a lovely creature she is," he nodded.

"Cat, my love?" Amon raised one eyebrow at me.

"Later, my darling," I answered succinctly. It was evident, from his expression, that he'd not gotten the dog for me.

"Bishop will see you to your room, Ulrich," Amon offered, his expression clearly one of displeasure at my dismissive comment.

The Witch Master nodded his thanks, then crossed the Great Hall to where Bishop stood waiting with a drink on a tray. Siri brushed against my leg briefly before disappearing up the stairs in a clicking of toenails on the marble tiles.

Looking back at Winter and Chimaera I mouthed "Did you know about any of this?" and both body guards feigned innocence, though both were clearly suppressing delight. I wasn't sure whether to be angry, annoyed, disappointed, intrigued, curious, or immensely pleased. Moving back into the game room, I returned my pool cue to the rack on the wall and retrieved my nearly empty wine glass.

"Gentlemen," I lifted my glass in a toast, "I shall bid you adieu." Downing the remains of the wine, I rinsed the glass in the sink behind the bar and left it on the counter before making my way around the pool table.

"Cat, wait," Winter moved close to me and murmured into my ear, "I was right. Your eyes did change."

"What do you mean?"

"When you were seeing," he paused, searching for the right words, "whatever you were seeing, your eyes were no longer white. It was like iridescent rainbows were shimmering on your irises."

"My eyes weren't closed when I was," I struggled for the right words, "experiencing this new ability?"

"At first you closed your eyes, yes, but then you opened them, 'tite souer," he nodded emphatically. "Your eyes were moving as if you were actually seeing, but you weren't looking at anything here. And your irises went, well, iridescent."

"What does that mean?" I wondered aloud softly.

"I don't know," he admitted, "but it's a 'tell'. Whenever you are reading someone's thoughts or memories your eyes are full of colors."

"So," I paused and sighed, "it's something I should only do when I'm wearing my contacts?"

"If you're trying to read them without their knowledge," he nodded, "then yes!"

"Beloved?" Amon called expectantly from the Great Hall.

Smiling at my much loved body guard, I nodded my thanks before exiting the game room.

"We have a lot of things to discuss," I offered, making my way to my mate and slipping my arm through his.

"Yes, we do, Passion," he patted my hand and looked down at me. "Indeed we do!"

Climbing the wide stone staircase, my mind was awhirl with all I'd experienced since I'd last seen Amon. I found myself sifting through what to tell him, what to avoid telling him, and where to begin any discussion. My mind was a mess and it wasn't a result of the wine. We reached the upstairs landing and turned down the hallway when Amon pulled me into his arms and pressed me up against the wall. As he pressed his lips to mine his tongue probed deeply into my mouth igniting my hunger for him and sparking the vision I'd shared with Chimaera. My body ached for my love and I grabbed fists full of his hair, wanting more than anything to be inside him and to have him inside me. He pulled away from me, looking deeply into my eyes.

"What has gotten into you, Little One?" His expression was one of concern barely masking delight. "And where are your contacts?"

"Long story, darling," I panted, nibbling the curve of his chin. "And it's a story that can wait. I can't!"

"By all means," he hoisted me in his arms and carried me quickly to his room, depositing me gently on the bed. "It is my pleasure to serve!"

Moving up beside me, resting on his left hip, he was undressing me with one hand while I was licking his throat, making my way to his mouth. I ripped open his shirt and ran my hands over the smooth skin of his chest, moving ever downward towards his belt. He kissed me hard as his hands found my breasts, electric shudders running through me when his fingers found my nipples. My hunger rose like a tidal wave and I could wait no more. Fumbling furiously, I managed to undo his belt buckle, unzip his trousers, and free him. Then I was throwing my leg over his body and mounting him like a steed. Finally he was inside me and my hunger, rather than being satisfied, grew more intense as I pounded myself atop my mate. His energy rose to meet mine and soon we were at the edge, about to crest the wave, but there was something missing and without thought or consideration, I leaned forward and drove my teeth into his throat. His blood rushed into my mouth as he grabbed my arm and sank his teeth into my wrist. The fire between us raged until a spine-cracking, eardrum shattering, mind blowing orgasm exploded between us. Gasping, I pulled my mouth away from Amon's throat and licked the wound closed, kissing the edge of his mouth gently. He lifted my wrist from his lips, kissed it after licking the wounds, and smiled at me.

"That was…" he looked at me curiously. "What was that?"

"I missed you," I rubbed my hands across his chest once more, making no attempt to remove myself from his body. "And I was worried, as I'd not been able to reach you as I normally do, I mean besides your cell phone."

"Ah," he nodded, "my apologies. Ulrich's availability came up suddenly and I was forced to go get him. He would only join us if I picked him up in the limo and if he was allowed to use his power to protect our journey. His spell of protection must have shut me off from you."

"It's just that," I paused to consider how much to share, "it was the first time I'd been unable to reach you. I mean, well, the last time I'd tried to reach you was when I was in your office and the vortex had nearly sucked me out of the room. Then tonight when I tried and got simply…nothing, I was worried."

"I am sorry, my darling," he murmured, a smile playing across his lips as he twirled a lock of my hair around his finger. He started moving slowly beneath me, his hunger rising again.

"You are not sorry," I breathed into his mouth as he kissed me and rolled me onto my back. "And at the moment, I am not sorry either."

Locking my ankles behind his back, his length plunging deep inside me, I tasted his blood on my lips and it stirred my desire as only it could. He pulled himself almost out of me before pounding into me again and again, the tempo increasing with each thrust. Finally he drove his length as far as he could into my depths and we once more exploded in orgasmic spasms. Lying heavily atop me, he heaved a deep sigh, moved his long hair aside, and planted gentle kisses along my collarbone. I sighed in satisfaction, delight, and exhaustion.

"So, my love," he lifted himself off of me, moving to lie next to me, one leg across my thigh, "would you like to sleep here this day or shall we adjourn to the coffin room?"

"It doesn't matter to me," I answered, still experiencing waves of lustful energy.

"Very well," he nodded and got off the bed, pulling up his trousers as he did so. After buckling his belt, he pulled his shirt up his arms but did not bother to try buttoning it, as I'd pretty much made that impossible. Broken buttons lay scattered atop the bed and I tried to avoid them as I retrieved what was left of my clothes. Without a word, Amon scooped me up in his arms and carried me from the room as I clutched my garments to my chest. Being carried buck naked from Amon's room, I could only hope that none of his security team or his house staff would see us. Though I didn't consider myself a prude, I was far from brazen, and I held onto a bit of my humanity through my modesty, or so I told myself.

Moving down the long hallways, around corners, and down various back stairs, we made it without incidence or witness into the coffin room. My mate placed me gently into our coffin, took my clothes from my hands, and removed his own clothes before climbing in beside me. We didn't always sleep naked, but there were times when we needed the feel of flesh against flesh. I slid my right knee across his legs, placed my right hand on his chest, and closed my eyes.

"Amon," I murmured as Thea's image appeared in my mind, "what does Sabre look like?" The witch's spirit had pleaded for my assistance, as had Sabre's sirelings, so I could not put off doing something about the matter. As I relaxed against my mate, I considered that my new-found ability might lend itself to further insights and investigations.

"What does he look like?" Amon parroted, and for a moment I thought he would refuse to answer, but at length he replied, "He looks young, as if he is in his twenties perhaps, and he has long brown hair that he wears pulled back. He is likely as tall as you are. Beyond that, I could not say. Why do you ask?"

"Just wondering what all the fuss was about," I half-shrugged against him, making light of the conversation in hopes that he'd let the matter drop. Making sure my mental shields were in place, I sent a secret prayer out to the universe that they would remain in place while we slept. My beloved said nothing further and I relaxed into the silence. Sighing deeply as he kissed the tips of my fingers, I slipped quickly and easily into sleep.

Once more I stood beside the auburn-haired witch as Thea appeared in my dream. Beside her stood Sabre, dressed in a black leather jacket, dark t-shirt, and jeans. With his hair slicked back into a ponytail, he looked like a biker or a fashion model. As I looked at him, however, his image shifted and his apparel transformed from modern to antiquated. The leather jacket became a royal blue velvet coat and the t-shirt was replaced with a white dress shirt, a cravat of gray tied neatly at the throat. I realized that I was 'seeing' the image of his origins, the man he'd been before he'd been made vampire. I could 'feel' his energy and even in my sleep I hoped I'd be able to find him once I'd awaken. Thea placed a ghostly hand against his chest and he cradled her other hand, brought it to his lips, and kissed her palm. She looked at me silently, the plea still clearly in her eyes, before disappearing into a mist. Sabre looked at me, our eyes locking in a profound moment, and then he too was swallowed by the mist. A tiny brown mouse appeared on the back of my hand and began whispering to me. It was clear the rodent had much to say, but its voice was so tiny and it was so excited that I could not understand what it was saying. As its frustration grew it began to jump up and down on my palm and I feared it would fall, but instead it merely winked out like a light and I slept without further dreams.

"I have discussed matters with your beast," Amon stood beside the coffin, looking down at me, brushing a lock of hair from my eyes. I had no idea what he was saying, but it was a most pleasant way to wake up. I blinked at him uncomprehendingly and did my best to refrain from grumbling as I moved around so I could stretch and sit upright.

"What?" I yawned and rubbed the sleep from my eyes. It felt like I'd been asleep such a short time.

"I have discussed matters with your beast," he repeated himself patiently, then stepped aside and nodded in the direction of the door where Siri lay curled sleeping.

"My beast," I sighed. "Yes, about that. I'd thought you might have gotten the dog for me, as you'd mentioned hiring additional bodyguards. But, from your reaction last night, I take it that's not the case."

"I did not get the dog for you," he admitted, "though it is a good idea. Had I considered the matter, I might have assigned one of my pack to your protection. I could do so still, but as the dog is here and she seems to be dedicated to you, any further action on my part seems unnecessary. I have discussed your protection with your beast and she has agreed to be your companion and be at your side as often as you will allow it."

"You discussed matters, huh?" I grinned as I clambered as gracefully as possible from the coffin.

"The creature seems quite intelligent," he offered, "and she understood what I was saying."

"Fine," I chuckled as I crossed the room and pulled a pair of jeans and black t-shirt from the shelf beside the door. At my approach Siri lifted her head and thumped her tail against the floor but she did not move from before the door. "Speaking of last night's reactions," I held up my index finger, "I noticed something!"

"And what was that, Beloved?"

"You didn't ask what you'd walked in on when you and Ulrich arrived," I raised one eyebrow.

"I did not," he nodded, moving to close the space between us. "I can feel that there is much there that, at some point, you and I will discuss, and so I am practicing patience."

"You?" I laughed, even though I knew it could be risky. "You are practicing patience?"

"You forget, my darling," he looked deeply into my eyes, "I waited centuries for your arrival and I waited until I was forced to act before touching your life. My patience is vast."

"Ah yes," I conceded the matter, "so it is. My apologies. So, is today my first day of school?" I changed the subject quickly as, it seemed I'd been gifted a reprieve and had no desire to get into the subject of this new ability of mine.

"Ulrich requested to be awakened at 8 pm so you have some time before he stirs," my mate answered, embracing me and kissing me deeply.

"Are you offering to entertain me until it's time for school?" I ran my hands up his chest and wrapped my arms around his neck.

"Alas, my darling," he sighed deeply, "I have a meeting with Chimaera and the Council. Chimaera's replacement has been selected and must now go through a series of…tests, if you will."

"If I will…" I smiled mischievously and wiggled my eyebrows at him.

"Cat," he lowered his voice and turned my name into a warning.

"Fine, fine," I pouted and released my mate. Stepping away to slip on my clothes, I paused a moment at the shelf on the wall and slipped a fresh pair of contacts in before running a brush through my hair.

"I shall drop in on your studies upon my return," he offered, taking my hand and kissing it gallantly.

"Siri," I patted my thigh with my free hand, "come on, sweetie. Let's go."

At my command, the dog leapt to her feet and came to me, nudging my hand with her big, warm nose. Amon led the way out of the room, down the hall, and up the stairs. Siri paced me as I followed my mate, and we were both rewarded when we reached the Great Hall. Lily was just coming out of the kitchen with a tray of coffee and croissants, and she pulled a dog biscuit out of the pocket of her apron and tossed it to my canine companion. Amon continued across the wide hall then paused, turning back to bow slightly to me, before disappearing through one of the doors leading to a sublevel of the mansion.

"Thank you, Lily," I smiled and took the tray from her, "I'll just take this into the study. Would you see if you can find a bowl for my new friend so she can have some fresh water?"

"I've already done that," the maid grinned and nodded toward the hall to the kitchen. "She's got a bowl of water and a bowl of meat scraps near the kitchen door. I'll have Lucius get her some real dog food when he can. I doubt she'll complain about what's in her bowl in the meantime."

"I'm sure you're right," I laughed, imagining the fare Siri was likely being offered. The refrigerator was constantly stocked with filet mignon, T-bone steaks, shrimp, lobster, and all manner of gourmet cuisine. I'd not be surprised if Lily found herself opening a bottle of imported beer for the dog.

Moving into the study, I put the tray down on the coffee table, seated myself on the couch, bare feet tucked beneath me, and sipped my coffee. The croissants were fresh and warm and I devoured over half of the first one before Siri came into the study and sat at attention near the bar. She stared at me, then stared at the croissant between my fingers, then looked at me beseechingly. When she cocked her head at me, I melted and tossed the end of the pastry to her. She snapped it out of midair and ate it in one gulp.

I was just about to break the second croissant into pieces to share with the beast when Ulrich appeared in the doorway. Wearing blue plaid pajamas beneath a navy bath robe, he looked bleary eyed and exhausted.

His long hair was slicked back from his forehead and the length secured into a ponytail going down his back. His beard, nearly as long as his hair, was combed and woven through an ornate leather-edged metal ring.

"Alas, poor Ulrich," I smiled in sympathy, "I knew him well."

"Surely it's too early in the day for butchering Shakespeare," he grumbled as he moved to the coffee table and looked at the empty mug.

"Awww…" I pretended to pout, "I thought thou wouldst enjoy my infinite jest!"

"The only thing worse than having one's sleep pattern interrupted," he offered, looking at the tray in obvious disappointment, "is having to deal with some-one…cheery, and having no tea!"

"Fine," I tossed a piece of croissant across the room and the dog once more caught it with ease. "Come Ulrich, have a seat and some breakfast. I'll have Lily bring tea and more food, though I must tell you I find anyone who doesn't drink coffee highly suspect."

"Please," he looked disappointedly at the tray, "ask her for something more substantial. Bread is fine, but I require protein. And I'd like Rooibos tea if she has it."

"Your wish is…" I stood and bowed, "well, you know." Laughing, I put my mug on the coffee table, put the plate of croissants and coffee carafe beside it, and took the tray. Siri stood and followed me from the room.

In the kitchen, Lily was already grilling sausages and she had ham in the oven. The room smelled wonderful. She took the tray from me and placed it on the counter.

"Master Ulrich would like tea," I said with an air of pomposity. "Rooibos, if you please."

"I have most every kind of tea under the sun, child, so Rooibos it is. Bishop's always cartin' strange herbal concoctions back here from New Orleans," she smiled as she started loading the tray with more croissants and a pitcher of orange juice. "It's good to have a man with a healthy appetite in the house. You and Mister Sin don't eat enough to keep butterflies alive."

"We have Siri to feed now too," I offered.

"She'll be eatin' dog food soon," the maid replied as she removed the tray of ham from the oven and began to plate the sausages.

"Yes," I sighed, looking at my 4-legged body guard, "and that's what's best for her."

When she'd properly balanced the loaded dishes on the tray, the maid tucked fresh linen napkins between them and covered them with silver domes. She then turned to pour hot water into a china teapot, added a silver tea ball, and placed the lid upon it. Beside the china teacup and saucer, she placed a bowl of sugar, a crystal dish of raw honey, and a delicate china creamer.

"I'll take it," I offered, "since I'm going that way anyway."

"Mister Sin got them people in a meetin' downstairs again?" She asked as she placed the tray carefully in my hands, offering an expression that suggested she did not approve of those attending.

"I knew he was having a meeting," I answered, considering the information she'd inadvertently given me, "but I didn't realize they were downstairs."

"They always come in that secret door," she admitted, "like no one will know they're here. But I know they're here. I can practically smell 'em!"

"I know what you mean," I grinned. "I have that reaction to them too. Come on, Siri,"

The black German shepherd moved to stand beside my left leg and when I started walking she paced me carefully. At first I thought it was because she'd been trained to 'heel' that way but, upon further consideration, I decided it more likely she was hoping I'd drop something from the tray so she could clean it up for me.

Ulrich was munching a croissant when I entered the study with the tray of food. He tossed the remainder of his bread to Siri, brushed the crumbs from his fingers on the lapel of his robe, and began to remove the silver domes from the dishes on the tray almost before I could set it down. Foregoing the offered plate, he picked up a piece of ham with one hand and a link of sausage with the other. Eating hungrily, he paused only briefly to fill his teacup, add a dollop of honey, and stir it with a silver spoon. Watching him eat as if he'd not eaten in weeks was actually fascinating and I found myself mesmerized, though I was not aware that I was staring.

"What?" Ulrich paused in chewing, his right hand bearing a sausage link frozen in mid-air.

"Oh," I startled myself, shaking my head, "I'm sorry. I didn't mean to stare. I've just never seen anyone eat so..." Unable to grasp the appropriate word to convey my thoughts without possibly insulting my mentor, I just stopped talking and took a sip of what was left in my mug, which was, unfortunately, cold coffee.

"I take it that you did little Craft before you became," he paused, searching my face as if he'd find the proper term there, "what you are."

"There wasn't much time between my arrival here and becoming His Lordship's mate," I admitted, delicately choosing my words. "Ok, I can't stand this verbal pussyfootin', I didn't mean to offend you. You just seem to be enjoying your food so. I think I'm jealous."

"So, we can be honest and forthright with one another?" He grinned, having finished the sausage link, he started on another piece of ham. "I would not offend My Lady, but if I spend so much time and effort watching my words, it may lengthen your training by… months."

Refilling my mug with fresh hot coffee, I stopped and looked Ulrich in the eye, "Trust me, you'll not offend me by being honest, and I'll try to not insult you with my honesty. Deal?"

"Deal!" He offered a bright smile in obvious relief. "And as to my eating, my dear, it took a tremendous amount of energy to protect the vehicle that got me here and to make sure that we traveled unobserved. That is why I'm eating so much and so quickly. My system is depleted."

"I'd not considered that," I confessed. "So, do all witches expend such energy when they cast spells?"

"That depends on the witch," he nodded, adding, "and the spell he or she casts."

"Ah, so I have a lot to learn," I observed, trying to hide my disappointment at how much time and effort this education might require.

"You do," he agreed, sipping his tea with a loud slurp. "And your first lesson begins as soon as I've finished this."

"Take your time, please," I smiled, "I have my coffee to finish."

"Time is of the essence," Ulrich replied cryptically.

At that moment, Siri rose to her feet and presented herself before me, pushing her nose under my hand and wagging her tail furiously. The look in her eyes was pleading, but it didn't seem to have anything to do with the food on the table.

"Oops," I sighed, "I just realized I'm a dog's person. Message received, Siri. Ulrich, if you'll excuse us, I believe nature is calling. I'll take my companion here out while you finish your meal and be back as soon as I can."

"I'll be finished by the time you return," he replied, popping a piece of croissant into his mouth and wiping his fingers on a napkin. Dismissing us easily, he turned his attention back to the tray of food.

Siri trotted to the French doors and waited patiently until I opened them, then she raced out across the veranda and into the garden beyond. She relieved herself on the grass then began to investigate the rose and butterfly bushes. I stretched my arms over my head and looked around at the darkness. The previous night's storm had not entirely moved on and low gray clouds still cluttered the sky. A slight hint of orange on the horizon heralded the dying sunset and promised a clearing, star-filled night.

Chapter 11

"Come, Catherine," Ulrich stood politely when I returned from the garden. Smoothing the lapels of his plaid pajamas, he straightened his robe and snugged the matching fabric belt at his waist.

"Please," I chuckled, "call me Cat. When someone calls me Catherine it usually means I'm in trouble."

"Alright then, Cat," he nodded with a smile. Siri rushed into the study, water still dripping from her mouth from a drink at her bowl, and stood on the rug in front of the bar. She walked a tight circle twice then plopped herself down and laid her muzzle on her paws. Apparently she was ready for a show or a nap, whichever came first.

"Do you maybe want to…" I started, then realized I was stumbling into tricky territory, but had no choice but to continue. "I mean, would you like to go shower and dress before we begin?"

"Trust me, my dear," he shrugged, "what I'm wearing is of no concern whatsoever and I'll enjoy a long and refreshing shower when your lesson for today is done."

"That sounds ominous," I chuckled, hoping he'd assure me that I was wrong.

"Come, just sit down here and we'll get started," he took a seat on the end of the sofa away from the door, leaving the center cushion and other end open for me. I took a seat on the far end and turned to him.

"No furry friend in your pocket today," I glanced at the breast pocket of his robe but there was no sign of Rufus.

"He chose to sleep in today; this change of situation upsets him," my instructor explained, though I couldn't tell if he was sincere or in jest. "Actually, for this particular lesson it was best he remain elsewhere anyway. This is one trip he cannot make with me."

About to make a comment about what kind of trip a rodent was not able to take with his witch, I was relieved when Ulrich cleared his throat.

"Now, you know that there's a meeting going on downstairs, yes?" He drew a deep breath.

"Yes," I answered slowly, not sure where he could possibly be going with the subject. "His Lordship is meeting with the Council of Five and I assume others are there as well."

"Correct," he nodded, "and you and I are joining them, though they'll not be aware of us."

"Wait, what do you mean?" A seed of foreboding suddenly took root in my gut and began to grow. This was so not going well.

"We're going to practice your ability to become invisible," he answered succinctly.

"I've um…" For a moment I was unable to gather my thoughts into anything cohesive, then finally my words returned, "I've never been invisible. Well, I've traveled out of body when I was in a coma, but I've never actually been invisible. I don't have any idea how to do that!"

"Relax, Cat," Ulrich smiled kindly. "You're a witch. This stuff is in your blood, so to speak. You'll take to it like a fish to water!"

"Sure," I laughed, thinking he was making light of my concern. "Oh wait! You're serious?"

"I'm serious," he nodded and straightened his shoulders. "Just follow my instructions as I give them and you and I shall make our way to the meeting."

"Wait, Amon," I shook my head, "I mean, His Lordship knows about this and he's okay with it?"

"He does," my mentor assured me, "and he is!"

"I've spent the majority of my life trying to avoid being invisible," I grumbled mostly to myself, "and here I go."

"Now," Ulrich began, "first I'm going to ask you to close your eyes, but this is only to help you to focus on my voice and what I'm saying." Looking me directly in the eye, the Witch Master captured my attention, captured my focus, and captured me. I couldn't help but notice his lips. They looked soft, moist, rosy and inviting. I wondered what it would be like to kiss those lips, then I shook my head and gasped with a start.

"What was that?" I cried, "Was that some sort of spell, some glamour or something?"

"My apologies, Ma'am," he bowed his head. "Forgive me. I was just…warming up, for want of a better explanation. A witch's power can be quite enticing. I should have warned you."

"Wow! So, will I someday be able to do that?"

"Cat, my dear student," he smiled brightly, "you are vampire. Already you possess a very powerful beauty and attraction. I'm sure your ability to cast a glamour would be quite formidable, though that's not something you need put effort into. So now, please close your eyes."

"So, you're going to hypnotize me with your voice?"

"No, Cat," he chuckled, "I'm not hypnotizing you. I just want you to concentrate on visualizing what I'm telling you and eventually I'll have you open your eyes."

"Fine," I sighed and closed my eyes. "Now what?"

"Just be calm and settle yourself, Cat," he intoned. "Visualize yourself. See yourself in your mind's eye. Can you see you?"

I saw the inside of my eyelids. I saw tiny bright streaks on a field of purple black, I saw the pattern of the rug upon which the dog now slept, and I saw the stars in the sky and the twinkling lights in the trees in the garden. I saw Amon's face, I saw Winter's eyes, and I saw...frustration. Determined to accomplish this feat, I refocused my intent and imagined what I must look like to Ulrich.

"Um," I hesitated then pretended I was seeing myself in a mirror as I'd once done, "I can see me, well, more or less."

"More or less is fine," he assured me, "and you'll not be able to hold the image for long, it will shift as your focus shifts."

"Yeah, I get that," I confirmed. One moment my face was huge and glowing, the next my chin was disproportionately long, then my forehead was massive, then my eyes large and bright. The sensation was like looking in a funhouse mirror, one aspect of my image growing while another shrank.

"Now, focus once more and see your image getting bigger," he instructed.

"Bigger," I replied uncertainly. I was having trouble keeping parts of my image from becoming gargantuan; I wasn't sure I wanted anything getting bigger!

"Bigger, expanding," he added, "from the molecular level. Visualize your cellular structure growing, the gaps between the cells expanding."

"Ah," I realized what he meant. "Okay, I think I understand." I imagined myself expanding, becoming lighter, more airy, and more ephemeral. Doing so actually stopped the funhouse mirror effect and I began to relax.

"Now, open your eyes," he offered, "and look at me."

Slowly opening my eyes, I turned to my instructor and did my best to squelch a startled gasp. His image was translucent; he was there but he was no longer solid matter.

"You see?" He smiled and held one weirdly see-through hand up between us.

"I do!" I laughed. He looked for all the world like a hologram from some computer generated movie.

"Now look at your hand," he nodded and I released a tiny shriek when my own translucent fingers waggled at me.

"Come Cat," Ulrich stood and offered his hand. I took his hand and he led me from the study and into the Great Hall. "I'll let you show the way, as you're more familiar with this place than I am. I've only seen the meeting hall once and I'm not entirely sure I can find it again."

"Oh trust me," I shuddered at the memory of the first time I'd seen the meeting hall, "I'll never forget that room or how to get there, and even more importantly how to get away from it."

Not long after the goddess turned sorceress who'd been hired to train me had arrived, Arathia had conjured a demon to uncover the origin of my powers and things had not gone well or as planned. The meeting hall was where the demon had been summoned, with me having been shackled to the wall and a large contingent of the vampire community in attendance. I'd been forbidden to protect myself, but it was not in my nature to take orders, so the incident had gotten ugly. I did have a fond memory of those in the audience scrambling for the doors when the demon, dragon demon to be exact, had gotten a taste of my power and had reverted to its winged dragon form.

Ulrich and I made our way into the sublevel of the mansion, going down flights of stairs and taking numerous turns into the labyrinthine basement. We could hear voices raised in excitement and celebration as we neared the closed doors of the meeting hall. I drew to a halt and turned to my mentor.

"This is it," I offered. "Do we open the doors and go in or do we just walk through them?"

"Eventually you'll be able to walk through solid matter in this state, but as this is your first experience, I suggest we carefully and quietly slip inside behind the next person who enters," he answered, ghostly hand resting lightly on the door.

"I don't know if I'm ready for this," I confessed.

"Trust me," he said confidently, "just follow my lead, be as silent as possible, and try not to draw attention to us. Don't knock over a chair or run into anyone."

When two vampires I'd never seen before stepped into the corridor from the outside entrance, I steeled myself and waited for them to rap on the door to be admitted. When the left door swung open the men nodded then disappeared into the meeting hall and I slipped inside behind them. I felt Ulrich follow me in as the noise of the crowd rose and sporadic applause erupted throughout the audience. Winter, in a formal black jacket and tie, stood guard to the left of the door, arms crossed at his chest, eyes scanning the room. Another vampire guard, whom I did not know, in similar attire stood to the right of the other door. At the front of the room, on a raised dais, the Council of Five were seated at a long table. Amon sat in a large, throne-like chair behind them all, and Chimaera stood beside His Lordship. I recognized the members of the Council, except for one man who had his back to the audience, as he had a private word with Thammuz, the Council head. Ulrich led me along the wall toward the dais, then paused before a bank of tall velvet curtains which would have been closed had the Council had any private matters to discuss before the rest of the community could join in the meeting. My mentor said nothing, just nodded silently and watched the proceedings. Chesmne, the calico cat-like vamp who delighted in theatrics, was her usual scene-stealer self in a silver, gold, and copper lame` sheath, her multi-colored hair piled elegantly atop her head and adorned with jeweled barrettes. Nephthele, the other female member of the Council, was subtly attired in a pale blue-gray brocade coat, a cascade ruffle of white silk at her throat. Whether she was in a skirt or trousers I could not tell from my line of sight, though I realized that I'd never seen either of the female vamps in pants. Mastiphal, whom I always thought of as Viking, sat beside Chesmne, wearing an expression of abject boredom. He wore a simple black long-sleeved dress shirt open at the collar and his hair, thick, wavy, and copper-blond, lay loose about his shoulders. He idly stroked his goatee as he inspected first the ceiling then his cuticles. Clearly he had somewhere more interesting to be. Thammuz wore an elegant charcoal gray jacket with white shirt and tie. His silver hair was smoothed back and secured at the nape of his neck, and a large black pendant hung from a heavy chain around his neck. Though I could not see the details of the necklace, I knew it was the Medallion of Office that he wore when the Council was in formal session. He glanced in our general direction as the stranger spoke quietly into his ear and I could only hope that he could not see us. Nodding smartly at whatever he'd been told, he placed his hands on the table and stood, the vampire at his side turning to look at the audience. My world tilted as I recognized the guru I'd met in meditation. He no longer wore saffron robes, but Zador stood beside Thammuz and when his eyes moved toward the wall behind us, I gasped, choking back a squeal of surprise, and took my hand from Ulrich's grasp. Suddenly I felt as if a strong wind had me in its clutches and I was hurtled past Winter, through the now closed doors, through the hallways, up the stairs, and back into the study where I was slammed back into my body. I yelped and leapt to my feet, Ulrich following suit. He clutched at his chest and wheezed loudly.

"Don't," he gasped and started again, "don't ever do that...again." He coughed, drew several deep breaths, and coughed again. "By Odin's eye, Cat, what happened? You could have gotten us both killed! Well, maybe not you, but I'm still a bit on the human side.

We could have been captured as spies or worse! What happened?"

Head still reeling, I began pacing the floor, careful to not alarm Siri. "You have no way of knowing this, of course, but I've seen the new Council member. I mean, well, we've not actually met, but he's spoken to me."

"What do you mean?" Ulrich moved unsteadily to the bar and helped himself to a glass of red wine from the crystal carafe in which it had been decanted. "I don't normally imbibe right after breakfast, but today I'm making an exception!" My obviously frazzled mentor drank deeply as I tried to gather my wits.

"I don't know what I mean," I confessed, chuckling at my own confusion. "The last time I meditated this guy showed up claiming that I'd called him and that he was there to help me. He looked like some Buddhist guru type and got a bit miffed when I told him that I didn't need his help. That was the guy on the dais with the other Council members which means he must be the new guy being sworn in, or whatever they do when they appoint a new member. I'm not really sure about the protocol and all that pomp stuff."

"You're sure it was the same person?" Ulrich raised his wineglass to his lips and raised his eyebrows in question as he took another sip.

"Sure looked like him to me," I shrugged, "at least enough to startle me into letting go of you. I had no idea I'd be rocketed back here so unceremoniously."

"Nor did I," my mentor admitted, "as I've not had all that much experience training a witch who also happens to be a vampire. I don't believe it was breaking the connection with me that drew you back to your body; I think it was just your surprise that broke your concentration. Your cellular structure just resumed its natural form when your intention and attention were scattered."

"Okay, wait, I'm confused," grimacing, I tried to put everything into some reasonable order, "were we invisible or did we leave our bodies here in the study and go for walk?"

"We were invisible," Ulrich looked pensive. "Well, let's put it this way, had you turned around and looked at the sofa, when we left to go to the meeting, you'd have found it empty."

"So, why did it feel like I was slammed back into my body when I messed everything up?"

"First," he explained patiently, "you did not mess everything up. Secondly, we were slammed back into our bodies in this study because..." Scrunching up his face, he paused, clearly trying to decide how to proceed.

"Because..." I urged him on.

"When I first suggested this exercise to His Lordship, he was quite concerned for our safety, yours in particular," he offered. "So, I offered a spell to ensure our success, well at least to ensure our safety."

"What kind of spell?" I couldn't repress my curiosity.

"Um," he tilted his head to the right and took a deep breath, "let me explain it this way. If you'd been startled or surprised and I'd not cast this 'spell of returning', we'd have both suddenly materialized in the middle of the meeting, which, I think we can both agree, would have been inconvenient, even possibly dangerous."

"So, you cast a spell that would draw us back into this room to return to our physical forms?"

"Yes," he smiled weakly, "that's exactly what I did."

"When you were doing that 'glamour' thingy?" I suddenly saw the truth of the matter. "That was what you were doing, wasn't it? That was when you cast your spell of returning!"

"I confess," he nodded, "yes, that was when I did it."

"So," I put things together quickly, if not smoothly, "you lied to me."

"Well, yes," Ulrich spread his hands, palms up, and shrugged. "Though it was not intentional. Before experiencing this form of invisibility there is simply no way to explain possible outcomes. But trust me, once you have some practice under your belt you'll be able to disappear and reappear easily and it will become almost second nature."

"Believe me, I'll never let myself get startled again when I'm invisible," I moaned, rubbing my forehead and my neck. "That was so not pleasant!"

"Wine, Cat?" He raised an empty crystal glass in offering.

"Yes, please," I smiled and moved to the bar, leaning my elbows on its polished mahogany surface. "This is going to take some figuring out, I think."

"I'll leave the figuring out to you," he nodded as he filled my glass with the ruby liquid. "I'll just have this glass and recover my wits before heading off to the shower. I'm in need of refreshing."

"Hey, if no one noticed us," I chuckled, "and apparently, as no one is rushing in with fangs drawn and guns at the ready, this is the case, I'll be a happy camper. A little wine, a little relaxing and I'm good to go."

"So, shall we take this opportunity," he rubbed his forehead, "to get to know one another while we wait for our brains to settle from this scrambling?"

"That would be nice," I sighed, aware that my own head was throbbing to an interestingly erratic beat. "How is it you came to be my mentor, I mean other than that Amon contacted you to do so?"

"As you might imagine, there are not that many Witch Masters who teach," he paused, glancing sideways at me, "special cases. I have something of a reputation in that regard."

"Special cases, huh?" I laughed. "I've been called worse, I'm sure. So, you've taught other types of beings that are also witches?"

"I have," he nodded and drank deeply of his wine, "though I am not at liberty to discuss the details of such things, I'm sure you understand."

"Oh, sure, sure," I agreed, then paused and looked him in the eye to make sure he was being sincere. Though his expression was kind and gentle, there was no sign of merriment in his eyes. "So, what's next for me?"

"First, we ascertain how successful this first lesson was," he answered matter-of-factly, "and then we'll analyze your weaknesses and work on improving your technique. His Lordship will be able to help with the analysis since he knew we were there and was looking for us."

"And then?"

"Then we'll proceed accordingly," Ulrich offered. "And I understand that you're a musician. You understand the energy in music and how to manipulate it?"

"I am," I brightened, "and I think I understand, at least somewhat. I think there are things I could do with my music that I've no desire to do."

"Such as?" He raised one eyebrow in question.

"I think that if I wanted to," I explained haltingly, "I could make people love my music. Um, which is to say, I think I could do with my music what you did to me before we began this lesson. I think I could glamour the audience if I really wanted to do so."

"But you're not interested in doing that?" He smiled, lips on the rim of his wine glass.

"Nah," I shrugged, "I want my music to do its own thing. I don't need to use it that way. I play for my own entertainment and pleasure and just hope that the audience gets onboard with me. I'm not performing to become famous."

"I should think not," Ulrich grinned.

"Yes," I chuckled, "it's not as if the Council of Five are my fans as it is. I can't give them anymore ammo. They actually think I'm dangerous!" I laughed a bit more, expecting my mentor to join in, but he only finished his glass of wine, put the glass on the coffee table and sighed deeply.

"If you'd be so kind as to excuse me, Cat," he gave me a tired smile, "I think I'll go take a shower and take a nap, or perhaps I'll take a nap and then shower. At any rate, I shall see you either later this morning or tonight, or tomorrow. How do you keep your days and nights straight? Being active primarily at night must be confusing."

"Happily, such details don't mean much to me, as my time is mostly my own," I agreed. "I'm currently booked to play a club outside of Houston two nights a week, so as long as I get there on time to play, the rest doesn't matter much."

"I see," he rose and carried his empty glass to the bar, "then I'll just say bonsoir for now and I'll see you again when I see you."

"Good enough!" I laughed and lifted my nearly empty glass in a toast. "Bonsoir, Ulrich!"

"Oh Cat," he paused in the doorway, pulled something from the pocket of his robe and tossed it at me, "this is your homework."

Startled, I nearly dropped my wineglass, but managed to catch what appeared to be a metal ball in my left hand. My first thought was '*I'm too old for homework,*' but I immediately dismissed that as wrong, then '*I'm too mature for homework,*' surfaced but that wasn't right either.

"Homework? There's going to be homework?" I tried not to whine but failed, "I'm too busy for homework." I thought that statement sounded reasonable and valid.

"That is, of course, entirely up to you," Ulrich bowed, "but you might consider how long you want the likes of me around here. The more you apply yourself, the more you study and learn, the sooner I'll be gone."

"Wait a minute," I stood, index finger of my right hand raised in protest, "just how much time are we talking about for this training? Is this going to take days, weeks, months, or years?"

"Again, this is entirely up to you," he answered.

"So, when will you know that my training is complete?" I insisted, "How will you know when I'm done? I'm already a witch, so it's not a case of me 'making witch'.

"When the student surpasses the teacher," he put his hands together as if in prayer and bowed again, "the teacher's work is done."

"Do you always speak in proverbs?" I quipped, my frustration getting the better of me. "You sound like Yoda."

"My apologies, Ma'am," he smiled, "and again, bonsoir. You have your assignment." He glanced at the weird metal ball thingy in my hand and the smile became a wicked grin. As he walked into the Great Hall and turned toward the back of the mansion, he laughed heartily, which made me oddly uncomfortable.

Sighing, I put my glass on the coffee table and resumed my seat on the sofa. I looked at the ball in my left hand, my assignment. It appeared to be metal, but it didn't really feel like metal. It wasn't cool or hard; it had some weight but wasn't really heavy. There were raised marks that appeared to be seams, or maybe, upon closer inspection I realized, they were an inscription. I didn't recognize the letters or symbols, but they were unusual. Turning it over and over in my hand, I could find no button or switch that might open it or make it do anything. Rolling it between my palms, I considered what it might be, then considered tossing it to Siri, but she was still sleeping on the rug and I didn't want to disturb her. In frustration I placed the ball on the table beside my wine glass and just looked at it.

"At this rate, Ulrich could be here until doomsday," I huffed, unhappy with my assignment, my mentor, and myself.

Chapter 12

As I sat staring at the ball, going over all that had happened with Ulrich in my mind, I heard voices getting louder as those engaged in conversation grew nearer the study. I recognized my mate's voice immediately and I thought I heard Chimaera comment, but there was laughter and other noise that kept me from identifying all who were approaching. I was torn between ignoring them and preparing myself for guests, but finally I picked up the ball and tucked it into the corner of the sofa, then plopped down on the cushion so my assignment was behind my back.

"I believe Her Ladyship Passion awaits us within," Amon announced as he reached the doorway, pausing to address those behind him. I stood, hands clasped before me, as regally as possible, wishing I'd had the foresight to dress properly for meeting new, um, vampires.

"I'd not go so far as to say I was awaiting you," I smiled and lifted my cheek so my mate could kiss me cursorily, "but I'm delighted to see you."

"My Lady Passion," Amon introduced me properly, "I present the new Council member and a fellow countryman, Bastiaan Dykstra. Bastiaan, this is my mate, Passion."

"Please, call me Ca..." is all I managed to say before Zador entered and took both of my hands in his. His eyes met mine and the energy between us froze me for a moment before I could look away. Then I saw shades of darkness, sensed warmth almost to the point of oppression, felt thick, soft fur, and heard a snuffling breath.

"I am," he kissed the back of each hand ceremoniously, lifting my hands so as to not release me from his gaze, "your servant, My Lady."

"Zador," I gasped at last. Pulling my hands from his, I realized he was pack, a member of Amon's brethren. Making a mental note to tell my mate about my new ability to sense things via touch, I turned my attention to the meditation guru.

"Pardon me?" Bastiaan looked confused at my utterance.

"You are Zador," I offered, "and I've seen you before."

"I don't know who or what Zador is," he smiled patiently, clearly thinking me mad, "but I assure you, I am Bastiaan."

"Sebastian?"

"No, Bastiaan," he politely corrected me. "I am, like your mate, from Friesland and the name is that of my ancestors."

His hair, though as long as Zador's, now appeared not gray but very pale blond. His features were identical to Zador's, the angles and planes of his face, the thickness of his eyebrows, even his voice was the same, yet I realized there were subtle differences. This vampire wore not saffron robes, but a tailored black shirt and blue frock coat with velvet lapels. Bastiaan 'felt' different, and not just because Zador was in my mind's eye when I meditated.

"I am sorry," I laughed probably more nervously than intended, "but I was sure I'd met you before. I must be mistaken. Please, pardon me." Looking at Amon for guidance, I wasn't sure if I'd made a faux pas by apologizing, I tried to be gracious without being too familiar. My mate merely looked at me with an expression of concern and a knowing, subtle blink of his eyes that said *'This is something we must discuss at another time!'*

"I am honored to meet you, My Lady," Bastiaan nodded smartly then took a step back and spread one arm behind him, "and I would like to introduce you to Elspeth. My Lady Passion, this is Elspeth."

The gorgeous, willowy, auburn-haired woman who stepped up beside Bastiaan made me regret once more that I was not formally attired. Her complexion was smooth and creamy, her eyes were brilliant green, and her simple black satin sheath was stunning. She bowed her head gracefully.

'And here I am, resplendent in my jeans and sleeveless t-shirt, and barefoot, even,' I grumbled silently. *'Amon had said he'd be dropping in after my lesson, not that he'd be bringing guests. He could have warned me!'* Without conscious thought, I glared at my beloved and saw him flinch at the intensity of my unspoken communication.

"My Lady," the beautiful vampire spoke with perfect diction and clarity, "I am honored to meet you. I have heard much of you."

"Elspeth," I responded, "I am pleased to meet you. Welcome to my home."

When she moved closer to Bastiaan I sensed that they were neither mates nor lovers. There was something between the two, but it was not romance.

"For you, My Lady," she offered her hand, upon which rested a lovely pendant on a fine chain.

"For me?" I was startled and surprised by the gesture, and when my fingers touched her hand I experienced the same sensations as I had when Bastiaan had held my hands. I felt 'pack'. They were siblings, I realized, and though they were both beautiful they looked nothing alike.

Elspeth's eyes flew open wide as our hands touched and she drew away as if scalded. She and I both sensed some energy that neither of us recognized or understood. I think we were both startled.

Laughing to dispel the tension, I took the pendant and held it gently, examining the details of the piece. It was a delicate metal sword, either white gold or platinum, perhaps an inch and half long, blade beveled, handle braided, and a sapphire decorated the hilt. It was exquisite.

"Thank you, Elspeth," I smiled, "it really is lovely. Thank you."

She stepped back without further comment, a slight blush coloring her cheeks. It always caught me off guard that some vampires were capable of blushing, though it was something I'd never been able lose. One would think such a reaction to emotional stimulus would change when one became, well, undead, but apparently this was not the case.

"So the meeting is over," I brightened, changing the subject, "and you are now a member of the Council of Five. Congratulations."

"Thank you, My Lady," Bastiaan responded, "and as the hour is growing late, I will beg your forgiveness for interrupting your evening and we shall take our leave. My Lord, I shall contact you at the earliest regarding the matter we discussed. Good night."

"Bastiaan," Amon nodded in response but made no move to shake the departing vampire's hand, "I shall await your call. Good night."

At that, the two vampires turned and made their way through the Great Hall and, presumably, back out the door through which they'd entered. Winter and Chimaera stood in the Great Hall on either side of the doors, though it was uncommon that they take such guarding positions when only two were being entertained.

"And what was that, my darling?" My mate turned to me, a quizzical look on his face. "Who, or what, is Zador?"

"Just a guru-looking guy who appeared in my meditation. He looked so much like Bastiaan, or Bastiaan looked so much like him, that it startled me. Must have been just a weird coincidence," I shrugged, making light of the matter, as I could see no other option.

"Interesting," Amon observed, "as it was my understanding that you do not believe in coincidence."

"Well," I admitted as I slipped my arms around his waist and laid my cheek on his chest, "that was a luxury I had in my old life. In your world, in our world now, there is so much more than black and white, so many shades of understanding, and so many impossible possibilities that I've decided to admit coincidence back into my vocabulary."

"There is more, precious?" He murmured, stroking his hand down my hair and along my spine. Handing him the necklace Elspeth had given me, I turned to offer my throat while lifting my hair out of the way. He slipped the chain around my neck, kissed beneath my ear, and fastened it as I placed the sword on my chest. A tingle stole through me as I released the tiny weapon and a spark of electric blue energy appeared in my vision before blinking out suddenly.

"They are pack," I announced, then turned to look up at him.

"How did you know that?" He looked back at me, surprise clearly etched on his face.

"That was another thing," I chuckled and extricated myself from his embrace. "You see, I seem to have acquired or developed a new ability. When Bastiaan took my hands I could sense 'pack'. I felt, heard, and smelled wolf. I got the same reaction when I touched Elspeth's hand. They are siblings?"

"They are," he affirmed. "And it is fascinating how your abilities are evolving. I love watching your powers develop. Have you told your mentor of this new power?"

"Not yet," I confessed, "as we've not really had time to get into such things, but I'm sure I will soon."

"I am going to see the remainder of the Council members out," he explained, "but I will return soon. I would like to take you somewhere if you would be so kind as to come with me."

"Where?" I couldn't help but ask, though I knew the way my love had made the comment that he'd not answer.

"It is a surprise, my dear," he wrapped me in his arms and kissed me deeply. "I shall return." Stepping back, he looked at the sword pendant curiously, and touched it gently with his finger. "Interesting," was his only comment, then he paused to kiss my forehead, an action which he knew irked me greatly. It always made me feel like a toddler being bussed by an elder and I didn't appreciate it. He chuckled and disappeared into the Great Hall as Winter and Chimaera entered. It disturbed me greatly that both he and Ulrich had been laughing as they departed and I was not in on the joke.

"So how went the meeting?" I asked the guards, as I plopped back down on the couch.

"As usual," Winter answered. "Though the ceremony was a bit tedious, if you ask me."

"I did like the treats," Chimaera added.

"Treats?" I asked with a creeping dread moving over me. The image of trays of artistically decorated, delicious cupcakes being part of any Council activity struck a "no" vibration in my mind.

"Human treats," Chimaera grinned, licking his lips and his index finger.

"Ewww…" I gasped, "You mean there were humans at this meeting and you guys fed on them like it was some Roman orgy?"

"I'm not aware of Roman orgies including blood feasts," Chimaera responded, "but if they did, then yes. It was just like some Roman orgy, without the sex."

"How did this happen?" I gaped, "I mean, where do these humans come from and where do they think they're going when they come here? Does this sort of thing happen all the time or is this an exception? What the heck?"

"It is okay, Cat," Winter grinned and sat beside me on the sofa, "Chimaera's just teasing you. Only the Council members fed and Thammuz provided the humans they fed upon. We have no idea where he gets them or what they think, but as he's Council head, and is well aware of the laws regarding our security, our secrecy, it's a given that their memories are wiped clean and there's no evidence of them having been fed upon."

271

"I don't care," I fumed. "It's still creepy! Does it happen at every Council meeting?"

"No, 'tite souer," he sighed, "it doesn't happen at every meeting. In fact, this is the first time it's happened in a very long time. It was on account of Dykstra's appointment."

"There was no Roman orgy feeding when I was appointed to the Council," Chimaera sniffed, then added, "but perhaps that was because my appointment was temporary."

"So, did anything else interesting happen?" I pried gently, "I mean, anything out of the ordinary?"

"No," Winter shook his head, "at least not that I'm aware of. Nice necklace, by the way." He nodded at the sword pendant. "It suits you. A gift from His Lordship?"

"No," I shook my head, "it was actually a gift from Elspeth, Bastiaan's sister. It's remarkable, isn't it?"

"It is," he agreed. "A fascinating weapon to add to your arsenal."

"Indeed," I nodded thoughtfully. "Well, I suppose I should get busy on my homework."

"My Lady Passion has homework?" Chimaera fairly crowed.

"Knock it off," I sneered. "This business was not my idea." I shifted forward and pulled the metal-looking ball from beneath the corner of the cushion. "I'm just going along with this for His Lordship, though why he thinks I need a mentor and such education is beyond me."

"Perhaps if you were properly educated the matter of why would not be beyond you," Winter teased and I smacked him on the bicep.

"That's it," I threw up my hands, "I'm done with the two of you. Tell His Lordship that I'll be in his office when he returns. I'll be working on my assignment at his desk and I'll await him there."

"My Lady," Winter stood and bowed, a wry grin on his lips.

Shaking my head, I rose, tossed the orb and handily caught it, and left the study. Siri rose silently and followed me across the Great Hall and up the wide stairs, her nails click, click, clicking on the marble.

Flipping on the lights as I entered Amon's office, I made my way to his desk, pulled his black leather office chair out and sat down. Siri followed me into the room and leapt on the couch, making herself comfortable on the smooth, cool, leather cushions. Turning on the desk lamp, I placed the orb beneath the light and opened the center drawer. Beneath a stack of papers I found a magnifying glass and held it above the ball as I closed the drawer. Though I could see the symbols on what looked to be the seams, I did not recognize them. If they were letters it was no alphabet I had ever seen before. On a whim, I grabbed a sheet of paper and a pencil and did my best to replicate the symbols, thinking to look them up online and in what archaic reference books I could find. Around and around I had to move the ball so as to copy the symbols as carefully and as exactly as possible. When I was done I was no closer to understanding anything than I'd been when I began. Frustration was building and I considered just tossing the ball as far and as hard as I could, but admitted silently that such a reaction was probably not wise.

"So let's see," I sighed aloud. "What does one do with a ball? One tosses a ball. One catches a ball. One rolls a ball. One plays fetch with one's dog and a ball." Looking over at Siri I tossed the ball in the air and caught it, whistling softly. The beast raised her head, ears alert, eyes bright, but made no further movement.

"Too good to play fetch, huh?" I asked her, holding the ball out on the palm of my hand. "What if we tried it this way?" Shoving my chair back, I rolled the orb across the hardwood floor and watched as it disappeared beneath the couch. Siri didn't even blink.

"Fine!" I huffed as I rose and got down on my hands and knees to scrabble for the ball in the darkness under the sofa. It rolled out, when the edge of my hand hit it, and came to rest beside my knee. Holding it before

Siri, I tried to get her interested in playing, but she just looked at me then laid her head back down on her paws. In defeat, I returned to the chair and put the ball on the corner of the desk. Studying the symbols I'd copied on the paper, I didn't notice when the beast rose from the couch and silently jumped to the floor. Nor did I notice when she snatched the ball from the desk, holding it gingerly in her mouth. It was only when she turned away from the desk that I realized what she was doing and that the ball was missing.

"Ah, so now we're going to play?" I grinned, excited at the prospect of getting some exercise with the dog out on the lawn. Siri didn't stop or look at me as she exited the office. I followed as she led me down the hallway, around the corner, down the stairs and across the Great Hall. She waited, tail-wagging, for me to open the French doors to the terrace, then disappeared into the garden.

"Okay, bring me the ball, Siri," I called, expecting some playful reaction. Instead she went directly to the edge of a flower bed, dropped the ball, and began digging. Suddenly I realized that she intended to bury my assignment and I went to get it away from her before she completed her task. As I approached she growled deep in her throat, but did not stop digging. When I got close enough to get the ball, she stopped and looked at me with something of a crazed look on her face.

"Okay, Siri," I spoke softly and in a calming voice, "I get that you don't want to play ball. I understand. And it's okay if you don't like the ball. I'm not especially fond of the thing either, but it is my homework. Ulrich gave it to me and I'm supposed to figure it out so…can I have it back?"

The black dog cocked her head and looked at me, then rocked back on her haunches and sat down. It was as if she was studying me and it made me uneasy.

"What's wrong, baby?" I cooed at her, concerned at her reaction.

She started to put one paw on the ball, then paused and nudged the orb to me with her nose. Apparently, though she couldn't make me understand what she knew, she understood me well and could respond accordingly.

"I'm sorry I'm just too thick to understand what you mean," I patted her head as I took the ball from her. "And I won't try to play ball with you again, at least not with this ball, okay?"

She licked my hand and panted, then sprinted away across the veranda, awaiting me at the doors again.

"Coming!" I called as I made it to my feet, brushing off the knees of my jeans. "I'll get the door and you can go get a drink." Laughing, I let her into the house and followed, inspecting the orb as I entered. There was no damage, no teeth marks, and no slobber spots. The orb was unchanged and unaffected.

Chapter 13

"My love," Amon greeted me as he entered the Great Hall from one of the back corridors. "Are you looking for me?"

"Um, no," I grinned at his tremendous ego. "I was out with Siri. But I am happy to see you."

He swept me into his arms, kissing the side of my neck and running his long hands up my back. Shivers rose along my spine at his touch and the desire to feel his teeth plunge deeply into my neck rose with enough force to make me shudder. On some level I resented that he could do this to me and on another level I was delirious at the sensations. I knew that I'd always been contradictory as a woman, I freely admitted if only to myself, and being witch and vampire had certainly not changed that for the better.

"Are you ready to accompany me, precious?" He murmured as he nuzzled beneath my earlobe. The feel of his tender lips on my neck drew my shoulders up and forced me to lean my head to one side.

"I don't know," I sighed, considering my options. "I don't know where we're going so I've no idea if I'm ready to go with you."

"Do you not trust me, my love?" My mate pulled back and looked at me with mock surprise on his face.

"Do you have to ask, my darling?" I feigned alarm, then broke into a grin. "Just let me tell Lily to keep an eye on Siri and grab a jacket and some shoes, then I'll be happy to accompany you."

"Your mentor is in the study," Amon offered, "perhaps you could have him keep your beast while we are away."

"Ah," I nodded, happy at the thought of talking to Ulrich even briefly, "good idea! I'll be right back!"

Leaning on the doorjamb of the study, I held the metal-looking ball thingy in the palm of my outstretched hand.

"Ulrich," I spoke to get his attention, as he was engrossed in the society section of the newspaper, "His Lordship and I are stepping out. Would you keep Siri company?"

"I'd be delighted," he smiled and folded the paper. He looked rested and refreshed, a vast improvement from his earlier appearance. "And what's that?"

"My assignment," I huffed. "You can have it back. I give up."

279

"Give up?" He patted Siri, who had trotted past me and entered the study to greet him, and raised one eyebrow at me. "You cannot simply give up! It is your assignment. You will complete it."

"I don't know what it is," I complained, "let alone what I'm supposed to do with it. How can I complete it if I can't even figure out how to start it?"

"Keep it, Cat," he said patiently, "and keep it with you. You will figure it out. You must have patience in the matter, but you will figure it out."

"If you insist," I sighed, tossing the orb gently. "But I can tell you that Siri doesn't like it. Her answer was to bury it in the garden." I expected he'd laugh at my comment, but he merely patted the dog again and looked at me. "All right then, we'll be going. 'Nite Ulrich!"

Stuffing the ball into the front pocket of my jeans, I ran past Amon, holding up my index finger to indicate he should wait for me. Racing up the stairs, I turned the corner and ran face-first into Winter's chest.

"Whoa there," he laughed and stepped back, pretending that I'd wounded him upon impact. "Are there demons chasing you?"

"In another time I'd know you were joking," I favored him with a wicked smile and smoothed an errant lock of hair away from my face, "but since around here that's an actual possibility… no, I'm just grabbing a jacket so Amon and I can go wherever it is he's taking me."

"I see," he grinned and actually looked relieved. "Are you in need of my assistance?"

"Getting a jacket?" I laughed at the thought, "I can't imagine I'd need your help."

"That was not what I meant, Cat," he looked at me soberly then tapped his left forearm with his right index finger.

"Oh," I startled that it had not occurred to me to put on my blades, "I'm sorry! I didn't even think of that. I don't know where we're going so…I don't know."

"If you need me," Winter bowed and started to walk away.

"No, wait," I paused, then added, "I think you may have something there, Winter. Please, come help me with my blades. We have to be fast because His Lordship is waiting downstairs."

"Then we'll be quick," he assured me as he followed me into the Sapphire room.

Yanking open the top drawer of the highboy, I dug under the neatly folded lingerie to find the blades in their holsters. I tossed them both to Winter as I made my way to the walk-in closet and pulled a long black duster off of its hanger. Tossing the jacket across the end of the bed, I offered my forearms to my beloved bodyguard and waited patiently, well, sort of patiently, as he strapped the holsters to me. Finishing as quickly as possible, he slipped a blade in first the left holster and then the right. As I made sure the weapons were stable and secure, Winter picked up my coat, turned it around and held it so I could slip my arms into the sleeves. He patted my back as I straightened the garment and turned to him. My body guard smiled at my bare feet.

"Boots!" I glanced down, "And gotta grab socks!"

Rushing back into the closet, I found my black boots, then moved to the dresser and got out a pair of soft socks. I considered trying to put them on hopping from one foot to the other, then decided it would be quicker to perch on the edge of the bed and get it done. Moving the length of the duster aside was a bit awkward, but I managed to get my footwear on, pulled the legs of my jeans over the shafts of the boots, and stood. I turned to Winter, posing.

"Perfect," he smiled. "You look great!"

"Thank you," I returned his smile and rose onto my tiptoes to give him a kiss on the cheek. "Good night, Winter."

"Good night, 'tite souer," he grinned. "Take care!"

When I reached the bottom of the stairs Amon was waiting patiently. He opened his arms and I stepped into his embrace.

"Okay," I announced, steeling myself for the unknown, "I'm ready to go…wherever!"

"You may close your eyes this time, precious," he looked down at me with an expression of kindness, "though the next time you should pay attention to the journey so you may return when you desire."

"We're going to be going to this place more than once?" I couldn't keep the surprise from my voice, "I mean, we'll want to go again? I'll want to go by myself?"

"We will," he nodded, "and yes, you will. You shall understand when we arrive."

"You're being very cryptic about all of this," I stepped back and looked at him closely, as if I could discover our destination by merely looking at him.

"Come, darling," he wrapped one arm around my shoulders and we walked out onto the veranda. "Let us go."

Tucking my face into the lapel of his jacket, I closed my eyes and held tightly to my mate as we rose into the night sky. I had grown accustomed to the sense of weightlessness and the disconcerting lack of anything solid beneath my feet, but it still made me slightly dizzy. Enjoying the solidity of Amon's back and chest, I relaxed and merely waited with my eyes closed. Time had no meaning when we were in flight, so I had no idea how far we flew or how fast, but I was relieved when

Amon's feet touched the ground and a moment later I joined him. I'd often had trouble getting my bearings upon landing and had, upon occasion, staggered, stumbled, even fallen flat on my backside, but this time I held on to my mate until I felt more settled.

"There," I smiled up at him as I stepped back, proud of myself for managing a decent touch down. "That wasn't so bad."

"Indeed, my love," he nodded and looked around.

"Where are we?" I turned and gaped at our surroundings. The view was breathtaking. Rolling hills were covered in rough dry grass, jagged slate boulders broke the ground here and there, and twisted, bowed trees clustered together at the base of a cliff. I noticed a trail running up the face of the stony mountain and followed it with my eyes until I saw the building rising from the top. It too was stone, many-columned, and looked like it might have been carved from the mountain itself.

"What is this place?" I murmured in awe, unable to take my eyes from the sight.

"This, my darling, is a library," my mate announced, "and it belongs to a friend of mine. Access has graciously been offered to you."

"You got me access to a library?" Obviously I was missing something, "Why? Can't I just buy books off the internet or visit the book stores in New Orleans?"

"Catherine," he held my hands to his chest, kissing first one and then the other, "the texts in this library are special, ancient, one-of-a-kind, and some are believed by most to have been destroyed. These books are for your education, for your training."

"Oh, my training," the light bulb over my head finally clicked on. "I wish you'd have told me we were coming here. I have some text I would have brought to look up."

"Come, Precious," he took my hand and began to lead me up the trail. "I will introduce you to the librarian and we shall go from there."

"Fine," I tried not to pout as I considered the page of symbols I'd left on Amon's desk and wished fervently I had it in my hot little hands. The metal-like orb moved uneasily in my pocket and I realized that the answer to the riddle might be just ahead. Grinning in relief, I picked up the pace as Amon drew me ever on toward the top of the mount. The trail was not difficult to climb, but it did cut back and forth on itself as it followed the natural features of the mountain.

"Why did we not just land up there near the building?" I asked as we trekked ever upward.

"The librarian does not like surprises," he responded succinctly.

"So," I wondered aloud, "by landing down there and making our way up this trail, we give the librarian a 'heads-up' that we're coming? Is the library the only thing atop this mountain?"

"It is the only structure atop this mountain," my beloved nodded, "and this is the reason the library was placed here. It stands alone, protected, and safe."

"Fascinating," I quipped as we followed yet another cutback and continued the climb. The air was crisp and I was glad I'd grabbed a coat. Though no longer affected by weather conditions as I'd been when I was human, I still preferred the warmth. There was no sun, nor was there moon or stars, so I could not even guess the time of day. The light was soft, but it didn't 'feel' like twilight or even predawn. I made a mental note to ask Amon about that at some point, though at the moment I could only concentrate on reaching the library.

As we neared the top of the mount, Amon turned and stepped into a tall, thin, crevasse where the trail became carved stone steps. The way was narrow, the walls of stone on either side were rough and I touched them as we moved as if to keep them from leaning in and crushing me. Finally, my mate stopped and moved his hand along the stone. I heard a 'click' and part of the wall slid away.

"Cool!" I gasped, "It's like in a James Bond movie!"

"I might have known that is where your mind would go, my love," Amon smiled and stepped aside. "Please, after you."

Moving past him, I made my way slowly, marveling at my surroundings. A short stone stair led into a vast, well-lit room. A rotunda of windows in the tall ceiling added an elaborately decorative circle of light on the polished stone floor. Ranks of shelves the height of the walls marched away into the distance. Massive wooden tables decorated the center hall of the room, each sporting a lamp at either end.

"Now, THIS is a library," I gaped, barely able to take it all in.

"Come," Amon took my elbow and propelled me forward, "I shall introduce you to the librarian."

We turned to the right, entering a wide, short room occupied by a large desk, upon which rested a beautiful Roman-themed chess set, and a man apparently intensely focused on an open tome before him. At first glance, I thought he was elderly, as his hair was silver and wispy, but when he looked up I realized that he was actually quite young. He smiled at Amon and immediately leapt to his feet.

"Amon, my good friend," he rushed to my mate and began pumping his hand excitedly, "it is always good to see you." With hooded brown robe tied at the waist and smudged fingers, he looked like a cleric just taking a break from transcribing some ancient religious text.

"Max," my mate replied with uncharacteristic warmth, "it is good to see you as well. This is my mate, My Lady Passion, though she prefers to be called Cat."

"I am at your service," Max took my hands in his and bowed gallantly. "Forgive my stained fingers, the scrolls I've been investigating are old, dusty, and sometimes the ink smudges. I am honored to have you here. My library is your library."

"Thank you, Max," I nodded, feeling a bit overwhelmed at the gushing sentiment. "This is an amazing place. But, you don't look like a librarian."

"I don't look like a Max either," he looked at me with a wry or bitter smile, I couldn't tell which. "My name is Maximus, an irony observed by most, as my slight build and stature would lead one to call me anything but Maximus."

"Are you…"I started to ask if he was vampire or otherkin, but I wasn't sure exactly how to proceed, given his comments, so I faltered.

"I am, My Lady," he offered with a bit more merriment in his voice, "of the Tuatha De Danann, which is yet another irony. We are a warrior race, and here I am studying, cataloguing, and caretaking books."

"Irony or not," I grinned at his humor, "I am glad you're here. I'm in need of your texts."

"This is what His Lordship told me," Max put his palms together in a tidy and thoughtful move. "With what may I help you?"

"I need some works on archaic symbols or alphabets," I answered, my mind going back to the paper on Amon's desk. "And if you have anything on witchcraft, I could probably use information there too."

"Any particular type of witchcraft?" His bright blue eyes shone with curiosity.

"In general," I laughed. "Just point me in the right direction and I'll see what strikes my fancy."

"Very well," Max nodded, and in a flourish of brown robes he turned, "follow me, please. I'll show you where you need to look and your mate and I will have a game of chess while you are busy."

"Wonderful," I answered, surprised that Amon played chess and admitting to myself that I still had much to learn about him.

Down long corridors created by towering shelves full of books, papers, scrolls, and other odd looking objects, Max led me, murmuring to himself as if ticking off the topics through which we strolled. At last we came to an antechamber which held not only shelves of books, but two comfortable looking leather wingback chairs with a low table between them. Max made a gesture with his right hand and the lights in the room brightened.

"This is where you'll find the reference material I have on ancient symbols and alphabets," he pointed to a large section on the right wall. "The texts I have on witchcraft are just through those doors," he indicated two tall, ornate doors standing ajar. "Please help yourself. If you have any questions or need anything, just call my name. I can hear everything in this place."

"Thank you," I turned to peruse the first shelf of books and when I did the ball in my pocket moved slightly as if to remind me of its presence. "Oh, Max," I added quickly as he turned to leave, "maybe you could tell me what this is?"

Pulling the metallic ball thingy from my front pocket, I held it out to the young man, noticing for the first time that, as he had tucked his hair behind his left ear, the slightly pointed tip of his ear was visible. It was one of the few signs I knew that would indicate he was Fae.

"A LeqonOrb," he brightened as he took the ball into his hands.

"A what?"

"A LeqonOrb," repeated himself, pausing to spell the term out for me.

"Again, what's a LeqonOrb?" I sighed, trying to rein in my impatience, feeling so close to the answer yet miles away.

"The term is French," he explained, "and it means 'lesson orb' or 'lesson ball'."

"Cool, so," I paused to consider the information, "what does that mean specifically?"

"I can tell you what the item is, My Lady," he laughed, his voice light and musical, "but I cannot tell you what the lesson is. That you will have to determine for yourself."

"Dang," I pouted, "I was afraid you'd say something like that."

"But I can tell you that if this is why you are researching ancient symbols and alphabets," Max brightened, "you're only partly on the right track. These markings are not letters, they are alchemical symbols."

"So," daring to hope, I raised one eyebrow, "you know what the symbols are?"

"Only in general," he nodded, "but I do have a text which will help you identify them. From that you may be able to discern what the lesson of the ball is."

"Great!" I clapped my hands gently, not wanting to disturb the quietude of the library, "So I'll just pick out a book or two on witchcraft and take the text you mention, then I'm good to go!"

"You need not take anything, My Lady," Max offered.

"But, I thought you said I could have access to any book here?" His comment caught me off-guard. "And please, call me Cat."

"Chose whatever texts you wish to read and study," he paused then added, "Cat. But you need not take them. Just learn their names and whenever you wish you may call and they'll come to you. This library is unique in many ways, this is one of those ways."

"Their names?" I hesitated at the term, "You mean their titles?"

"No, Cat," he almost grimaced as he forced himself to use the more familiar name, "I mean their names. They each have a title, of course, but they each have a name as well. Once you know their names, you may summon them anytime."

"Well," I imagined a huge, leather-bound book named Joe, or a small leaf-bound text named Amelia, "that's fascinating! I trust you'll show me how or where to learn their names?"

"I shall indeed, Cat," he grinned and his countenance brightened. For a moment he truly looked like a fairy, at least what I imagined a warrior fairy would look like. "Now if you'll excuse me, I have a game of chess awaiting."

"Enjoy!" I called out to Max's disappearing form before wandering through the tall doors into the stacks of witchcraft books.

Chapter 14

Amon and I arrived back at the mansion just as the sun was beginning to rise. Darkness still held onto the sky, but it was weakening as the morning approached. Max and Amon had played chess while I entertained myself with books on all manner of witchcraft. Finally settling on two reference pieces, one on Traditional Witchcraft and one on Seidr, a type of Norse witchcraft, I took the books to Max and he literally introduced me to them as well as to the book on Alchemy that he'd recommended. He showed me where their names were magically woven into their spines and taught me how to pronounce them, as they were not the traditional names that I'd imagined them to be. And he made sure I could remember by writing the information down. I'd tucked the parchment, upon which I'd made phonetic note of the names, into the pocket of my jeans, right next to the LeqonOrb, and thanked the librarian for his time and generosity. Amon had shaken his hand and leaned down to whisper something into the librarian's ear, then they both laughed. My mate and I departed the library, made our way back down the side of the mountain, and took to the sky. When I asked why we didn't just take off from the top of the mount Amon had answered succinctly that I needed to learn the path and that was the end of that matter.

As I walked past the study where candles burned low behind their glass chimneys, I paused to appreciate the sight that greeted me. My mentor, Ulrich, lay snoring softly on the leather sofa, Siri stretched out alongside him with her head resting on his leg. The dog lifted her head and looked at me as if in question and before I realized what I was doing I mouthed '*No, you stay put. Sleep. You're fine!*' She lay her head back down and watched silently as I moved away. It was something of a relief to realize that she'd not insist on being with me every moment I was around the mansion.

As Amon and I made our way into his room, he paused in the hallway and drew me into an embrace.

"So your beast will not be joining us?" He grinned lasciviously and kissed me deeply.

"Apparently not," I murmured softly, enjoying the sensation of his lips.

"So I have you all to myself," he sighed.

"You do!" I flashed him a wicked smile before putting my lips on his throat, running my tongue up its length and nibbling his earlobe gently. He slid my coat down my arms and tossed it to the floor. As he drew his hands down my arms his fingers touched the blades in their holsters.

"You were armed?"

"I was!" I shrugged, "Since you didn't tell me where we were going I had no idea how to dress or accessorize myself, whether to go armed or not, so I erred on the side of safety. Apparently the Tuatha De Danann are not adversely affected by silver?"

"The Fae have issues with iron," he smiled as he unbuckled the forearm holsters, "not silver. Though since the blades were covered by your coat it likely would have been of no consequence had the blades been steel." He folded the leather straps around the blades and placed them on the dresser, then returned to rub my naked arms with his long, elegant fingers. His eyes burned with passion and I yanked my shirt over my head and wiggled out of my jeans with unbridled anticipation. Stretching out across the bed, I watched my mate slowly remove his clothing. He knew the effect he had on me and he was milking it for all it was worth.

Later, after luxuriating in making love slowly and intensely, we lay spent and comfortable on the massive bed under the gaze of Dave the dragon, Amon's ancestral crest carved headboard. Running my fingers up and down his smooth, perfectly muscled torso, I replayed the events of the day in my mind and as I did so several issues arose.

"Amon, my love," I cleared my throat and rose to rest my weight on one elbow.

"Yes, Little One," he responded, eyes closed, long lashes lying delicately on his high cheekbones.

"Tell me about Max," I suggested.

"What would you like to know?" He patted my hand and opened his eyes.

"You are obviously fond of him," I explained, "and he's fond of you, yet you've never mentioned him to me. In all the time I've known you the librarian has not once come up in conversation."

"The subject of Max has never come up because the need for a librarian, such as he, has never arisen," Amon replied. "I have met and known many people and many creatures in my time and to discuss them all with you would be impossible, as well as a waste of time. Would I ask you to tell me about everyone and every creature you have encountered in your life?"

"Of course not," I laughed. "But then again, you've been watching me practically since the day I was born. I've no need to do so."

"Point taken, my love," he nodded with a wry grin. "Very well, I will tell you about Max."

"Cool," I sat up further and rested my back against a stack of pillows.

"When my sire made me what I am…" he began.

"Vampire," I interjected.

"Yes," he paused and gave me a slight look of reproach. I adopted a penitent expression. "When I became what I am, after the rage passed and the blood lust exhausted itself, I felt the need to know what I had been made."

"Vampire," I nodded sagely.

"Yes," he sighed, "so I searched the various libraries and learning institutions of the world at that time. My reading ability was not extensive then, but I was able to make do and eventually I happened upon the Laurentian Library in Florence, Italy. At the time Maximus was curator and librarian there and we struck up a friendship. My knowledge of the game of Chess was sufficient to give him a challenge, and he repaid my kindness by helping me improve my reading skills."

"So, did you know what he was back then?" I interrupted him, "I mean, did you know what Tuatha De Danann were then and that he was one?"

"Not when I first met him," he shook his head, "no. But over time that did come up and he was kind enough to educate me on the history of his kind and touched lightly, at least, on what powers some of them possess."

"So how long did you hang out with Max?"

"I frequented the library in Florence over the course of three years," he answered. "Then Max was arrested and imprisoned and I facilitated his release."

"Arrested?" I gasped. "Max was arrested and imprisoned? For what?"

"Maximus had been taking texts from the library and making them his own. He is a Fae who possesses the power to travel through time and he had used his power to go to Alexandria before the great fire and rescue many important texts and scrolls. He had accumulated quite a collection."

"Wow!" I couldn't help but utter my surprise and delight.

"When the authorities discovered that he had been purloining books from the Laurentian Library he was arrested and put into prison, though the crime was not considered very severe so his sentence was not a long one. When I learned of his predicament I greased the palms of a few dignitaries and managed to get him released into my custody, with the proviso that I escort him out of the country."

"He had to leave Italy?" I was startled, "That's kind of harsh, isn't it?"

"Perhaps," my mate nodded thoughtfully, "but it seemed a small thing at the time. Maximus did not seem to mind when he realized that he would be able to take what books he had hidden with him where ever he was forced to go. I knew some people in somewhat powerful positions, what you would now call 'contacts', and eventually I managed to barter and trade until I could get him and his collection into the library he now inhabits."

"And it's a little more than just a plain old library, right?" I pried gently.

"It is," he nodded succinctly. "And that is the story of Max."

"So he actually has ancient books and scrolls there that he's stolen from the course of time, so to speak?"

"He does," Amon smiled at my speech. "And it is likely that he will continue to steal and protect those records he deems too important to be lost to time or destruction."

"That's amazing!" I replied then added, "Wait, so did you find what you were looking for regarding 'that which you became'?

"Vampire?" He retorted.

"Yes," I huffed, "did you find out what you wanted to know about being vampire?"

"I did to some degree," he nodded, "yes. But what has been written throughout the ages is scant and was often destroyed as heresy or the insane ramblings of those possessed of demons. Some information was obscured by the use of arcane language and cryptic symbolism. But Maximus did finally turn up a scroll of the lineages of several vampire clans and members. That, I discovered, was most helpful in putting everything into perspective."

"Is that where you learned of Arathia?" I wondered aloud, "I mean, is that where you first encountered her name?"

"It is, as a matter of fact," he admitted. "And of course, that too was part of the prophecy that led me from where I was to where I am now, and where you are too. And now, my love, you should sleep. The day has begun."

"Yeah, yeah," I grumbled, "I know. I still don't like it that now I'm nocturnal and you're, well, you're not! It's not fair that we've changed places."

"Fair or not," he kissed my forehead, "you need your rest."

"Yes, I do have homework to do when I get up," I sighed, "but at least now I have some idea of how to do it, thanks to you and Max and his wonderful library."

"I am delighted that you are happy," Amon drew me down next to him and wrapped his arms around me.

"Wait," I struggled in his grasp, "there's one more thing. My lesson with Ulrich today, you know about that, right?"

"I do," he answered succinctly.

"So, how did I do?" I looked at him expectantly, "Did you see me? Could you tell Ulrich and I were there?"

"You did well, as far as I could tell," he nodded. "I did not see you, nor did I see Ulrich, but I could sense your presence the moment you arrived. And, I felt you very abruptly leave."

"Yes, well," I pulled the covers up and tucked them under my arms, "you can thank Zador for that. It was not my intention to get zapped back into my body."

"Yes, this Zador concerns me," Amon admitted. "Though I do not know the name, there is something there that strikes a familiar chord with me."

"Well, the Zador that appeared to me looked like Mister Zen guy," I chuckled, "but he looked so much like Bastiaan, too. It was startling."

"Sleep, my love," he insisted. "Be quiet and rest. The night and I will await you when you awaken."

Though I wanted to protest that I was not tired, nor sleepy, I was actually exhausted. The moment I closed my eyes I fell asleep. I don't know at what point the dreams started, but once they began they held me hostage.

Faces, some familiar, some not, flashed by me as if I was rushing through a crowd. I saw Bastiaan and Elspeth, I saw Thammuz, I saw Thea, and then the creepy old lady who had approached me in the church parking lot. A giant spider crouched in a corner then began to spin a gigantic web that seemed to reach everywhere. I actually felt the tickling sensation as a tendril of web encircled my wrist and I fought to free myself as the web began to pulse and sing. A masculine voice came out of nowhere, saying *"Relax, Catherine, don't fight. Just watch. Relax, don't fight!"* And I glanced down to find myself holding a tremendous sword in my hands. As I was considering how the sword might cut through the silken web that had me, the weapon shrunk and I found myself holding 'Wicked Little Thing' between my hands. Siri ran up to me and knocked me down, then the creepy lady appeared again pointing one bony finger at me as if accusing me of a crime. I scrambled to my feet only to find that I now held the little sword pendant, the chain dangling off the edge of my right hand. Then I was in the deep woods, the scent of mold and decaying leaves heavy in my nostrils. Before me gathered a group of small, stout, dark-skinned men wearing coarse cloth garments and sporting a variety of wicked dangerous looking weapons. As if it was the only logical thing to do, I offered the little pendant to them and the one nearest me accepted it with a thick-fingered, heavily calloused hand. The leader, if indeed that's what he was, returned to the group and they gathered in a circle, backs to me, apparently discussing something. At length the circle opened and all but the leader simply disappeared. *'You're gnomes!'* I blurted out with irrestrainable delight. *'Aye, Madam, 'tis gnomes we are, and we thank ye for retarnin' the wee wheepon, as it was stolen away froom us lang agoo. We ne'er tought ta sae it agin, 'tis true,'* the gnome replied in such a heavy accent it was amazing that I could understand him at all. *'You're most welcome. I'm happy to return it to you,'* I smiled, feeling a twinge of regret that I'd be without the lovely necklace. *'We'd be een ta way oof tankin' ye, Madam, by givin' eet back ta ye. Please, keep eet wit ourr blissins,'* he bowed deeply and stretched up on his tiptoes to place the necklace across my palm before disappearing. I clutched the necklace tightly in my hand and suddenly I found there was a heavy wooden beam across my shoulders. Nearly buckling beneath the weight, I managed to step out from under it and let it thud to the ground behind me. Max appeared tossing the LeqonOrb nonchalantly in his hands. He smiled at me then threw the orb into the air where it disappeared. Zador floated into view wearing his saffron robes and a leering smile. *"You summoned me, you must allow me to help you,"* he chanted, and I could feel myself shaking my head, vehemently denying his assertion. Oola lay on the wet highway in a heap of blood and feathers. A state trooper's vehicle drove by, not bothering to stop and help as the owl lay dying.

"Catherine!" Amon shook me by the shoulders, "Beloved, wake up!"

As I struggled from my dreams, I felt the sword pendant in my hand. I was sure I clutched the delicate necklace tightly, but when I was finally able to open my eyes I found my hand was empty, save the discolored mark on my palm where I'd stabbed the athame through my hand. I blinked in confusion as I looked from my hand to my mate's eyes.

"You were having a bad dream?" He looked deep into my eyes, obviously concerned.

"I was having..." I shook my head in hopes of clearing my mind, "helsa! It definitely qualified as a bad dream, if indeed it was a dream. I'm glad to be awake though, I'll tell you that!"

"Would you like to tell me about your dream, Pet?"

"No," I shook my head again, "absolutely not. This is something I need to chew on by myself."

"Chew on?" Amon looked at me curiously.

"Consider," I explained. "Contemplate, analyze, that sort of thing."

"Ah," he nodded, "I see."

"Or, I could just chalk it up to brain de-fragging and never think about it again," I laughed. A sudden scratching at the door brought me up short and I looked at my beloved.

"Your beast awaits you, it appears," he offered as he rose from the bed. I realized he must have been awake for some time as he was dressed and his hair was neatly pulled back from his brow, secured on the back of his head with a leather thong.

"Seems so," I shrugged and exited the bed, scrabbling for my clothes which were still strewn about the floor. Realizing the dog would be shredding the wood finish off the bedroom door, I gave up my search for attire and grabbed a robe from the closet. When I opened the door, Siri gave a 'woof' and jumped up and down in greeting. In her excitement she jumped on me, front paws landing very near my shoulders.

"Holy crow, dog," I gasped, "I knew you were big. I didn't realize you were HUGE!"

The black German shepherd licked my chin in her exuberance, then moved back and favored me with a loud, deep, and very odiferous belch.

"Oh, my heavens!" I waved my hand between my face and hers, "What has Lily been feeding you? Was that Mexican?"

Siri just grinned, wagged her tail furiously, and dropped to all fours. The look on her face was one of clear expectation. I couldn't help but laugh.

"Fine," I tied the belt of my robe, "let's go. I'll take you out and grab some coffee."

"I shall be leaving for a meeting, my love," my mate moved up behind me and wrapped his arms around my waist. "So, I shall leave you to your beast and your studies."

"See you later, sweetie," I turned in his embrace and kissed him chastely on the cheek.

He just smiled, stepped back, and bowed chivalrously.

Following Siri down the hallway, around the corner, and down the stone steps, it was all I could do to keep up with her. Though I expected her to go to the French doors, she instead turned to the right and bolted down the short kitchen hallway to her water dish. I heard her drinking loudly as Lily stepped into the Great Hall.

"Before you say a word," she announced, clearly unhappy, "don't you be blamin' me for that dog and her digestion. That Viking friend of yours invaded my kitchen earlier and insisted on making what he called a breakfast burrito. Whatever kind of meat he used, it was plenty spicy and plenty strong, and as you know everyone here eats spicy food. Anyway, he's the one that shared his burrito with your dog, so he gets the blame for whatever happens." She handed me a mug of hot coffee. "I'm used to sharin' my kitchen with Bishop, not sure I like sharin' it with another one."

"That explains it," I chuckled and took a sip of the steaming brew. "She burped at me and I swear she was bragging."

"You gonna want some food in the study, Miss Cat?" the maid looked at me.

"Nope," I responded, "I'm going to take Siri out, then I'm going to Amon's office to do some work."

"That Viking done had your dog out a couple of times," Lily offered. "He's in the study either readin' or sleepin', I'm not sure which."

"All right then," I nodded, "I'll just poke my head in and have a word with him, then go on to work. Thanks for the coffee, Lily."

"Welcome, Miss Cat," she smiled and wiped her hands on her apron before disappearing into the darkness of the kitchen hallway.

Leaning into the study, I found Ulrich awake and deep in studying what appeared to be a large and intricately illustrated leather bound book. Apparently he'd brought the book with him as I'd never seen it here in the mansion before. He glanced up when I tapped my fingers on the doorjamb.

"Ulrich," I nodded, "I trust you're well?"

"Good day, Cat," he responded, closing the book with his index finger between the pages so he'd not lose his place. "Fancy a lesson today or do you wish to work on your homework assignment?"

"Homework, please," I smiled. "And by the way, though I'm grateful to you for spending time with Siri, I'd appreciate it if you'd NOT share your breakfast with her."

"Share?" He guffawed, "That's rich! I was cooking, stacked my chorizo onto a platter on the counter, and when I turned my back the beast helped herself! When I turned back around I was shy two sausages and she was smacking her lips."

"That explains it," I nodded. "It seemed she was boasting when she burped in my face. Now I know why she was so proud of herself."

"She's one to watch, alright!" He grinned, shook his head slightly and opened his book again. "I'll see you later then, Cat."

"You will," I agreed. "I'm off to dress then to tackle my assignment. Later, Ulrich!"

As my mentor returned to his studies, I sipped my coffee and made my way up the stairs. Behind me I heard Siri's nails click across the Great Hall. When I paused to look back, I saw her disappear into the study and heard my mentor greet her warmly. It was cool that the two of them got along, I mused silently, so they could entertain one another and give me the free time I needed to handle my studies as well as my other obligations.

Slipping into Amon's room, I picked up the clothes I'd tossed on the floor the previous morning, as well as my long black duster, and headed back to the Sapphire room. Hanging up the coat, I shoved my hand into the pocket of my jeans and withdrew the metal-looking orb, turning it over and over in my hand. Apparently having been stuffed in my pocket had no ill effects on the thing and I tossed it lightly onto the bed where it landed near the pillows. After pulling the folded notes I'd made at the library from my pocket, I tossed my worn clothes into the hamper then pulled a fresh pair of jeans from the closet before extracting my black Led Zeppelin t-shirt from a drawer in the dresser. Though I had no plans to go outside, I grabbed a pair of socks and short boots just in case. Recent experience had taught me that it might be prudent to take footgear with me even if I did prefer to be barefoot. I took off my robe and dressed before running a comb through my mane, putting green contact lenses over the white irises of my eyes, and grabbing my tiny black sunglasses. Pausing to glance around the room, I checked to see if I'd forgotten anything then spied the orb resting against the pillows.

"You're comin' with me, sweetheart," I cooed to the ball before tossing it gently into the air. "I'm going to get to the heart of your puzzle!" Tucking the folded notes into my pocket, I stepped into the hallway, socks and orb in one hand, boots in the other.

Chapter 15

Once settled in Amon's office, orb resting on the leather desk blotter, I hit the button on the intercom and asked Lily to bring me a fresh cup of coffee at her convenience, assuring her that there was no hurry. Carefully, I unfolded the paper on which I'd written the texts' names and smoothed it out beside the paper where I'd copied the orb symbols. Closing my eyes, I took a few cleansing breaths then opened my eyes to concentrate on calling the book I needed. I held the page up and refreshed my memory on the phonetic pronunciation of the text of alchemical symbols.

"Arb dgleet ithn zle uthka," is what it sounded like, but it was as close to what Max had taught me as I could recall. Nothing happened. Peering around the office, I inspected every horizontal surface expecting the book to be there, but there was nothing.

"Max," I called in frustration, "this isn't working!"

"Try again, My Lady," came the librarian's voice from nowhere.

"Fine," I grumbled and picked the paper up once more. "Aarrrb dgleet ithn zleeee oothka," I drew out the vowels and rolled the 'r' as dramatically as I could. Suddenly the book twinkled into the room, landing on the corner of the desk.

"Cool!" I gasped at the leather bound tome, "You didn't materialize, you twinkled into the room! How neat is that?" I was so delighted at the text's entrance that I considered calling the other books on the list, but Max had been quite clear about calling the book I needed only when I needed it, so I refrained. Instead, I moved the book to the center of the desk blotter and placed the page with the symbols beside it. I just concentrated on the first symbol and ran my finger up and down the list of alchemical symbols on each page of the book until I found a match. Systematically I went from the beginning to the end of the script on the orb and when I was done I sat back and read what I'd written.

'*Touch me not, tarry not, I will escape, I will consume,*' and there was a symbol I recognized from my astrology studies. It was the symbol for Mercury, a cross with a circle atop the center bar and stylized horns atop the circle.

"Mercury," I murmured, then it felt like a gong resonated in my head. "Quicksilver! This thing is filled with quicksilver? My assignment is poisonous?" Glaring at the orb, I shoved the office chair back from the desk. "No wonder Siri wanted to bury the darn thing!" Standing and pacing, I considered aloud what this might mean.

"Okay, this orb is full of mercury," I reasoned, "which means that, eventually, whatever material the thing is made from will break down and the quicksilver will be free, free to poison anyone or anything it comes into contact with. This is witchcraft? How is this witchcraft?"

Carefully I placed the orb on a clean sheet of paper and fashioned something of a cradle for it by folding the corners together. Shuddering at the thought that I'd had it stuffed into my pocket and had been tossing it around, I no longer had any desire whatsoever to touch the thing.

"You are going back to Ulrich," I snarled at the orb, "and he can deal with you!"

Lifting the cradle of paper gently, I placed it on my left palm and headed for the door, pausing only to turn off the light.

"Oh," I turned back and called to the book, "thank you. You may return to Max."

Moving quickly down the hall, I held the corners of paper cradle together in my right hand and lifted the weight of the orb from my left hand. So busy concentrating on the poisonous orb was I that I nearly ran into Lily as she came up the stairs and reached the landing just as I did. She managed to avoid me, stepping aside holding a tray laden with pastries and a fresh mug of coffee.

"Miss Cat," she gasped, "I don't know what that is you've got, but you're holdin' it like it's a snake!"

"Yes, well," I smiled at the image, "it's as close to a snake as I care to get! I'm just getting rid of it."

"You want me to put your coffee in Mister Sin's office," she cocked her head, "or are you comin' back?"

"Oh yes," I nodded as I started down the wide stone stairs, "I'm coming back. Just put the tray on His Lordship's desk and I'll be there. Oh wait, Lily, is Ulrich in the study?"

"No ma'am," she turned and smiled down at me, "he's in the pool."

"The pool?" I tried to imagine my mentor swimming and simply couldn't do it, "Really? The pool?"

"Yes, ma'am," she chuckled, "and you really should see it."

Intrigued by Lily's comments, I turned to the right at the bottom of the stairs and made my way to the lower level of the house, down the halls and to the natatorium. Carefully I opened the door while balancing the orb and stepped into the chlorine scented room. Distant splashing drew my attention and I saw Ulrich standing in the pool, water up to his shoulders, slapping the water surface. Siri stood at the edge of the pool, her attention fully on the Witch Master. He said something which I could not clearly hear and suddenly the dog leapt into the water and splashed happily to him.

"Oh my heavens!" I gasped at the sight, "I had no idea Siri would swim, or that she'd enjoy it."

"Many German shepherds like to swim," my mentor turned to me as he watched the dog swim to the shallow end of the pool and climb out onto the concrete deck. She stood stiff-legged and shook herself from head to tail, the spray of water flying from her fur in a spiraling sheet.

"Here," I held up the folded paper cradle, "I'm done with my assignment. You can have it back now."

"You're done with it?" He wiped his hands up his face and shook the water off of them, blinking to clear his eyes. "What do you mean you're done with it?"

"I know what it is," I announced, "and I don't want it. It's quicksilver inside and it's poisonous."

"Indeed it is," he nodded, smoothing his wet hair back from his face. "And what is it you wish me to do with it?"

"You made it," I held the orb out, "so I'm giving it back to you. I can't understand how this has anything to do with witchcraft. How is this witchcraft? Is this a spell?"

"Ah, you've gotten to one aspect of the assignment," he smiled broadly, "and that is determining what is witchcraft and what is not. Knowledge of chemistry and alchemical workings would have once been considered the work of the devil. Those studying and practicing would have been arrested, imprisoned, or even put to death."

"So, now I'm confused," I sighed. "Is this witchcraft or is it not?"

"Indeed, that is a question," he nodded and began moving to the pool's edge. As he climbed up the metal ladder and stepped across the concrete to his towel, I noticed that though he was a big man, he was not fat. His body was massive but firm and well-muscled. He squeezed the water from his hair and his beard, then grabbed his towel and dried his face and arms. Tucking the towel around his waist he walked toward me with a questioning look on his face.

"So why are you carrying the orb in paper?" He added, "Surely you know that paper would be of no protection against the quicksilver were the orb to open."

"I know," I moved uneasily from one foot to the other, vehemently wishing he'd just take the thing from me. "I just really didn't want to touch it once I found out what's in it."

"But you've been handling it for some time," he reasoned, "and nothing happened. Why would you be fearful now?"

"I'm not fearful," I exclaimed. "I'm cautious!"

"Part of the assignment, My Lady Cat," he bowed graciously, "is to determine how to deal with such a deadly object once it's been created. You may one day face such a situation of your own making."

"So, what am I supposed to do with it?" I probably sounded like I was whining, but at that point I didn't really care.

"Do what you will, Cat," my mentor responded. "But you might consider the thing's purpose when determining how to deal with it."

"But, it's a LeqonOrb," I offered. "Its purpose is to teach me, whatever it is to teach me, like how to investigate and discover its nature?"

"Yes," he smiled encouragingly, "that is part of it. But such an item is also a weapon. It is used to destroy one's enemy."

"So," I sighed, "what if one has no enemies? What do I do with it then?" Turning, I started toward the doors then paused and looked back.

"Do you truly have no enemies?" Ulrich gaped at me, "Or do you just wish to believe it so?"

"You tell me," I quipped, more than a little concerned.

"Think on it, My Lady," he responded cryptically.

"I trust you'll dry the pooch?" Changing the subject, I nodded at the beast who stood wet, panting, and happily wagging her tail at the pool's edge.

"Consider it done, Cat," he bowed and snapped his fingers. Siri trotted to his side and sat beside his left leg, looking at him adoringly.

As I neared the hallway to the kitchen an idea popped into my head and I made my way through the swinging galley doors to find the maid up to her elbows in soapy water, washing the dishes. Recessed lighting enhanced the warm glow of the cherry wood cabinets and glanced off the black stone countertops. The copper range hood gleamed above the center island cooktop where a copper kettle sat above the flames of a stove burner. Lily's kitchen was always spotless.

"Lily, do you have an empty jar with a lid somewhere around here?" I asked as I peered around the immaculate room. There wasn't a jar, a bottle, or anything else on the counter to indicate the room was for culinary use. Even the small appliances were kept discreetly hidden in cupboards or the pantry.

"How big a jar you need?" she responded.

"Um, oh, not huge," I considered aloud. "Maybe a quart jar?"

"I have a pickle jar," she nodded. "Just washed it out and put it in the pantry yesterday. It'd be about the right size, I think." She pulled her hands from the sink and wiped the soapsuds from them with a white cotton towel. "Hold on, Miss Cat, I'll get it for you."

When she returned from the pantry, she placed the empty pickle jar on the counter before removing the lid and sniffing the container.

"Clean and odor free," she smiled brightly. "Whatcha want a jar for?"

"This," I held the paper up then lowered it to the counter and removed the orb. "I'm putting this into the jar."

"What is it?" she looked puzzled.

"Heaven only knows," I laughed, "but I'm taking no chances with it. I figure it will be safe under glass." There was no way I could explain the LeqonOrb to her, and having known her as long as I had, I was fairly sure she really didn't want to know anyway.

"Well, hope that works for you," she smiled again and returned to her dishwashing. "You best get back to your work, your coffee will be getting' cold, ma chère."

"Yes ma'am," I smiled as I screwed the lid onto the pickle jar, safely containing the quicksilver orb. "Coffee is just what the doctor ordered." Holding the jar at arm's length I made my way from the kitchen, across the Great Hall and back up the stairs.

The coffee Lily had brought me was barely warm when I got back to the office, but the pastries looked good and I was so relieved to have the LeqonOrb hermetically sealed that I really didn't mind. Placing the jar on the desk, I sat in the leather chair and sipped the brew as I munched on a cream cheese Danish.

Ulrich's comment about me possibly having an enemy, or worse many enemies, perplexed me. I knew I wasn't considered Glenda the Good Witch by anyone, but I was surely not Public Enemy Number One either. No memories of drama or trauma from my previous life, that of Catherine Alexander-Blair, Celtic fiddle player, ex-wife, and average woman who lived on Enterprise Boulevard in Lake Charles, Louisiana, came to mind. Though I might have unintentionally or accidentally ruffled some feathers or bruised some egos in that world, I could not recall any transgression on my part that would have created an enemy left in my wake. Besides, as far as that world was concerned, I was long gone, missing, presumed dead. So, I reasoned silently, if I had an enemy it had to be in this world, Amon's world, this world of vampires, witches, demons, and all sorts of other entities.

"Demons," I whispered, swallowing my coffee too fast. Grateful that the brew wasn't as hot as it should have been, I coughed to keep from choking. The image of the demons I'd encountered since I'd been at the Montjean Estate scrolled through my mind like a slide show. There was the panther demon that disappeared post-haste when he met me, then there was the dragon guy, I couldn't immediately recall his name, then there was Arioch, the demon I'd destroyed.

"Okay, well, we can scratch Arioch from our list of possible suspects," I reasoned aloud to myself, "and I really don't think panther boy would have the cojones to even consider me an enemy, so that leaves..." Chewing on the inside of my lip, I struggled and searched for the demon's name, then realized it had been Arathia who'd summoned him and all the memories of that ritual came flooding back with intense clarity and color. The sensation of the tiny brush Arathia had used to paint symbols on my body shivered through me. I heard the tinkling of the charms she'd woven onto cords around my hips, waist, wrists and ankles. The scent of the demon wafted to me and I had to toss the pastry onto the tray as my stomach roiled.

"Agathodemon," I coughed at the sudden memory.

"Should you really be calling on old friends?" Winter leaned in the doorway, grinning.

"I'm not calling," I coughed again, "on anyone! I'm thinking aloud."

"What's got you so deep in thought, petite soeur?" He sauntered into the office and sat down in the leather client's chair in front of the desk, crossing one long leg over the other. Resting his elbows on the arms of the chair, he steepled his fingers and peered at me as if he were a psychiatrist and I his patient.

"This," I pointed at the LeqonOrb in the jar.

"Why do you have what looks like…" he paused to look closely at the contents of the jar, "a steampunk ball in a jar?"

"Steampunk ball?" I countered, realizing that's exactly what the thing looked like, right down to the burnished gold metallic-looking material and the raised, almost welded-looking, seams.

"Looks like that to me," he offered. "So, why is it in a jar?"

"It's a LeqonOrb," I replied. "You know what that is?"

"No," he shook his head thoughtfully, "but I know enough French to know it means 'Lesson Ball', so what's the lesson?"

"Apparently it's a multi-layered lesson," I laughed at the thought. "Not only do I have to determine what it is, I now have to figure out what the heck to do with it!"

"And it is…" he prompted me.

"It's got quicksilver in it," I answered, "and it's a weapon to destroy an enemy. However, I don't think I have an enemy."

"Ugh," he coughed into one fisted hand to choke back a laugh then added in a sing-song voice, "Have I told you lately that I love you…"

"Relax Winter," I sighed, "I know you're no enemy. I'm well aware that the Council of Five don't trust me, I don't think they really like me, but surely they're not enemies. Chimaera will never be a trusted friend, but again, he's no enemy either, or at least if he is he's hiding it well. And that brings me to where I was when you walked in. I was considering my demon enemy, Agathodemon. He announced when he walked away from me that the next time we met one of us would not survive."

"You took that seriously?"

"Nah," I shook my head with a grin, "I've no doubt that was posturing for the crowd to save his wounded ego. However, our meeting did probably, um...not make him especially happy. Do dragon demons hold grudges?"

"It's my understanding that they age quite slowly," he explained, picking up the jar and looking at the LeqonOrb closely, "and that they live a very long time, have very long memories, and yes, they do hold grudges."

"Great," I tossed a pencil onto the desk, pulled a sheet of typing paper out of the drawer and placed it on the blotter. "That gives me a few ideas." Not stopping to explain to Winter what I was doing, I began jotting down ideas for possible issues I could weave into the story of the next book, if nothing else to see if there was enough material for an actual book.

"So, I remember that when Arathia did her ceremony or spell, or whatever it was," I shifted the focus of the conversation, "she painted symbols all over me and I had little dangly charms here and there. Is that sort of thing actually necessary to summon Agathodemon or was that theatrics?"

"I can't say for sure," Winter responded with a shrug, "but I should think that you could summon him simply enough without the symbols and charms. But, would you really do it? Would you really even want to destroy Agathodemon?"

"I don't know," I admitted. "To be honest, I really don't care about destroying him. I'm just trying to figure out how to get rid of this stupid quicksilver thingy."

"Could you not just save it and store it," he asked, "like, for a rainy day? Have it on hand in case an enemy ever shows up?"

"I could," I nodded, "but only for so long. According to my research, eventually the mercury will eat through the material and escape the orb. The jar will keep it safe for now, but I really don't like the idea of having it around forever. Part of me would like to cheerfully choke my mentor for creating this thing." I scratched out a list of thoughts on the page before me then put the pencil down and sat back in my chair.

Silly, arbitrary vampire laws

Vampire paranoia, is the world ready for us to 'come out of the closet'?

Star-crossed lover otherkin

Vampire Armageddon

Catherine Alexander-Blair, demon assassin

My list was becoming more outrageous the longer I continued to scribble, I realized. It was long past time I stopped the madness.

"I trust that whatever you decide to do with your lesson," Winter offered me a wry smile, "you'll discuss the matter with His Lordship first?"

"Maybe," I pondered a moment then went on, "but I'm a bit torn on the matter. It is, after all, my lesson so it should be my decision, so to speak, what and how to deal with it. It is, again, a witchcraft thing and as he's not a witch…you catch my drift?"

"Ah yes," he nodded and rose to his feet, "that drift which might get us both drawn out to sea. Well, if I can be of no service to you, I'll take my leave." The ceiling lights danced off of the golden curls of his hair and created a halo around his head.

"Actually," I lifted my index finger in the 'wait a minute' gesture, "there is something you can do for me. Tell me how to summon Agathodemon."

Sighing, he closed his eyes, long dark lashes resting lightly on his high cheekbones. When he opened his eyes, gold the color of a cat's eyes, he looked at me seriously.

"You are playing with fire, 'tite souer," he warned. "If you do this thing and it goes bad..."

"It's not going to go bad!" I insisted perhaps a bit too vehemently.

"If you do this thing and it goes badly," he reiterated, "His Lordship will be beyond angry. I really think you should discuss this with him."

"I may," I put my hands on the desk and pushed myself to my feet. "I mean, I'm not saying that I won't talk to Amon about this, but in any case, please, just tell me how to summon the demon."

"Ah, you'd throw me to the wolves," he queried, "so long as you get the information you need, huh?"

"Wolves?"

"Fine then," he sighed dramatically, "wolf. As in THE wolf."

"Oh," I laughed, "Amon. I can see how this might be a problem for you if it went badly for me. Okay, never mind."

"Really?" my bodyguard looked both relieved and suspicious.

"Yep, I don't want to risk you," I admitted, "so as far as anyone's concerned, this conversation never happened. C'est compris?"

"Are you sure, Cat?" Raising one eyebrow, he looked me straight in the eye. I didn't flinch or blink. I knew he was asking more, but I wasn't taking the bait.

"I'm sure, Winter," I nodded, "this conversation never happened. Now, go do whatever it is you were going to do."

"And what are you going to do, 'tite souer?" I couldn't quite recall at what point Winter had begun to call me his 'little sister', and from anyone else I might have considered it an insult, but from him it was a sweet term of endearment so I took it as a compliment.

"Research, Bro," I laughed and escorted him to the door. "I have more homework to do, and miles to go before I sleep."

"Are you performing tonight?" He paused at the door.

"Nope," I patted him on the arm, "tomorrow night. Tonight I have other things to do, including further study on Oola's issue. Any word on Sabre?"

"No, My Lady, at least not that I know of," he bowed gallantly. "Bonsoir!"

"See you later, Winter," I called as he started down the hallway. "Maybe we can do some shooting later?" Amon had a shooting range built behind the guards' barracks shortly after I'd arrived at the Montjean Estate, and though it was intended to be for the guards to practice their marksmanship and even qualify for new positions on the security team, I soon discovered that I enjoyed using it tremendously. Were I the suspicious type, I might have wondered if my mate had it built just to keep me busy and out of trouble, but he'd made it clear that he would prefer me to develop other abilities with regards to self-protection. Whatever the case, Winter and I often spent hours shooting at various target distances, and though I'd probably never make 'sharp shooter' status, I did enjoy something of a natural ability and loved challenging myself.

"Just let me know when you're free," he responded as he turned the corner and disappeared from view.

Relieved that he'd not pressed me on why I'd let him off the hook so easily, I returned to the desk and resumed my seat. I'd remembered that the text I'd discovered in Max's library had information in it regarding working with demons and hoped that what I was in need of would be in it. Carefully searching the desktop, I found the paper upon which I'd written the books' names and prepared to utter the name of the witchcraft tome.

Chapter 16

"Narhen snayb lootz dohor," I announced to the silence of the room. The instant I finished the last syllable the book glistened into view, landing lightly on the desk. Not even pausing to appreciate the mode of the thing's arrival, I opened the front cover and looked over the list of chapters. Naturally, the chapter on demons was chapter 6 and I was surprised there was no additional '66' in parenthesis. I thumbed through the pages until I found the right chapter then started going down a rather extensive list of demons' names and attributes. As the list was arranged alphabetically I found Agathodemon quickly, but couldn't help but peruse the rest of the demons, purely out of curiosity, of course.

"Hmmm...." I murmured, "all things considered, Agathodemon was not the most objectionable demon Arathia could have contacted. There are some seriously icky critters on this list. Yikes!"

Turning to the Agathodemon profile, I skimmed the text then turned the page to find both evoking and invoking spells. The thought of invoking a dragon demon made my skin crawl, but I did read about it before continuing to the spell for evoking one. It appeared that Arathia had personalized her spell a bit, and in all likelihood the painted symbols and charms or amulets she'd put on me had been intended to prove to the demon that I was hers with which to barter his services. Some of the text was in at least one language I did not recognize. I could neither understand nor pronounce any of it. However, to my relief, there were a few brief descriptive paragraphs in English so I was able to ascertain that it was possible to evoke Agathodemon without all the complicated ritual. The final paragraph was a warning that to focus on Agathodemon extensively was, in essence, enough to summon one, and that if one were not sure of one's ability to control the demon one should not think about, concentrate on, study, or speak of the entity.

"Well, that's a bit vague," I sighed to the text. "How do you know if you're focusing too much? How much is too much?"

"Little witch," the smooth hissing sound came out of nowhere a moment before Agathodemon appeared beside me.

'Question asked and answered,' I thought as I bolted to my feet, knocking the book to the floor as I did so. Standing so close, basically penning my right arm to my side, the demon appeared in his human form. His long, thick, wavy charcoal hair hung loose about his shoulders and his eyes glittered gold. He looked very much like Amon, but he didn't smell like my mate, and there was a disturbing rasp in his voice which put me very much in mind of a snake.

"Crap!" I yelped as the demon captured me with his eyes and I froze.

"I've not seen you since that unfortunate incident with your sorceress," he purred. "How curious it is that you summoned me. I take it you've changed your mind and wish to play with me now until your mind and body breaks?" Nictitating lids closed and opened on his reptilian eyes and his vertical pupils widened slightly as he tried to hold me entranced.

"No!" I managed to close my eyes and gritted my teeth. "And how did you get in here?"

"You called me, pretty morsel," he leered. "Your shields are of no use when you summon me."

"I did not summon you!" I growled. "And back off!" Shoving as hard as I could, I managed to force the demon to move only a couple of steps back, but I was at least able to breathe and I was free of his power. Turning my back to the desk, I faced Agathodemon as I reached behind me and carefully picked up the pickle jar.

"So, if you do not wish to play with me," he pouted, making my stomach lurch, "why have you called me? And what has happened to your sorceress?"

332

"Arathia was destroyed," I answered, fascinated to be having an actual conversation with a dragon demon despite myself. Sure, I'd been in Amon's world for a while and I'd run into some impossible creatures, but to be standing in the same room talking to a being that the rest of the world considered myth still made my mind wobble.

"Good," his smile widened. "Such beings are so tedious, always insisting on controlling others and demanding sacrifices and offerings. I've encountered many in my time and they all seem to be the same. I'm glad she's gone."

"I, um..." I stammered, not really knowing what to say.

"So," he brightened and moved to the other side of the desk, taking the chair Winter had not long ago vacated, "why am I here? I must admit, I've not tasted human flesh in some time and you do look delicious."

"This is why you're here," I turned, presented the jar with the LeqonOrb in it and removed the lid. I was not sure what to expect when I showed the demon the orb, but his reaction was strange indeed. At the sight of the thing, his nostrils flared, his image blurred, and he shimmered into his dragon form. An aura of green energy rippled along his silvery scales as his body transformed. Golden eyes glittering larger, his sharply-fanged mouth spread wide and his long snake-like tongue lolled out, dripping. He was drooling!

"Little witch," he sprayed saliva as he spoke, "is that what I think it is? Is that quicksilver?"

"It is," I nodded, heart sinking at the realization that he was not threatened by my weapon but seemed to actually be attracted to it. "It is a weapon to destroy my enemy!"

"Awwww..." he mocked me with a sigh, "you would destroy me? Silly witch, do you not know that quicksilver is a delicacy to me? Greedy humans hold and carefully keep the stuff these days. I've not had any for centuries." As he rose from the chair that barely held his more massive, natural form, his wings spread up and out behind him. He towered over me.

"This is for you," I offered, hoping to change tactics without his notice. "It's a gift!"

"Wait," the demon looked around the room carefully, "where is your vampire? Is this a trap?"

"No trap," I assured him, "and Amon is not here now. The orb is yours, no strings attached."

"And what would you have in trade?" He stared at the orb, drool dangling from his lips.

"Nothing," I responded. "I want nothing in return. The orb is yours."

"What if I take the orb," he hissed, "and have you too?" Leaning across the desk, he reached out with one claw and wrapped it around my throat. "I would have two delicacies." As he lifted me off my feet, the pressure closed off my windpipe and had I still needed to breathe to survive I'd have been in trouble. Breathing was a habit of mine, but since turning vampire I'd come to discover that it was no longer absolutely necessary.

"You would," I admitted, not sure where to go next, "but the orb is a gift. Would you take a gift and destroy the gifter?"

"I might," he lifted his immense head, nostrils flaring again, and sniffed loudly. "Wait, you are no longer human. You are vampire!"

"I am," I nodded at the glimmer of hope, "and I'm more than that."

"I do not associate with the dead," he snarled, released me unceremoniously, grabbed the jar from my hand and stepped back. With surprising dexterity, he gently pinched the LeqonOrb between two claws and removed it from the pickle jar, then handed the empty jar back to me.

"I'm not dead!" I snapped, then paused to consider, "Well, maybe I am, but I'm not just dead. I'm not just vampire, I'm witch too and probably a few other things. And who are you to discriminate against vampires?"

335

"Your kind and mine have a long history of battles and destruction, and the destruction was not always just the combatants, if you get my meaning. We have agreed to survive by avoiding each other," he explained, cradling the LeqonOrb in one claw. "And the world continues due to that agreement."

"Ah, I see," I nodded, "and on behalf of this world, of which I'm quite fond, I thank you. The orb is yours. You are free to go."

"Just like that?" he raised one heavy eyebrow at me in suspicion. "The quicksilver is mine?"

"It is," I affirmed. "And as vampire, I too will honor the agreement."

"What are you called?" Agathodemon looked at me as if I'd just entered the room.

"I'm Cat," I retorted. "And what are you called, I mean besides your name of power? What do those who don't wish to control you call you?"

"I'm Snarl," he closed his eyes and bowed his head politely.

"Snarl," I smiled, "I'm happy to meet you, well, not exactly, but you know what I mean."

"You are called Cat, but you are not a cat," he looked up as his image shifted back to that of his human form. I noticed once again that his eyes remained those of a dragon.

"This is true," I admitted, not wanting to get into the subject of nicknames and shortening proper names. "I am not a cat, but I'm Cat."

"Humans are fascinating," he observed, "and they often make no sense."

"Our business is finished, Snarl," I changed the subject as politely as I could. "Please, be gone."

Whether it was my words or just that the matter was done, Agathodemon cradled the LeqonOrb in long, delicate hands and...just wasn't there. To say I felt a flood of relief would be an understatement, but I did manage to make my way to the office chair before my legs gave out beneath me. The scent of sulphur hung heavy in the air so I picked the book up from the floor and fanned it around furiously hoping to dispel the odor.

"Thank Gods and Goddesses that Amon wasn't here," I wrinkled my nose at the smell then began to tidy up the desk. I wasn't really interested in making a neatness of the desk, but I was having trouble processing all that had just happened. My mind was awhirl and I wasn't sure what to do next.

"The orb is gone," I rationalized to no one. "The lesson is over with, apparently. Snarl is gone." I would make a point of thinking of and speaking of the demon using his more familiar name from now on, I told myself. "Things could have gone badly, but they didn't. I think I should be not only relieved but pleased with myself. At least, I think that's what I think."

I neatly stacked the few sheets of paper I'd used and turned them face-down on Amon's blotter. It occurred to me that I probably should look further through the text I'd called for from Max's library, but I suddenly lacked the patience for it and sent it back to the librarian in the manner in which it had arrived. I wanted to be outside in the night, in fresh air, and walking in warm grass, but I had to find Ulrich and tell him about the assignment. Surely by now he and Siri were done with their swim so I decided to try looking for them in the study.

Carrying the empty pickle jar down the stairs, I called out to my mentor, but there was no reply. I called Siri and heard a 'woof' in return, then the doors to the veranda swung open and the beast came trotting in, tail wagging. Ulrich stepped into the Great Hall and smiled up at me. He was neatly dressed in a pale blue denim shirt, sleeves rolled up above the elbow, and dark blue trousers. His hair was pulled back into a ponytail on the nape of his neck and his beard sported delicate beads in braids. Tiny black eyes peeked above the edge of his shirt pocket just before Rufus poked his little pink nose out and twitched it curiously.

"Cat," my mentor bowed politely, left hand gently supporting his pocket. "Siri and I have just had a lovely walk and now, if you'd care to join us, we're going to find something to eat, as we've worked up quite an appetite."

"Thanks for the invitation," I replied as I scratched the dog beneath her big fuzzy ears, "but I think I need some exercise myself. I'm done with the assignment, by the way."

"Trying to give it back to me again?" He grinned mischievously.

"Nope," I presented the empty pickle jar, "it's gone. The assignment's done!"

"Very good!" His eyes brightened. "Would you like to give me the details?"

"Do I have to?" I tried not to sound petulant.

"Of course not," he looked almost insulted. "I can sense that the orb is no more. You need not explain your actions to me if you don't wish to do so."

"Really?" I was surprised at his response.

"At some point in the future I would like an explanation, of course," he admitted, "but it need not be right now at this moment. Please, go get some air and enjoy your night."

"Thanks, Ulrich," I smiled as I passed him, "and please don't let Siri get anything to eat that she shouldn't have."

"Will do, My Lady," he laughed. "I'd like to think that I learned my lesson on that matter."

Feeling much like a child released from class on the last day of the school year, I opened the French doors and stepped onto the veranda. The night was fine, if a bit cloudy, and the lights in the trees twinkled an enchanting greeting. In the distance I overheard Winter talking with someone and started toward the stables to find out what was going on. Just inside the stable doors, my beloved bodyguard stood talking with Lucius, Lily's brother, and the moment they saw me all conversation abruptly ceased.

"Am I interrupting something important?" I adopted my most demure demeanor but stopped short of batting my eyelashes.

"Nothing important, My Lady," Winter turned to greet me. "I was just going over some details with Lucius. He's going to drive one of our guests home later." Nose wrinkling subtly, he winced and looked around as if in search of the source of some odor, but said nothing about the matter.

"One of our guests?" I couldn't help but ask, as I had no idea who was on the estate beyond the 'usual suspects'.

"I'll just be drivin' Mister Dykstra and his sister home." Lucius laughed then added, "Well, not really to their home, but to the dock where their yacht's moored.

They're sailing south to the Caribbean when they leave here, or so I've been told."

"Bastiaan and Elspeth are here tonight?" I wondered what that was about, before recalling that Amon had mentioned something for tonight, either a phone call or a meeting, with the new Council member.

"So, are you ready to go waste some ammo?" Winter clapped his hands together as if they were dusty.

"Of course," I smiled at the thought, "there's nothing I'd rather do than go blast some paper targets. Later, Lucius!" Lily's brother smiled and threw me a salute as Winter linked his arm through mine and escorted me into the courtyard beyond the stables.

"Cat," he said soberly, which was very unlike him.

"Winter," I responded with a parroting tone.

"Not to be indelicate," he cleared his throat, "but, well...you smell."

"Hey!" I punched him in the bicep. "It's not my fault!"

"You reek of dragon demon," he feigned holding his nose. "Tell me you didn't summon Agathodemon!"

"I didn't!" I insisted, then laughed, "Well, not on purpose anyway."

"You did! You summoned him! Have you lost your mind? What happened?" The barrage of questions only served to amuse me further.

341

"Relax Winter," I chuckled, "everything's fine. The LeqonOrb is gone, the dragon demon is gone, everything's gone but the smell, apparently."

"And His Lordship is okay with this?" my bodyguard stopped in his tracks and raised one eyebrow at me. "He does know."

"Well, not exactly," I nodded. "I haven't had the chance to tell him about it yet, but I will! I told Ulrich that I'd completed my lesson, so he's good. Once I tell Amon, everything's done and done."

"I'd feel better if he knew about it," he confessed, "but that's up to you. I'm just happy that you survived and that the demon's gone."

"So, let's do some shooting," I pulled him to the shooting stations and hit the levers to move the paper targets. "How far shall we aim tonight?"

"Your call, 'tite soeur," he suggested as he unlocked the weapons safe secreted in the wall adjacent to the stations. "Pick your weapon."

The variety of handguns and rifles in the safe was extensive, and the weapons ranged from ugly but effective to exquisite but 'iffy' when it came to firing. As I was fond of my Beretta Tomcat, I chose a similar model and checked the safety before making sure it was cleaned and loaded. Bear was in charge of the gun range and he kept all the weapons in perfect condition. I was not disappointed. Winter chose a Lugar 9mm, identical to the one he carried patrolling the estate, and checked his weapon as I had done.

We shot at various distances, trying to best one another at the 'kill shot' on the closer targets and just trying to make a hole in the human shadow shape on the more distant ones. I was pretty sure Winter encouraged me by making a few wild shots so as to make my shooting seem improved, but he denied it when I accused him. When we were done, we placed the used weapons in a bin so Bear would know to clean them, then Winter offered to escort me back to the house.

"I'm on estate grounds, Winter," I complained. "I'm quite safe. You don't need to walk me back. I'll be fine. Go ahead and check in with the rest of the team. I'll just mosey on back."

"Are you sure, Cat?" He actually looked concerned. "It's no trouble. You know it's my job."

"I know, sweetie," I smiled, "but I'm just walking from point A here to point B there. You have other work to do. I'll be fine."

"If you insist," he nodded and bowed. "Thanks for the shooting practice. I'll check on you in a bit."

"As you wish, mon capitaine!" I saluted before I started off down the gravel path that led to the garden. The lights in the trees offered just enough light to see the flowers and soft shadows here and there. Crickets chirruped and wolves howled in the distance. I hopped up on the low concrete wall that surrounded the main flower bed and pretended to be a wire walker, arms extended out to the side for balance. Just amusing myself, I was startled to catch a glimpse of movement ahead and to the side of the house. Someone was stealing quickly and furtively along the tall garden wall. Frozen, not daring to move, I watched silently as the shape moved in and out of the shadows until it passed into a patch of light. To my dismay it appeared to be Bastiaan.

My mind spun, as I couldn't imagine why the new Council member would be outside and skulking around the grounds in such a manner. I had no choice but to follow, and I tried to do so quickly and quietly. The vampire's pale blond hair gleamed like a beacon in the darkness, its length gathered at his nape and resting down the back of his dark coat. As he continued along the wall, I realized he was going to the arched doorway I'd been through when I found Siri. As I'd forgotten to mention the door to anyone, I was surprised that someone new to the estate would be aware of it and that just piqued my interest further. When he disappeared into the bushes surrounding the doorway, I paused for a few moments, the amount of time I figured it would take him to open the door and go through, and then I followed, wishing I had either my throwing blades or my gun. I had no intention of engaging the guy; I was just following him to find out what he was doing. One quick peek to see what he was up to, then I was going back inside to have a shower and maybe a glass of wine.

When it felt safe to do so, I moved quietly to the door, pushed it open and stepped through into the open field. Behind me, from the house, I heard Siri let out a blood-curdling howl and Amon's wolves quickly joined in. Suddenly, I no longer cared what Bastiaan might be doing. There was something seriously wrong in the mansion and I needed to get back there! I turned to go back then realized that I couldn't move. My feet were trapped, my arms were pinned to my sides, and tape was slapped over my mouth. Course fabric was pulled down over my head and body. My head spun as I was hoisted into the air.

"Crap!" I thought, as I realized I'd just walked into a trap.

Chapter 17

My head hurt. My mouth was dry and foul tasting. There was grit on my hands and the air was musty and warm. Something wet trickled down my forehead where apparently I'd been hit, or perhaps dropped on my head. That thought amused me and I chuckled softly as I gently touched my face. The stuff was mostly dry, just a little bit of it wet and moving. I had no idea where I was, how long I'd been out, or what was going on, but I knew well that things were going to get uglier before they got prettier. Though my wrists were bound, my hands were free and before I even fully formed the intention, I was reaching for my head wound, my Healing Hand thrumming in anticipation. The pain receded as soon as my palm reached my head. The bleeding stopped immediately and I could feel the tissue mending as the healing was completed. When I opened my mouth and stretched my lips I could feel the adhesive from the tape stinging and the dry skin cracking slightly, but at least the tape was gone.

Suddenly my thoughts went to Amon, then Winter, who would likely be facing the wrath for letting me insist on walking back to the house alone. I imagined my mate unaware of my absence, then upon discovery of it, raging from pillar to post in search of me. Calming myself, I sent my thoughts to my beloved and though the response was weak, I did 'hear' him as only I could. I knew that he'd heard me, but communication, for whatever reason, was difficult, almost impossible. That took my thoughts back to my situation, and who might have committed this abduction and why.

The room in which I was being held was without light; it appeared that there were no windows and no light peeked from beneath the heavy wooden door on the adjacent wall. If I removed my contact lenses I would be able to see clearly in the dark, but as my hands were covered in grit and I'd not be able to put them back in, I quickly dismissed the idea. My vision was fair in the darkness, I just couldn't see much in the way of details. If there was a key to my prison on the table across the room, I couldn't see it. The floor was hard-packed earth, cool and dry, and reminded me of an old fashioned root cellar, but I discerned that more by feel than by sight.

"Maybe if I'm deep underground," I whispered to myself, "that's the reason I can't communicate with Amon. Maybe there's something in the walls or in the ground that's blocking our signal." The image of antennae poking out of my head and sending signals to similar antennae on Amon's head sent my mind back to 'My Favorite Martian' and I chuckled softly.

"Doesn't matter why I can't reach him," I sighed, "I can't. So, what do I do now?"

Once upon a time I'd been psychically connected to Chimaera, and his voice had actually led me back to the physical world, but it had been a long time since I'd tested that link and I wasn't even sure it still existed. Figuring I had little to lose, I closed my eyes and tried to focus on my mate's Lieutenant and pack member. I envisioned his icy, violently blue eyes looking at me, his expression inscrutable as it always seemed to me. Briefly I felt a brush of fur over my skin, but there was nothing more. Either the link no longer worked or the same thing that was blocking me from Amon was blocking me from Chimaera.

One last hope remained, that I might reach Winter as he was owl and under my dominion. He and I were not only friends and confidants, he was my creature, so I hoped beyond hope that I could connect with him. I started focusing on his image, the curly blond hair, the golden eyes, the broad cheekbones and cherubic lips. Then his snowy owl image superimposed itself and I could hear his screech as he spread his wings and shot into the sky. I was reaching him! I could feel him! But, after a few moments, it became clear that though I was connecting with him he was unable to sense or connect with my energy. Well, helsa! I opened my eyes in defeat.

Looking around the room brought me no inspiration, no insights, no brilliant ideas on how to make my escape. I wondered idly how Siri was doing with Ulrich and remembered the dog's strident howl just as I was attacked.

"Could she have known?" I wondered, not at all concerned about talking to myself. "Are we that connected? Could I contact her as I tried to do with Amon?" Though it seemed unlikely to work, I closed my eyes and imagined the black German shepherd in the study, most likely in the company of Ulrich. She was curled up asleep on the rug in front of the couch and I touched the top of her head just between the ears. She twitched, whimpered in her sleep, and then exhaled loudly. Whether it was because she was asleep or because it was just impossible, I was unable to reach her and withdrew my thoughts.

I was being held against my will. I was a prisoner. I had no idea who had abducted me or what they wanted. My power should have been stirring, revving up to explode at anyone or anything that was a threat to me, and yet it was quiet. I was calm, a bit irked, admittedly, but neither angry nor upset. This was unusual, I realized. Closing my eyes I centered myself and listened to the sounds of the room. On the surface level, there was no sound, but on a deeper level I could hear the soft susurration of moving water and a deep, heavy vibration, like the purring of a distant engine. The sound must have comforted me more than I expected. I slept and I dreamed.

Thea stood atop a gentle hill, the breeze stirring her long auburn hair and billowing green cape. She was obviously angry, her brow furrowed and hands gesticulating wildly. She was screaming or yelling at me. I couldn't hear what she was saying, and I couldn't read her lips, but the message was clear. She was not happy! An owl swooped down from the sky and lit on her left shoulder, peering at me intently. It opened its hooked beak and screeched at me.

"You!" A voice rang out of the darkness as I bolted awake. A heavy boot nudged my knee. "Wake up, you. Now!"

When I opened my eyes I was blinded by a bright light. I blinked, then closed my eyes tightly, seeing purple blobs on the inside of my eyelids.

"I said, wake up!" The voice came again and I realized that it was female, clear, and resonant. The dream of Thea swam back into my consciousness and I opened my eyes, looking away from the source of the glare. Once my eyes adjusted to the light, I could just make out the gleam of a shining crucifix right beside the barrel of a handgun. Both were pointed at me.

"On your feet, witch," the woman brandishing the weapons commanded as she bent down and grabbed me by the elbow, yanking me upright. "Don't try anything stupid. Don't utter a curse or spell at me and I won't stab you in the heart with this crucifix."

"I don't utter curses or spells," I replied, trying to wipe my hands on my jeans.

"Fine," she nodded as she marched me from the room and into a narrow, poorly lit corridor. I stole glances at her as she half-shoved, half-dragged me down the musty hallway. She was young, but severe looking with features sharp, harsh, and angular. Whether it was because she was playing jailor or it was her natural state, I couldn't tell, but I'd not want to meet her in a dark alley unless I had a Louisville Slugger or at the very least the powers bestowed upon me by the deities. I was more curious than fearful, more amused than angry. This situation was an enigma and I greatly anticipated getting to the heart of it.

At the end of the hallway, a weathered, wooden door swung open and fresh air hit me in the face. It was morning, though the sun had not yet risen, thankfully. My eyes were unprotected, but for contacts, and I had no idea where my dark glasses were, so I put my head down instinctively. It was a short walk across damp grass and through another door, this one newer and in better condition than the last. Inside the door hung a wall of heavy velvet drapes and before I knew what was happening I was sailing through them to land on a hard stone floor. Whether my escort tossed me or something tripped me, I couldn't tell, but my entrance was less than graceful. Wrists still bound, I couldn't easily push myself up so I just moved my legs around, scissor-like, until I could roll into a seated position. I sat on the grime covered floor, blinking, and looking around the room. There was a desk several feet away with a tall, brown leather office chair behind it. The room itself was fairly non-descript with one window, behind the desk, which was mostly concealed by the same heavy velvet curtains that covered the door through which I'd been deposited. An unremarkable ceiling light bearing two florescent tubes flickered, sputtered, went out and then strengthened, casting the room in a wan, ugly pink. The wood paneling on the walls, which might have once been warm and stylish, was covered with at least one thick coat of cream colored paint and pipes covered in matching insulation ran from floor to ceiling in two corners. There were no touches of warmth or personality, certainly no decorator's touch, in the place.

"I apologize that we must meet this way," a masculine voice reverberated around the room. I tried to follow the sound to its source until the desk chair swung around, grabbing my attention.

"Bastiaan," I gasped at the long-haired man sitting behind the desk. Thoughts of intrigue and betrayal ran through my head as I considered what having been abducted by a member of the Council of Five might mean.

"Ah," he smiled brightly, "I'm glad that you appreciate my little ruse. I thought I'd done an excellent job with my disguise. So glad that you agree."

"Disguise," I murmured in confusion, "wait, you are..."

"My name is Zador," he stood and bowed slightly before moving around the desk. "I trust you'll forgive me for having entered your mind during meditation, you see it was just too tempting to resist."

"Zador," I responded, clarity not forthcoming, "and in my mind you said that I'd summoned you so that you could help me. How did you do that, and why?"

"I was having a spot of fun," he shrugged. "I have a dramatic flair." At that, his features shifted, and suddenly he no longer resembled Bastiaan. His dark eyes sparkled and his smile made it clear that he was quite proud of himself, and rightfully so, I had to admit. He was the same height as he'd been as the new Council member, his hair was still long but was now a rather dull chestnut, and his brow became his most prominent feature. Bushy brown and gray eyebrows shaded his deep-set eyes and a poorly-trimmed mustache fringed his ample lips.

"Who are you," I snarled, losing patience with the theatrics, "and what do you want?"

"First," he stepped forward and bent down, lifting me by the elbows to my feet, "I'm sorry for your accommodations. Things moved more quickly than we'd anticipated and we had no choice but to act. We were unprepared and had to make do with what was available. I promise, you'll have a nicer room from now on."

"Fine," I tucked an errant lock of hair behind my ear and looked at Zador, "so, what do you want?"

"Perhaps this will give you some idea," he moved back around the desk and pulled the heavy velvet drapes open. What was behind those curtains was not, as I'd thought, a window but a large, ornately etched, sheet of glass. It might have been a mirror, except that it didn't reflect the room; it held the image of Arathia. The sorceress looked as she had in my dream, but in the glass she did not move or speak.

"What the..." I was speechless at the image.

"You remember my Queen, Arathia," he cocked his head in the direction of the glass. "It has taken us a long time to make this much progress towards her return. This is her essence, her shell, but she is not within. You have the missing piece, that which will enable us to bring her back to her followers."

"I have nothing," I shook my head, having no idea what he was going on about. "And you can't bring her back. She was destroyed by her kind!"

"She was destroyed by your mate," Zador exclaimed, dropping the façade of being polite and civil. "Amon destroyed her and now I have his mate."

"Amon did what he was directed to do by Nemesis and the other deities," I insisted, "and though he certainly had cause to do so on his own, he did not."

"Nonsense," my abductor retorted, "your mate did what he wanted to do, just as I'm doing what I want to do. And now that I have you, you will give me that which I seek and I will return Arathia to her former glory."

"I don't have anything," I responded, trying to quell the power that was beginning to stir in my gut. Fear didn't clutch at me, but anger was beginning to simmer and impatience was fanning the flames. "What are you talking about?"

"Her athame," he slammed one hand down on the desk. "Where is it? We've been able to track it to you; we know you have it."

"I didn't even know it existed," I laughed, "until recently. And yes, I've seen it, helsa, I thought it was a letter opener, but I don't have it!"

"You want me to believe that you've not had it since the moment your mate destroyed my beloved Arathia?" He looked like he was losing his patience too. I was beginning to like the situation.

"I don't care what you believe," I pasted a wry smile on my face, "but I'm telling you the truth. I've no idea where her athame has been these past years, but I assure you that neither Amon nor I have had it."

"But you've admitted that you've seen it," he countered, "so where is it?"

"I don't know!" I laughed.

"You have it," he glared at me, "and I will get it."

"You may get it," I shrugged, "but I do not have it. And between you and me? I wouldn't give it to you if I did have it."

"So, this is how you want it," he grimaced. "Fine. Naomi!"

She of the warden disposition entered the room and stood behind me. She placed one hand on my left shoulder and squeezed firmly, ostensibly to let me know that she was in charge. At that moment I felt the Mark of Obedience on my back roar to life and knew that Amon had discovered my absence and was less than pleased. I stiffened and stilled until the pain passed

"Take her away," Zador commanded. "In time she'll see things our way."

"Don't bet on it," I grumbled under my breath as Naomi, now known in my mind as 'The Screw', pushed me not toward the door I'd come in but a door on the adjacent wall. Apparently my new digs would not be in the same building as the dungeon. Things were looking up!

Down a short hall, past a few doors on both sides of the corridor, Naomi paused to unlock a room on the right, opened the door, and stepped back so I could enter. The room, to my dismay, wasn't much of an improvement over the one I'd awakened in earlier, but at least it wasn't a jail cell. Judging from the dimensions of the place, it had once been a janitor's closet or large supply room. Again, there was no window but a small door near the far wall opened into a bathroom with toilet and sink. There was, I noted, no mirror, so the idea of breaking it to gain a weapon was eliminated. Still, I was happy to have the means to wash my hands. The zip-tie that secured my wrists rolled up and down on my wet skin, but it would not stretch or break to afford me freedom. The water felt good, however, so I took my time and enjoyed cleaning and refreshing myself.

When I stepped out of the bathroom I discovered that my 'prison' had not improved. The springs moaned when I sat down on the cot and the legs squealed when I scooted back against the wall. Heaving a sigh, I closed my eyes and sent my thoughts out to Amon. The energy moved, as it always had, but there was nothing in response. I waited as patiently as possible, then tried something akin to a scream, amping up the projection of the energy in hopes of breaking through whatever barrier was thwarting me. My energy came right back at me, slamming into my third eye like a runaway locomotive. Yelping, I opened my eyes and leapt to my feet. I paced and rubbed my forehead and temples, waiting for the pain to subside.

"Well, Cat," I moaned, "that was less than brilliant! And we've discovered that our theory, regarding having been underground and that being the cause of our inability to reach Amon, was probably incorrect. This room doesn't feel like it's underground, but we still can't reach himself. So…" Pondering the possibilities, I paced, swore a bit under my breath, and paced some more.

Finally, I sat back down on the edge of the cot and held my head in my hands. The pain was diminishing, but I felt wobbly, frustrated, and exhausted. Closing my eyes, I thought if I could sleep for a bit I'd awaken with a clear head, so I lay back on the cot and curled into the fetal position. Just as I yawned and was settling into sleep, I felt the air stir around me. It started out as a soft breeze then quickly increased, pulling my hair up and away from my face. Sitting up suddenly, I saw a maelstrom between the cot and the door. The vortex I'd seen in Amon's office had found me once more and this time I had nothing to anchor myself from its power. At the moment the realization hit me, so did the pull and I was yanked from the cot, weightless and airborne.

At first, my eyes were closed tightly in defense of the rush of energy, but as the sensation of motion continued I dared to open my eyes and was dumbfounded by what I saw. Streaks and smears of various colors rushed past me, or perhaps I was rushing past them, in a crazy kaleidoscope effect. I could hear music, sirens, voices raised in song and screams, mechanical bleeps and ratcheting sounds, a cacophony unlike anything I'd ever heard before. The sensation seemed to be going on and on, as if I was hurtling through an extremely long tunnel, and my concern about how and where it would end grew by the moment. The colors around me finally shifted into a blur of white, which then broke open into blue the color of a clear sky. My feet touched solid ground, but I couldn't grasp what surrounded me. It made no sense that I was on the ground yet nothing but sky was around me. Turning, I saw a spot in the distance and it rapidly grew larger as whatever it was approached at blinding speed. I closed my eyes tightly and threw my arms up over my head, instinctively trying to protect myself from what was approaching. Energy, like a large puff of air, pushed at me for what seemed like a long time, though after the fact I realized it was likely only a moment. When I opened my eyes I found myself standing on a grass-covered hill above a walled city. The sky was still blue, and white clouds scuttled across the sun, casting shadows across the land below. Looking down at my clothes, I found I was wearing a simple robe of brown wool with a rope tied about my waist. I could feel the chemise beneath the rough garment and fine dust on my feet made the leather sandals I wore feel loose and unpleasant. My hair was pulled back from my face and gathered into a braid that lay down my back.

Not far from where I stood was an orchard of some sort and I made my way to the trees, curious as to the variety. Touching a leaf on the lowest branch of the first tree I encountered, I realized it was an olive and was full of soon to be harvested fruit.

"Well, Cat," I sighed, "I think it's safe to assume that we're no longer in Kansas!" Feeling once more like Dorothy finding herself in Oz, I looked around the orchard, searched the horizon for any more clues as to where I might have landed, and listened for any familiar sounds. The distant city looked quiet, but a small earthen road wound around the base of the hill upon which the orchard grew and a few horse-drawn carts and wagons made their way toward the open gates in the wall. Having no idea specifically of where I was or why I was there, it seemed a reasonable thing that I should follow the wagons into the city, so I neared the edge of the orchard and waited until the last of them passed. Pulling the hood of my cloak up over my head, I trotted onto the road. My plan was to keep up with the last slow moving cart, to stay near enough to it that anyone seeing me would think I was part of the entourage, but that didn't work. The wagons easily out-distanced me and I ended up walking alone quite far behind them.

After some time I realized that the city was farther away than it appeared and the sun was slipping beneath the horizon as I finally neared the city walls. Torches were being lit along the parapets and hooded sentinels were cranking a huge pulley to close the city gates just as I entered. To my relief, no one stopped or even seemed to notice me so I relaxed and pulled the hood of my cloak back to take in the sights.

At first glance, everything appeared normal. People walked about carrying goods, pulling carts loaded with crates of live animals or casks of wine or beer. Some bore bundles of wood on their shoulders, a few carried stacks of what appeared to be scrolls. Most folks wore simple garments, tunics and leggings, skirts or shifts, capes and cloaks, though a few were dressed in elaborately adorned fine silks. I was enjoying myself people watching when I noticed my vision was blurred when looking at some people but not others. The more I observed the situation the more I came to realize that some of the individuals I passed were hardly there at all, and others were overly vivid, almost too 'there'. Whether it was a trick of the dying sunlight or dust in my eyes or something else entirely, the phenomenon became more pronounced as I made my way deeper into the city. Eventually, the blurred effect overwhelmed most of my perceptions and only a few people in the city appeared to be 'real'. The sensation was quite disturbing, so I concentrated on looking at the architectural details of the city, the shops, or the stones in the road. Apparently, only what was inanimate appeared real, solid, and normal. The vision was giving me a headache and I was relieved to find myself standing alone before what looked like a very ornate and beautifully spired ancient cathedral. The tall arched doors stood open and I could hear music coming from within. The thought of resting in a pew near the back of the church and enjoying the music lifted my spirits and I eagerly stepped inside.

Chapter 18

Candles burned in the alcove just inside the door, emitting curls of greasy smoke that rose to the soot-stained ceiling. An ornate, even grotesque, crucifix hung on the wall, weakly illuminated by the tiny flames below. The air was cool, dry, and heavy with the fragrance of what I guessed was Frankincense. Moving quietly, I stepped into sanctuary and slid into the pew nearest the door. Voices, one very powerful, masculine, and raised in obvious anger, reverberated and bounced off the stone walls, echoing from behind the altar all the way to where I sat. I had no idea what was going on somewhere in the building, but from the sounds of it I had no desire whatsoever to get involved. The music I'd heard on the street had ceased and there seemed no other reason to remain so after I gazed and gawked at the flying buttresses, steepled stained glass windows, and carved stone statuary, I got up to leave. A young, soft, voice whispered from behind me and I sat back down quickly.

"That's Señora Zapata," the little boy's hand brushed my shoulder as he held onto the back of the pew then slid in to sit beside me. "She's with Bishop De La Cruz.

She's been accused of witchcraft!" His hands placed palm to palm as if in prayer, the boy spoke Spanish, and, though it was not a language familiar to me, I could understand him as if he were speaking English.

"Is Señora Zapata a witch?" I asked in English, though what came out of my mouth was the same Spanish my young companion spoke. It was an unusual sensation.

"She is not!" He raised his eyebrows in surprise, "But…" He suddenly went silent as a woman crossed from a nave near the altar, paused momentarily to glance in our direction, then disappeared behind heavy velvet drapes. "She accused Señora Zapata," he whispered in a lower register, nodding subtly at the woman, whose form was suddenly familiar to me.

"Naomi," I gasped in recognition of my guard. "How is this possible?"

"Señorita Mirelda, she is Bishop De La Cruz's eyes and ears in the village," the child explained, his big brown eyes unable to contain his emotions, his dark curls bouncing as he nodded. "He listens to her and she tells him what she thinks he wants to hear. They are dangerous."

"What are you doing here?" I turned to look at the boy, worried that he might be placing himself in danger by being seen with me.

"I help out here," he smiled, straight white teeth almost beaming against his dark skin. "Sometimes I get to be acolyte."

"I see," I returned the smile. "That's a very important job."

"Yes, and I'm very good at it." His grin was infectious and I couldn't help but be impressed at the way he spoke. "You should probably go now. Bishop De La Cruz will be leaving soon and he should not see you."

"Thank you," I whispered conspiratorially, "I'll go then."

"Wait!" he touched my shoulder as the curtains beside the sanctuary parted and a man who could only be Bishop De La Cruz stepped into the sanctuary. Speaking to Naomi's double, the man, dressed in elaborate vestments, was distracted momentarily so I took the opportunity to slip the hood of my cloak up over my head. I figured that such an important man as Bishop De La Cruz probably wouldn't bother to take notice of a lowly parishioner so I took my place on the kneeling bench before my pew, rested my elbows on the back of the pew before me, and placed my hands together as if in prayer. When he was finished speaking with his assistant, the Bishop made his way down the center aisle in a flurry of rustling fabric, and though I peered at him from beneath the edge of my hood, he took no notice of me or the young boy beside me.

Had I still been human, I think my blood would have frozen solid when I saw the Bishop's face. Without question, the Bishop was Zador. The hairstyle was different, but the face was absolutely that of Arathia's consort. Once he'd passed us and had exited the cathedral, I pulled the hood of my cloak back down and turned to my young friend.

"Thank you for your help," I smiled. "I'll be going now."

"May God bless you, Señorita," he bowed, crossed himself, and then disappeared down the center aisle.

"He may indeed," I responded beneath my breath before leaving the cathedral. It seemed a reasonable assumption that the reason I'd been delivered to this place and time was to witness Zador and Naomi doing, whatever it was they'd been doing, whenever this was. Judging from the clothing the people wore and their activities, I guessed I was somewhere perhaps in the sixteenth century, possibly in Spain, but where and when didn't seem as important as what and who I'd seen.

As I stepped through the tall, arched wooden doors and onto the steps of the cathedral, the vortex reappeared, and before I had time to even think of a response, I was once more on my way, feeling like a bug sucked into a vacuum sweeper.

Fortunately for me, this time through the vortex the travel was brief and when it ended I was deposited in familiar terrain. Once more I found myself in a forest of ancient trees, surrounded by a throng of people, some bearing torches, surging forward into the night. I was swept along with the crowd knowing already that what lay ahead was the beautiful tree-throne of the Goddess Arathia, the sacrificial stone on the ground before it deeply grooved and darkly stained with the blood of her worshippers and their victims. She perched, as she had when I'd witnessed this scene before, on the wide, bent back seat of the tree, her finely woven silver gown twinkling in the lights of the myriad torches and bonfires that lit the grove. The crown atop her head was white, sharply barbed, and made of twigs and bones. In her left hand she held a stone chalice, and after taking a long draught of the contents, she daintily wiped her lips of the blood she'd spilled. Beneath the throne, and near the sacrificial stone, stood Zador with a long, heavy, wickedly sharp blade in his hands. To his right stood Naomi, holding a wide, deep platter, apparently used for collecting the sacrificial blood.

The crowd was moving quickly and I really had no desire to be brought before the bloody Goddess and her henchman, so I moved to the right, cutting between cloaked worshippers and what appeared to be merely curious villagers. However briefly I'd been there, I was hoping that I'd seen what was important as well as seen enough. Surely the vortex would snatch me up again, I hoped. As I neared the edge of the crowd a phalanx of hooded and cloaked beings presented themselves as a human wall, blocking my escape, so I ducked my head and moved back toward the center of the throng. Though I had my eyes on the ground before me, I kept noticing the hems of scarlet robed worshipers at the edge of my vision and I turned away again and again. Was I inadvertently moving into the devotees of Arathia instead of getting away from them as I intended? They seemed to be everywhere and I could feel my panic rising. Where was that darn portal anyway? Surely there was somewhere else I needed to be by now!

The crowd around me suddenly parted and a chorus of voices rose in exaltation. I froze in my tracks and dared to look up. To my dismay, I found myself directly before Arathia's tree throne and the sacrifice stone was mere steps ahead of me. I couldn't imagine how I'd gotten so turned around, but I realized I was precisely where I did not want to be. Strong hands grabbed me by the wrists and my hood was yanked back from my face. Suddenly I was lifted from the ground and my feet flailed and kicked uselessly in the air. Though I tried to scream I had no voice and realized I was only able to thrash about to little avail.

Arathia rose from her perch and pointed a finger in my direction. Suddenly the ground was once more beneath my feet and I struggled to gain my equilibrium without stumbling. I staggered a few steps then righted myself. Naomi's double was right beside me, one hand roughly holding the back of my neck. Zador stood beside the stone, sharp blade at the ready and a wicked, too eager, smile on his lips. Struggling against the weight and force of the hand on my neck, I tried to kick my captor's legs, step on her feet, elbow her in the gut, but she was simply too strong.

'Where are my powers? This isn't right! Why isn't the energy deep inside me stirring to come to my aid? This is wrong!' My thoughts were doing a circle dance in my head as I tried to find rhyme or reason for the scene in which I found myself. I realized I was tiring quickly, trying to fight such a greater force, so finally I stilled and drew a deep breath. Besides the left hand on the nape of my neck, a well-muscled right hand held my right wrist and I looked in confusion at my own hand. I was still me inside, but the body I now inhabited was not that of an adult female; it was apparently that of a young boy! My fingers were spatulate and the nails were

ragged. My hands were covered in grime and there were scratches caked with dried blood on my palms. Beneath the cloak I wore a simple tunic and breeches. As I was shoved to my knees the memories of my all too short life came flooding back to me. I saw my mother and father in our small but cozy home, my little sister played with a doll before the hearth on a snowy morning, and our huge horse pulled the plow before me as I struggled to balance both the leads and the awkward implement. I was James. I was 11 years old and I knew that I was about to be murdered. Terror blinded me for a moment before all the other emotions rose and I found my voice. I screamed to the sky. I screamed for mercy. I screamed in outrage and fury! I might have tried to beg for my life had there been time, but before I could draw breath and begin my appeal, Zador stepped forward, pulled me from Naomi's hands, and tossed me down before the stone. I could smell the blood of the previous victims emanating from the ground and the channel of darkness in the carved trough was clearly visible. On my knees, hands flailing in the air, head pulled roughly back by my hair, I knew what it was to be powerless, to be victim, to be sacrifice. Had my eyes not rolled back in my head, I might have caught sight of the sharp blade as it arced down before me. Had I not been so terrified, I might have felt the pressure of the edge as the knife smoothly cut from the left side of my throat to the right. Had I not already exited my body, I might have felt myself drop onto the ground as my blood rushed down the sacrifice stone and into the ewer at the end but I was beyond all of that, in the air above the scene, when the vortex finally came for me.

"Holy crow!" I gasped. "What the hell was that?" Still reeling from the emotions and memories, I shuddered as I took in my surroundings. Patches of snow lay melting amidst the rows of simple arch-topped headstones and one lonely, barren tree stood twisted and gnarled by years of harsh weather. A harbor gleamed in the distance, glowing with the light of the sun, and for a moment I couldn't tell if it was rising or setting. As I stood looking at the headstones around me, I noticed my shadow growing across the ground and realized that, wherever I was, it was morning. Wrapping my cloak tightly around my shoulders to ward off the strong wind that threatened to topple me, I hunched forward and made my way onto a small path that meandered through the cemetery. The village that lay ahead looked quaint, well-maintained, and surprisingly active for this time of day. People walked in pairs and small groups, or rushed by singularly, and I noticed their odd dress with a deep, inward groan. Their garb reminded me of what the pilgrims wore and with a sudden awareness, I stopped in my tracks and took in the details of the village. Though there was no statue of Elizabeth Montgomery in her 'Bewitched' role, I knew without question that I was in Salem, Massachusetts, and that it was the time of the Salem witchcraft trials. Ironically, I recalled the episode of the situation comedy when Samantha had been transported back to that time and was accused of witchcraft after her memories had been taken from her. Something told me that I would have no well-meaning 'Darren' to come to my aid were I thusly involved, so I raised the hood of my cloak, concentrated on the muddy ground ahead of me, and willed myself to be invisible. I could feel the denim of my jeans rubbing against my legs and the familiar and comfortable leather of my boots surrounding my feet. Touching the contours of my face and hair, I was relieved to discover that in this place and time I was once more, apparently, myself; I was Cat and hoped to remain so. Though my cloak kept me well protected from the rising sun, I noticed that in this 'reality' the solar rays caused me no discomfort and I hoped to have a moment or two to take advantage of that at some point before the vortex moved me on.

Low stone walls and split rail fences surrounded cozy cottages and two-story houses alike on either side of the well-worn, hard-packed earthen road. A cluster of bright yellow crocuses broke up the black and white appearance of the winter scene and I found myself staring at them as if they were the only real things around. The cheeriness of their color lifted my spirits and I smiled. Suddenly I was surrounded by three dark rough wood walls and before me stood a wall of iron bars. Two women huddled in the shadows behind me and just as I started to offer them words of comfort I glanced down and saw that I wasn't there. I could see as if I was looking out of my own eyes; I could hear as if I had two good ears; I could smell the acrid smoke from the oil lamps on the walls outside the cell and I could even taste the fear and desperation that wafted through the room, but I had no physical body with which to interact in this time and place. Frustration began to build in my mind as I realized that I was helpless, a mere shadow of a being, even, but that quickly gave way to fascination when the sound of heavy boots walking across the wooden floor drew my attention. The darkness was suddenly split by the light of an oil lamp on a simple wooden table on the other side of the bars. An iron key was inserted into the lock and the bar door of the cell swung open with a dry, rusty, squeal. To my amazement, Zador, dressed in early colonial attire, took three steps in, bent down, and brusquely yanked one of the women up by her elbow, pulling her away from her friend amidst sobs and pleas of innocence. His hair, now silver, was shorter and secured at his nape with a leather thong. He wore a neatly trimmed goatee, but his facial features were the same as they were in that 'other' world, the one in which I was physically his prisoner. It made sense, I suddenly realized! All the times and places I'd been taken by the vortex had been those in which Zador and his partner Naomi were busy manipulating power. They'd been doing their thing throughout history and now they were continuing their work in my 'present' day. These two were apparently more than just mere mortals who happened to find their way to worshipping Arathia. There was more…and I was hurtling through the vortex tunnel once more, no longer amazed or even surprised, though I remained curious as to where I'd land next.

The smell of warm earth and dry grass woke me. I was lying on my stomach on the ground, scorching heat pressing on my back like a massive weight. A flapping sound drew my attention and I sat up to find myself beside a dark brown canvas tent, its edges, though anchored by heavy ropes, being beaten by the warm wind. I could hear vehicles nearby and car doors being opened and shut. Struggling to my feet, I saw a grass-choked field adjacent to the tent was filling up with old fashioned cars. My knowledge of cars was limited, but from the length of the 'noses' on a few of them I'd guess they were vehicles made in the nineteen-thirties or forties. There were a few pickup trucks parked in the field and along one edge, nearest the road, stood half a dozen horse-drawn wagons, horses tethered to split-rail fence posts. Men dressed in dark suits escorted women wearing below-the-knee dresses, tailored coats, and various style hats. Children, their hands held tightly by their parents, bounced and skipped along wearing what could only be their good 'Sunday clothes'. Everyone looked hot and uncomfortable in their formal attire, but they seemed in good spirits, laughing, smiling, and greeting one another as they made their way to the tent. I brushed myself off as best I could, noticing that I was once more wearing my jeans, black Led Zeppelin t-shirt, boots, and black cloak. Certainly I was not dressed to blend in with the crowd, but if I stayed near the back of the tent where the two corner panels met, I could see and hear what was happening inside without anyone taking notice of me.

I stood near the tent, one hand holding onto the wooden support pole, for what seemed like a very long time as the crowd arrived, parked, made their way into the tent and found seats. Rows and rows of uncomfortable looking wooden folding chairs marched from one side of the tent to the other, with only a gap of four feet or so for the center aisle. Paper fans had been placed on the chairs and most of the women seated were whipping them about intensely trying to cool themselves in the festering heat. A small wooden dais had been built at the far end of the tent and beside it stood a small piano and bench. A stern looking elderly woman with gray hair braided and piled atop her head rose from her seat in the front row and made her way slowly to the bench, pulled it out, seated herself primly, and then adjusted its proximity to the keyboard until she was satisfied. At last she put her hands on the piano and began to play a ponderous hymn. A few of the seated began to sing along to the music, but as there was no choir director to lead them, their voices quickly fell silent. As the last of the chairs at the back of the tent were being taken, a man in a black suit stepped up onto the wooden dais, bible in hand. He wore a crisp white shirt with a black string tie at the throat and his dark hair was plastered back on his head. He was clean shaven, but was still easily recognizable. Zador, the evangelist, had arrived, and behind him, standing off to one side of the wooden platform, stood Naomi, her high-necked, long-sleeved, black cotton dress starched and as uncomfortable looking as anything I'd ever seen. She too had her hair pulled back from her face, drawn into a chignon at her nape, and small wire-framed glasses perched on her nose.

"Holy crow again!" I murmured at the scene, amazed at how the pair had moved through time using religion, apparently any religion, as a means to use and control others. Zador lifted the bible in his left hand and gained the audience's attention. A hush fell over the tent.

"The Lord came to me last night," he bellowed then paused for effect, "with a message for each and every one of you." The silence in the tent was palpable and beneath it simmered excitement. The flock was ready to be led and their shepherd was in rare form. As Zador lowered the bible and began to speak in a lower more relaxed voice, Naomi opened a large wooden crate that sat on the ground beside the platform and withdrew from it two large brass offering plates. Soon the fleecing would begin, as the devout dug deeply into pockets and purses in an attempt to buy their way out of sin and into Heaven. Zador paused in his introductory comments, raised his hands and invited the crowd to stand for prayer. As the audience rose, he began the plea for forgiveness, for patience and kindness, for generosity and guidance. When the 'amen' came, the woman at the piano began a hymn and everyone began to sing as the offering plates were passed from hand to hand down row after row. Two men in black suits stood at the end of the aisle on either side and made sure the plates made it safely from one row to the next without spilling. The music grew louder and a few members of the congregation began to sway on their feet, though whether it was due to the Holy Spirit or oppressive heat, I couldn't say. To my dismay, I was actually beginning to enjoy the scene when it began to fade. The music grew faint, the heat disappeared and, more gradually than before, I was once more in the portal.

Chapter 19

When my eyes fluttered open I found I was once more in my makeshift prison. My wrists were still bound by the zip tie. My body felt stiff and a bit battered. Disoriented, I struggled to sit upright, my balance having not yet returned to my physical form. The images I'd seen beyond the portal were quite fresh and vivid in my mind as I glanced around the room for evidence that the vortex had been real. A faded, ripped, and brittle looking calendar hung on the wall beside the door and a worn whisk broom lay on the floor not far from my cot. If a vortex had actually opened, as I'd experienced it in Amon's office, those things would have been pulled away from this room and deposited elsewhere. Sure, what I'd seen and experienced could have been a dream, but it all felt like much more than a mere dream. I'd felt myself moving through the corridor of energy beyond the portal; I'd even felt my body as a young boy and recalled his memories before I'd been sacrificed. I had seen, felt, smelled, and heard things in my visions, which surely meant they were more than just dreams, didn't it?

Giving up the analysis for a time, I inspected my surroundings more closely. The cot was old, its legs screwed into the metal frame that supported the springs and what passed for a mattress. If I could remove the screws from a leg I might be able to use it as a weapon, but the screws appeared snugly seated and I could find nothing suitable to use as screwdriver. For a moment I considered removing the sword pendant from around my neck and trying to loosen the screws with its blade, but I knew it was too small, the blade was too narrow, and the screws were rusted into place. It would take more than my tiny sword to move those screws. Obviously, my captors didn't think the pendant was dangerous or of any use or I'd not still be wearing it, but I lamented that the sword was not magic and capable of springing off its chain to full evil-slaying size.

My hopes soared when I got down on my hands and knees to look beneath the cot, as I saw part of a vent in the wall and immediately thought of it as an escape route. However, upon moving the bed aside, I discovered the vent was a cold air return and was maybe large enough for me to get one arm through, but no more than that. Slamming the cot back into place, hopes dashed, I pushed myself off its squeaky frame to stand on wobbly legs. Seething with frustration, I moved into the small bathroom and clicked on the lights. Sudden glare off the stained porcelain sink, ancient mirror, and pockmarked chrome fixtures made me wince for a moment until my eyes could adjust. My contacts were dry and made my eyes itch, but the thought of taking them out to rinse them off and rest my eyes made me more uneasy than bearing the discomfort. Turning on the faucet, I rubbed my hands beneath the running water then splashed my face. I wet my fingertips and ran them around the edges of my eyes in hopes of getting a little moisture beneath the contacts, but I couldn't tell if it did any good. At last I turned off the water and patted my hands and face dry on the tail of my t-shirt. Besides the shower, that looked like it might have been fashionable in nineteen-fifty, and the sink and mirror that appeared only slightly newer than that, the only other things in the room were a can of powdered cleanser and a roll of cheap toilet paper on the lid of the toilet. An ancient looped toilet brush stood propped in the corner beside the toilet tank. Two dead flies and a partially decimated moth lay on the ugly green linoleum floor, which had never been fashionable, but was clearly cheap and mostly functional.

Sighing deeply, I turned off the light and walked out of the bathroom, only to find that I was no longer alone. Naomi stood at the door, one hand resting on the door knob, the other holding a gun.

"Ah, my favorite person," I grinned. "I'm so delighted to see you and I can tell you're equally joyous over being here. Are we going somewhere again? Don't tell me, let me guess…we're having a 'girls' day out', drinks at the club, getting mani-pedis, maybe having our hair done if time allows, right?"

The woman didn't return my smile or even react to my attempt at humor. She just waved the nose of the pistol at me to indicate that I should move into the hallway and glared. Now that I had a better idea of who and what I was dealing with, my mind kicked into overdrive and it was all I could do to relax and not make my guard suspicious. Holding my hands up to prove that I was still bound, I moved past her and stopped just beyond the door to give her time to close it behind us. As before, she put her left hand on my right shoulder and firmly squeezed as she muttered "Move!"

With only moments to think and act, I waited until we moved away from the door then pretended to stumble on some imaginary object before me. Naomi's hand on my shoulder stayed put, as I'd hoped it would, and when she moved forward, almost doubling over with me, I drove my right elbow as fast and as hard as I could into her ribs. I heard her utter "Oof!" as the breath was driven from her diaphragm and the crisp snap of bones breaking gave me an obscene rush of satisfaction. Though the hand on my shoulder tightened briefly, I was able to wriggle out from under it, turn quickly and while Naomi was still bent double, drive my knee up into her nose. She screamed before the force drove her up and back, landing her with a thud on the floor. Broken nose bleeding profusely, my guard lay semi-conscious, writhing in pain and gasping for breath. She squeezed off two rounds from the gun before I could kick it out of her hand, which probably meant reinforcements were on the way so I had to make up my mind and do it fast.

Picking the gun up off of the floor, I transferred it to my left hand and used my right hand to grab Naomi's collar. The zip ties were beginning to cut into my flesh and annoy me greatly, but I was determined, committed, and frankly had no other choice but to push on. Using whatever supernatural strength of body I had, I hoisted the moaning, bleeding, woman to her feet, pushed her ahead of me, and shoved the nose of the gun into her back. I felt a bit better with the weapon in my hand and a human shield before me, and I strove to steady myself as I moved her forward.

"Now, I know you're in a great deal of pain and I'm not a cruel person," I explained as calmly as possible. "Take me to Zador and I'll let you go tend to your wounds."

"Ashh chew whish," she wheezed, one hand cradling her ribs and the other trying to catch the blood streaming from her nose.

As we moved down the narrow hallway, the scent of the woman's blood reached my nose and hunger reared its ugly head. I had no idea when I'd last fed, but I forced myself to ignore the pangs and tend to the situation at hand. The image of me sinking my teeth into her neck, drinking my fill, and then ripping out her throat did dance around in my head, briefly, before I finally managed to shake it off. I was not about to start a blood frenzy.

To my surprise, no one came running at the sound of the gunshots, no one raced to Naomi's defense, and we made the short trip to Zador's office unchallenged. When we stepped into the room I understood why no other guards had responded, two lay bleeding and unconscious, or dead, on the floor, and Zador stood behind his desk with a stricken look on his face. A man with brown hair pulled back into a pony tail long enough to just touch his back had the priest in a restraining hold, arms pinned behind his back, elbows locked. His charcoal gray suit strained across his back and broad shoulders and the navy tie at his chest hung loose on his crisp white dress shirt. Another man, silver hair cropped military style, stood before the desk wiping blood from his mouth with the back of his hand. His black suit was impeccably tailored and was, I suspected, Italian and expensive. Narrow satin lapels accented the cut of the single breasted jacket, and the black shirt and tie beneath made an understated yet dramatic statement. For a moment "Cosa Nostra" went through my mind but, unless Zador was trafficking in more than just magic, that made no sense. With sudden clarity I realized what was happening and I knew what and who the newcomers were. Both men were vampires and I knew without question that the brunette who held Zador was Sabre. How I knew that the other vampire was Cesare, Amon's sire, was not clear, but that he was rang loud and true to me. His features were sharp and his dark eyes were piercing. He had the look of a bird of prey and I took an immediate dislike to him, a personal one in addition to the one I harbored for him for what he'd done to Amon.

"Crap!" I uttered as I realized freedom was not as close as I'd hoped.

"Ah, and the guest of honor arrives at the most opportune moment," Sabre looked me in the eye and smiled. "It is good to see that you are no longer a prisoner, My Lady Passion. Allow me to introduce myself, I am…"

"Sabre," I finished his sentence. "I know who you are. And I know who you are, Cesare." I turned to the more menacing looking man before the desk and nodded succinctly. "Though I am confused as to how it is you're here and what you have to do with Arathia's priest."

"This?" Sabre laughed, released Zador's arms, grabbed the priest's head and snapped his neck with a twist. "I have nothing to do with this sycophant. Cesare and I came to rescue you, of course."

"Rescue me," I brightened. "Hallelujah! I'm not one to look a gift horse in the mouth, but how did you even know where I was or that I was being held prisoner? The Council has been searching for you since you disappeared after your beloved Thea died." It wasn't that I didn't want to believe the vamp before me, I truly did, but that small quiet voice that often got overruled by logic and reason would not be shushed. She wasn't just giving me a gentle warning, she wasn't yelling or screaming in alarm, she was banging a gong loud enough to render me deaf momentarily until I accepted her insights.

"Beloved Thea," he shook his head and laughed again. "Ah yes, my beloved witch. Let's just say that relationship didn't work out as planned."

"Didn't work out as planned," I gaped at his surprising response and another sudden insight. "You didn't love her! You set her up! Why? What possible reason could you have had to play her as you obviously did?

She loved you enough to kill herself for you! Why did you use her?"

"My, my," he chuckled at me, "you certainly do live up to your name. Passion indeed! And what a romantic you must be. Surely you can see how my darling Thea and I could have replicated you and your Master Vampire? The power you two share is amazing and I wanted it, no, I deserved it! Things just didn't work out as I'd expected."

"You're not even sorry she's dead," I shuddered at his indifference. "You never loved her at all, did you?"

"I loved what I hoped she and I could create," he shrugged, "but no, alas, I did not love her. Love is for the weak."

A sudden vision blinded me for a moment as Thea appeared, bowed her head, and gave me a look of silent understanding. I knew that I'd been released from my promise to protect her beloved Sabre and I sighed in relief as my sight returned to normal. Wondering if Thea's ghost had touched me and somehow accessed my new ability, I had little time to ponder the matter and forced it to the back of my mind.

"So...you knew I was here how?" I looked with suspicion at first one vampire then the other.

"We have our ways," Sabre responded with grin. "Let's just say that we've control over creatures that know things and these creatures live to serve us, to make us happy."

"I'm sure," I grimaced at the mental image. "So, let's go! You can take me back to the estate now. I can't wait to get home!"

When no one moved I looked from one vampire to the other, then Cesare stepped forward and pulled Naomi away from me. She whimpered pathetically as the vampire sank his teeth into her neck then she fell silent. It took mere moments for Cesare to drain her completely and drop her empty husk of a body on the floor.

"First," Sabre bowed theatrically then straightened and kicked the large sheet of glass that held Arathia's form. Her image shattered as easily and as completely as the glass and she was just...gone. "Now we have some business of our own to complete," he turned to me.

"Did you know that Thea begged me to protect you," I tried to change the subject as the dark haired vampire drew near, "and that I agreed to do so? Did you know your sirelings have come to me for protection?"

"And you're doing such an excellent job," he laughed as I pointed the gun at his head. "You would shoot your rescuers? How rude is that?" He kept moving toward me, his dark eyes never leaving mine, pacing like a feline about to pounce. "And you know that gun won't stop me. It might slow me down, but that would only make me angry and as we've just met it would be impolite to make me angry, don't you think?"

"So," I said unsteadily, "what do you want?"

"You, my dear," he bowed gallantly, "are going to be my bargaining chip. Amon won't dare take action against me if I have you in my possession and when he discovers that Cesare and I rescued you he'll fall all over himself to keep the Council from punishing me for the unfortunate incident with that other witch."

"Are you serious?" I managed to utter just as he reached out and snatched the gun from my hand.

"Quite serious, love," he smiled wide and took my elbow. "Come, let us leave this place."

"If you're not taking me home, where are we going?" I tried in vain to yank my arm from his grasp. I wasn't sure his touch on my arm was enough but I focused and opened my mind to Sabre's. I realized as I did so that I'd not experienced anything when Naomi had touched my shoulder, but then again I'd not actually opened myself to her so I was hoping intent was the linchpin to this ability. Like a key slipping into a lock and turning, or the first domino in the line falling forward, as soon as I focused Sabre's memories were mine. I saw scenes from his childhood as well as when his sire made him vampire. I felt the elation that he experienced when he made his first kill. I tasted the blood that he savored, heard the rapid thud of the hearts of his victims, felt the bitter-sweet remorse when the feeding was done and his prey lay empty. Visions of his time with Thea moved through my mind and I knew the hunger he had for power, the jealousy of Amon and me burning in his cold, unbeating heart. His thoughts and memories gave me an idea of just how far he would go to get what he wanted and I realized that he literally had nothing to lose.

"Out of the frying pan into the fire," I murmured as I finally broke the link to Sabre's memories and looked into his face. Oh yes, this was one seriously rabid dog and I was at his mercy, for a time anyway. I'd have to be careful, watch my words and actions, so as to not set him off. As he was Master Vampire, I wasn't sure if he could tell if I was trying to contact my mate or not, but I'd not risk it for now. Inwardly, I chuckled that I now looked forward to being alone in a cell, even one as spare as the one from which I'd just escaped. '*This keeps getting better and better!*'

"Sabre," Cesare called out as my captor started dragging me toward the door, "keep your head straight. You forgot this!" A projectile arced through the air and Sabre caught it easily with his left hand, his right hand still clutching my elbow firmly.

"What's that?" I blurted out the question before thinking and was surprised when he turned and looked at me, a look of dominance and glee on his face.

"That, Princess," he smiled broadly and opened his hand so I could see, "is your blood. I'll bet you didn't even know Dr. Feel-good and his girlfriend had harvested it from you, did you?"

"My what?" I touched my throat with my fingertips, but there was no mark there, neither needle nor tooth had broken the skin. Drawing my hands away, I extended my arms and, sure enough, there in the bend of my left elbow was a needle mark, barely visible. "That son of a motherless goat…" I swore but Sabre's laugh cut me off.

"Don't worry, My Lady," he chuckled, "your blood is safe with me for now."

That 'for now' did nothing to reassure me that what lay ahead was going to be a day at the beach for me. In fact, my power was beginning to stir uneasily in my gut, so I knew what was coming would require not only my attention but my magic.

"Now, I know that as Amon's mate and vampire you're capable of flight," Sabre offered, "but I'm sure you'll understand if we insist that you be accompanied by Cesare or myself. I'm in a genial mood so I'll let you decide. Would you prefer to fly with me or your mate's sire?"

I felt like I'd been handed a ticking time bomb. The thought of flying with either one of the vampires made my skin crawl and my stomach lurch, but of the two Cesare was the more troublesome entity to me. Sabre's energy was more blatant, his ego wouldn't let him conceal anything, but Amon's sire hid much. He spoke little, but his eyes gave away his thoughts and they were neither kind nor good. The dilemma, as I saw it, was whether or not Sabre was being straight with me or testing my mettle. I had to play a hunch.

"Cesare," I lifted my chin, squared my shoulders, and nodded at the vampire across the room. "I'll fly with him."

"Indeed?" Sabre brayed like a donkey, "Princess, I am crushed!"

"You asked," I raised one eyebrow at him.

"I did," he leered, "and I lied. You're flying with me."

Propelling me forward with one hand on my elbow and the other on the back of my neck, Sabre guided me up a short flight of steps to a door I'd not previously noticed. Cesare, ahead of us, opened the heavy stone door and stepped outside. Sabre pushed me through and followed me into the darkness. Glancing over my shoulder, I realized that we'd escaped through a stone crypt into what appeared to be a very old cemetery. I truly had no idea where I was or where I'd been.

"What was that place?" I gaped at the ornate but neglected crypt.

"Just a place," Sabre replied and then added, "but if you must know it was once part of a rather successful and lucrative smuggling operation. As is where we're headed for that matter, but that smuggling is no more."

"What time is it," I whispered, "in fact, what day is it, or what night is it?"

"Thursday morning," Sabre answered absently as he turned me and tucked me under his arm, "just past midnight, if it's of any importance."

"I lost track of time," I murmured, more to myself than to my captor. "I don't know how long Zador had me."

"No matter now, My Lady," Sabre wrapped his arms around me, "time to go."

"Wait," I froze in his embrace, "if I have to fly with you I need to turn around. The lights hurt my eyes in this position."

"Ah yes," he lowered his mouth and whispered into my ear, "I've heard about your eyes. By all means, turn around."

Closing my eyes, I tried to hold myself as far away from Sabre's body as I possibly could, but flying tandem required a certain amount of bodily contact. The Master Vampire held me in his embrace, his arms pinning my arms to my side, my bound wrists and hands lowered to an area on his anatomy that I had no intentions of touching. I laced my fingers together so any contact would be clearly understood as accidental and unavoidable. I would not hide my face in his lapel as I did with my beloved when we flew together. I was torn between wanting to appear experienced and powerful when it came to flying and wanting to whoops my cookies all over his exquisitely tailored shirt and pants. As I'd not consumed any sustenance for several days the latter was not likely, but a part of me vehemently wished it otherwise.

Without further comment, we rose into the night sky and I felt the earth's gravity pull at my body, felt the wind whip my hair around my head. Sabre's heart did not beat, nor did his body feel warm, but he had the annoying habit of humming as he flew and I spent the remainder of the journey trying to identify the tune and wishing for all I was worth that he'd just shut up.

Chapter 20

When at last we landed, I managed to keep from tumbling as my feet touched the ground and Sabre released me as we both righted ourselves. A row of shoreline promenade lamps cast rivers of light on the water before us and the scent of swamp hung heavy in the air. A gator, a few feet away, took exception at our arrival and slithered into the water with a smack of his heavy tail.

"Smell that air," Sabre lifted his face to the sky and pretended to breathe in deeply. Before I could respond, he was upon me, yanking my hair aside and opening his mouth wide, about to sink his teeth into my throat. So startled was I that I couldn't even move or call out, but that didn't mean the world went silent. On the contrary, the howling that rose into the night was deafening and the screeching that fell from the sky was equally strident. Amon's pack, his wolves, felt I was in immediate peril. My owls likewise knew what I was experiencing and they responded as only they could.

"Sabre!" Cesare was suddenly beside us and brusquely tore the other vampire from me. "Have you lost your mind? Do you hear that? Her creatures have sent up the alarm and it will be no time before Amon and his men are here. If you can't keep your mouth off of her throat, you're going to ruin everything!"

"I do what I want, old man," the younger vampire roared. "And I don't care about her mate. By the time he gets here, I could have her drained and be gone."

"And then what?" Cesare reasoned, "Are you going to spend the rest of eternity on the run? All for the taste of witch blood?"

"It's more than that," Sabre licked his lips. "I know it's so much more than that!"

"It doesn't matter," his cohort quipped. "You've got the vial, that's enough. Now let's get going before our whereabouts become common knowledge. The boat's tied to the dock, let's move!"

Still stunned, I blinked repeatedly and shook my head to clear my mind. Clarity would not return and I had no strength to resist my captors, so I stumbled along between Sabre and Cesare, each of them holding an elbow. Water slapping beneath the short dock echoed in my ringing ears and when Sabre let go of me to untie the boat, I had to grab onto Cesare's hand to steady myself. He startled at my touch and froze when he looked into my eyes. I had no way of knowing what he was seeing, but what I saw just past him brought great joy to my heart. Behind the vampire, along the shore and in the distance on the horizon, wolves moved stealthily toward us. In the night sky, owls soared and banked on the wind, offering silent witness to my plight. It seemed the other vampires did not see what I was watching, or they were too distracted by other matters to care, but I was heartened to think that somewhere out there my beloved Amon was learning of my whereabouts and the details of what was happening to me. Then, as I looked back at Cesare, I noticed his expression was one of... it took me a moment to recognize it, but he appeared to be in a stupor. His dark eyes were wide and shimmered with shafts of silver light, his mouth and jaw were slack.

"Cesare!" Sabre barked sharply at the vampire before me and, with what seemed to be great effort, Cesare finally shook himself and blinked at me. Grumbling something incoherent beneath his breath, he turned me roughly and pushed me toward the end of the dock where Sabre stood in the boat holding onto one of the steel piles that anchored the pier.

"Get in," Cesare commanded and I knew that whatever he'd experienced looking at me, he'd not leave himself open to in the future. Wrists still zip-tied together, I squatted, then turned as gracefully as possible, and sat on my right hip. Sabre swung my legs around and pulled me forward into the boat, then guided me to the middle bench seat and helped me down.

"So, why the boat? Why didn't we just fly to where we're going?" I blurted out abruptly, as the questions suddenly leapt into my mind. Unfortunately, the tact and diplomacy editor in my brain wasn't always on duty and when she was away my mouth was free to get me into trouble.

Cesare climbed in after me and took the seat in the prow.

"Some vampires lack the ability to fly over salt water," he answered, trying to hide a grimace as he glanced at his younger partner. "Vampires' abilities are varied. Master Vampires have more than others, but abilities do vary."

Somewhere in my befuddled mind, I grasped that Cesare was alluding to the fact that Sabre, though Master Vampire, couldn't fly over salt water. I found this curious because Amon had explained to me that Cesare was not Master Vampire and he seemed to be implying that he was more than able to perform this feat. It had never occurred to me to wonder what powers or abilities different vamps enjoyed, I just figured there were standard things that all vamps could do, and perhaps I was wrong!

Sabre started the outboard motor at the stern without comment. Two sharp tugs on the rope and the engine roared to life. He turned the boat away from the shore and we were soon racing over the water's surface into the early morning, away from the lights of civilization and any hope I had of escape.

The drone of the outboard motor was broken only by the insistent slapping of the waves on the hull of the boat. Had communication been necessary between us we'd have had to yell, so I hoped the noise and vibration would cloak my actions as I steeled myself, closed my eyes, and sent my thoughts in search of Amon. Lowering my head so my captors might think I was fighting sea sickness, I opened my mind to my beloved and this time I was rewarded.

'Catherine! Where are you? I have searched for you!

'My love, I don't know where I am. I am in a boat on sea water, but I've no idea where.'

'You are weak. You have not fed!'

'I don't remember the last time I fed. I've lost track of time.'

'In your weakened state I cannot feel your whereabouts. Can you see anything around you that might be used as a landmark?'

As I raised my head to look around, Cesare pinned me with a glance and I just had time to realize he knew something was afoot before he called out to Sabre.

"She's doing something!" He leaned sideways so he could see his partner behind me. "Get us to safety now!"

"We're nearly there," Sabre replied and pulled me back by the shoulder so he could speak into my ear. "I suggest you refrain from doing whatever it is you were doing. I'd prefer not to injure you, but I will do what I must do to see that things go as planned. Understand? Nod if you understand, My Lady,"

Nodding as clearly as was possible, I closed my mind to my beloved Amon and hoped that our brief communication was sufficient to at least point him and the security team in my direction.

In the distance a shadow in the darkness loomed and grew larger as we made our approach. The silhouette of a massive structure rose from the water like a leviathan, and as we got closer, I could see that it was a very old plantation house perched on a small island, surrounded by water and completely cut off from civilization.

Sabre throttled the outboard down and we slowed to make a sharp turn around an outcropping of stone and weeds, then idled into what could best be described as a shallow cave.

"Home sweet home," Sabre smiled as he maneuvered the boat to a narrow dock running along a concrete bulkhead. "Smuggler's home, to be more exact, but the smugglers are long gone, the owners of the place dead and buried, and even the family cemetery and crypt were reclaimed by the water decades ago. This is what's left, but it serves our purpose nicely."

"Very homey," I grumbled as I looked around the moss and mold-covered dirt and stones. A path led from the dock up a slight incline between weatherworn boulders and disappeared beyond. Mold-covered, corroded oil lamps hung from pegs that had been driven into the stone walls of the cave, but neither Sabre nor Cesare moved to use them. I stepped out of the boat and onto the dock with as much grace as I could muster with my wrists still bound as Sabre led the way and Cesare fell in behind me.

"You know, I'm not likely to try to escape," I offered to whichever vamp would take heed, "and I'd be a lot less troublesome if you'd cut these zip ties off my wrists. It's not like I'd try to leap into the water and outswim the gators, you know!"

At first Sabre didn't slow his pace but kept moving ahead, then finally he paused and turned to look back at me.

"You're not going to try anything if I remove your bonds," he looked at me pointedly, "and you will do as we tell you to when we tell you to do so?"

"Scout's honor," I held up three fingers of my right hand, as I could only guess at the Boy Scout's salute. "I mean, you've got me, you've got my blood, it's clear that you're in charge so if I ever hope to see my mate again I have to play along, right?"

"Play along," Sabre parroted as he pulled a small pocket knife from his pants pocket.

"Wait," Cesare chimed in and not for the first time did I wish him painful bodily harm, "are you sure you should release her? We don't know what kind of powers she has, for all we know she could hurl lightning bolts with those hands!"

"Dang!" I laughed, "You've nailed it! You've uncovered my super dooper secret power. That's it! I hurl lightning bolts. Zeus and I used to practice from Mount Olympus. Ah, the good old days…" Sure, my theatrics were a bit over the top, but then again, I wasn't out to impress anyone; I was just trying to drive home my point.

"I think we can be reasonably sure," Sabre replied to his partner, "that could she hurl lightning bolts she'd have done so by now. Meager zip ties probably wouldn't have stopped her." Flipping open the blade of the pocket knife, he grasped my right hand with his left and slipped the sharp edge beneath the plastic tie, snapping it easily. I yanked my hands away from his and immediately began to rub my wrists. The deep red grooves would take some time to disappear, but I didn't mind. I was free!

"Come on, this way," he nodded as he closed the knife and slipped it back into the front pocket of his pants.

It was easier to walk with my hands free, more comfortable to move with my center of gravity back where it should be. Finally unbound, I relaxed and even realized I was curious about the tiny island and the house perched upon it. The term 'rundown' would be a kindness for the dilapidated two story home. What was keeping it from collapsing into a heap of rubble escaped me. Maybe it was just intent on continuing its existence like some elderly, disease-ridden matriarch who refused to go to her heavenly reward simply because her will was indomitable or she was just too freakin' cantankerous. The railing along the second story balcony was broken, hanging, and swinging dangerously in the slight breeze. Broken shingles lay scattered on what was once the front lawn, but which was now an overgrown weed-choked tangle. Windows on either side of the front door were covered by weathered sheets of plywood and the wide planks of the front porch floor were broken in several places. I started to go up the wide stone steps, expecting to enter the place despite its wretched condition, but Sabre turned back and looked at me, shaking his head.

"Not there," he offered. "We go in this way."

Beyond the front stairwell and just around the corner of the porch, narrow cobblestone steps led down to an all but invisible door. Sabre extracted a key from his pocket, slipped it into a padlock suspended on a shiny new-looking swivel hasp door lock. He removed the padlock, hung it on the metal loop, and swung the door open. A soft blue light pulsed from within and, though it offered little in the way of illumination, it was encouraging that there was, at least, electricity in the cellar. Well, I assumed it was a cellar.

Sabre stepped aside and gestured with a grand wave of one arm that I should enter first. I nodded and moved as carefully as possible into the underground chamber. The floor, highly polished concrete and completely out of place, dropped away slightly from the threshold so naturally I entered with my usual grace. As I stumbled forward, pin wheeling my arms for balance, Sabre grabbed me and steadied me.

"You are weak," he observed. "You need to feed."

"I'm very particular about what I consume," I grumbled as I pulled away from his grasp.

"Relax, My Lady," he nodded with a mischievous grin, "I have just the thing for you." He turned and called out, "Ian!"

From the darkness of a hallway across the room a figure appeared. When he stepped into the softly lit room the man bowed officiously and looked at Sabre.

"Master Sabre," he addressed the vampire with something akin to delight, a reaction that disturbed and confused me, "how may I be of service?"

"My Lady Passion," Sabre gestured that sweeping arm in my direction, "must feed. See to it."

"Of course, Master Sabre," he smiled broadly and turned to me. "I am Ian. I am happy to serve you."

I looked uneasily at the willing young man, strong, well-muscled and attractive though he appeared. I knew that Sabre was a Master Vampire, but apparently Ian considered him much more!

"You're going to erase his memory before you release him?" I turned to Sabre, my mind spinning.

"Master Sabre is not going to release me," Ian interjected brightly.

"Ian is not being held here against his will, Princess," Sabre chuckled. "He may come and go as he pleases, but he is loyal to me and he remains here."

"Why?" I couldn't hide my skepticism, "Why would anyone stay here so you can feed..." My thoughts suddenly slid down a hill and I didn't like what I saw at the bottom. "Wait, are you?"

"Yes, Master Sabre has promised to make me one of you," the man fairly beamed. "I'm going to become immortal."

"Oh yes," I nodded, the fog clearing, "I saw that episode of 'Buffy the Vampire Slayer'. One of her classmates is diagnosed with a fatal disease so the guy offers Buffy up to Spike in exchange for being turned into a vampire. As I recall, it didn't turn out well for the classmate. Spike had no intentions of turning him and the guy ended up ultimately really dead, not just undead. So, do you have a fatal disease or are you just in love with the concept of being a vampire?"

"Oh, I'm healthy," Ian laughed. "I have my own reasons for the deal with Master Sabre. So, how would you like to feed, from my neck, my elbow, wrist, or thigh?" At the last word of his question the young man waggled his eyebrows and winked. My concern for his safety quickly became distaste and something like a chill crawled up my spine. Feeding from his neck would put my body up against his and I had the feeling he'd enjoy that entirely too much. Though I tried to avoid the mental image of feeding on his naked thigh, my mind went there as swift and sure as an arrow. Shaking my head to clear my mind, I sighed loudly.

"Elbow, please," I answered succinctly.

Ian unbuttoned the cuff of the left sleeve of his blue chambray shirt and started folding it up his arm. It was a lovely arm, I noticed, tanned, smooth, and muscular. He strode forward, offering the appendage, and I could see his eyes light up as I took his left hand in mine and slid my right hand to cup his elbow. I had noticed long ago that vampires had a preternatural beauty about them, but Ian's beauty was natural and very human. His features were even and balanced, his nose long and straight, lips full and slightly scarlet. Dark brown curls framed his face and tumbled down the back of his collar. He was clean shaven, but a hint of stubble darkened his chin, which bore a cleft worthy of Lloyd Bridges.

Closing my eyes, I sank my teeth into the crook of his elbow and drew his blood into my mouth. It was hot, rich, and delicious and I found myself enjoying it probably more than I should have. When at last I drew away from Ian, licking my lips, my mind was clear. I felt renewed and refreshed, able to think for the first time in what felt like a long time.

"Escort our guest to her accommodations, Ian," Sabre commanded, as he and Cesare left the room. Apparently, I'd been dismissed in favor of more interesting or more pressing matters.

Ian politely offered his arm and I took it without thinking. Images of the man's past life rushed through my mind until I managed to raise my mental shields. We walked down the dimly lit corridor without further conversation, and when we reached the open door to what would be my room, he reached inside and turned on the light.

"There is an intercom on the wall by the door," he explained. "If you need anything I am at your disposal."

"I don't suppose you'd supply me with a map, a boat, and a key to the doors," I chuckled.

"No," he grinned, "but I can supply water, wine, music, reading material, anything that will make your stay here more comfortable."

"Thanks, Ian," I sighed as I stepped into my room and he closed the door behind me. I heard a crisp 'snap' as the lock was driven home. "A cup of black coffee would be great!" Calling through the closed door, I first thought I'd not been heard.

"As you wish," Ian responded. "I'll bring it right away!"

Chapter 21

My prison was not entirely uncomfortable, I realized as I looked around the room. There were, of course, no windows and the walls were stone, but it was dry and nicely decorated. There was a large, comfy looking bed with small tables on either side, each sporting a pewter based lamp with a pristine white shade. An old, but well maintained, ruby Oriental rug covered the floor beneath the bed and a similarly colored and patterned smaller rug lay before two gray fabric upholstered chairs arranged in a conversation area adjacent to the door. At first glance it appeared that I'd be doing without the comforts of a bathroom, but when I peeked behind a painted silk screen to the right of the bed I discovered an open doorway that led into an alcove with a sink, toilet, and tub. It wasn't exactly the Ritz, but it was comfortable enough. I had no plans on staying any longer than was absolutely necessary and now that I was finally alone with a clear mind, I could think and hopefully figure a way out of my current situation. A sudden insight flashed into my mind like a neon sign when I realized I felt no need to weave a ward of protection around myself, and yes, I did find that curious.

Taking a seat in the upholstered chair nearest the bed, I threw my left ankle across my right knee and sighed. My thoughts bounced from how to escape to how to alert Amon about what was going on with the occasional detour of wondering how and why Cesare was involved and replaying what had happened to Zador and Naomi. I wasn't entirely sure that coffee would help the situation but, with little recourse, I decided it was better than nothing.

"Your coffee, Ma'am," Ian announced as the door swung open. He carried a large tray upon which rested a white porcelain coffee pot, a delicate matching cup and saucer, cream and sugar, cloth napkin, and a delicate little teaspoon. He placed it on a small trolley parked against the wall and poured the steaming brew into the cup. As if a professional waiter, he draped the linen napkin over his left forearm and presented the cup and saucer to me. I carefully accepted and placed the coffee on the table between the chairs, then took the napkin and placed it on my lap.

"Thank you, Ian," I smiled, genuinely grateful.

"If that will be all?" He raised his eyebrows in question.

"Yes, thank you," I nodded. "This will be fine."

"The intercom is just by the door if you need anything else," he reminded me. "It is my job to see to your comfort."

"Understood," I responded succinctly. "Thanks again!"

He bowed slightly and backed out of the room. I heard the bolt slide smoothly into place as he locked the door and left me alone once more.

Carefully lifting the cup and saucer, I brought the steaming brew to my lips and blew gently to cool it. I had to admit that it smelled delicious, but I had no patience to wait for it to cool. Returning the cup to the table, I stood abruptly and paced. I was not anxious as much as restless. The blood I'd taken from Ian was coursing through my veins, renewing my energy and my body. I felt like there was rocket fuel in my system and it demanded release... so I paced. It occurred to me that this fresh energy might help boost my ability to contact my beloved Amon so I stopped pacing, planted my feet, and concentrated my thoughts on my mate. I sensed nothing and immediately withdrew, pulling my psychic energy back into myself. My pacing resumed.

"Wish I had a weapon," I thought aloud, "but what would I do with it? I don't want to kill these guys, morons though they may be. So, maybe I don't want a weapon, but then again...I do! I should so never leave the house unless I'm wearing my blades. I've grown complacent and this is where it's brought me."

Silence echoed around the room. My pacing continued and I found myself swinging my arms, smacking my right fist on my left palm.

"Wish I had a demon," I chuckled at the thought of releasing such energy on my captors. "Yep! That's what I need. I need me some demon." As I made my way to the table where the coffee sat cooling, a sudden image of Agathodemon appeared in my mind and I spun suddenly when I heard movement behind me. To my surprise and relief, what I'd heard was 'Wicked Little Thing' hurtling into the room and lodging its sharp tip in the wooden frame of the silk painted screen outside the bathroom.

"There you are," I cooed as I once more took in the details of the lovely blade. "I'd ask where you came from, but I doubt you'd answer me." Pulling the athame from the wood, I examined the blade and the handle making note that there was no visible damage. As I balanced it on the edge of my hand, I appreciated its weight as well as its beauty. An idea twinkled into my mind as I glanced at the door, and before I knew it, I was at the door jamb looking for hinges I might dismantle with 'Wicked Little Thing'. Starting at the floor on one side and following the arched jam all the way to the floor on the opposite side, I found three hinges. To my disappointment and dismay, they were inset hinges with no way for even the small sharp tip of the athame's blade to reach them. Anger quickly usurped disappointment and I turned and hurled the blade across the room where it once more lodged itself into the silk screen frame. Wicked Little Thing vibrated briefly as the force that had driven its point into the wood dissipated. I sighed as my anger and frustration disappeared almost as quickly.

"So, I'm not escaping through that door," I reasoned aloud, "but there's got to be another way. Maybe there's a weak spot in the stone wall or an air vent or something." I looked around the room with renewed hope and started to systematically inspect every inch of my prison. I moved furniture, I moved rugs, I moved everything that stood between me and the walls but my search was in vain.

"Maybe the bathroom," I snapped my fingers and moved the silk screen back against the wall, exposing the carved arched entrance. As I turned on the overhead light my eyes quickly scanned the room, searching for any possible means of escape or anything that might be hiding said means. There was actually very little in the room. A simple toilet sat with its back against the wall on the right, a small carved shower stall with a tiny drain in the floor stood partially hidden behind an ugly psychedelic print shower curtain on the far wall, and a small sink and mirror occupied the wall to the left. My meager hopes were dashed once more when I realized that the mirror was not a medicine cabinet that was set into the wall, one which I could remove and slip through the hole in the wall behind it, but merely a framed mirror suspended on a bolt by a wire. My search beneath the sink proved futile as well as the only holes in the wall and floor were those for the waterlines and drains, all much too small and currently filled with difficult to remove obstacles. At last I found the ventilation ducts, which were indeed open and accessible, but were long, horizontal, and set into the walls just below the edge of the carved and rounded ceiling. If I stood on my tiptoes I might be able to slide my hand into one, but that was probably all that would fit. Sighing in defeat, I switched the light off and left the bathroom, pausing only long enough to retrieve Wicked Little Thing from the silk screen frame.

"Well, that sucks," I shrugged my shoulders and stretched my neck. "How can I use you to escape, Wicked Little Thing? As you've suddenly come to my aid I assume there's a reason." Chuckling at my own absurdity, I placed the tip of the athame against the pad of my index finger and twisted it gently. "No doubt about it, you are one seriously sharp knife. I should apologize for ever having thought you a mere letter opener." As I slipped the knife into the shaft of my boot, and pulled the leg of my jeans down over it, I wondered if it would be there when and if I needed it.

Dropping into the upholstered armchair beside the table, I crossed my legs and drummed my fingers on my thigh. I picked up the coffee cup, peered at the cold brew, and returned it to the saucer.

"This just keeps getting better," I moaned at the coffee and at my current circumstances.

"*You are witch*!" A deep voice seemed to come from no specific direction, it just echoed around the room, or maybe, I considered, it was just in my head. I froze in hopes that the speaker would appear and clarify the statement. Nothing happened as the seconds ticked by.

"*You are witch*!" The words came again, reverberating into silence.

"Yeah, well, I'm a lot of things. Okay, I'm witch. I'm also vampire, I'm Celtic fiddler, and I'm one seriously ticked off entity at the moment!" I spoke to the empty room, feeling a bit foolish for doing so.

Glancing once more at the cup of cold coffee on the occasional table beside my chair, I had what I hoped was a spark of inspiration. Snapping my fingers, I rushed to the intercom in the wall near the door and stabbed the 'talk' button.

415

"Ian," I called, trying to sound business-like, "are you there?"

There was a brief pause, some static crackled through the speaker, then the clear, masculine voice of my appointed servant.

"I'm here, Ma'am," he replied brightly. "How may I help you?"

"My coffee got cold," I sighed theatrically, hoping my angst would be clear through the mechanical contraption, "so could you bring me some that's fresh and hot?"

"The coffee that's in the carafe on the trolley is cold too?" He queried.

"Well, yeah," I chuckled, "it's not really cold but it's not as hot as I like it. Do you mind?"

"Of course," he answered. "I'll be right there. Is there anything else you wish?"

"Just coffee," I quipped and released the button on the intercom. I'd considered telling Ian that I wasn't feeling well and that I'd be lying down to rest, but I wasn't sure how much he actually knew about vampires and if he was aware that we seldom are affected by the minor physical complaints that humans endure. Instead, I pulled the pillows off the bed, yanked the comforter back, and put them end to end before pulling the comforter back up. I plumped the pillows and rearranged the bed clothes until it looked something like a person might be sleeping there, then crossed the room. Hoisting the heavy lamp from the table, I grabbed the electric cord and snapped the plug out of the outlet. Turning the weighted base up, I dropped the shade to the floor, and held the neck of the lamp between my hands as one would a baseball bat. Placing my back to the wall, I waited silently. I waited, and I waited, I tapped my toe in impatience, and waited some more.

"What's taking so long?" I murmured to myself. "Did he have to go to Columbia to meet Juan Valdez to get coffee beans? Is he walking back from South America with a burlap bag of coffee slung over his shoulder? Sheesh!"

As the moments ticked by I considered many possible outcomes to the situation, and even took time to determine my best reactions in various circumstances, but I soon admitted that such thoughts were folly. There was only so much my mind could fathom so rather than try to foresee possible futures, I let my imagination run free.

Cloaked completely in black and wedged, spider-like, in the slightly rounded corner above the door, Ninja Cat waited silently and motionless. Her eyes and mind alert to everything, she waited for her prey to enter the lair. When Ian stepped into the room, she leapt onto his back, uttering not so much as a grunt as she grabbed his chin, yanked his head sharply sideways, and broke his neck with a resounding 'snap'. Ninja Cat then gracefully floated to the floor, handily catching the tray of coffee and china service without spilling a drop. She then calmly placed the tray on the bed, poured herself a scant cup of the dark brew, and removed the black scarf that had hidden her pale skin before imbibing the aromatic coffee. Considering the broken form of Ian lying crumpled on the floor, Ninja Cat felt not a twinge of remorse, knowing that deep in her heart she'd done no more than precisely what had been necessary and that she'd done it expertly. Above admiring her work, Ninja Cat emptied her coffee cup, returned it to the tray, and then made her escape, careful to turn out the lights and close and lock the door behind her.

How I wished I was Ninja Cat when the door finally opened. To my delight, and as I'd hoped, Ian was distracted trying to balance and carry the tray of coffee, and he paused just inside the room, his attention drawn to the pillows piled on the bed. Silently, I stepped forward and swung the heavy lamp at the back of his head, feeling only a slight pang of guilt at my actions. A slight miscalculation on my part brought the base of the lamp ricocheting off the wall behind me and the added force caused the poor man to actually be lifted from the floor and flung forward on contact. The sound of the lamp cracking against his skull preceded the crash of china and splash of coffee on the polished stone floor by mere seconds. Ian went down face first without a sound.

"Ninja Cat would have done better," I sighed at the mess.

I did feel remorse, for a moment at least, then recovered the lamp, yanked the cord free, and used it to bind the man's hands behind his prone form. I'd not intended to do him any permanent damage and I hoped that I'd just knocked him out, but I couldn't take the chance that he might recover sooner than expected and sound the alarm before I'd made my escape. I ripped a strip of sheet from the bed and bound his mouth, in case he woke up and tried to call out for help. On sudden impulse, I touched Ian's shoulder and opened my mind to his. At first there was only darkness, then I saw Sabre's face and felt Ian's joyful expectation. I sensed his distrust and fear of Cesare and his confusion and even awe of me, then his memories opened and I tumbled through his past. I'd no intentions of plowing through his experiences and willed myself to take a mental 'step back' and stop. Moving slowly through the images of his mind toward the most recent, I watched him move from the kitchen on the ground floor of the crumbling mansion to the underground level and the room in which I'd been held before releasing his shoulder and breaking our connection. It took a moment for my mind to clear and my vision to return to normal. I looked around the room, hoping to find something, anything, which might aid me. I had Wicked Little Thing in my boot, I reminded myself, and that would have to be enough, apparently.

Moving to the slightly opened door, I listened for movement down the hallway but heard nothing. As Ninja Cat had, I turned off the light then closed and locked the door behind me as I stepped into the corridor. Now to make my escape!

The carved stone corridor was dark, illuminated only by pale, pulsing blue lights near the floor reflecting gently in the highly polished stone floor. Keeping my right hand free in case I needed to quickly withdraw Wicked Little Thing from the shaft of my boot, I guided myself along with the palm of my left hand touching the wall. Somewhere in the distance, unknown equipment beeped, whirred, and whooshed, making a strange electronic orchestration, and I did my best to determine from where the 'music' came in hopes of avoiding it. I reasoned that my captors would most likely be where the power and electronics were, though of course I had little on which to base my theory. It was blind hope, I admitted with a grin.

When I'd exited my 'prison' I'd turned to my right, thinking it was from that direction I'd 'seen' Ian's memories unfold and expecting to reach the steps leading up to the kitchen above at some point. As I followed the dimly lit corridor I soon came to realize that I'd made an error either in trusting Ian's memories or in my ability to interpret them, as I walked far enough that I should have reached those steps but had not. Several possibilities crossed my mind at once. First, it could be that Ian just had a faulty memory or bad sense of direction. Secondly, it could be that his connection to Sabre somehow cloaked, or at any rate affected, his perceptions so that his memories would be of no help in my escape, though I was unsure of just how much Sabre knew of my powers. This possibility seemed highly unlikely as this 'new' ability of mine had only just made itself known, so logically Sabre could not have armed his minion against it. Thirdly, and most distressing to me, it could be that I tapped into not memories but imaginings. Though my newly acquired 'gift' had thus far granted me access to memories, perhaps it was still evolving and now I was getting into imagination rather than actual memories. Had I read somewhere at some time that memories and imaginings were stored in the same place in the brain? Or was that memories and dreams? Shaking myself out of my musings, I squared my shoulders to focus on the issue at hand.

"Crap," I whispered, pausing with my back against the corridor wall. Now I could only hope to stumble upon the exit on my own or find somewhere to hide before the alarm went up and the place was a riot of goons looking for me. My plan was quickly dissolving!

With no alternative, I kept moving slowly along the corridor, left hand moving along the wall to steady and to reassure myself. I had always maintained that I was never lost so long as I kept moving, so on I went. Glancing back over my shoulder to make sure no one was following, I suddenly realized my left hand was touching nothing. Stopping short, I waved my hand around in the darkness for a moment before I realized it was an open doorway. My hopes soared at the thought that perhaps beyond this archway of stone steps might lead to the kitchen and my freedom.

In but a moment my eyes adjusted and welcomed the total darkness, my vision now keen with no glaring or pulsing lights to disrupt it. I could clearly see, unfortunately, that the steps I'd hoped would lead me upstairs to freedom instead were going down to yet another lower floor. I could feel cool, damp air rushing by my face and I noticed an oddly familiar and somewhat unpleasant scent riding the soft breeze. Wrinkling my nose, I stepped quickly down the stone steps counting them as I went. Thirteen steps, I counted, thinking it was fortunate that I wasn't superstitious once I stood beyond them. The darkness here was absolute and would have been impenetrable for mortal creatures, but to me it was comforting and soothing. The smell, however, was more pungent and more insistent. What was that smell?

Just to my right there shimmered dark script seemingly suspended in mid-air and I knew that it would be invisible to anyone else unless illuminated by overhead lights. Curious what it was doing there, I realized that it was actually separated into several panels, five distinctly different panels, in fact. Without conscious thought I began to read the script aloud, then stopped suddenly when I realized what the spell was, and that indeed it was a spell. The words were ancient, yet I recognized them and could smoothly verbalize the magic. The words were a trap, as strong and as unyielding as a door of iron bars.

"Little witch," a voice hissed from behind one of the panels.

Smacking my forehead with my palm, I suddenly realized why the scent in the room was so familiar.

"Snarl," I sighed. "Is that you?"

"Yessssss," the demon's voice reverberated around the room.

"What is this place," I asked, "and how is it you're here?"

"Release me," the dragon insisted, "and we shall discuss matters."

"I don't know," I paused, shrugging in the darkness. "I'm not sure that's such a great idea."

"Release me," Agathodemon raised his voice.

Considering things further, I realized that the dragon demon might be in the very situation from which I'd just escaped and hoped to escape further. How Sabre had come to trap the dragon demon and why...piqued my curiosity.

"Promise me that you'll behave if I let you out?"

"I will behave, little witch," he replied. "I promise, Cat!"

"You'll not hurt me," I clarified, "and you'll not even try to hurt me?"

"I promise, Cat," the timbre of his voice dropped and he almost purred, "I promise!"

Once more I began to verbalize the ancient words on the panels, reading from right bottom to top left of the first panel then up and down through the other four, unweaving the spell. Each panel, in turn, began to dissolve then collapse to the stone floor, its energy dissipating. Suddenly the room was awash in bright lights and I was forced to close my eyes tightly against the assault. Rough hands, no, not hands, rough claws grabbed my arms just above the elbows and beneath my ribs. My feet kicked uselessly as I was hoisted aloft.

"Snarl!" I called out above the sound of hissing and slithering movement. "Snarl, you said you wouldn't hurt me! You're going back on your word!"

"Little witch," the dragon demon cooed as he neared me. "I am not hurting you. I can't make promises for my brothers and sisters, however."

At the mention of sisters I stopped moving momentarily and opened my eyes to peer around at the other Agathodemon surrounding me. I'd never seen a female dragon demon, and in dragon form I wasn't sure I'd be able to recognize one, but a bit of side by side comparison and it was clear which gender was which. The males in the group, two besides Snarl, were his size give or take an inch, which meant they were between 6'7" and 6'10" tall. The other two, obviously female, were not only larger, they were taller! The shorter of the two had to have been at least 8 ft. tall and both females hunched over with their backs touching the stone ceiling. They looked neither comfortable nor pleased.

"Snarl, please," I gasped in the overwhelming stench of Sulphur, "remember the LeqonOrb, remember the quicksilver! I gave you a gift, remember?"

"I do remember, Cat," he sighed, "and it was tasty fare, but the Agathodemon holding you received no such gift, so they have no qualms with dispatching your body and taking your power."

"Wait, wait," I struggled against the demons that held me, "there must be something we can barter."

"Do you have more quicksilver in your pocket or can you draw it out of the air?" Snarl licked a strand of drool from the corner of his mouth. In human form he appeared socialized, even suave, but in dragon form, well, he was all dragon. He clicked long, sharp, black claws together nervously as he neared me. The room was still too bright for me to see comfortably so I was forced to squint. The Agathodemon in their natural state and in their anger, were glowing, their silver reptilian scales emitting a green white aura. I realized the bright light that had almost overwhelmed and blinded me when the dragon demons were released had been their natural energy and it had built up and was trapped, as they were, in their magically wrought cells.

"No, I don't have any in my pockets," I shrugged, or at least tried to do so but my mobility was quite limited in the claws of my captors. "And I don't know if I can draw quicksilver out of the air. I've never tried. How is it you came to be here, anyway?" I changed the subject, hoping to buy some time to talk my way out of my situation. Stall, Cat, stall!

"Mglurshly blarn," an Agathodemon behind me growled, apparently in their native tongue.

"Ngasheen," Snarl snapped back, then turned to me.

"You should know," he cocked his massive dragon head and looked at me closely. "You are vampire, after all, and you are here."

"Yes, I'm vampire," I swallowed hard, "but I'm not here of my own free will. I was captured and brought here by Sabre and Cesare. I've only just escaped and have been trying to find my way out of this place and off of this island. And I obviously don't know how it is you and the others came to be here or I'd not have asked."

"Bluck lorp," someone behind me called out, "emdirthenan clayjub arflot."

"Ngasheen," Snarl insisted, and though I had no understanding of their language I got the impression that he was suggesting his companion kindly hold his tongue.

"Why should we believe you, little witch?" Snarl drew a deep breath into large nostrils and exhaled warm, moist, sulphurous air.

Turning my head to try to avoid the cloying stench, I noticed that one of the female Agathodemon, the smaller of the two, had a wound on her side. Black liquid oozed slowly down her torso and she kept trying to cover it with her claws but couldn't, apparently, bring herself to do so. The wound must sting, I figured from her movements, and a wonderful idea popped into my head.

"I can heal," I turned back to face Snarl. "I see one of you has a wound. I have a Healing Hand and can mend wounds."

Silence fell over the demon dragons as they looked first at me then at one another. Some communication seemed to pass from one to another. Either they shared telepathy or some other language I could not perceive.

Snarl stepped back and rose to his full height. The dragons lowered me slowly and I was relieved to have my feet back on the ground. Claws released my arms and withdrew from beneath my ribs as the dragons stepped back. Air, not exactly fresh, but better, flowed around me and I drew a deep breath in relief. Though I'd not had to breathe to survive since being made vampire, it was a habit from my earlier life that I still felt uneasy doing without. It would likely, I thought, always be a part of me.

"You have a Healing Hand?" Snarl looked questioningly, if a dragon is capable of such an expression. One brow, over his left, vertical-pupiled eye, rose anyway.

"I do," I nodded succinctly. "And I'll heal any of you that are wounded."

"Any of us," the Agathodemon before me asked, "any at all? Of any wound or illness?"

"Yes," I responded with a sense of unease. What could Snarl possibly mean by 'any wound or illness'?

"Very well," Snarl took two more steps away from me and his image became ephemeral as he shifted into his human form. Tall and slim, his dark gray hair long and wavy, he resembled my mate so much that it always startled me, yet there was something to his appearance, some aspect that I couldn't quite pin down, that remained reptilian despite his transformation. I knew that his eyes were always those of a dragon, but there was something more subtle that was always Agathodemon.

Brushing myself off and smoothing my Led Zeppelin t-shirt, I hitched my jeans up and started to walk toward the wounded female Agathodemon, then paused and turned back to Snarl.

"How is it you came to be here?" I repeated my question.

"Obviously we were lured here and trapped," he responded cryptically.

"How?"

"Sabre and Cesare made it known that a certain treasure, really just a bauble to anyone or anything else, but dear to us, was here," Snarl explained, "and they knew that to reach this place we'd have to be in dragon form.

There are, shall we say, a few physical limitations when we are in our natural state, which is how we became imprisoned behind the ancient spells."

"So this wound," I gestured toward the female, "was inflicted while she was as she is now?"

"It was," the dragon demon, now in attractive male human form nodded, "which is the reason she still lives. Were such a wound dealt her in her human form she would have perished."

"So, you were all trapped here just like I was?" I looked around at the group of Agathodemon to find them nodding their massive dragon heads in agreement.

"We were," Snarl replied. "Now will you heal our sister?"

"I will," I smiled as my Healing Hand began to tingle and itch, anxious to be doing its thing.

The female dragon demon moved her claws away from the wound on her side and drew a sharp breath as I approached her. Double rows of what appeared to be razor sharp teeth shone in the light when she opened her mouth, leaving me unsure whether she was smiling or giving me a warning. Either way, I intended to proceed carefully. My palm tingled as I placed it gently over the black oozing puncture wound and I could feel the flesh stitching and mending as soon as I touched it. As my Healing Hand was busy, I glanced up to see the dragon peering down at me with, what at first glance I took to be, black eyes. Then I realized her eyes were violet, such a deep purple red that without actual inspection they would be dismissed as black. Her pupils, vertical and black, contracted as she stared at me and suddenly the world tilted as I fell into her eyes.

Chapter 22

Visions from the Agathodemon beneath my hand washed through my mind. Eggs clustered together in dark caves cracked as infant dragon demons made their entrance into their world. Clouds of red and black vapor swirled through caves illuminated by glowing crystals. Agathodemon towered over bodies and body parts of various prey as they gnawed bone and sinew, those smaller, younger, or elderly, being relegated to what scraps were left when the adult, strong, and able-bodied were done. I couldn't tell if what I was seeing was the memory of this one dragon demon or a genetic memory of the entire species. Beneath my hand, something stirred and I shook my head, opening my eyes as I took a step back.

"Wow," I gasped as I pulled my Healing Hand from the dragon's body.

"Sniiittthhhh," the female Agathodemon hissed. I looked at Snarl for interpretation.

"She said thank you," he explained. "Her name is Gnash, by the way. And this is her sister Gnaw." He gestured toward the larger dragon demon.

"Ah," I bowed slightly. "I'm happy to make your acquaintance, and you're welcome." I looked once more at Gnash, she with the violet eyes, and then at her sister, whose distance left me unable to determine the color of her eyes.

As I stood there surrounded by Agathodemon, I realized that my Healing Hand was picking up memories, or the thoughts or imaginings, of she whom I touched. I'd assumed that the healing would have overridden anything that I might be opening myself to by touching a wound, but this 'new' power seemed to be changing and my control of it was sketchy, I admitted to myself.

"So," I rubbed my palms together, "is there anyone else wounded? Anything else I need to heal?"

"Well," Snarl grinned, "now that you ask. Can you heal this?" Looking at me with the golden eyes of a dragon in the face of a man, he pulled his long hair back and tucked it behind his ear, showing me a rough and ragged scar that ran from his left cheek bone to the edge of his chin.

"How is it that the wound healed but left a scar?" I asked as I touched the shiny, deep red slash that marred an otherwise perfect face.

"I received the wound from an iron blade," he explained, "while I was in this form. I was able to trans-

433

form into my dragon form to heal the wound but the scar remains when I'm as I am now."

"Dare I ask who inflicted this?" I stepped back to inspect the scar further.

"You should know the author of this," he glared at me as he touched the scar.

Numerous responses went through my mind, many of which repulsed me, but I was not about to guess which was correct.

"I don't," I shrugged.

"Your kind," Snarl spat, "and one of our captors. Cesare did this!"

"He may be my kind," I admitted, "but I don't approve of him or his actions. I don't approve of his cohort either, for that matter."

"Can you heal this?" He asked hopefully, lowering his hand from his face.

"I'll try," I squared my shoulders and stepped closer to the Agathodemon. "Just stand quietly."

The tingling sensation in the palm of my Healing Hand had not subsided from its previous action so I couldn't tell if it was anxious and willing to do its thing or not, but I figured I had little to lose in trying. Placing my palm against his face, I steeled myself against the possible onslaught of images. After a few moments I realized that none were surfacing in my mind so either

I'd shielded or Snarl was intentionally blocking his thoughts and memories. Either way, I had no desire to go mining for them. The tingling in my hand became a burning sensation and I noticed the dragon demon's eyes closed as if in relief or rapture. Iridescence shimmered across his skin and surrounded him like an aura as the healing continued, then my hand began to hurt, to burn intensely. I snatched my hand away from Snarl.

"What was that?" I snapped at him as I rubbed the palm of my right hand.

"What was what?" He smiled hugely and feigned innocence.

"Never mind," I sighed, realizing that he'd never confess what he had done, which was, I suspected, to draw into himself some of my energy.

"Thank you, Cat," Snarl touched his cheek to check for the scar that was no longer there. He bowed deeply.

"Anyone else?" I looked around at the other Agathodemon, but none stepped forward or made comment. "So, do you know how to get out of this place?"

"Of course," Snarl laughed and the other dragon demons, as one, shimmered into human form and, for a brief moment, I stood in a crowd of unusual but mostly normal looking people. Then, before the shimmering clouds settled, they all disappeared! I was alone, coughing in the dust of the vanishing Agathodemon.

"Hey!" I called out in the darkness resulting from their departure, "That's not what I meant! I meant do you know how I can get out of this place." I stressed the 'I' for effect, hoping Snarl could somehow still hear me. Silence settled around me as hope dwindled.

"What's this?" A familiar voice boomed from the top of the stairs behind me and I looked around the room for something to hide behind or somewhere else to be. I scuttled back and stood pressed against the stone wall beneath the stairs, hoping Cesare wouldn't notice. Overhead lights snapped on, flooding the place with blinding light and I moved deeper into the shadows of the corner. Motionless, I recalled the invisibility lesson Ulrich had taught me, calmed myself and 'scattered' my cells. I could only hope that I was doing it right as I waited for my mate's sire to depart.

"Dragon demons!" Cesare barked to no one, "They've escaped! The Agathodemon are gone! This is not possible!" He fumed, pacing the width of the chamber, then turned on his heel and dashed up the stairs, calling for Sabre as he left.

Figuring my opportunity to escape might never be better, I silently followed the vampire up the stone steps and watched him disappear down the hallway to the right, so I naturally took the corridor to the left. Angry and disappointed that Snarl and his dragons had left without me, and after I'd freed them, I clinched my jaws and tried to focus on finding my way out. If only I could find the stairs to the kitchen, surely it would be a small thing to get to a door or get out through a window. Behind me I could hear Cesare and Sabre arguing, voices raised and fury obvious, but no alarms sounded.

Down the arched corridor I went, tiptoeing so the heels of my boots wouldn't clack on the stone floor and give my whereabouts away. My eyes had to adjust once more to the softly pulsing blue lights that ran along the base of the stone walls, but they did so quickly and I soon came upon a partially hidden alcove, a recessed door barely noticeable just around a corner. Hoping against hope, I took hold of the old metal doorknob and whispered a silent prayer to anyone and anything listening.

"Please," I breathed softly, "let this be the way out!"

Oddly, I found the door swung toward me rather than away as I'd expected, and to my delight stairs rose into gloom beyond.

"Bingo!" I almost giggled as I closed the door behind me and took the stairs two at a time. Another door stood at the top of the stairwell, but I didn't even pause to consider what might be on the other side as I turned the door knob and shoved it open. The door banged back against the adjacent wall but the noise it made was slight and I could see no one in the room. The kitchen, old, sad, and barely recognizable, was blissfully empty! Two small, high, windows perched atop what was probably once a lovely farmhouse sink, but the idea of clambering into it to climb outside seemed too complicated and time consuming so I peered through a wide doorway on my right. To my relief, the dining room was empty and boasted three floor to ceiling windows, two of which were missing their lower panes. I'd found my way out!

The wood floor was dark, dusty, and covered with the scuff marks and shoe prints of many who'd passed through the room, so at least I didn't need to be concerned about having my tracks followed. I was concerned about the boards creaking so I stepped quickly and lightly, ducking beneath the horizontal rail of the first window onto the wide wooden porch. The sky was slate gray, the light so diffuse that I couldn't tell if it was dusk or dawn, but a fine rain pattered softly on the grass surrounding the house. Well aware of where the boat launch was, I considered leaping off the porch and running for it as fast as I could, but that seemed a bit too daring, as I'd be racing across open terrain possibly in view of anyone inside who happened to glance out a window. Unsure of the success of my previous attempt at invisibility, I was reluctant to put any energy into that spell. Quickly a plan came together in my mind; I'd get off the rickety, and likely squeaky, wooden porch and sneak around the far side of the house, then come around the back where I could watch the boat launch for a while to make sure my escape would be unobserved and successful. If those in the house started a search of the island surely I could keep one step ahead and away from them, I reasoned hopefully.

A sharp, protruding, splinter of wood snagged my jeans, ripping a long gash in the fabric and my flesh beneath it as I clambered over the porch railing and dropped silently into the grass below. Overgrown bushes and vines choked the foundation of the house and I had to gingerly pick my way around them to gain open terrain. I was farther from the protection of the shadows than I'd have liked, but had little choice if I was to make a speedy exit. Treading carefully, so as not to slip on the wet grass, I rounded the porch and reached the west side of the house, well, what I thought was the west side, anyway. I was fairly sure that we'd left land and boated south to reach the north, possibly North East, side of the island. The house faced the south, and my plan was to make my way around it and come up on the North West side, find cover, and watch. I was counting on the Agathodemon's escape to keep my captors busy and unaware that I was no longer in their control.

Walking sideways, glancing back to make sure I wasn't being followed, I rounded the north west corner of the house only to bump into something tall and solid.

"Crap!" I yelped as my sight went from the pointed toed boots to the slightly damp European cut suit and the long-haired male wearing it. "Oh, helsa no!" I back pedaled as quickly as I could, the heels of my boots slipping and losing purchase in the wet grass. Down I went on one hip and one elbow as I scrabbled away from Sabre.

"Now, now, My Lady," he purred smugly as he bent over and extended his hand, "no need for such hysterics. I assure you, you're safe." As he reached for me I rolled over, dug the toe of one boot into the ground and launched myself up and away. Physically running away from someone on a small island probably wasn't the brightest idea I'd ever had; I knew my chances of escape now were slim, but I was running on pure adrenaline and getting away was my only concern.

Back the way I'd come, I raced around the front of the house, trying desperately to keep my footing in the wet grass. I heard voices throughout the house and knew it was only a matter of time before Sabre wouldn't be the only one after me. '*THIS could be going better,*' I thought as I made it to the east side of the house and recognized the steps of the boat launch ahead. '*On the other hand, why not?'* I considered as Sabre called out behind me to those inside that I was out and trying to escape.

Before I covered half the ground that lay between the house and the steps to the boat launch the air around me lit up, blinding me, and I skidded to a halt in the muddy grass. Gasping in surprise, I turned to see more Agathodemon standing on the island than I knew existed in the world, or otherworld even. They were all in their human form, tall, powerfully built, and none were wearing an especially pleasant expression. Snarl stood at the head of the phalanx, feet planted firmly, shoulders squared, arms crossed at his chest. This was the first time I'd seen female Agathodemon in their human form and, I had to admit, they were wicked cool looking! There were, at a glance, maybe half a dozen females and they all had long braided hair and wore bands of gold resting on their brows. In their human forms they were similar in size to their male counterparts.

Sabre, rushing up behind me, tried to come to a halt but met with little success as the wet grass thwarted his intentions. He hit me squarely in the back, propelling me forward, and I went down, skidding in the mud on my knees.

"Snarl!" I called out in confusion, looking behind me to see Sabre getting to his feet. He wore a look of distaste as he brushed mud and wet grass from his suit jacket. Taking two steps forward, he once more leaned over and offered me his hand. The polite thing would have been to accept and let him help me to my feet, but I wasn't feeling particularly polite and, frankly, anger got the best of me. As he bent down, I struck out with one booted foot and kicked him squarely in the knee. He yelped and went down, holding his knee in both hands, rocking back and forth. I knew that the injury wouldn't keep him down for long, as vampires heal at a vastly increased rate compared to humans, but I took certain satisfaction in his pain.

"You came back for me," I turned my attention to Snarl, "and you brought friends?" As I looked from one Agathodemon to another, I realized the absurdity of that comment.

"Little witch," Snarl sighed dramatically, "do you really think that much of yourself?"

"Well, I…" confused, I made it to my feet and wiped my wet hands on my jeans, "I don't know. I thought we were friends."

"Friends," Snarl echoed the word. "Though you and I may be friends, Agathodemon do not meddle in the business of vampires."

"So why are you here?" I cocked my head, "And more importantly, why are you all here?"

"We have," the Agathodemon announced pointedly, "unfinished business with those who trapped us and sought to use us!"

Snarl's words brought Sabre to his senses and he stopped rocking himself and released his wounded knee. He looked startled, but there was no fear in his eyes.

Cesare and four large men I'd never seen before rushed from the house, rounded the porch and were brought up short by the sight of the Agathodemon standing shoulder to shoulder, faces sober and determined.

"Oh, Helsa!" I muttered at the realization that I was witnessing an otherworldly version of the shootout at the OK corral and I was too close to being caught in the crossfire. Not sure whether to run or just throw myself to the ground and cover my head, I watched in dismay as the Agathodemon shimmered into their dragon forms. I'd never seen dragons in battle, I realized, and as fascinating as the notion of witnessing such was, I had the sense that I should probably make myself absent. Looking from Snarl, his silver scales radiating iridescent green, powerful wings spread up and out behind him, to Sabre and Cesare, their faces contorting into full on vampire mode, I could almost hear the menacing music soundtrack playing. The four guys behind the vampires also transformed so this was clearly a dragons versus vampires fight and I had no desire to be anywhere close.

"Wait," Snarl hissed, covering the space between us much more quickly than his size would indicate possible. Before I could move or comment, he'd slipped one scaly, long clawed arm around my middle, lifted me into the air, and spun around, putting himself between the vampires and me.

"What," I shook my head in confusion as he put me down amidst the army of dragons. "What am I doing here? I thought this was between you and them!"

"Though you are vampire," he spoke through his now large and sharply toothed dragon muzzle, "it is clear that you are not with them, as you released us and healed us. We now protect you."

"Um," I tried to wrap my mind around what was happening, as well as what was clearly about to happen, "thanks?"

At that, Snarl turned his back to me to once more face our mutual enemies. The other dragons moved closer together and forward, but there was a secondary line of them behind the first so I was effectively encircled, though I felt less than safe.

A shot rang out in the misty gray morning, or evening, I'd never figured out which. The dragons roared, yes, they ROARED. The sound of their ancient cry of anger deafened me and I clapped my hands over my ears as the battle began.

Three of the Agathodemon surrounded me, their wings spread, large tails overlapping in a circle around my feet. I couldn't have moved had I the desire to do so and cover to which I might flee. My line of sight was somewhat limited, but I could hear and sense that both the vampires and the dragons had taken to the sky. Apparently, besides their guns, the vampires were using their fangs, but the dragons had some sort of energy balls they were hurling at their enemies. These orbs of electricity, at least that's what they looked like to me, would knock the vampires back and out of the sky, but didn't visibly wound them or destroy them, at least not at first.

As I watched assault after assault, I noticed that the orbs the dragons were hurling were changing colors and becoming smaller and smaller. Suddenly a ball that Snarl hurled at Sabre shifted to violet and when it made contact with the vampire he screamed as if severely wounded, then turned to ash and collapsed. The Agathodemon fighting next to Snarl hurled a purple orb at Cesare and as it left the dragon's claw it too shifted to violet. Cesare tried to duck and dodge the orb but to no avail. He too screamed as the ball hit him, the violet energy traveled over his body, and he became ashes that fell silently to the ground. Two of the other vampires tried to fly away from the carnage, but their fates were the same as their leaders. One vampire, determined and angry-looking, hovered silently, taking his time to aim at the Agathodemon. As Snarl released another orb at the shooter, the vampire pulled the trigger and released a barrage of bullets at one of Snarl's lieutenants. The dragon took a hit, at the edge of his chest where the scales of his armor were the weakest, and he fell from the sky, black blood oozing from the wound. A moment later Snarl's energy ball hit the shooter and he dissolved, his gun making a splat in the mud as it hit the wet earth.

One vampire remained aloft, and to my dismay he raised his arm and pointed to the sky.

"Reinforcements," he chuckled. "Now you'll pay!"

Gnaw hurled an energy ball and it turned violet, but the vampire dodged and it hit the side of the house not far from what was once the kitchen window. The violet energy spread out and flames erupted from the wooden wall. Gnash stepped up beside her sister and volleyed an orb, expertly hitting the target. The vampire screamed briefly before turning to ash and scattering to the ground.

"Well," I looked around at the dragons, their excitement and energy still palpable, "I'm glad that's over!"

"It's only just begun, little witch," Gnaw looked at me almost sadly then turned her massive head to the north east, "for indeed more vampires are coming!"

Stepping gingerly from between my protectors, I looked across the water into the sky and what I saw would have taken my breath had I been breathing. At first glance it appeared that dark clouds rode across the sky, stretching from horizon to horizon, but as I continued to watch it became clear that the clouds were many, many vampires and they were all headed in this direction.

"Oh no," I gasped as I realized that my protectors would soon be tremendously outnumbered. "What do we do now?"

"First," Snarl landed silently before me, his golden eyes wide and lungs heaving, "please, see to the wounded."

"Um," I looked around the battlefield to find only two dragons lying wounded. The one that had been shot out of the sky lay on its side in a pool of dark blood, its vertical pupils narrow in heavy lidded dark eyes. Another, slightly smaller, dragon stood with what had to be tears running from its eyes as it held an obviously broken right wing between two gnarled claws. I'd never seen dragon's tears before, and I was amazed at how beautiful the shimmering drops were as they trickled down the wounded beast's cheeks.

"Gristbite first," Snarl nodded at the bleeding dragon, "then you can see to Chomp."

"Gristbite and Chomp," I muttered, shaking my head, "you Agathodemon sure do have fun names!"

"These are the English words closest to what our Agathodemon names are," Snarl offered, "for you lack the physical equipment to pronounce our real names."

"Ah yes," I nodded, "your dragon language. I see."

Making my way to the wounded dragon demon, I turned back to Snarl as a thought occurred to me.

"I've only healed one Agathodemon in dragon form and her wound was slight," I called out with a shrug. "Can Gristbite transform into his human form if needs be?"

"That depends on the severity of the wound," the dragon demon answered, "and how much energy he has left. It would likely be easier on him if you could heal him in his natural form."

"Got it," I nodded and tossed him a salute. "And now, we see how the Healing Hand works on serious Agathodemon wounds. Just remember, Cat, every day is a learning thing!"

To my relief, my Healing Hand began to tingle and burn even before I reached Gristbite and I was beyond hopeful that I could heal his injury. Kneeling at his side, I looked into his eyes and tried to convey calm reassurance, as I was not sure that in his dragon form he could understand my words.

"I'm here to help," I smiled softly as I gently moved his claw from the wound and placed my Healing Hand on it. My palm began to thrum and what was normally a tingling sensation became a burning pull, zinging from one side of my hand to the other. Gristbite closed his eyes and heaved a sigh as the black blood ceased its flow and his dragon flesh began to heal. My hand continued to burn, in fact the feeling increased to almost unbearable before I was finally able to pull it away from the now healed injury. Rubbing my Healing Hand with my other, I inspected it closely for blisters or inflamed tissue, but there was nothing there and even the scar from my using Wicked Little Thing to anchor myself from the vortex was gone. The hand looked perfect!

"Well," I sighed, "will wonders never cease!"

"Grddleaagh," Gristbite spoke as he gained his feet, "bloot dar."

"Um," looking up into his now bright eyes I could read 'thanks' in his expression, "you're welcome Gristbite."

When the newly healed dragon demon was making his way back to his companions, I turned my attention to Chomp, the poor beast with the broken wing. Having dropped to one knee, he looked up at me with eyes more orange than golden and clearly pleading for help.

"Bear with me, Chomp," I tried to sound confident and reassuring, though I felt no confidence at all. My Healing Hand still tingled a bit, and the burning had all but stopped, but I was almost certain that I'd have to realign the cartilage of Chomp's wing and, if dragons had pain sensors anything like humans, it would probably smart. "Maybe, look over there at the water," I suggested as I placed my Healing Hand on the broken cartilage and my other hand on the stronger outer 'bone' of his wing. As the dragon demon turned his head, I quickly 'snapped' the misaligned sinew and brought it back into alignment. Chomp howled briefly then leapt or fell away from my touch. He blinked surprised orange eyes at me.

"Better?" I raised my eyebrows and waited for some response. For a moment he just looked at me then seemed to come to his senses.

Nodding succinctly, he rose to his feet and silently bowed his head to me. I touched his massive brow.

"You're welcome, Chomp," I smiled at his chivalrous gesture.

He rose, running his left claw along the now healed right wing. Without comment, he suddenly spread both wings and rose into the sky, apparently excited and happy to be whole.

"By the way, Snarl," I raised my voice to reach the group of dragons across the yard as I made my way toward them, "what are those balls of light you dragons are using as weapons?"

"Those, little witch," the dragon demon swung his head toward me with a smile, "are all thanks to you. We owe you a great debt!"

"Thanks to me," I echoed his words. "Now, how exactly is that?"

"The LeqonOrb you gave me," he smiled baring a mouthful of long sharp teeth, "returned to the Agathodemon that which had been denied us for centuries!"

"Wait, what?" My thoughts began to spin at the possible ramifications of Snarl's explanation. I didn't think "Oops!" was going to cover it.

"We Agathodemon were spawned in the bowels of the earth where we availed ourselves of the natural elements around us," he spoke as if telling a fairy tale. "But when man became so numerous and began to mine for gold, silver, copper, gems, and crude oil we were displaced. Sent to the farthest reaches of the world, we eventually ran out of quicksilver and were denied access to it by those who held it dear, specifically vampires who would keep us limited to defending ourselves by our strength and our ability to shift forms and fly. Your generous gift, which I shared with my brothers and sisters, has re-fueled our ability to create and use dragon fire, the orbs you just witnessed us using."

"My tiny LeqonOrb did all that?" I wanted desperately to discount Snarl's story.

"It did, indeed," he nodded succinctly, "for it takes merely a drop or two for us to fuel our bodies in dragon form."

"Can you use dragon fire when you're in human form?"

"That has yet to be determined," he spread his claws in an opening gesture. "Our ability to shift into human form came about long after we'd run out of quicksilver and we've yet to have the time or opportunity to experiment."

"Was that what Sabre and Cesare used to entice you to the island?" The notion popped into my head and I blurted out the question before considering what reaction I might receive.

"Was that the bait?"

"It was NOT!" he growled low in his throat.

"So, what was it that was so desirable, so cherished, that it would get five Agathodemon caught and trapped?" My curiosity got the better of me and though the dragon demon growled I just kept talking. '*Hmmm…who was it that once suggested one day my mouth would get me into trouble?'* popped into my mind.

"That which was sought may not be named," he looked at me pointedly with vertical black pupils narrowing to barely a slit. "You will speak no more of it, Cat. Besides, we have more pressing matters to attend to, as you can see." He raised his huge dragon head to the sky and released a ragged sigh.

The thought that Sabre and Cesare might have sent out a call for reinforcements when it was discovered that the Agathodemon had escaped had crossed my mind, but would they have access to the number of vampires that were now approaching the island? The sky was almost black with vampires though it appeared that a small group had broken away from the large contingent and were moving more quickly toward us.

"Now what?" I turned and looked at Snarl, my mind a blank.

"Now we stand," he said succinctly, "and we wait."

"But…" I started to object.

"Agathodemon!" Snarl bellowed and the others snapped to what could only be described as dragon attention. "Prepare to fight!"

"Wait, are you insane?" I yelled at Snarl, "Do you see how many vampires there are out there in the sky? Even though you Agathodemon are big and bad, and there are more of you than I knew existed, those vamps must outnumber you many times over!"

"Little witch," Snarl looked down at me and simply said, "Hush! You will be protected as before."

The three dragons that had encircled me before did so again, their massive bodies and spread wings shielding me as well as blocking my view. I could look up at the sky, but the view was very limited. The Agathodemon began to growl as one, their deep resonating voices powerful and obviously inviting a fight. Peeking between the two dragons blocking my view of the approaching vamps, I struggled to catch sight of what was about to ensue.

Finally, I saw a small group of well-dressed vampires land several yards away from the front line of dragon demons. When the foremost vampire spoke, my heart trip-hammered and my stomach dropped. Nothing was going to keep me trapped, I determined, and started squeezing between the dragons, stretching one leg high over the haunch of the nearest protector. My exit was graceless, a bit awkward, but I finally was free of my shield.

"Amon!" I screamed as the lead vampire stepped away from the others and addressed Snarl and his brood. I raced across the open ground between the two armies, desperate to throw myself into my beloved's arms. Nothing else mattered, all other considerations were brushed aside, so excited was I.

The sky shifted colors suddenly. I saw Amon's expression change from one of surprise to alarm, then to one I didn't recognize. His lips moved and I could tell he was calling out to me but I could hear nothing. A force hit me from behind and suddenly I was tumbling feet over forehead through the air, then everything was dark and eerily quiet.

Chapter 23

I was falling. I could feel the wind whistling by my face. Though I awaited the impact of my body hitting the ground, it did not come. I continued to fall, and fall, and fall, and fall. Finally the sensation of falling just... stopped. I was in darkness, but could see nothing. The air around me felt cool and smelled of earth and brackish water. I could hear a deep, heavy rumbling coming from somewhere beneath me, though I had no idea how I knew that, as I had no idea where I was.

"Home," a soft voice echoed around me and suddenly I could see. My balance returned when I saw the solid ground upon which I stood. Rough stone walls arched high overhead and stalactites decorated the vaulted ceiling of the enormous cave. "Home," the voice repeated and I realized there was a thumping, much like the beating of a heart, all around me. The path upon which I stood was wide, sloping gently, and scattered with small pebbles. A sudden and intense urge drove me forward and I struggled to keep from running. This need to see what lay ahead, to reconnect with it, though I wasn't consciously aware of what it actually was, burned deep inside and I was powerless to deny it.

The path curved sharply to the left and just abruptly disappeared. A sheer drop of the cave floor opened the huge cavern into a black chasm. To my surprise I realized I was feeling elation and excitement. Delight overwhelmed me, blocking the horror struggling to rise, as I leapt off the path and into the darkness ahead. Releasing a triumphant cry, I spread my arms as I plummeted. From my shoulder blades I felt wings unfurl and stretch out and up. I had WINGS!!! I could FLY! I was not going to land in a broken heap somewhere at the bottom of this chasm. The sensation of flight was amazing, even more than when I'd flown with Amon, and the one time with Chimaera. This time I was doing the flying and I had wings! Somewhere deep in the recesses of my mind the Cat I had always been was screaming, trying to get my attention to alert me that something with this situation was not only 'not right', it was very wrong, but I was having too much fun to listen to her. I was flying!

With a little experimenting, I found if I dropped my left shoulder and lifted my right, I could bank to the left. If I dropped my right shoulder and lifted my left I banked to the right. By pushing both shoulders forward simultaneously I rose and became stationary, idling even. If I lifted the wings up and together I dropped

457

gently straight down. This was AWESOME! I couldn't refrain from giggling, so freeing was the sensation. I wondered amusedly if I had a 'reverse' with these wings, but the idea of bringing my wings together in front of my body and being propelled backwards blindly held little appeal.

Dropping my right shoulder and lifting my left, I began a wide, slow descent into the chasm. The walls were devoid of detail, merely coarse stone, and when I got tired of spiraling to the right I shifted and went to my left continuing down and down. Eventually I noticed a soft, pulsing light rising to meet me. It shimmered green, blue, and violet and became brighter and more intense as I neared it. Before my feet touched the ground I slipped through what turned out to be a layer of myriad colored gases. The scent that assaulted my nostrils was both repulsive and strangely familiar. The throbbing 'pulse' sound continued and became more pronounced, reverberating around the cavern. I brought my wings to a stationary position and drew them up behind me then down along my back. *'This is so cool!'* I thought as I smoothed my wings down, still amazed and delighted to actually have wings.

The cavern I'd landed in was large but not huge. It was warm, very warm actually, and it was occupied. Before me sat a dragon, white with electric blue eyes, gold tips on its horns and wings. She raised her massive head and regarded me coolly. Her posture and demeanor could only be described as 'regal', and though she didn't seem threatened by my presence, she didn't seem particularly thrilled either.

To her right, my left as I looked ahead, a dark dragon stood as if at attention. His skin color was impossible to determine in the shifting light of the cavern, but it was definitely dark and the scales on his chest formed a shield that appeared much lighter, and were possibly silver. In his left claw he held a long staff, which explained why I immediately thought of him as a guard. He nodded his huge head at me in acknowledgement but said nothing.

On the other side of the white dragon, on her left, sat another pale dragon, neither white nor dark, but somewhere in between. He had a wispy white beard on his chin, tufts of white hair peeking from his ears, and a drooping white mustache framing his wrinkled muzzle. His appearance brought to mind the memories of Muppet dinosaurs and I struggled to not laugh or smile at the obviously aged male dragon.

Here and there around the cavern young female dragons of various colors sat atop nests of dragon eggs. Piles of bones and sinew, chunks of raw and fetid flesh, were scattered along the edge of the cavern, leaving the center relatively clean of gore and keeping the stench below the swirling layer of gaseous vapors. I realized, finally, that I was experiencing the origins of the Agathodemon. Relief flooded my thoughts at the logical conclusion. I must have somehow touched Snarl or one of the other dragon demons and been transported back in time through their memories. Whew! Now I could understand what was happening!

The aged male Agathodemon rose slowly and then rocked back on his huge haunches, curling his tail around his feet, resting its tip across his lap. He cleared his throat with a bellow then smacked his lips.

"Sit child," he said in dragon demon language and I was delighted to realize I could understand him. "When time was young, when I was young, we Agathodemon found a precious stone deep in Mother Earth and we accepted it from her body. We cleansed and consecrated it, we made the crystal orb talisman and it was protected and cherished. We offered it sacrifice and it empowered us. All was well."

As the aged dragon demon spoke, I felt a tingling itch beside my nose and absently scratched at it with my claws. WITH MY CLAWS??? I was startled to see that my hands were not hands at all for they had been replaced with reptilian claws. My nose was not a nose either, it was a snout, a muzzle, and my jaw was elon-

460

gated and horizontal. I ran my tongue across my teeth only to find they were sharp, widely separated, and some were long enough to be fangs. Now I knew this had to be a dream.

"Son of a motherless goat!" I yelped as the realization that I was Agathodemon set in. "I'm a dragon demon!"

The elderly dragon paused in his story telling and blinked at me calmly.

"Well, of course you are," he sighed before continuing. "Now do please be quiet, as I'm telling you this for a reason."

"But, but," I whined as a whirlwind of thoughts crowded the ability to reason out of my head.

"Be quiet and pay attention, please," the Agathodemon cleared his throat once more and looked to his companions. They nodded silently and he continued. "When man began to dig into the earth for her riches, we withdrew deeper into her depths, taking our talisman with us, naturally, and for a time we were able to avoid their notice. The few humans we did have contact with understood our situation and were practical enough to acknowledge our existence, but to relegate us to myth and fantasy. Those humans were rewarded."

"How were they…"I raised one claw to interrupt, about to ask how those humans were rewarded, when the dragon glared at me, silencing me with those eyes.

"How they were rewarded is of no consequence," he waved one gnarled and wickedly sharp claw, "and please do not interrupt me again."

"Sorry," I mumbled, lowering my head.

"When vampires showed up in the course of history things took an unexpected turn," he looked at me, cocked his head, and closed his eyes. For a moment I thought he'd fallen asleep, but he soon heaved a deep sigh and continued. "The undead knew we were neither myth nor fantasy, because you see, they were considered as such also. For a time we were able to avoid each other, then one of the humans we'd had contact with was, what is that term? Oh well, he was made vampire and with that power came a hunger he was unable to quench. He cut a swath through the humans of several villages until his hunger for blood and flesh was satisfied and then his hunger turned to greed and power. He caused war between his kind and the Agathodemon, he lured us out to battle and to defend our kind. While we were drawn away, he snuck in, killed those Agathodemon guarding it, and stole the talisman. He spirited it away and we've not seen it since that time. What he did with our beloved crystal we do not know. We do know that he exists no longer and that what vampires survived the war, as we Agathodemon did, withdrew from the world for a time. Since then we have been diminished in numbers and in our powers. Once our wounds had healed we realized that to continue to war with the undead would serve no purpose. We would win very little and lose too much so we entered an agreement. Vampires and Agathodemon would remain sworn enemies, but would not actively seek out one another for war. Should a single vampire happen upon one of our kind they had the choice to try to slay one another, but we would not engage in a war of numbers."

"I see," I nodded, understanding that this was the matter to which Snarl had alluded. Relieved that the vampire the elderly dragon spoke of was no more, and more importantly was not my beloved Amon, I focused on what I was being told. "So for the good of the world, Agathodemon and vampires have agreed not to war."

"Just so," the elderly dragon nodded. "And your time here is coming to an end."

"But," I stood up suddenly and almost tripped on my own tail. My feet were HUGE! "But I have so many questions! There's so much more I want to know!"

"The light calls," he responded, lifting his huge head up and looking at the swirling column of glowing gas that was rising from the cavern floor up the chasm. "You must fly!"

"No, no, no," I shook my massive head emphatically, "I am not flying. I'm not going anywhere. I have no idea how it is I came to be here or how it is that I'm Agathodemon, but I suspect you do and you must tell me."

"I cannot," he replied succinctly. "I only know that your coming was foretold and that it was given to me to tell you what I did."

"Wait, that's not right," I fumed. "How could my coming have been foretold? I'm not one of you! I mean, I'm not usually Agathodemon, I'm mortal. I mean, I was mortal, and then I became a witch, well, a witch and then a vampire. I was touched by a Goddess, but I've never been a dragon demon."

"I can only tell you what I know," he drew his arms in and moved his narrow shoulders in something of a shrug.

"If I fly up there," I pointed to the column of spiraling gases, "will I still be dragon demon when I reach the top?"

"I do not know," he shook his head sadly. The other two Agathodemon shook their heads as well.

"Well this stinks!" I huffed in frustration.

"The light calls," the dragon demon reiterated, "and you must fly!"

"Wait," I tried to snap my fingers as a sudden thought occurred to me, but dragon claws really are not designed to snap. "Who are you? What are your names? Tell me, please. I need to know."

"I am Kur," the aged Agathodemon replied with a gesture I took to be a polite bow. "This is Dodola," he gestured toward the regal looking white and gold female, "and this is Zir." The dark dragon with the shield of silver scales turned his massive head slightly and nodded at me. "Now you must fly!"

"But why?" I looked around the cavern at all the dragon demons, the beautifully swirling gases and the shimmering stones twinkling in the walls. "I don't want to go!" Even as I said it I realized that it was true. I really did not want to leave the cavern.

"The colors are rising," Kur insisted, "and you must follow them. If they cease their motion before you enter you may not make it all the way up."

"Fine," I sighed, spreading my wings. "I thank you, Kur, Dodola, and Zir." Bowing my head briefly, I took two quick steps forward and leapt into the air. The updraft caught my wings and lifted me effortlessly up, up, around, and up. I felt like a feather being borne aloft as I glanced down at the receding light. When I could see no illumination beneath me I lifted my eyes to what was above me, even though it was nothing but darkness. The force beneath me diminished as I rose until it suddenly released me and I opened my wings to fly on my own power. At first it felt liberating, I felt strong and capable, but as time went by and I continued to fly, but noticed little change in the light or appearance of the chasm, I started to wonder. Had I waited with the Agathodemon too long? Could I make it to the cave and the path from which I'd jumped what felt like ages ago? Would I plummet to my death if the strength in my wings gave out? A litany of questions marched through my mind as I continued to rise.

Chapter 24

Suddenly I gasped, yelping softly as I came back to myself. My eyes were open, I could feel myself blinking, but I could see nothing. Taking stock of myself, I touched my face with my hands.

"Hands," I whispered and heard myself doing so, "I have hands again!"

Running my fingertips over my skin, I noted my nose was once more a nose, my jaw and mouth again those I'd always known. Though it seemed likely that I was no longer Agathodemon, I could not rest until I ran my hands down my arms and legs and touched my feet and toes beneath the cover. I'd apparently been resting beneath a luxuriously soft silk blanket.

Listening intently, I found all I could hear was the soft purring of some machine and the beating of my heart. I could hear my heart beating! Wait, I could hear the blood pulsing through my veins! I wasn't sure what that meant, but it brought me great joy.

"Hello," I called out, turning my head to the right then the left, "is anyone there? Hello! Um…where am I? Something's wrong here!"

The sound of booted footsteps quickly drawing near broke the silence.

"Cat, thank the stars you're awake!" Winter's voice sounded like music to me and my unease departed instantly. When my beloved friend sat beside me on the edge of the bed, he reached out and took my right hand in his. "How are you, 'tite souer?"

"Winter," I sobbed in relief, tears welling in my useless eyes, "I'm so happy to hear your voice. Where am I? What's happened?"

"What do you mean you're happy to hear me?" he rubbed the back of my hand and I could hear the concern in his voice. "What's wrong with your eyes?"

"Besides them not working, you mean?" I chuckled sadly. "I've no idea. I feel pretty good except that I can't see anything and my heart's beating. Tell me what's happened. How did I come to be here and where is here?"

"You're home, Cat," Winter spoke softly, comfortingly. "You're safely back at Montjean. We've been taking turns watching over you since your return. His Lordship will want to know that you're awake. He wants to talk to you about all that's transpired. Just rest for a minute and I'll call him."

"Winter," I spoke quickly as I felt his weight lift from the bed, "could you get me a drink of water? My mouth is dry, throat feels like sandpaper."

"Of course, 'tite souer," he replied and I heard him cross the room, pour water, and return. "Here," he placed the cool crystal tumbler in my right hand then brought my left up to help cradle its weight. "Cool water for you. Now, I'll be right back!"

"Thanks Winter," I called out then lifted the glass to my lips and took a long quenching draught. It felt amazing to have my heart beating in my chest again, but it raised some serious questions. Was I now human once more? Was the entire 'being transformed into vampire' thing a bad dream? How was this all possible?

Propping the pillows behind my back, I leaned back with a sigh as I smoothed the soft blanket across my lap. A thicker, heavier blanket lay across my lower legs and I ran my fingers across the sumptuous fur-like fabric, relishing the sensation. Delight was suddenly swept away as a wave of sadness washed over me. The memory of flight rose in my mind and I felt amazing remorse at the loss of my wings. Leaning forward I ran my right hand down my left shoulder blade and back, then did the same with my left hand on my right shoulder blade and back. As I suspected, there were no wings, no sign I'd ever had wings. But I remembered flying! I remembered the strength and elegance in my wings. Having felt so free only to have that freedom snatched away, if even by reality, hurt deeply and I wept bitter tears. The cool liquid cut streaks down my face and I let it go with a keen sense of self-pity.

"Catherine," Amon's voice reached my ears long before I heard his footsteps on the marble floor. "Beloved, I am so relieved that you are awake."

"Amon," I sobbed again and threw open my arms.

He took the empty crystal glass from my hand then slid his hands around my ribs to embrace me. I wrapped my arms around his neck and burrowed my face into his throat, relishing the feel and the scent of my mate. I held him tightly as the tears flowed and the crying continued. He patted my back gently and just held me until my sadness was spent. At length he lowered his lips to my forehead and I raised my mouth to his. As he kissed me deeply I felt a hunger stir within me and realized with a growl that it had been too long since I'd fed my body and my passion.

"Beloved," Amon pulled away from me and held me by the upper arms, "I feel your hunger, as it stirs my own, but first I want Bishop to examine you."

"My darling," I smiled at where I felt his face probably was, "didn't you notice? My heart is beating! Didn't you feel it? I'm alive again!"

"Passion," he responded carefully, I could hear it in his voice, "alas, you are not alive again, as you say. Remember when I once made my heart beat for you so you would not think you were sleeping with a corpse? Remember when I made my body warm for you so you would feel more comfortable?"

"Well, sure," I sighed, already 'seeing' and not liking where this was going.

"That is what is happening to you," he explained, taking my hands in his and kissing my fingers. "You now have the ability to will your heart to beat and to make your body warm."

"So, I'm not alive again," I pouted a bit. "Well, crap!"

"Beloved," Amon chided softly, "you cannot return to how you once were. No magic or power can return you to mortality. You were hit by dragon fire. It is enough that you were not turned to ash as the others were."

"Yes, I remember," I cocked my head, "at least I remember being hit by something. And why is it I didn't turn to ash?"

"No one knows precisely why, though the Agathodemon that hurled the energy was able to retract some of it from your body," he responded matter of factly, "but I am thankful."

"Amon, I..." my thoughts dwindled to nothing as his outline appeared before me. Blinking repeatedly, I shook my head to clear it. Slowly the details of his face emerged and I could see his beautiful eyes, blood red, peering deeply into my own. "I can see you!"

471

"Your eyes," he gasped, unable to hide his surprise, "are changing! Your pupils have gone from vertical to round! Your eyes are still silvery white, but they are as they were. Welcome back, my darling!"

"I can see you," I whispered in delight as I took in every detail, every inch of him. "I have missed you so!"

"And I you, Beloved," he embraced me once more, "and I you."

When he released me, I leaned back on the pillows once more and gazed around the room. I was home, resting in my beautiful Sapphire Room. My hands were the long-fingered, calloused appendages they had always been and were no longer the claws I'd had in the presence of the three Elder Dragon Demons. *'Where did that term come from?'* I wondered, as I was sure it had not been uttered while I was Agathodemon. At that thought I realized how much there was to discuss with my beloved mate and I was truly at a loss at where to begin.

"Amon," I swept my mind clean and changed the subject, "would you be terribly insulted if I asked for my blades?"

"Passion," he cocked his head at me, "you know that you are safe in this house."

"I do," I nodded vigorously, "but this whole nightmare began when I walked outside without my weapons and frankly I have no desire to be without them again."

"Very well," he nodded and smiled slightly, "I understand your feelings and though I could take offense at your feeling the need to arm yourself while in my protection I shall not do so. That you are now willing to take your safety and your security seriously is a wonderful thing, as my ability to teach you this was apparently insufficient." He rose from the bed and crossed the room to the chest of drawers against the wall. Pulling open the top drawer, he withdrew my throwing blades and their holsters. Turning back to me, he lifted my hand gun from the drawer and held it aloft in a questioning gesture.

"No gun," I smiled, "just my blades please."

"Very well," he returned to weapon to the drawer, closed it and returned to my bedside, blades and holsters in hand. "Here you are, Passion."

"Amon," I looked up into his beautiful eyes as I accepted my weapons, "we have a whole bunch to talk about."

"We do indeed," he nodded and resumed his seat on the edge of the bed.

"Okay, first," I began as I strapped the leather knife holster onto my left forearm with my right hand, "you know that Cesare and Sabre were destroyed, along with their minions?"

"I do know that, yes," he murmured thoughtfully, "and that brings up another matter."

"Yes, yes," I grinned, "it actually brings up many matters, but I need to know what happened to Snarl and the other Agathodemon. Tell me they're okay."

"Thanks to you the Agathodemon are well, mostly," he took my hand in his. "When you were injured what happened changed everything."

"Wait," I snatched my hand from his, barely able to contain my excitement. "I can see what happened through your eyes. At least, I think I can."

"Your newly developed power?" My mate looked at me with a mix of wonder and pride in his eyes. "You have continued to experience this phenomenon?"

"I have, yes," I smiled, "and I'm learning to turn it off and on. Well, that's what seems to be happening. This is so far out of the realm of my understanding that I'm just kinda…going with the flow and trying to apply patterns and reasoning to it."

"Very well, my love," he returned my smile. "How does this work?"

"I touch you," I explained, unable to refrain from a lascivious wink, "and I open myself to you. Through my touch I can now access thoughts and memories."

"But you have accessed my memories before," he paused to look at me. "How is this different?"

"This is different, my beloved Amon," I touched his face with the palm of my hand, "because now I am able to do so while awake and alert. When I experienced your memories before it was only while I was asleep or even in coma."

"Ah, yes," he covered my hand with his own, "I understand."

Placing my other hand on the other side of his face, I cleared my mind and looked into his eyes. Nothing happened for a moment or two, then suddenly my vision shifted and my perspective was not my own.

Once more I was on the island, my booted feet touching wet grass, but now I stood at the head of a battalion of vampires and before me lay open ground. Across the short field stood a line of Agathodemon in their dragon forms and there, running toward me, calling my name, was my beloved Cat. With such relief at her appearance, I took two strides forward to meet her when I glanced over her shoulder to see an orb of violet energy heading for her back. I called out to get her attention but there was no time for her to hear me and react. The orb hit her squarely and sent her tumbling through the air. She landed in an unconscious heap in the middle of the open field, but at least she did not turn to ash. Horrified, I raced to her prone form but even before I could get there, as fast as I move, another reached her first. One of the female Agathodemon had gotten to Cat's body and threw herself over it in a protective pose. The other

Agathodemon moved quickly to support the female and suddenly they were a wall, my beloved's body behind them. My first instinct was to cut them down and destroy them, but the way they were shielding Passion, protecting her, even though it was one of their weapons that had taken her down, it was clear from their actions that it had been a mistake. Though they spoke in their own unintelligible language, I could glean from their tone that they were concerned, not for themselves but for her.

"That is my mate!" I put my hands on my hips and announced. "I would have her back."

"If this is your mate," an Agathodemon I recognized answered, even as he shimmered and his body transformed from dragon to human, "where were you when she was captured? Why are you only now here for her?"

"She was taken by a traitor of my own kind," I admitted reluctantly, "and I have only now realized the truth of the situation."

"And what is the truth of the situation?" the beast responded.

"I did not come here for her," I explained, "but to do battle with you on behalf of two of my kind, Cesare, my sire, and Sabre, a vampire possibly gone rogue whom the Council sought to answer charges. My connection with my mate had been somehow severed and I was unable to find her."

"And you would do battle with us?" One of the leader's lieutenants interjected.

"Had one of our scouts not witnessed what occurred here just now," I answered, "we would have. But we know now that it was you who destroyed Cesare and Sabre, the traitors who stole my mate away. Cesare and Sabre are no more. It is clear that you intended no harm to Catherine. There is no need for battle, though I am curious as to how and why you are here."

"A few Agathodemon were lured by the very two traitors you mention and held captive," the lieutenant replied. "When she released them they returned to us and we all came to mete justice." He pointed one long-nailed claw at Cat's body.

"I seem to recall a time when you yourself used Cat as a bargaining chip," the familiar demon raised one eye brow and favored me with a wicked grin. Was he trying to incite me?

"You dare to bring that up?" I growled, shoulders squared I clenched my fists in barely contained anger.

"You're right, Master Vampire," he nodded, looking properly admonished, "that was the past. She who orchestrated that is no more, thanks to you. At least, this is what Cat told me."

"You call Her Ladyship Cat?" I felt a twinge of anger at his familiar use of her human name.

"At her insistence," the Agathodemon replied succinctly.

"Yes," I sighed, "that sounds like her."

The leader turned back to the other Agathodemon and they exchanged words in dragon language. At length, the female dragon who had been protecting my beloved stood up and backed away leaving Cat lying on her side in the wet grass.

"There is no bad blood between us?" One called out from the ranks of the other Agathodemon.

"None," I replied as I lifted my beloved Passion's body in my arms. "We are done here." Turning back to the other vampires, I strode forward and rose into the air, Cat's crumpled form cradled against my chest.

My eyelids fluttered open and I found Amon holding my wrists, my hands still in the position I'd had them against his face but now away from it. It took me a moment to realize what I'd seen and where I was once again.

"So," I looked into Amon's eyes and smiled at the love I saw there, "there was no battle. The Agathodemon are okay?"

"They are," he nodded, "and I should like to know how it is that you became such good friends with those creatures."

"Well, first I guess it was because I gave Snarl the LeqonOrb full of quicksilver," I shrugged, "but then when

I escaped Sabre and Cesare I found the basement where the Agathodemon were being held and released them."

"Snarl?"

"The leader," I replied before adding, "You know the dragon Arathia offered me to? That's his name, his dragon name."

"I knew who he was," my mate nodded slowly, "though I never knew his name. He was called at Arathia's behest."

"Anyway, at first I think they wanted to eat me," I laughed, "but I convinced them to let me heal them instead. After that we were good!"

"You were good," he echoed my words, shaking his head. "Oh, how I have missed you, my love."

"And I have missed you," I growled, "in more ways than one."

With reckless abandon, I grabbed him by the back of the neck and pulled him into a kiss so intense I thought I'd end up swallowing his very soul. I had all sorts of plans running through my mind, most involving unusual and even acrobatic carnal fun, but when the kiss ended at last he pulled away from me and stood. To my disappointment, I saw Bishop standing in the doorway, medical bag in his hand.

"Hi Bishop," I sighed wistfully. "I'm happy to see you."

"Welcome back, My Lady Cat," he bowed slightly, dark curls spilling across his face. Lifting those brilliant blues eyes, he smiled. "You don't look that happy to see me."

"Timing, Bishop," I chuckled, "it's just a matter of timing."

Amon stood and stepped away from the bed so Bishop could draw near.

"I shall talk to Lily about getting you some food," he announced, "and drawing your bath. Those bloody tears of yours, as beautiful as they are, will likely be uncomfortable once dry."

"Oh!" startled I looked at the counterpane in dismay. It was splattered and stained with quickly drying blood. "I forgot about that. I just needed to cry."

"And you will tell me why that is at another time," Amon smiled wryly at me as he left the room.

"I hate it when he gets the last word," I grumbled to myself as Bishop set the leather medical bag on the bed beside my right leg, opened it, and pulled out an ophthalmoscope.

"Please, look up," he suggested gently. Peering through the scope he looked at first my right eye then my left. "Fascinating!"

"What's fascinating?" I queried as he unscrewed the funny shaped end of the scope and replaced it with an equally funny shaped end.

"Once more," he murmured as he examined one eye then another.

"Bishop," I huffed, "what's fascinating?"

"The effect of the dragon fire you took," he answered as he put away the scope and prepared a hypodermic. I was hoping fiercely that the needle was for himself and not me.

"What do you mean, Bishop?" I tried to hide the impatience, "And why is getting information out of you like pulling teeth?"

"Please, Cat," he smiled reassuringly at me, "be calm. I'm just correlating information here. You have to keep in mind that Agathodemon have not been able to wield dragon fire in centuries. What information there is on the weapon is sketchy and in some cases outright impossible. You saw what the dragon fire did to the other vampires, yes?"

"I did," I muttered as the image of Sabre, Cesare, and the others being hit with violet energy orbs and turning to ash came to mind. "It wasn't really pretty."

"You are unique, Cat," he offered as he peered once more into my left eye. "And why you survived, even

481

with a dragon demon trying to remove the dragon fire charge, when others would not is a mystery His Lordship would like to see solved."

"Um, well," I groaned, "that's not the first time I've heard that. What are you looking for?"

"I don't know," he admitted as he shifted his scope to my right eye.

"What do you mean about the dragon demon trying to remove the charge?" I suddenly realized that Amon had alluded generally to this, but it was not something I witnessed in his memories.

"Did His Lordship not tell you?" Bishop paused in his ministrations.

"Tell me what, Bishop?" I was starting to lose patience.

"A female Agathodemon threw herself on your prone body," he responded, "and tried to pull the dragon fire charge from your body."

"So, she was obviously pretty successful, huh?" I shrugged.

"And paid with her life," he nodded.

"Wait, what?" I was suddenly awake, alert, and not at all happy. "You mean to tell me that one of the Agathodemon died because of me?"

"She died trying to save you, yes," his blue eyes regarded me evenly. "Rest assured she chose to do so.

She felt it an honor. It was one of her kind that lobbed the dragon fire that hit you. She took personal responsibility and acted. It's likely what kept you from turning to ash, though we don't know what else the charge you received may have done to you." Stretching a rubber tourniquet around my left arm just above the elbow, he extended my arm and expertly slipped the needle of the hypodermic into a vein before releasing the band.

"What was that?" I held an alcohol-dampened cotton ball in the crook of my elbow as he turned to dispatch the empty syringe.

"Nothing really," he responded, "just a bit to strengthen your blood."

From the hallway came the raucous sound of clicking nails on pounding paws, followed by Ulrich's voice calling, "Siri, come back here!" Before I had a chance to comment, the black German shepherd dashed into the room and bounded onto the bed, reaching me in a rush of fur and wagging tail.

"Siri," I laughed, trying to push the great beast away from me, "you are not a feather, but I'm happy to see you too!" I scratched her ears and beneath her chin as she licked my chin and cheeks in obvious joy. "Maybe I won't need that bath after all!"

Ulrich entered the room panting almost as much as the dog and, leaning on the bed post, he paused to catch his breath.

"I'm sorry, Cat," he huffed, "I tried to hold her back, but there's no controlling that beast when it comes to her reaching you."

"That's okay, Ulrich," I laughed as the dog rolled onto her back so I could scratch her tummy, "I'm happy to see her. And I'm happy to see you too!"

"Welcome home," he nodded and straightened himself. "I'm sure you and I will have much to discuss when you're better. For now, I'll take my leave of you, and I'll take Siri with me."

"Probably best," I chuckled and shoved the huge dog away. "Go, Siri! I'll see you later."

With that, the dog rose, looked at me as if slightly dismayed, then turned and leapt off the bed. She ran out of the room with my mentor quick on her heels. I could hear him calling to her as they made their way down the hallway.

"Well, that was fun," I grinned at Bishop who had jumped away from the bed when Siri arrived. "But, now back to business. You were explaining the effects of the dragon fire, I believe."

"I was," he agreed, "but alas I've little to explain. There simply is little known about the weapon the

484

Agathodemon wields as it's been so long since they were able to do so."

"But, you can tell me a bit more, surely?"

"I can tell you that when you returned," he offered, "your eyes were similar to those of the Agathodemon. You had vertical pupils. And Winter told me that when you first regained consciousness you were blind?"

"I was," I nodded, "and that was scary!"

"But when you began to cry your pupils returned to normal and your sight returned?"

"Well," I thought about it a moment, "yes, that's right! You think there's a connection there?"

"I truly don't know, Cat," he shrugged as he put his scope back into the leather medical bag, "but it's possible. What's important is that you seem to have made a complete recovery. I'll keep an eye on you for a few days, of course, in case any other issues from the blast arise. But you seem to be fine. How do you feel?"

"I feel," pausing to take stock of my body I then continued, "I feel great! And now I'm looking forward to a hot bath and some food."

"I'm sure Lily will be here with your meal any minute so I'll take my leave of you," he bowed slightly then grinned at me. "Welcome home, Cat. You have been much missed!"

"A girl can't help but love to hear that, Bishop," I laughed and pulled the sheet and blanket back from my legs. "Thanks."

As he left the room I put my bare feet on the cool marble floor and looked around the room. It was so wonderful to once more be home. The white t-shirt and panties I wore were comfortable though they probably looked silly with my blades strapped to my arms, but at this point I was not worried about looks. I would never again be without my weapons, I swore as I stood on slightly wobbly legs.

Chapter 25

I was going through the shirts in the middle drawer of the chest of drawers when Lily entered the room behind me. She carried a large tray loaded with plates of food and a carafe of wine as well as a pot of coffee. The fragrance of the delicious fare wafted in around her.

"Welcome back to the land of the living, Miss Cat," Lily said brightly. "Mister Sin wanted me to bring you food and he chose the menu himself. He's such a thoughtful man."

"He is that," I agreed as I made my way to the upholstered occasional chair on the far side of the bed. Lily waited until I was seated then placed the tray before me on the ornate glass-top table. "So what's on the menu?"

"You got rare steak, Cajun shrimp, dirty rice, fresh baked bread, black coffee, red wine, and of course chocolate beignets," she gestured grandly as if hosting a game show. Had she offered me a year's supply of Rice-A-Roni I'd not have been surprised.

"Wine, Lily?" I looked dubiously at the crystal carafe. "Wine for breakfast?"

"This may feel like breakfast to you, child," she chuckled as she arranged the exquisite flatware on the pristine linen napkin, "but it's nigh on 8pm."

"That late," I marveled. "It doesn't feel that late. How long was I asleep?"

"Mister Sin brought you home asleep or unconscious three days ago," she replied, "and he's been worryin' and frettin' over you since then."

"Okay, Lily," I prepared myself for bad news, "just how long have I been gone? I mean, how long was I away before Mister Sin brought me home?"

"Let's see," she paused in her tidying and wiped her hands on a towel she had tucked into her apron, "I guess it was about...nine days! Longest nine days in the world, by the way. Mister Sin had everyone turning this place upside down lookin' for you. I think he'd have called the police but his security guys are much better than them. And they did find you!"

"They did," I nodded as I cut into the succulent, juicy steak.

"So what happened to you, Miss Cat," Lily asked then added, "I mean if you don't mind me askin'."

"I don't mind you asking, Lily," I paused, bite of food on the fork suspended in mid-air, "but I'm not really sure! I wonder if I hit my head." Having no choice but to be creative with explanations until I had time to consult with my mate about any scenario he'd concocted to explain the situation to those non-vampires in our world, I fibbed a little.

"My beloved should eat, Lily," Amon announced as he entered the room, "please leave us."

"Yes sir, Mister Sin," the maid curtsied slightly, "you just let me know if I can bring you anything else or if you want this cleared when you're done. Welcome back, Miss Cat."

My love took the upholstered chair across the table from mine and leaned forward to pour wine from the carafe into the cut crystal goblet. He handed it to me then leaned back, making himself comfortable to watch me eat, apparently.

"Thank you," I raised the glass in a toast before taking a sip. The liquid was rich, warming, and not entirely just wine. "Merlot and AB positive?" I grinned.

"Let us just say that the wine is fortified," he responded. "Would you like to eat and then discuss matters further or shall we talk while you eat?"

"I'm good with talking while we eat," I responded, putting an amazingly delicious Cajun spiced shrimp in my mouth with my fingers.

"Shall we begin when you first disappeared?" He raised one eyebrow at me, an expression so...Amon that I had to stifle a laugh.

"Well," I thought back to that time and realized how long ago it felt, "if you had this power I now have, you could just touch me and experience everything I did. That would save us a lot of time explaining!"

"I am sure it would, my darling," he replied, "however I do not have your gifts."

"How do you know?" Pausing in my chewing, I regarded him closely, "Have you ever tried it?"

"Beloved," he sighed, "we do not even have a word for your new ability. I would have no idea how to, as you say, try it."

"You just place your hands on me," I offered, "and open your mind!"

"I am certain that if I had such an ability I would know about it by now, Pet," he asserted, intentionally adding the 'Pet' name I disliked the most.

"Fine," I huffed, "and how many times have I told you not to call me Pet?"

"Once or twice, I believe," he chuckled. "Very well, back to matters at hand. How is it you were spirited away, my love?"

"Through the old wooden door in the wall that surrounds the estate," I answered, taking another sip of wine before continuing. "It's mostly covered by bushes and vines, but I found it when I found Siri. In fact, I found Siri when I went through it to the field beyond the wall."

"Catherine," Amon said soberly, "there is no door in the estate wall, old or otherwise. The only gates are the steel security gates we have pass codes to use."

"Well, yes," I nodded, putting another bite of steak in my mouth and following it quickly with a forkful of dirty rice. Chewing thoughtfully before swallowing, I added, "That's what I had always thought until I found this door. I can show you where it is!"

"Cat, I assure you there is no such door," Amon insisted.

"But," I stopped and looked at him. He was dead serious. "But there has to be! That's where I found the dog and that's where I was captured by Zador, and his cohort Naomi."

"Zador?" My mate looked at me in surprise, "You were taken by Zador, Arathia's High Priest?"

"I was," nodding enthusiastically, I added before shoveling more food into my mouth. "They held me in some ratty underground room. I didn't know what kind of place it was or where it was, but they held me until Sabre and Cesare rescued me. Sabre later told me I'd been held in a smuggler's keep that happened to be beneath a cemetery."

"That might explain this," he leaned forward and pulled Wicked Little Thing from behind his back. "Arathia's athame. Zador must have been searching for it. How is it he didn't find it on you when he captured you?"

"Easy," I laughed, looking at the beautiful blade with delight that it was still with me, "I didn't have it when I was being held by those two. Wicked Little Thing only came to me while I was being held by Sabre and Cesare."

"Came to you, my love?"

"Appeared out of nowhere," I assured him. "Apparently it has a mind of its own."

"So my sire and Sabre rescued you?"

"Um," I paused to consider, "technically I guess I shouldn't use that term. They actually captured me away from Zador and Naomi. In fact, Sabre took great joy in destroying them and all their people."

"Zador is dead," Amon looked at me curiously.

"For now," I smiled, "but not for long, I'm sure. I don't know what kind of entity he and Naomi are, but they don't stay dead. Not at all!"

"Yes," my mated agreed, "you are correct. So, Cesare and Sabre rescued you from Zador and Naomi and then kept you for their own purposes?

"Yep! Sabre was going to use me to secure his continued existence," I explained. "He had big plans of, I think, trying to replace you, and trying to replicate what you and I have."

"I knew he was power hungry," Amon sighed, "but I had no idea his appetite was so huge."

"So," I grinned, "I can haz Wicked Little Thing back?"

Amon looked at me with what I could only describe as resignation.

"You may haz, as you put it, the athame," he sighed, "once you have finished your meal, bathed, and dressed."

"Are we going somewhere?" I quipped, expecting to be disappointed.

"We are," he responded as he stood and straightened his beautifully tailored trousers. "I shall draw your bath while you finish eating."

"Wait," I coughed, nearly choking on the last bite of beef, "wait a minute. What about Sabre's people? What about Oola and his other sirelings? Please tell me they won't be destroyed because of their sire's actions."

"Had the Council been forced to mete justice to Sabre," Amon explained, "they may very well have been destroyed. But as the Agathodemon destroyed Sabre and the Council had no hand in it, Sabre's sirelings are indeed safe. You may rest easy now."

"I'd rest easier if he hadn't been such a jerk," I complained bitterly. "I promised the witch who loved him that I'd find and protect him, but when it came right down to it, he'd never loved her at all. He was just hoping to find in her what you found in me! She released me from my promise to help, but I still feel bad for her. She committed suicide because of him."

"No one shall ever find in another," he leaned down and kissed me on the forehead, "what I found in you."

"Awww...." I giggled, "That's sweet!"

"Eat," he feigned a stern countenance before smiling broadly. "I'll draw your bath."

"I have a better idea," I brightened at the notion. "I think a shower is in order."

"Very well then," he turned back to me, "you may shower."

"I may shower," I parroted his words as I shoved the last shrimp into my mouth and washed it down with the last of the wine. "I may shower."

My mate stood motionless and speechless as I rose, wiped my fingers off on the linen napkin, and dropped it on my mostly empty plate. Crossing the room to where he stood, I batted my eyelashes coquettishly, well, what I thought might be coquettishly, and placed my hands on his chest, running my palms up the smooth black silk shirt.

494

"I probably shouldn't shower alone, you know," I looked deeply into his eyes, running the tip of my tongue along my lips. "I might be weak and need some support in there."

"You might be weak," he murmured as he lowered his lips to mine. "You should not shower alone."

Slipping my hands around his neck, I pressed my mouth on his and opened his lips to slip my tongue through his oh so sharp fangs. I drank him in as my hunger rose. Suddenly he bent and lifted me in his arms, crossing the room into the bathroom beyond in four long strides.

Though I wore only a t-shirt and panties which took no time to remove and Amon was fully dressed, it took him mere moments longer to undress. I turned on the water and adjusted the temperature and the spray as my love moved up behind me. When he wrapped his strong arms around me I leaned back, looking up to receive his mouth on mine once more. Damn, it was great to be home!

Chapter 26

Waiting at the bottom of the grand staircase, Amon was resplendent in tight black jeans, polished knee-height boots, white tailored shirt and red paisley satin vest. His hair was drawn back from his face, secured at the nape of his neck by a black leather thong. Black onyx cuff links and collar pin twinkled softly when he moved. He stood and straightened himself as I made my way down the stairs.

As it was a mild night, I'd donned a black lightweight knit ballet gown, sleeveless with a scooped neckline. The full skirt moved gracefully with me and the deep slit pockets offered a place to carry Wicked Little Thing with me. My blades were strapped to my forearms and the black shrug that covered them was draping and comfortable. I'd secured the delicate blade pendant around my neck and, frankly, I thought it looked way cool, since it was the only blade anyone else could see. I'd donned contacts to protect my eyes as Amon had refused to divulge our destination. As I went down the stairs, I slipped the little black sunglasses up my nose and gave my hair a final toss.

"You look lovely," my mate smiled and extended his hand.

"Thank you, my darling," I returned his smile as I took his hand. "And are you going to tell me where we're going now?"

"I am not," he replied succinctly.

"Well, can you at least tell me if I'll need shoes, sandals, hip boots, snow skis?" I pouted.

"Odd you should ask," he retorted, "for you need none of those."

"Wherever we're going I can go barefoot?"

"You may," he patted my hand and commented no further.

Possibilities ran through my mind regarding our destination. We might very well be going out the big French doors onto the veranda to enjoy the twinkling lights in the trees and the fragrance of the night blooming jasmine in the garden. We might be flying anywhere. We might just be walking to the study to share a glass of wine and further canoodling.

When Amon slipped his arm in mine and turned me, not toward the French doors or the massive front doors on the opposite side of the Great Hall, but toward the door that led down to the labyrinthine lower level of the mansion, the little voice in my head started yelling at me.

"Holy Crow, Cat, this cannot be good! Pretty sure we're not going swimming in the pool down there and we wouldn't have dressed to hang out in his coffin room. There might still be rooms down here we haven't explored, but the obvious place we're headed is the meeting room where, frankly for us, nothing really good has happened!"

The memory of the crowded hall where I'd been subjected to various discomforts in an effort to ascertain the origins of my power were still very clear in my mind. The scene when Arathia had been dealt with, finally, and I'd been absent from my physical form so the goddess Nemesis could use it, stood out clearly in my mind as well. It too had taken place in the lower level meeting hall.

"Told you, chick! Nothing good has ever happened to us here. Maybe we should consider an alternative move, like, say, running like crazy? True, we probably wouldn't get far, and ultimately we'd likely be dragged back here kicking and screaming, but at the moment this is my only suggestion." My inner being was stating the merely obvious, and when we entered the hallway that led to the lower level, and Winter and Chimaera greeted us with a formal salute, my unease increased. When the two vampire guards fell into step behind us, I

looked back at them with growing concern. Both merely nodded silently when I mouthed 'what's up' at them.

"Um, Amon," I stopped walking and refused to go further, "you love me, right?"

"Of course," he looked at me calmly.

"And you're not looking to replace me with a newer model, are you?"

"Replace you?" A small smile played around his lips. "I would never replace you with a newer model."

"So, why are we going down here?" I gestured toward the door to the meeting room. "Don't tell me the Council of Goobers is down here."

"I thought it was the Council of Goons," Winter interjected.

"Winter!" Amon turned and admonished my beloved body guard with a look of derision.

"Whatever," I huffed. "Are you going to tell me that they're not through those doors?"

"I am not," my mate quipped as he pulled me forward by our linked arms. He paused only briefly to pull open the double doors, then took my arm once more and led me into the room. As before, it was crowded with people I didn't know and the Council of Five sat on the dais at the far wall. To my dismay, the crowd began to applaud, the sound filling the room and deafening me. Everyone stood as Amon led me to the dais and helped me up the step. The members of the Council stood smiling at me.

'Okay, this has got to be a dream,' I thought amid the din. *'Am I naked in class, unprepared for an oral book report? How do I wake up?'*

Moving my arms behind my back, I actually pinched my left forearm with my right hand when Amon released me and took a few steps away. The pain shot through my arm and the scene before me didn't change in the least.

'Holy mercy, Mary of,' I failed at the proper expletive even in my head, *'I'm awake and this is really happening!'*

To my surprise, no, my shock, Snarl and several other Agathodemon, in their human forms, stood before the chairs in the front row and they too were clapping. Ulrich stood smiling, arms crossed over his chest, against the wall with Siri sitting by his right leg. I stood mutely looking over the crowd trying to figure out what could possibly be happening to me and around me.

Finally, Thammuz, attired in a stunning black suit and white shirt and tie, moved up beside me. He raised his hands then lowered them, palms down, in a 'quiet now' gesture. Once the crowd was silenced, they took their seats and all eyes turned to the head of the Council. He smiled at me and then turned to address the audience.

"Ladies and gentlemen, thank you for coming. As you all know by now, the truce once wrought by and accepted by vampires and Agathodemon is no more!" Soft overhead lights glanced off his gleaming white hair and his dark eyes revealed nothing.

Applause erupted from the crowd once more.

"And that's not to say that the truce has been broken," Thammuz added. "The truce no longer exists because it is no longer needed. His Lordship Amon's mate, Her Ladyship Passion, has, inadvertently or intentionally, ended the barely contained hostility between us."

My mind was spinning, as I tried to grasp what the head of the Council was saying. He must be mistaken; he was surely speaking of someone else. Boy, was there a mistake made somewhere! I was speechless!

"And because of her actions," he continued, "she is being honored with this." He turned and accepted a huge book from an obvious assistant. When he turned back to me, he smiled. There was a glint in his eye that spoke volumes, and what it said was not in agreement with his words. This man was in no way honoring me. There was a defiant challenge in his eyes.

As he handed the ancient-looking book to me his hand brushed mine and I touched his thoughts, no I grabbed his thoughts. Suddenly I was transported behind the eyes of this Master Vampire before me and his emotions hit me like a pile driver. This entity not only didn't like or trust me, he held a deep and vehement loathing for me. There was a seed of hatred buried in his thoughts and memories, but it was so deep and long-held that I had no time to reach it. I saw a meeting with Council members Nephthele, and felt vague memories of a passionate relationship, Chesmne, the feline female who warranted little regard, and Mastiphal, a Master Vampire whose Viking appearance belied a cunning mind.

'She's a danger, I tell you,' I (Thammuz) insisted. *'His Lordship cannot see the risk he puts us in by indulging her!'*

'What do you expect?' Nephthele replied with a soft chuckle, *'He's besotted by her! She fulfilled a prophecy for him, so of course he indulges her. What can we do about it?'*

'If she were to anger him,' Mastiphal held an index finger up as he considered aloud, *'to the point that he finished her Mark of Obedience, that would put her at his complete control, would it not?'*

'It would,' I (Thammuz) remarked. *'But how do we make that happen?'*

'She's passionate about her writing,' Chesmne interjected, *'and we all know that Amon let her write her book with great reservation. Perhaps a sequel would be the straw that breaks the camel's back?'*

'Offer her a contract,' Nephthele clapped her hands in delight. *'We own Dark Ours Publishing. Dangle the bait in front of her and wait until she bites. Her human ego won't let her walk away and whether she writes another book or not is beside the point. We just need a bone of contention between the two of them. Surely this can't be that difficult.'*

'Bone of contention,' I (Thammuz) snorted, *'I'd prefer her destroyed utterly and completely, but as she's Amon's mate and protected, I guess this is our only option at the moment.'*

"And as added insurance," Nephthele interjected, lifting a tiny, gleaming, blade by a delicate chain, *"we shall gift her with this. It's wrought of the elementals, though she'll not know it. Its influence will be quite subtle. Even if we can't cause a rift between His Lordship and his mate, in time this will control her!"*

"She would never accept such a thing from one of us," Mastiphal pointed out. *"She would be suspicious!"*

"So we have someone else give it to her, someone she'd have no reason to suspect," Nephthele reasoned.

"Bastiaan," I (Thammuz) suggested.

"Better yet," Nephthele smiled wickedly, *"Elspeth! Our new council member's sister would be ingratiating herself to His Lordship's mate and would seem to only be trying to make a new friend."*

"Excellent!" I (Thammuz) nodded at the reasoning

'So, we're agreed!' Chesmne rose from her seat and slid one long pale hand along Mastiphal's shoulder to caress his neck, a display of affection that neither surprised nor interested me much.

'We are in agreement,' I (Thammuz) announced, feeling a twinge of satisfaction and anticipation for the plan we were about to initiate.

In the blink of an eye, literally, my connection with Thammuz ended and I returned to myself, shaken, surprised, and relieved to be away from the wicked emotions of the Council Head. My first instinct was to grab the blade pendant and yank it off its chain then hurl it across the room, but reason stayed my hand, as I realized I couldn't divulge my newly gained knowledge. I was also a bit relieved that the mystery of the origins of the book contract deal had been solved. For a brief instant I felt sorry for Doug, as he'd be sorely disappointed that I'd not accept the offer and he'd lose out on his commission. Then fast on the heels of that thought came another, I didn't have to refuse the offer! Even if the Council was Dark Ours Publishing, the offer existed and I could have some delicious fun playing with them. I suddenly felt smug and content, if still somewhat dazed. I'd have to investigate what power, if any, the blade pendant held over me, but I had time. I needn't leap into action, apparently.

"Um," I blinked at Thammuz, whose expression was a mixture of confusion, surprise, and suspicion. "Thank you?" It was literally the only thing I could think to say. I feared that my eyes had done that 'rainbow effect' thing Winter had told me about and that Thammuz, standing so close to me, had seen it even through the contacts I wore. It was clear that he'd noticed something, but I wasn't about to hang around and find out what. I smiled at the white-haired Master Vampire, glanced down at the book in my arms, and then looked at Amon with pleading in my eyes. He read my expression and returned to my side.

"My Lady Passion is overwhelmed," he announced to the crowd with a smile, "but I am sure she is grateful for your attendance. I assure you, she accepts this Grimoire and thanks you all."

Applause rose once more and the crowd stood. Amon took my left arm, as I cradled the huge book in the crook of my right elbow, and led me down the dais steps. Hands reached out and touched my shoulders, my arms, and my hands. A sea of strange faces rolled toward me, mouths moving but the words drowned by the noise, then receded as another wave surged forward. I struggled to keep from being overwhelmed and running away. Tightening my hand on Amon's arm, I pushed forward through the crowd. Winter and Chimaera stood sentry at the double doors, and when they saw us, they opened them. Relief washed over me when at last we stepped into the hallway.

"Okay," I released my mate and raised one hand in the air. "Someone tell me what the heck just happened please! What was all that about and what is this?" I thumped the cover of the book I held. "What is this honor or reward I was just given and why was it given to me?"

"That is Arathia's Grimoire," Amon answered soberly, "and in one way it is an honor to hold it. In another way it is anything but that. It is a huge responsibility and one I would not have had you accept were it possible for me to stop it. Your actions brought this about."

"My actions," I fumed. "What actions? What did I do?"

Behind us, the doors swung open briefly and Ulrich stepped into the hallway with Siri at his side. Behind them, the Agathodemon followed. We all stood in a group in the corridor until Amon suggested we step into another room as the meeting could end at any time and we'd be overrun by departing audience members.

Beyond the meeting room doors and on the opposite side of the hallway, two white panels stood almost seamlessly in the wall until my mate pressed one with his hand and it sprung back. He opened one door while Winter opened the other and we all stepped inside what turned out to be an office, settee and wing back chairs in the foreground, ornate desk and file cabinets beyond. The three Agathodemon took the settee, Ulrich took a chair and Siri wagged her tail as she made her way to me, pushing her head up under my hand. I sat on a leather ottoman near one of the wing back chairs and Amon took that chair. Winter and Chimaera stood on either side of the closed doors.

"Now," I looked around at the small gathering, "would someone, anyone, tell me what I did and why whatever it was seems to be such a big deal?"

"If I may," Snarl held up a finger and looked at Amon, who nodded silently in response. "You actually did several things, but there are two that are of greatest importance. Firstly, you gifted me the LeqonOrb and the quicksilver within it served to reignite the Agathodemons' ability to wield dragon fire, no pun intended."

"Okay, yes," I nodded, "you mentioned that before."

"Yes, and that enabled us to destroy our captors," Snarl continued, "from which you delivered those of us captured, thank you!"

"You're welcome," I responded, "but what else?"

"If you recall, one of the dragon fire orbs went astray during the battle and hit the side of the building," he explained, "which at first merely singed the structure, but after you'd been hit and your mate spirited you away to safety, the fire grew. Eventually the house was consumed and what was left collapsed into the chasm below."

"Okay, and…" I gently coaxed further details.

"The Agathodemon talisman was, at last, discovered in that chasm. It has been returned to us!"

"That's wonderful," I murmured, trying to act excited while actually replaying my time with the Agathodemon Elders in my mind. "Wait, so Sabre and Cesare had the talisman?"

"No," Amon interjected, "we would have known had either of them been in possession of the talisman."

"So if they didn't have it," I shook my head in confusion, "how is it that it was there?"

"There was a small cave off the main cavern that held a cache of treasures. Our talisman just happened to be among them," Snarl offered. "And we're keeping the other items as they're not of interest to others."

"So, my giving you quicksilver," I reasoned aloud, "and freeing you from Sabre and Cesare…"

"And using your healing hand on those of us wounded," Snarl's lieutenant added.

"Yes," I nodded as I recalled the battle, "I remember. So all of that led to the Agathodemon getting the talisman back. So that's what all the pomp and circumstance in the meeting room was about?"

"In essence, yes," Amon sighed, "but there is more."

"When is there NOT more with vampires," I grimaced. "Okay, hit me with it. Spill the rest of the details."

"Arathia's Grimoire is now in your keeping," he touched my hand and looked into my eyes, "and that will make you a target to those who would have it. You shall have to find a way to keep it safe."

"Oh, yippee skippy," I threw up my hands and stood up. I needed to pace. "So, I have to protect this thing and keep it safe. Is there a certain way it has to be handled?"

"It is alive," Ulrich offered, breaking his silence, "so you must keep that in mind. It has a will of its own."

"Just like Wicked Little Thing," I suggested. '*And this little blade pendant,*' my inner voice added silently.

"The athame, yes," my mentor responded.

"So how I protect the Grimoire is up to me?" Moving from the desk to the doors and back again, I was basically thinking out loud, as if hearing the issue would clarify things in my mind.

"It is," Ulrich nodded.

"Damn," I hissed, smacking my palm with my fist. "Challenge accepted, Thammuz!"

"My Lady," Snarl drew my attention away from my angst, "if you would be so kind. I'm given to understand that when you recovered from the dragon fire your eyes were..." He was obviously unsure how to put it.

"As yours are," I finished his sentence, nodding. "Yes, that's what I've been told, though my eyes were useless when I came to and only when they returned to, well, what's normal for me could I see again."

"Yes, I understand that," the dragon demon responded politely, "but you survived the blast. Can you explain what you experienced?"

"I think I became you," I scrunched my forehead and wiped a lock of hair from my cheek. "At least, I'm pretty sure that I was Agathodemon. Oh, yes! I met three Elder Agathodemon. They told me their names, but I can't remember them right at the moment. My head's kind of spinning."

"They spoke to you?" Snarl's lieutenant interjected, obviously surprised.

"Yes," I tried to remember what I'd been told, but it was like trying to grasp a whisper. "I know there was an older male and he told me the tale of the talisman, but what I mostly remember is the joy of flying on huge wings. I don't think I'll ever forget that."

Snarl and the other Agathodemon shared knowing looks or perhaps exchanged some silent information then, as if satisfied, they stood in unison.

"My Lady," the dragon demon closest to me, to whom I'd never been introduced, took my hand, "thank you for sharing your experience with us. Might we meet sometime in the future to discuss this matter further?"

Glancing at my mate, I raised an eyebrow in silent questioning. He closed his eyes and nodded in affirmation.

"Sure," I responded, not entirely clear what was going on, "I mean, yes, of course."

"Excellent!" He patted my hand, "And I am Thrash, by the way. It is an honor to make your acquaintance. I was one of your body guards on the battle field, but there was no time for introductions."

"Thrash," I smiled, "it's nice to meet you, and thank you for your protection."

Suddenly realizing that he still held my right hand in his, Thrash bowed, kissed my hand and released me, a slight blush reaching his face as he moved toward the door. Then, one at a time, each Agathodemon stepped before me, kissed my hand and moved away.

'Could my day get any stranger?' I couldn't help but think, knowing darn well that doing so was likely challenging the Universe to prove that it could.

511

Chapter 27

Our impromptu meeting broke up after the Agathodemon paid their respects, each insisting on calling me "Her Ladyship Passion" which annoyed me greatly. I much preferred plain old Cat, but evidently I'd become something of a special person to the dragon demons and we'd never be so 'familiar' with one another again. Ulrich took Siri out for a walk and Winter and Chimaera returned to the meeting in the other room. Amon and I made our way upstairs to the Great Hall then stepped through the French doors onto the veranda beyond. The night was giving way to morning as the dark sky was tinged with streaks of pink and gray. My mate held me in his arms without comment and, as my mind was still awhirl with the news of all that had occurred, that was just as well. I was having a hard time mentally digesting everything. In fact, I was beginning to have a headache.

"Come, my love," I shook off my malaise and stepped away from his embrace. "I want to show you something!"

"Catherine," Amon responded sternly, "morning is coming soon. You should be inside. You are still recovering and you need rest."

"I know, I know," I grumbled as I grabbed his hand and dragged him from the veranda to the yard. "This will only take a few minutes. I want to show you the old door in the estate wall. I know exactly where it is."

"Precious," he sighed, "I have told you that there is no such door."

"Yes, I know what you've told me," I insisted, "but I want you to see it. It's there, I swear!"

As we rounded the corner of the mansion, I moved closer to the stone wall that enclosed the property. It was, I guessed, probably eight feet tall, at least one foot thick and solid. No cracks or fissures were visible.

"It's right up here," I gestured ahead where bushes clustered near the base of the wall. "It is right here hiding in these vines and bushes. I remember because at first glance I only saw the outline of the door and I kind of had to push my way through the overgrowth."

"Cat," Amon sighed but followed me reluctantly, "there is no overgrowth and there is no door."

"See?" I pointed at the bushes, "I told you! The door's right in here."

When I reached the cluster of bushes I came to a sudden halt. Amon was right, there was no overgrowth.

There were three perfectly manicured camellias, their creamy white blossoms fairly glowing in the darkness. There were no vines climbing up the wall or around an arched doorway. The landscaping was immaculate.

"It was right there," I insisted as my mate stood beside me. I was looking at the wall, but I could feel him looking at me.

"I told you that there was no such door," he said patiently.

"Dammit, Amon, it was there! I know it was right there!"

"Catherine, my love," he turned me to face him, running his hands down my upper arms, "I believe you. I believe you."

"How can you believe me when I was clearly wrong?"

"There is another explanation," he assured me. "You need not be wrong or mistaken."

"So," I looked into his eyes, hopeful that he had reasoning that made sense.

"I believe that what you saw and what you went through was an energy portal," he held me by the elbows and looked at me seriously. "It was likely an energy portal, Little One."

"So, it was like," I fumbled for the words, "like a magical doorway? It appears and disappears on its own?"

"Not entirely," he responded. "A portal is created by someone for a specific purpose and it is placed where it is to further that purpose."

"Somebody put that doorway there so I'd find it and go through it?" An uneasy feeling began to grow in my gut.

"Indeed, beloved," he nodded, "that is the most likely explanation."

"It was a trap," I threw off his hands and stepped back from my mate. "It was a trap and I stepped right into it!" Now I was angry, no I was furious. Part of my ire was for the author of this trap and part of it was at myself for being so easily manipulated.

"What is important is that you are home once more," Amon changed the subject in an obvious attempt to diffuse my anger, "and you will never step foot off the estate without your weapons again. Rest assured that we shall find the creator of this portal and deal with the entity accordingly."

"So, was it Zador who put it there? Was it Sabre or Cesare who did it? I want to deal with the culprit," I fumed, relishing the power of my anger and at the same time feeling a twinge of regret that if it were those who previously held me captive they'd been dispatched and were beyond my grasp. About to smack my palm with my fist once more I glanced down and was startled by the sight. My fist was giving off an eerie glow!

"Amon, my love," I drew his attention to my hand, "um, this is, um, something new!"

"Not entirely new, my darling," he offered, gently taking hold of my wrist. "You have wielded energy before. This is merely a different energy."

"So, um," I muttered uneasily, "what do I do with it?"

"I suggest that it is a side effect of the blast of dragon fire you took," he said calmly, "coupled with your own power and the anger you have just experienced. The energy has accumulated and needs to be released."

"Released," I repeated.

"Yes, beloved," Amon assured me, "you need to release that charge and probably the sooner the better."

"Where do I aim it?"

"At the wall," he suggested to my great surprise.

"Wait, won't that destroy the wall," I worried aloud, "or at least damage it?"

"Do it, Cat," he insisted. "You shall see what happens."

With a shrug, I drew my arm back and hurled the energy that had built up in my right hand at the wall several feet from where we stood. There was certainly a 'boom' when it hit, but there was no explosion, no broken shards of stone sailing through the air, no crumbling hole in the structure. The energy, much like dragon fire, not violet as dragon fire is but closer to indigo blue, hit the stone and spread out from the impact point in pulsing tentacles. The blue light crackled and spread, racing away from the center in both directions, shimmering as it moved. The color dimmed, but I could still feel the energy in the atmosphere.

"It is traveling all the way around the perimeter of the wall," my mate smiled. "It will continue until the ends meet."

"You knew that would happen?" I rubbed my hand as it tingled.

"I did," he nodded.

"So what will happen when it connects or when the ends meet?" I wondered aloud.

"Nothing, my love," he smiled slightly. "When the charges meet they will cancel one another out."

"So, they'll disperse?"

"For all intents and purposes, yes." He nodded succinctly "But now the day is approaching and you need rest."

"I do," I sighed, suddenly more exhausted than I'd ever been before. Light-headed, I tried to take a few steps toward the mansion, but my ears started ringing, spots appeared before my eyes, and the world threatened to tilt. Amon was beside me when I threw out my hand for balance. He caught me in strong arms, scooped me up, and carried me quickly to the veranda.

"I can walk," I whined when we reached the stone steps before the French doors. "You can put me down!"

"I will put you down inside," he responded, opening the doors and stepping sideways to allow my length to clear the opening. "You will rest in the study and you will feed, precious. You must regain your strength."

"Whatever you say," I sighed, too tired to argue.

In the cozy study off the Great Hall, Amon put me down at last, lowering my bare feet to the beautiful rug atop the stone floor. When my hand touched the skirt of my dress, I dug my hand into my pocket and yelped.

"Helsa!" I turned to Amon in a panic, "Wicked Little Thing is gone! I had it in my pocket and it's gone now."

"You still wear your throwing blades?" He lifted one eyebrow at me.

"What does that matter?" I complained, "Yes, the blades are still on my arms."

"Fine," he nodded, "then I shall contact security and they will search the yard for the athame. I will have Bishop bring your food." My mate bowed slightly, then turned and left the room.

Alone, I looked around the room at the softly burning candles on the credenza against the wall, the crystal decanter and goblets atop the wine cart, the leather sofa and chairs. The room was beautiful, and I felt grubby and unworthy as I looked down at my dirty wet feet and the damp hem of my skirt. Perching on the edge of the leather couch, I wiped the top of my feet with my skirt, having accepted that it would require serious cleaning anyway.

Just as I was considering pouring myself some wine, Bishop came in carrying a glass on a silver tray. Beside it was a hypodermic, dark with whatever substance filled it, resting on a tidy, folded white cloth.

"His Lordship had me bring this to you," he bowed his head politely. "He said you need to feed so you have two options."

"Ah," I nodded at the tray, "I see. I can drink what's in the goblet or you'll poke me with that needle?"

"You must take nourishment," Bishop replied matter of factly. He placed the tray on the coffee table before me then smiled. "Is there anything else you would like?"

"Well, this isn't really the bacon double cheese-burger I was hoping for," I shrugged, "but I guess it will do for now." Picking up the goblet, I raised it in a toast. Drinking blood from a glass would never be the same as drawing it from the warm, throbbing, throat of a human, its beating heart causing the fluid to surge into my mouth in generous waves, but it was better than feeling that intense hunger. Once that was sated, clear thinking returned, but blood wouldn't hold the warmth of its host beyond a few moments and drinking it luke-warm or cold was just strange. Rather than dawdle over its odd taste and feel, I downed the contents of the goblet and placed the empty crystal on the tray.

"I'll leave you now," Bishop retrieved the tray then paused to turn back to me, "unless you need something else? "

"No, thanks," I answered, wiping my mouth with my fingers, "I'm good."

"No more after effects from the dragon fire?" He cocked his head and looked at me as if searching.

"Who knows?" I laughed, "I guess time will tell that tale."

Alone once more, I relaxed against the back of the sofa and stared up at the ceiling. I felt full, warm, and happy. A pang of remorse rose as my hand brushed against my empty pocket. The thought of Wicked Little Thing lying outside in the wet grass made me cringe. It was all I could do to keep myself from leaping to my feet and rushing through the French doors into the yard to find and rescue it. Instead I closed my eyes and sighed.

'The athame is not lost,' a voice whispered in my mind, or in my ear, I couldn't really tell which. *'Wicked Little Thing is yours now. It has tasted your blood and*

accepted you as its mistress. All you need do is call it to yourself. Extend your hand and will it to come.'

As if in a dream, I extended my right arm, turned my right palm up and imagined the athame there. When nothing happened, I mentally commanded it to appear, feeling a bit foolish for doing so. Again, nothing happened so at last I opened my eyes and focused on my palm. I willed Wicked Little Thing into my hand and closed my fingers around its handle, the hilt resting comfortably atop my curled index finger and thumb. Lifting the blade, I watched the candle light playing along the sharp edges, relief at Wicked Little Thing's appearance.

'Well done,' the voice echoed in my head and I wondered if I should thank it for its assistance. *'Welcome home, Wicked Little Thing.'*

Giddy at the blade's return, I called out to my mate, using that unique spiritual telepathy we shared, and told him to suspend the search as I'd found the athame. He assured me that he would be with me momentarily, as he was giving directions to the security team before the sun rose.

Holding Wicked Little Thing firmly in my right hand, I exited the study and made my way up the stairs. The bed in the Sapphire room was tidy, the polished surfaces of the furniture gleamed in the soft overhead lights, and the Grimoire rested mutely on the upholstered bench at the end of the bed. I swear it glared at me in defiance, even as Thammuz had given me a similar look. With all that had happened, I'd forgotten the book and my responsibility to keep it safe.

"Hmmm…," I sighed as I lightly touched the edge of the ornate and obviously ancient cover, "am I supposed to, like, read you?"

The Grimoire said nothing.

"Fine," I huffed. "You don't speak to me and I won't speak to you!"

Though I was weary, the idea of a relaxing hot bath was just too enticing to ignore so I placed Wicked Little Thing on the bedside table, away from the Grimoire for some reason, and entered the en suite bathroom. As I drew a hot bath, I lit the three black column candles decorating the ledge around the tub then added a few drops of patchouli essential oil to the water. Removing my contacts, I paused to imagine what I might have looked like with vertical pupils and the sensation of being dragon demon swept over me like a wave. I removed my blades and holsters, gathered my hair into a large clip on the back of my head, then slipped out of my dress and undergarments. I opened the clasp on the chain around my neck and removed the blade necklace, wondering again what Nephthele had meant when she said the pendant was alive and that in time the Council would control me. Carefully, I placed necklace atop a hand towel folded on the vanity, making sure it could not slip off into the sink and disappear down the drain. Stepping gently into the tub, I hissed slightly at the sting of the hot water. The heady, earthy scent of patchouli wafted around me and I relaxed, resting my back against the tub recline.

"*Ca-at*," A sing-song voice called from the other room.

"In here," I responded, expecting Amon to enter the bath and respond.

"*Ca-at*," came the voice again and I realized that no one I knew ever called my name in such a manner. My name simply didn't require two syllables.

As tempted as I was to ignore the voice, I knew that something was wrong and I suddenly felt vulnerable naked in the tub. As quietly as possible, I stepped out of the bath and dried quickly on a thick white towel. I waited for the voice to come again, in hopes of recognizing it and following it to its source. With no time or patience to dress, I grabbed a blade from one of my holsters resting on the vanity as I wrapped an oversized dry towel around my body and tiptoed to the door. Holding onto the doorjamb with one hand, I leaned into the Sapphire room and peered about. Nothing moved and nothing had been moved.

"Is someone there?" I called, trying to sound more confident than I felt.

When no answer came I took a few hesitant steps into the room. Nothing had been disturbed and there was no one there. Had I imagined the voice? Had I fallen asleep in the tub and dreamed it? My eyes fell onto the Grimoire and I had an almost overwhelming urge to open it. It was just such a curious thing and the possibility of having all the power that must surely rest within its covers felt enticing, I had to admit.

"Catherine," Amon was behind me, his hands on my upper arms, suddenly as if out of nowhere.

"Amon!" Startled, I spun around and glared at him. In relief, I put my palm on my chest, as if to still my heart, and laughed. "Where did you come from?" Relaxing the death grip on my blade, I placed it on the upholstered bench beside the Grimoire.

"From the hallway, as usual," he replied, concern obvious in his expression. "You seemed to be in a trance. I called your name but you did not answer. Are you well?"

With a dismissive laugh, I assured him, "I'm fine. I just got out of the bath and was trying to decide what jammies to wear to bed." The lie tumbled easily from my lips and I heard it as if someone else had said it. My inner self reared back in a 'Say what?' response, but I had no time to stop and analyze things.

"That was some deep pondering for sleeping attire," he observed, taking me once more into his arms. "Would you like my opinion on the matter?"

"You know that I LIVE for your opinion," I smiled, delighted that my attempt at diversion had been a success. "What jammies should I wear?"

"Well," he grinned as he bent to kiss my throat, "there are many possibilities." Slowly, he slid his tongue up my jugular to nibble on my left earlobe. He stroked his fingers up my right arm, across my shoulder and cupped my head in his hand. Before I could think or speak, his lips were on mine, his tongue invading my mouth. Wrapping me in his strong embrace, his hunger reared its head and mine responded with equal excitement. I slipped my hands into his long silky hair and grabbed fistfuls as I drew him into me. Suddenly I wanted nothing more than to have him inside me, to be one with my beloved Master Vampire. My lips still on his, his tongue in my mouth, I hastily started unbuttoning his shirt, anxious to have his skin against mine. He pulled the towel I wore away and lifted my naked body against his to move us to the bed. Gently, he laid me on the pristine white counterpane, then stepped back to finish removing his clothes. I pulled down the spread, mostly just to be doing something while waiting for him to join me, and fluffed the pillows as he slipped into bed beside me. Whether it was from the blood I'd drank or just my wanton self, I suddenly felt invigorated, full of energy, and elated to be flesh to flesh with Amon. He took me in his arms and I wrapped my legs around his hips, his member sliding easily and expertly into my depth. A slowly increasing rhythm developed as our passion and hunger grew. Every cell in my body seemed to be throbbing and thrumming as if electricity was racing through me, as we approached sweet release. Suddenly Amon embraced me and rolled us as one, leaving me sitting astride him looking into those blood red eyes of his. As we simultaneously orgasmed, I found myself behind his eyes looking up into my eyes and was startled to see that my eyes were those of a dragon. My silver pupils were vertical slits and appeared incapable of sight. The sensation of being in more than one body, having more than one awareness, was dumbfounding and the words *insane, looney tunes, meshugas, and asylum bound,* popped into my head like neon signs along a dark night highway. I felt my fingers turn into claws and momentarily felt the essence of a huge tail extending from my back. As the climax subsided I suddenly found myself back in my own body, muscles quivering, and nerves jangling. Amon's eyes met mine with shared confusion.

"Cat," he began, then said no more.

I couldn't blame him for his reaction. I was pretty much speechless myself!

Lying down atop his body, resting my head on his shoulder, I went still, unable to think for a time. Thankfully, he seemed willing to allow me time to gather my thoughts and try to make some sense of what had just happened.

"First off," I lifted my head and looked at the face of my beloved, "I want to thank you for that."

"You are most welcome, my darling," he responded hesitantly.

"And secondly," I grinned, not knowing how else to approach the issue, "I think I just experienced my new ability with you."

"I see," Amon raised one eyebrow. "And?"

"Well, about that 'and' thing," I scrunched my brow seeking how best to explain things, "I think I also just experienced a side effect of the dragon fire blast. Or, at least I hope that's what it was."

"I did see your eyes go iridescent and your pupils went vertical for a bit."

"Yes," I nodded, "I was looking out of your eyes at myself and I saw that, and yes that was freaky."

"Are you well?" He sat up and straightened the pillows behind him, resting his back against the headboard. "Should I call Bishop?"

"I think I'm fine," I answered slowly, taking stock of my physical and mental state. "I'm maybe a little wobbly, but I think I'm okay."

"Then you should sleep, my love. You need your rest."

"Promise me that you'll stay with me for a while?" I looked up into his eyes and noticed the concern there. I wondered if he saw the same in my eyes because my own concern was growing.

"Of course, Catherine," he gently brushed a lock of my hair away from my forehead and I caught his hand in mine. "Now sleep."

Closing my eyes, I nuzzled down into the pillow, curled into an almost fetal positon, and relaxed. Amon's hand in mine felt like a physical anchor and a sense of security settled on me like a warm fuzzy blanket.

Chapter 28

My eyes fluttered open and, yawning, I stretched my arms over my head. I let the stretch run the length of my body right down to my toes, then brought my arms down, surprised at having my left elbow bump the edge of the coffin in which I'd been sleeping. Startled, I sat upright and looked around the otherwise empty room. I had no recollection of how I'd come to be here sleeping alone in Amon's coffin. I recalled the previous evening's ceremony, Thammuz presenting the Grimoire to me and being behind his eyes, I remembered my bath and making love with Amon, and I remembered feeling dragon demon in the throes of passion. I'd not disclosed everything I'd experienced to my beloved, as I was still trying to process it all myself.

As I climbed out of the deceptively comfortable coffin and my bare feet hit the powdery stone floor I recalled that I'd been dreaming. In my dream I'd been in Amon's arms in a bed of fragrant, dry leaves on the forest floor and we'd been discussing the Grimoire. I'd asked if there were any rules I had to follow, if there was any specific means by which I had to keep it safe and he'd admitted that there were no rules, well, beyond that it had to be me who crafted the protection. I could just almost remember another dream, but when I tried to replay it in my mind it scattered like dandelion puffs in a strong wind. Stretching once more and making my way across the room to the shelves where some of my casual clothes were neatly folded and stacked, I wondered if what I remembered actually was a dream. It felt like a dream, though, unlike having experienced being Agathodemon. That, whatever it was, felt real. I could still remember the feel of my wings lifting my body, and the weight of my tail lying atop my huge feet.

Shaking off the memories and the dreams, I slipped into a pair of blue jeans and opened Amon's ornate wooden wardrobe on the other side of the doorway. Normally I wore light tops and t-shirts, but occasionally I wanted to be even more comfortable, so I pulled one of my mate's long-sleeved white poplin dress shirts from the hanger and put it on, buttoning the front and folding the sleeves up on my forearms. My blades and their holsters had been carefully placed on the shelf between a stack of jeans and a stack of tops and I strapped them on with little difficulty. Some days I was all thumbs when it came to putting them on, other days it was surprisingly easy. I dug a comfortable old pair of leather boots from the closet and plucked a pair of soft white socks from the dresser before sliding them up my calves, pulling on the boots, then tugging my jeans down over them. Crossing the hallway, I stepped into the half bath and turned on the light. Brushing out my hair, I noticed that at some point in the previous night I'd removed my contacts and my little black glasses. I had no idea where they were now, but I figured I'd run across them eventually. Since I kept a spare pair of dark glasses in the drawer of most every bathroom and bedroom in the mansion, I was never far from protection for my eyes. Brushing my teeth and rinsing with cool water, I wiped my mouth and hung the towel back on its loop. Sliding open the vanity drawer, I grabbed the glasses, not a favorite pair, slipped them on, then snapped off the light.

"Time for coffee!" I announced as I clacked along the hall. Sneaking up on someone wearing boots in this place was just an impossibility, I mused.

"*Ca-at,*" came the sing-song voice again. I stopped and looked around, assuring myself that I was quite alone.

"*Ca-at,*" the sound reverberated around me, but I knew with every fiber of my being that the voice had to be in my head; it didn't seem to be in the room. It was not the deep, masculine voice I'd heard from out of nowhere before, nor was it female. What was odd was that it almost sounded like a child!

"Listen," I responded softly, "I don't know who or what you are, but if you want something from me you'd better make it clear and do so now. Calling my name is just annoying me, got it?"

Bright laughter, almost like jingling bells, cascaded around me and then there was silence. A gust of energy blew past me, then I could actually feel whatever had contacted me withdraw. Shrugging off the sensation, I continued along the hall and made my way up the stairs, analyzing the possibilities.

When I reached the main floor, I found it quiet and deserted. The crystal chandelier gleamed softly from the vaulted ceiling and cast dancing orbs on the white marble floor below. Crystal sconces flickered on the walls and I could see the lights in the trees through the glass panes of the closed French doors.

"Hello?" I called out to the emptiness. "Anyone home?"

"Miss Cat," Lily came out of the short hallway that led to the kitchen, "I'm sorry, I didn't hear you. Can I get you some coffee and some breakfast?"

"Coffee, please," I nodded, "and where is everyone?"

"Well, Mister Sin is downstairs with some of them others," she responded with an expression of disapproval. I didn't even want to think about who, exactly, 'them others' might be.

"Where's Ulrich?"

"Him and that dog that follows his every step are out on the veranda. They've both eaten, in case you're wonderin'."

"Excellent," I beamed at the maid as a sudden idea popped into my head, "I'll join him out there and you can bring me some coffee if you'd be so kind. I have questions for him."

"There's other folks out there with him," she added as she turned to disappear into the kitchen.

"Other folks," I murmured wondering who that could possibly be. "Alrighty," I smiled, heading for the French doors, "I'll just be out here."

The sun was long gone, judging by the color of the sky. Deep blue-black stretched from horizon to horizon, broken only by clusters of stars and a few wispy clouds. The air was cool and damp, a slight breeze stirring the strings of lights draped in the boughs of the trees between the mansion and the garden. Fireflies bobbed and flickered through the fragrant night.

To the right of the double doors a long teak table stood flanked by matching benches. My mentor sat on the bench facing the garden and, to my surprise, across the table Winter sat beside Oola. My beloved body guard looked delicious in a soft chambray long sleeved shirt, his blond curls pulled back from his brow and secured with a suede hair tie. Oola's blond tresses were braided down her back and tiny glimmering crystals had been woven into them here and there. The newest Council member, Bastiaan, and his sister Elspeth were relaxing in the two teak Adirondack chairs near the edge of the veranda, he in a navy blue waistcoat and matching shirt and she in an elegant plum colored satin sheath. Her rich auburn hair had been curled and piled atop her head, her lipstick, eye shadow, and eyeliner, artistically and perfectly applied making her look like she'd just stepped out of the pages of a glamour magazine. There was no sign of Siri, but I figured she must be nearby as she seldom left Ulrich's side. A pang of jealousy that she'd become more his dog than mine surfaced briefly, but I shook it off, just happy that man and beast had found each other and were fulfilled in one another's company.

"Greetings, Cat," Ulrich rose at my approach. In fact, everyone rose as I neared the table. "Won't you join us?" My mentor added, stroking his beard, then petting the red mouse that perched in its tresses. He had Rufus with him and that pleased me greatly.

"This is an unexpected little party," I nodded in greeting. "Ulrich, Winter, and Oola. It's nice to see you. Bastiaan and Elspeth, it's lovely to see you again. What brings you here?"

"The Council is meeting," Bastiaan bowed deeply, "and as it is old business they're dealing with, I was not needed. So Elspeth and I excused ourselves to enjoy the night in His Lordship's beautiful garden. I do hope you don't mind?"

"Not at all," I shook my head, "you are most welcome here. Please, take your seat. And Oola, I am surprised to see you, though you too are welcome. What brings you here?"

"Winter contacted me when my sire met his fate," the blond vampire looked at me with sadness in her eyes. "I have announced his demise to his other sirelings and they appointed me to come see you." She looked uneasy, pulling one lock of curly hair and twisting it around her index finger.

"Ah," I glanced at Winter as I took my seat beside Ulrich. "Please, everyone, sit down, sit down. So how did the others take the news?"

"Well," Oola started to speak then stopped abruptly when Lily stepped onto the veranda.

"Pardon me," Lily announced to everyone then turned to me, "Miss Cat, here's your coffee and I took the liberty of bringing some Danish in case you're hungry."

"Thank you, Lily," I replied, reaching for an empty cup atop a matching saucer. The maid beat me to it and

535

poured a cup of steaming dark fluid from the footed coffee pot then replaced it on the tray. "Have you seen to our guests?"

"Yes, Ma'am," she nodded enthusiastically. "I've offered them food and drink, but they all said no."

"That's fine, Lily," I blew the steam off the top of my coffee before taking a tentative sip. The brew was hot, black, and delicious. "I'll call you if we need you."

"Yes, Miss Cat," she replied and turned on her heal, quickly leaving the veranda.

"You were saying, Oola?" I returned my attention to the beautiful blond vampire seated across the table.

"Yes, well, the rest of Sabre's sirelings took the news fairly well, I think," she paused as if to consider what to say next. "And they wanted me to come to you."

"And that would be because…," I felt the vampire's unease. She was here to tell me something she thought I would not like.

"Some of them would like you to become their adopted sire and protector," she answered and I caught the issue she'd skimmed over.

"Some of them," I parroted her words, "and some of them have other plans?"

"Well," she looked down at her long, delicate hands feigning an expression of surprise, as if she'd never seen them before. She had no idea how to tell me what she had to tell me.

"Oola, please," I put my hands out on the table to draw her attention and she finally lifted her eyes to meet mine. "Just tell me. It's okay."

"Twenty-nine of Sabre's sirelings wish to become yours," she sighed, "and the rest are either going off on their own or approaching other masters."

"Only twenty-nine, huh?" Raising one eyebrow I forced a smile onto my face though I couldn't help but feel disappointment. Truthfully, I didn't really like the responsibility of being 'master' or in my case 'mistress' of anyone, and I certainly had enough responsibility having dominion over the owls. Still, that so few of Sabre's sirelings trusted me enough to want my protection…it did bother me.

"Oola, Sabre's sirelings are in the unique position of being able to choose whom they serve or choosing to serve no one at all. I don't know what I would do in such a situation. However, I am happy to accept any and all who seek my protection," I offered after a brief consideration of the situation.

"Even me?" She looked at me doubtfully.

"Of course," I laughed, "even you! Welcome Oola."

"My Lady Passion," she spoke formally as she stood, "I am honored to serve you and to accept your protection."

"You are welcome, Oola!" I responded before adding, "And please convey my response to the others who would be mine."

"I shall, My Lady," she nodded, "and I shall take my leave now if you don't mind. The others are waiting to hear your answer."

"By all means," I smiled, "go. I'm sure I'll see you again soon."

"You will, My Lady," she almost laughed, the relief on her countenance clear to see. "Good eve, everyone," she glanced at the others before turning away, gliding down the steps of the veranda, and disappearing through the garden.

"I see you have Rufus with you," I turned to my mentor, who was busy feeding the red mouse what I took to be either a piece of cheese or a piece of cracker. The tiny rodent was holding the morsel Ulrich had given him in both delicate mouse paws, chewing intently.

"Yes, he insisted on coming out tonight," Ulrich smiled. "He told me that the night was too nice to miss."

"He told you that, huh?" I grinned at the notion of Rufus talking to Ulrich.

"Oh yes, indeed," my mentor insisted. "His voice is tiny and not easy for some to hear, but to my ears, he roars!"

"Of course," I retorted with a giggle at the thinly veiled reference to 'The Mouse that Roared'. "And where is Siri?"

"Off chasing a squirrel or a rabbit, I should think," he answered, gently lifting his head and taking in the view of the yard from one side to the other. He obviously didn't want to disturb Rufus. "She shot out of the door when we stepped out here. I heard her bark once or twice then she was gone. I expect she'll be back when she's tired, hungry, or thirsty."

"Winter," I turned to my guard and friend, "she can't get off the estate, can she? There are no open gates or places in the wall that are low enough for her to jump over, are there?"

"No, 'tite souer," he shook his head, "there is no way for her to escape. I'm sure she'll be back here soon."

After draining my coffee cup, I walked to the far edge of the veranda and called Siri's name as loudly as I could. There was no response. I repeated the call and again there was no answer. I turned to Ulrich and Winter with barely contained panic rising.

"Um, maybe we should go look for her," I tried to sound unconcerned, but was fairly certain that I failed.

"Of course, Cat," Winter stood and wiped his hands on his jeans, "I'll walk down to the guard house and check around the stables."

"I'll go through the port'a cochere and take a look at the lawn beyond," Ulrich offered. "Maybe she caught what she was chasing and is absorbed in dining on it."

"Ewww," I grimaced, "thanks for that visual, Ulrich. I'll go walk the perimeter of the property following the wall. Between the three of us we should cover the property."

"Please," Bastiaan stood and offered me a sheepish grin, "I would be happy to help you search and I'm sure Elspeth would be delighted to walk with you." His sister stood and silently nodded her agreement.

"Fine," I replied, "the more the merrier. Come Elspeth, you can come with me."

Bastiaan and Winter took a step back as the lovely Elspeth crossed in front of them and stepped up beside me. She held up one hand, index finger raised, then bent over to remove her strappy sandals, first one then the other.

"Ready," she smiled with an odd expression.

"Something wrong?" I asked, curious at the look on her face.

"You use those?" She nodded and glanced at the throwing blades on my forearms.

"When necessary," I chuckled at her query, "I do, yes."

"That's wonderful!" She replied, "Bastiaan won't let me touch weapons. He claims it's his job to protect me."

"In all deference to your brother," I sighed, "it is your job to protect yourself. Come, you and I need to talk."

As we stepped off the veranda and started our walk I knew darn well that I was stepping into forbidden territory. I knew that it was not my business to interfere, and I certainly understood how Bastiaan felt, to a great degree Amon had once felt the same, but that was not going to stop me. The tiny voice in my head was moaning "Noooooooooooo," but it knew that I wasn't listening either.

Once we rounded the corner of the mansion I cleared my throat.

"Elspeth," I began, "can I ask you something?"

"Of course," the lovely vampire responded with a demure smile.

"How is it you became," I hesitated briefly then blundered ahead, "what you are? I mean, you and Bastiaan are sister and brother. How is it you became vampire?"

"Ah," she nodded, "yes. Well, my brother made me as I am now."

"Are you kidding?" I gasped, suddenly full of righteous indignation, "That's obscene!"

"No, no," she shook her head emphatically. "I begged him to do so!"

"You what?"

"Please understand, My Lady," she smiled weakly.

"Cat, please," I interjected.

"Fine, Cat," she continued, "please understand. My brother and I were on our own at a fairly young age. Our parents died during a plague that decimated many villages in our land. He was all I had and I was all he had. When he was attacked and made vampire I was lost. He wanted me to go on and live a normal life, marry, have children, that whole story, but I could not bear to be without him. I forced him to let me join him in this world."

"Forced?"

"Yes, I threatened to kill myself if he didn't make me vampire. I truly gave him no choice."

"And how long ago was this?" I queried, suddenly curious as to how old the siblings might actually be.

"Almost three centuries ago," she answered wistfully.

"Wow, so you two have been together for that long," I marveled, "and you've not had the desire to strangle him or put his head on a pike?"

"Cat, I..." she stammered, looking at me in abject horror.

"Just kidding," I laughed and watched as her expression turned to one of relief. "That's just a very long time for any two people to be together."

"I can't imagine being without him," she sighed softly, "though there are times I wish he trusted me more."

"Look, Elspeth," I stopped in the cool, moist grass and looked at her pointedly, "I'm not about to start a feminist revolution and I don't want to cause trouble between you and your brother, but if you'd like I can have one of these made for you." Pushing the sleeve of Amon's shirt up a bit higher, I slipped the throwing blade from its holster and held it up in the meager light of the stars and waxing moon. It softly glowed in the night.

"Really?" she brightened as I carefully handed the weapon to her.

"That is if you can keep it from Bastiaan," I added quickly. "Can you shield your mind from him? I mean, can you keep a secret from him?"

"I can," she nodded. "I noticed that I have that ability long ago. There is not much I have cause to keep from my brother, but yes, if necessary I can do so."

"Excellent," I sighed, relieved greatly, "and if you're interested you can join me and Winter at the gun range and we can teach you about shooting. Whether you bring that up to Bastiaan or not is entirely up to you."

"He might actually find that a good idea," she admitted. "I could be honest with him about shooting, and just secret the blade for my own protection."

"You do what you feel is right," I offered, "but rest assured that I'm not mentioning any of this to Amon. This is between you and me."

"I understand, Cat," she smiled, "this is between us."

Elspeth gently placed the short, stout blade in the palm of my left hand. I picked it up and deftly slid it back into the holster on my forearm.

"On more thing," I straightened the rolled up sleeves of my shirt and looked my companion in the eye, "where did you get the pendant you gave me?"

"Well," she shrugged almost imperceptibly and looked askance, "I was not supposed to say, but I can't imagine there'd be any harm now. The Council of Five wanted you to have it. That female member, oh, I'm terrible at names, um, was it Nancy?"

"Nephthele?" I offered.

"Yes, yes," Elspeth brightened, "that's it! She gave it to me to give to you and said that I should just let it seem that it came from me. I didn't feel quite right about that, but since Bastiaan's a new Council member, I didn't want to cause problems by refusing. Was that alright? Should I have kept it a secret?"

"Everything's fine, Elspeth," I assured her, "and I won't let on that you told me anything, okay?"

"Oh," she smiled sweetly, "thank you, Cat. It really is a lovely pendant, isn't it?"

"It is indeed, and now let's go find my dog," I chuckled as I called Siri's name into the night.

Chapter 29

S iri was nowhere to be found. We searched every-where to no avail. There was no breach in the wall surrounding the estate, so it seemed unlikely she'd escaped and run away. The search of the stables, guard house, carriage house and garages proved unfruitful. Eventually Bastiaan and Elspeth departed, both apologizing for our lack of success finding my beast. At Amon's suggestion, which he offered after the Council meeting ended and he joined the search, we even inspected every room, closet, and cubbyhole in the mansion, several of which I had never before seen, but she was not there. I did find a lovely antique rocking chair, which I claimed as my own the moment I laid eyes on it. My mate had Winter carry it downstairs and put it in the study. It didn't actually go with the décor, but I loved it and didn't care.

"The dog arrived on her own for whatever reason, yes?" Ulrich offered his understanding, "And now she seems to have disappeared on her own. I'd suggest she had reasons for both, and if she wishes she'll be back."

"Yes," I sighed, "you're right. I know it. Logically I understand, emotionally I can't help but be worried."

"We can always find you another," Amon smiled, "if you want a canine companion."

"No," I shook my head adamantly, "no replacement for Siri. If she comes back, fine. If not…"

"The security team will continue to watch for the beast," my beloved mate assured me.

"And in the meantime," Ulrich cleared his throat and changed the subject, "I believe you have a Grimoire to deal with, yes?"

"Yes," I responded reluctantly, "yes, I do."

"Then let us make that your next lesson, shall we?" My mentor looked at me with amusement twinkling in his eyes.

"Fine," I nodded, thinking about the large book even now resting on the upholstered bench at the foot of the bed in the Sapphire room. How was I ever going to figure out how to keep it safe?

"Am I supposed to read this thing," I started to leave for the Sapphire room when the question popped into my head, "or just guard and protect it?"

"Interesting question, Cat," Ulrich just smiled. It was obvious he had no intentions of answering further. Having a cryptic Witch Master as a mentor was, I was coming to understand, sometimes infuriating. Why in the world could he not just…ANSWER ME?

"Alrighty then," I fumed, "inscrutable is the color of the day!"

As I made my way up the stone steps and then along the marble-floored corridor I considered my options. The Grimoire was given to me, granted for protection, but it was technically mine now. I wasn't sure I really wanted to know what spells or secrets or evil plots Arathia had written in the book, but then again maybe I did! Maybe it was true that forewarned is forearmed and the knowledge hidden within those pages might one day be of value.

The Grimoire still lay silently atop the upholstered bench. Was it my imagination or was it taunting me, daring me to open its cover and read what was inside? The book was unimpressive looking but for its size, which was massive. The cover, apparently once black leather, was tattered and worn, and if there had ever been a title or cover art there it must have been lost to wear long ago. I stood just staring at it for the longest time. Part of me wanted to snatch it up and dive into the contents while another part wanted nothing more than to toss it in the nearest blast furnace. My thoughts went back to Thammuz and the expression he'd had when he 'honored' me with the Grimoire. That twinkle in his eye angered me, and his hatred of me, for no good reason, perplexed me. It seemed to clear that he believed I'd fail to protect the book.

Finally, I turned away from the Grimoire and shook off its effects. As I turned, I spied my violin case atop a wardrobe against the wall. Apparently in my absence either Lily or Amon had moved it from the shelf in the study where I usually kept it for ease of access. More often than not I played outside on the veranda or in the garden, but I was happy that the fine instrument was here in the Sapphire room. Maybe playing for a while would clear my mind and it had been so long since I'd played I knew I needed the practice.

After rosining the bow, I perched on the bench, placed the violin beneath my chin, and began to play. It felt so good to feel the vibration of the strings and to hear the rich tones. 'Somewhere Over the Rainbow' wafted through the room, though I had no conscious reason to choose such a tune. Deciding it was a bit too melancholy for my taste, I followed it with some short bluegrass rifts then launched into some Loreena McKinnett numbers I usually played in my performances. *'My performances!'* My thoughts were brought suddenly back to earth when my absence from the stage popped in. *'I wonder what Estella was told!'* Estella Green was the manager of Lamey's and she and I had generally gotten along well. I hoped that whatever explanation she'd been given had been reasonable and had kept the door open for my return. Making a mental note to ask Amon about the matter, I placed the violin back in its case, securing the bow, then returned it to the top of the wardrobe.

"*Ca-at,*" came the childlike voice, and I spun in the direction from which it came.

The Grimoire glared at me from the bench.

"You?" I gaped at the tome, "Is it you that's been calling me?"

Again, the bell-like laughter shimmered around me.

"Fine," I sighed to the Grimoire, "let's see what you've got!"

Picking the book up gently, I turned around and sat down on the bench, lowering the Grimoire to my lap. Placing my palm atop the cover I closed my eyes and just allowed myself to sense the collection. It felt both powerful and guarded, as if I'd have to work to unlock its secrets. Opening my newly arrived ability, I was transported into the pages of the text, seeing first Arathia then others unknown take quill pen, paint brush, and some pin ended instrument I didn't recognize write, draw, and paint on my pages. There was anger within me, a thirst for vengeance, a hunger for power, a sense of satisfaction at gaining power, a voracious appetite for…everything!

"Whoa!" I gasped as I lifted my hand from the Grimoire and shuddered at the residual feelings. "You are one seriously nasty book! Well, okay, I guess that's not really fair, but some of what's inside you is just not nice!"

The book didn't respond, though I half expected it to, so I took a deep breath and opened the cover. The first page was empty but there was writing on the second page, though it was not a script or language I recognized. It was in paragraph form so it was a message of some sort, but its meaning escaped me. There were symbols drawn on the third, fourth, and fifth pages, some of which were pretty and artistically rendered, others looked like chicken scratches or attacks on the pages with nothing smooth or flowing to them. Flipping to the center of the huge book, I rifled the pages back to the beginning, taking random peeks. One page in particular caught my attention and I went back to it after it flipped by. The page was black with a very narrow paper border and as I spread the book open fully to get a better look something appeared at the bottom of the darkness. At first I thought it was my imagination, but as I blinked and looked again I recognized first the sharp nail then the first and second joint of a finger. It was trying to grasp the edge of the page and quickly a second and third finger joined in. On the opposite edge of the page another 'hand' was trying to gain purchase and when I realized that something was trying to come out of the darkness, out of the book, I slammed the tome shut. Though I really wanted to toss the thing across the room, I placed it back on the bench before standing and releasing a shudder.

"*Ca-at,*" the voice taunted me.

"You alright?" Winter was leaning on the door frame, head cocked, with a look of concern on his face. His gorgeous mane of blond curls framed his face and lay gently on his shoulders.

"Of course," I smiled in relief. "Yes, I'm fine. You?"

"I am well, 'tite souer," he replied entering the room with his fingers in the front pockets of his well-worn jeans, elbows wide, arms relaxed. "Busy?" He looked at the Grimoire then shot me a look which wavered between curiosity and bemusement.

"No, just trying to figure out what to do with this sucker," I gestured at the book, trying to hide another shudder of distaste. "Did you escort Oola to…wherever it was she was going?"

"I did not," he looked surprised by my question.

"Sorry, just thought I caught a 'friendly' vibe between you two," I made quotation marks in the air with my index and middle fingers extended.

"Are you upset with the news she gave you?" He smoothly changed the subject. "It can't make you happy that so few of Sabre's sirelings want you as protector."

"To be honest," I shrugged, "it does kind of upset me. I mean, I know that I've not been in this world so very long and I'm sure I'll never have the reputation that Amon does, but jeez!"

"I understand," he nodded. "His Lordship's reputation is great. Everyone knows that before you he created no sirelings and that those who serve him do so out of respect for his strength and power."

"So how many of Sabre's sirelings are petitioning my mate for his protection?" I asked without really thinking it through.

"An emissary is meeting with His Lordship and other Council members as we speak," Winter brightened, "and I believe the number is near three hundred fifty."

"What?" My head spun for a moment, "How can that be? I'm sure Oola told me that Sabre's sirelings numbered two hundred seventy!"

"Yes," he nodded, raising one eyebrow at me, "that's correct. The number of those who are Owl is two hundred seventy and of those twenty-nine are soon to be in your keeping. A few have not decided or chosen with whom to align, but of that number one hundred eighty seek protection from His Lordship and the rest are other species."

"How is that possible?" I murmured, trying to wrap my head around the sheer number of vampires Sabre had sired. "Out of three hundred fifty sirelings two hundred seventy are Owl? Doesn't that seem strange?"

"Sabre preyed on the weakest humans," Winter shrugged, "or, at any rate, those least likely to put up much resistance. Though owls are birds of prey they do not fight for the mere joy of the battle, unlike many of Amon's 'pack' to whom the fight is a rite of passage as well as a means to establish hierarchy in the group."

"What other species are there in Sabre's people?"

"I do not know," he admitted, "but I can find out for you if you'd like."

"No," I brushed it off with a wave of my hand, "never mind. I'm sure His Lordship will tell me about it if I need to know. In the meantime I'm still dealing with this blasted Grimoire."

"Any thoughts on how to protect it?"

"I was playing the alphabet game in my mind," I laughed. "You know, A is for acid, B is for burning, C is for crushing, that sort of thing. I really wasn't getting very far."

"What about Max?" Winter smiled, his eyes dancing in delight with the sudden inspiration.

"Max? What do you mean?"

"He deals with books all the time," my beloved body guard explained patiently. "Who would know better how to deal with such as this?"

"I hadn't thought of that," I nodded enthusiastically. "This could be the perfect answer! Maybe Max will take the Grimoire and keep it safe in his library for me. You think he would?"

"What harm could there be in asking him?" Winter replied.

"Can you take me there now?" I tried to refrain from jumping up and down with excitement. "I mean, Amon is busy, right? I really want to see Max now."

"Um, well," he looked doubtful.

"Come on Winter," I pleaded shamelessly, "please take me to the library. Surely you've been there. You must know the way. Max would let you in, wouldn't he?"

"Yes, 'tite souer," he sighed theatrically and rolled his eyes in mock exasperation, "I've been there and I know the way. But I'm not sure His Lordship would approve of me taking you."

"But," I reasoned as logically as I could, "we could be there, get this thing dealt with, and get back even before Amon knows we're gone. And besides, it was your idea!"

"It was, Mon Chèr," he grinned and I knew I'd won my way. "Fine. Get ready, get your weapons, your travel gear, whatever you'll need. We won't have much time before the sun rises so we'll have to travel fast."

"Yay!" I spun around a few times before reaching him then I placed my palms on the sides of his face and planted a kiss on his lips. "Thank you! You won't be sorry. I promise. This feels right!"

"Why does your saying that I won't be sorry make me think that I probably will be?" He looked deeply into my eyes, his hands holding my hands on his face.

"Um, 'cause you're silly?"

"Oh yeah, Cat," he grinned softly, "I'm known for my silliness. Meet me in twenty minutes on the veranda?"

"Yes sir!" I stepped back and threw him a salute. "I'll be there!"

"Wonder if I should just fly into the sunrise and get it over with," he mumbled to himself as he sauntered into the hallway.

"Hey Winter," I ran to the doorway and leaned out into the hall when a sudden thought popped into my head, "why did Thammuz hand me the Grimoire in front of everyone if he wanted me to protect it? Wouldn't it have made more sense just to, I don't know, give me a medal or a certificate of achievement in front of the crowd and then put me in charge of the Grimoire in private?"

"He wanted everyone to know that it would be you who has the book in your keeping," Winter answered simply. "Perhaps it was proof that he and the other Council members feel you're worthy of the task?"

"Or," I offered absently, recalling what I'd learned from touching the Council head's hand in passing, "maybe he's painted a bullseye on my forehead and hopes someone will destroy me in taking the Grimoire? I'd be out of the picture and the Council would be innocent of any wrong doing."

"What?" Winter turned to me, surprise clearly written on his face, "Why would you think that?"

"Never mind," I started to chew on the inside of my bottom lip as I considered my next move. "First things first, Winter," I laughed then turned back to the Sapphire room. "See you in twenty!"

Grabbing my long duster and tossing it over one arm, I pulled the Tomcat from the drawer and checked that the safety was on and that it was fully loaded. The leather shoulder holster lay in the drawer and, on a whim, I picked it up before stepping into the en suite. My hunch had been right, the sword pendant and chain still rested atop the vanity and I fumbled with the clasp for a moment as I put it on. Clicking off the bathroom light, I moved into the bedroom, retrieved the book from the bench at the end of the bed, crossed the room, turned off the bedroom lights, and closed the door. As I walked down the hallway, Grimoire tucked in the crook of my left elbow, I slipped the empty leather holster up my right arm and onto my shoulder then transferred the book and coat to my right arm and slipped the holster up my left arm, settling the back strap across my shoulder blades. Tucking the Tomcat into the holster, I rolled the sleeves of Amon's shirt down and buttoned the cuffs, then donned the duster. By the time I made it down the grand stairway, crossed the Great Hall, and opened the French doors to the veranda, I was put together and ready to fly.

Winter stood waiting for me, his short brown leather bomber jacket now covering his denim shirt.

"Ready?" He clapped his hands together and glanced at the night sky.

"Yep," I smiled, stepping up next to him and sliding my right arm around his neck. "This won't give us any trouble, I mean flying with it, will it?" I motioned with my left arm around the Grimoire.

"It shouldn't," Winter responded, muttered in jest, "probably, I hope." He just laughed then wrapped his arms around me, putting his body against mine. "Let's go."

Closing my eyes, I clutched the Grimoire in one arm, and held on for dear life to Winter with the other arm. I'd not flown with my beloved bodyguard before, but I did trust him. I just wasn't comfortable watching as the world beneath us changed from 'normal' to a reverse energy picture, looking more like a film negative than the world I knew and loved. The dark sky turned to brightness and the twinkling stars became throbbing dark spots. It was always surreal feeling to me and I wondered if, in time, that would change.

"When are you going to start doing this yourself, petite souer?" Winter lowered his mouth to my ear and spoke loud enough that I could hear him over the sound of the wind rushing around us. "You still don't fly alone."

"I know," I lifted my face and risked a peek at my flying companion, "and I don't know why I don't fly by myself. It just doesn't feel right to me, yet."

"You're a Master Vampire, Cat," he added, "and eventually others are likely to take this as a sign of weakness, if they find out."

"And thank you for pointing that out, Grand Frere," I teased, as he was always referring to me as 'little sister' in French.

When we reached the Library, having raced up the narrow path along the sheer vertical cliff feeling the moments rushing by, we were surprised that no one greeted us. The huge doors were unlocked and we stepped into the silence of the main hall to find soft lights illuminating the place, but there was no sign of Max. My hopes fell, thinking that the librarian, and possible answer to my dilemma, was nowhere to be found.

"Max," I called out as loudly as I dared. It seemed almost profane to disrupt the quiet of the place, but I had little choice. At first there was no response and then, to my delight, a door sounded in the distance and I could hear footsteps hurrying toward us. "Max?" I called out again, my hopes once more on the rise.

Chapter 30

"Catherine," Max smiled as he stepped through an open doorway and moved behind the work counter strewn with parchment rolls, bottles of ink, various pens, rulers, and many little piles of eraser dust and pencil shavings. The librarian looked positively dashing in a tidy black suit, pristine white shirt and black tie. His kerchief was neatly folded and tucked properly in his breast pocket. His hair was combed, his face was clean and shaved, and there were no visible ink stains or pencil smudges on his hands.

"Max, you look," I had to step back and think about how to end the sentence. We didn't know one another so well and I didn't want to offend him. "You look amazing! Have you been out on the town?" True, I had no idea where the Library actually was or if there were any cities with nightlife around, but it seemed a reasonable question.

"As a matter of fact," Max beamed, "I was! I was in the company of a lovely young woman."

"A date?" I couldn't hide my surprise. I thought the odd little guy was a hermit.

561

"Just so!" He laughed, "And I'm as surprised as you are. It's been longer than I care to think about since I had a date and out of the blue this angel came into my life and she's actually interested in me!"

"That's great, Max," I couldn't help but laugh with him. His joy was that infectious. "So are you going to see her again?"

"I hope so," he nodded enthusiastically. "If I have any say about it I'll see her again."

"That's so wonderful," I leaned on the counter, my thoughts awhirl.

"So, Cat," Max sobered and straightened the work space before him, "how can I help you?"

"Take this book off my hands?" I plunked the heavy tome down and stepped back, hoping the librarian would snatch it away so I might never need think or worry about it again.

"Um, Cat," he touched the book hesitantly, turned it around to glance at it, but did not pick it up. "I can't take this."

"So you can't help me?" I feigned pleading, well, I mostly feigned pleading, but some of it was real.

"I didn't say that," he held his index finger up and grinned mischievously. "I can't take it off your hands, as you say, but I may be able to help you."

562

"I'm supposed to protect it," I explained, "and keep it safe. It's Arathia's Grimoire. I swear I'm never going to get rid of all that sorceress' influences. Parts of her keep coming back from the dead!"

"Arathia's Grimoire," he looked at the book with increased interest. "I've heard of this but I've never seen it. It's said to be quite powerful, and a bit danger-ous." He licked his lips nervously and his fingers flut-tered over the Grimoire as if he really wanted to touch it but dare not.

"Yeah well," I grimaced, recalling the creepy fingers trying to crawl out of the dark page, "it probably is that! Winter suggested I come to you because you deal with books all the time. He thought you might have some idea of how to deal with this."

"Winter, my friend," Max looked up, startled, as if just noticing my bodyguard, "nice to see you again." The two shook hands and the librarian turned back to me. "As I said, I can't take it off your hands, but I do have an idea of how you can keep it safe."

"Anything," I laughed. "What's your idea?"

"You are a witch so you know how to become invis-ible, yes?"

"Um," I hesitated then replied, "yes. I've made myself invisible successfully, once anyway!"

"Fine," he bobbed his head up and down with enthusiasm, "so what I suggest is that you make the Grimoire invisible. You may then place it on a shelf here in the library and I will watch over it. Anyone who comes here with the sight will see that there's something on the shelf there, but they'll not be able to see what it is. It will be safe so long as it's invisible."

"Excellent!" I clapped my hands in relief. "So what do I do first?"

"Wait, wait," Max lowered his head and raised that index finger once more, "there are conditions that must be agreed to!"

"Fine, what conditions?" I was trying to hold back my impatience.

"First, you'll need to keep the spell of invisibility activated. This place," he raised his hands, palms up, and looked around, "has a unique atmosphere so your spell will last longer than it would elsewhere, but it will need to be refreshed every year or so. Should something unexpected cause the invisibility to start dissolving I will alert you immediately, of course."

"Great," I smiled, thinking I was getting somewhere. "And anything else?"

"There is the matter of payment," he looked almost embarrassed at his words.

"Payment," I thought, of course there would be payment involved, "Sure! I can pay whatever it costs. You name the amount."

"Oh, I'm sorry," the librarian blushed. "I didn't mean money. The payment would be in the form of a service, a deed."

"A deed," I echoed. "That's all? Just a service or a deed? I will just need to…do you a favor in the future?"

"Something like that, yes!" Max looked relieved.

"Deal," I stuck out my hand and the librarian shook it. "So how do we do this?"

"Well, first we must find the perfect place on the perfect shelf in the perfect room where this will be happy," Max smiled broadly.

"Wait," I drew back, "are you serious? We have to find a place for the Grimoire to be happy?"

"Oh my," the librarian startled and looked at me, "I was exaggerating, of course. Silly me! We just need to find the right place for it where it won't be too obvious that there's a space, since an empty space is what anyone else should see."

"Ah," I nodded my head in sudden understanding, "I see what you mean. Okay, is there any specific room of this place you need it to be?"

"This room, I should think," he looked around the main hall at its various tall library cases, each likely 10

565

feet tall with 8 to 10 shelves each. "I'll need to have it near me."

"Alright," I responded, taking a few steps to the case nearest and adjacent to the librarian's counter, "what about here?" I stepped back and bent down, looking at the shelf above the bottom shelf. Near the end on the right there was an empty spot easily four inches wide, which would fit the Grimoire nicely. "There's a spot empty here and it's near enough to the ground that it's almost out of view normally. I think this would be perfect!"

"Well done, Cat," Max clapped his hands together, "now the next step is up to you. First, do you have any magical tools you'll need to cast the spell of invisibility?"

Thinking back to the one time I'd made myself invisible at my mentor's request, I shook my head.

"Nope!" I responded in relief, "I need no tools."

"Fine," Max too looked relieved, "then all you need to do is to make yourself invisible then pick up the Grimoire and hold it. It should be that, eventually, the book too will become invisible then you can slide it onto the shelf, set the spell, and be done with it."

"Should be?" I caught the possibility that the spell of invisibility might react other than expected.

"It's magic, Cat," the librarian explained patiently, "and as you know, magic is a living, breathing thing. One can't always expect it to act as intended."

"Um, 'tite souer," Winter interjected, "it will soon be sunrise and our time is limited. We should be leaving very soon!"

"I know, Winter," I huffed, "I'm trying to hurry! You adding pressure will not help things!"

"Sorry, Cat," my beloved bodyguard and friend replied, "take your time. We'll make it back to the estate in plenty of time. Just, do what you have to do!"

"Okay, now," I squared my shoulders, closed my eyes, and tried to recall what I'd done when I'd made myself invisible before. I remembered the feeling of expansion, as if every cell in my body was separating, creating spaces from one to the other. I stepped into that feeling, closing everything else out of my mind. It seemed my lungs drew a great breath then my eyes popped open and I could see. Looking down at my feet assured me that I was indeed invisible, so I took a few steps forward and picked up the Grimoire to cradle it in my arms. To my relief, neither Max nor Winter spoke a word. I held the tome gently, willing my energy to envelope it and at first it seemed nothing was happening, then finally the edges of the book became invisible. It actually looked like an invisible cloth was being drawn

567

together around the thing until it suddenly stopped. I blinked and saw my hands holding the book.

"What happened?" I looked at Max, "Why didn't it work? It was starting to work then it just…stopped!"

"It may take some practice to cast the spell here, Cat," he shrugged, "for as I mentioned before this place has a unique atmosphere and that affects energy."

"So, what? Can I just try it again?"

"If you feel you have enough energy," Max nodded, "of course you can try it again."

"Okay, here goes," I announced, placing the Grimoire onto the counter again before returning to the spell. Once more I expanded myself, I concentrated on clearing everything from my mind and my energy field. I stood patiently as my magic found its equilibrium then opened my eyes. Again, I was invisible and stepped forward to pick up the book. I focused on its cellular structure and willed it to expand as I had done. It shimmered a few times then became invisible. It took every ounce of concentration I had to keep from jumping up and down in the joy of success, but I managed and as I slipped the invisible Grimoire onto the shelf, slightly below my knee level, I breathed a sigh of relief. Turning to smile at Max and Winter, I let my invisibility dissipate and watched my hands and arms reappear.

"Yay," I laughed a bit nervously, the tension leaving my body, "I'm so glad that's done!"

"Um, Cat?" Max responded soberly, one eyebrow raised at me, "I don't believe it's done." Moving forward, he pointed at the obviously not invisible Grimoire on the shelf. "It's where it should be, but it's still visible!"

"No, no," I shook my head, "that's not possible! I made that thing invisible. It should still be invisible!"

"Did you 'set' the spell?" Max asked timidly.

"Well, um," I bit the inside of my lip, "maybe not! How do I do that?"

"You don't know how to 'set' a spell so it remains?" the librarian looked surprised.

"No time for that now, just tell me how to do it!"

Winter was obviously getting more agitated by the minute and my energy was really draining away. I needed to get this done and now.

"Very well," Max instructed, "just make yourself and the Grimoire invisible, as you've already done, slip the book onto the shelf, then break the connection with it and smooth the rift in the energy between yourself and the tome. You may have to physically calm the space before you can step fully away from the Grimoire."

"Okay, one last time then," I sighed, picked the Grimoire off the shelf and returned it to the counter before making myself invisible again. When I stepped forward and cradled the book once more in my arms my energy swam around it making it disappear quickly. When I slid it onto the shelf, making sure it stood upright, I pulled my right hand back drawing the tips of my fingers to a point then snapping the connection sharply. It broke cleanly, but I could feel the disruption in the energy between the Grimoire and me, so I used both hands to smooth the atmosphere as one would smooth a wrinkled sheet or a toddler's messy hair. After a few moments the disruption disappeared and I stood up and back, confident that this time I'd done everything right.

"Dare I ask?" I sighed as my invisibility spell once more dissipated, "Did it work?"

"Congratulations, Catherine," Max stepped forward and at first I expected him to pat me on the back or arm, then he caught himself and extended his hand. "It worked!" He pumped my hand enthusiastically. "And it should be that you'll not have to repeat this spell for a year, more or less, but we'll deal with that when the time comes."

"I did it?" I looked around in amazement and delight, "I actually did it? The spell worked and the Grimoire is safe? Woohoo! Yay!" I couldn't help but imagine

Thammuz's face, his expression one of disappointment that I'd out-maneuvered him.

"Congratulations, Cat," Winter chimed in then swept me up into his arms for a bear hug surely intended to snap ribs. "You did it, 'tite souer!"

"I did it," I sighed, looking down at the shelf where only an empty space between other books was visible. "I did it!" It was such a relief to have that matter off my mind that for a moment I couldn't focus on what to do next, what to think, how to feel.

"You really should be going now," Max suggested, taking my elbow to escort me to the door. "As Winter said, the sun will soon be rising and you have far to travel."

"Oh, um, that's right," I nodded, confusion and exhaustion threatening to sweep me off my feet.

"Come, Cat," Winter was suddenly right beside me, his left arm around my waist, his right arm pulling my right arm around his shoulders. With a slight swooping gesture, he lifted me in his arms and carried me through the doors and down the steps.

"Take care of her, Winter," Max called as my eyelids began to droop. I couldn't seem to stay awake.

"I'll do so," my beloved Grand Frere responded, "and thanks again, Max!"

There were no more voices. I could feel Winter's strong arms supporting me, felt the weight of my head resting against his broad shoulder, then the rush of weightlessness. Darkness swallowed me.

Chapter 31

Luckily for me, the exhaustion I'd experienced after making myself invisible three times did not last long. I came to my senses as Winter was flying us back to the estate. When he realized I was awake, he released my legs and let me swing myself back into an upright position, my body once more against his. He held me around the middle and I had my arms around his neck as we flew. I'd opened my eyes to look at him and was about to say something when something slammed into us with a force great enough to separate us. Tumbling sideways, I could see my beloved Winter also being hurled in the opposite direction.

I didn't know how high we were when whatever hit us did so, but the force quickly dissipated leaving me in that pregnant moment before my body began its downward journey. Winter called my name as I began to plummet, and briefly I welcomed the earth rising up to greet me, then a flash of memory rose up from somewhere. I recalled the sensation of flying, my great wings spread out and up, pushing downward against the air and lifting me higher. Of course, I had no wings now, but apparently the sensation of flight was enough. It was as if a part of me still did have wings and I caught myself before nearing the ground. My beloved's voice wrapped itself around me like a warm, comforting blanket and I knew in that instant that he was aware of what had happened and that he was pleased with me. Without conscious thought I rose in the night air to where Winter hovered, having righted himself and recovered his wits.

"Cat," he beamed, "you're flying! You did it!"

"Seems I had little choice," I laughed and took his hand.

"True," he nodded, the smile on his face lighting up the night. "Come, we must hurry."

"What was it that hit us?" I asked as we headed toward home, now just holding hands, "I didn't know we could be run into by other flying things!"

"I don't know what it was," he shook his head, his gold locks shining in the growing light.

'*Growing light!*' A little voice in my head screamed. '*It's sunrise!*'

"Winter, the sun's breaching the horizon," I yelped, trying to refrain from panicking. "I'll be blind shortly!" My dark glasses had tumbled from my nose when the energy had forced us apart and the contacts I had covering my white irises would be protection, but not especially helpful to see in daylight. I wasn't about to turn to cinders or explode, but I wouldn't be able to see very well either.

"Come 'tite souer," Winter pulled me once more into his arms, "close your eyes and tuck your face into my coat. I'll get us safely home!"

"But what about you?" I insisted.

"Don't worry," he smiled, cradling the back of my head in his hand, he tucked me into his jacket collar. "I am uncomfortable in the sunlight, but my eyes are not as sensitive as yours. So long as I'm not in direct sunlight I won't turn to ashes, probably. We'll be home before the sun's fully risen. We're very close now."

Though I'd wanted to protest, Winter held me tightly and it made further conversation impossible. Vivid images started parading through my mind and I realized that I was 'reading' my beloved body guard, so I slammed the power shut firmly. It was one thing to see information for a specific purpose, it was another to invade someone's memories and thoughts just for fun.

True to his word, Winter set us down on the veranda of the Montjean estate just before the sun came up fully. The French doors were open and soft lights burned in the Great Hall beyond. Amon stood at the bottom of the stairs, a look of relief on his face as we entered the mansion.

"I flew," I smiled broadly and launched myself into my mate's arms. "I flew, I flew, I flew!"

"You did indeed," Amon hugged me tightly, lifting my feet from the floor. "I felt it the moment it happened."

"It was awesome!" I admitted. "But I wondered if it would have injured or killed me had I tumbled from the sky and hit the earth."

"Impossible!" My mate replied, "Firstly, my blood is your blood. It would have never permitted you to fall. Secondly, my love, technically you are already dead, though not in the traditional meaning of the word. Had you fallen to the ground your body would have sustained some minor damage, but your accelerated healing rate would have dealt with it almost immediately. It would have been nothing but a slight inconvenience."

"Wow, so there was never really any risk in my flying alone?" I wondered aloud, peering deeply into my love's blood red eyes seeking understanding.

"There was not," he nodded succinctly, then added, "and I often wondered why you were so reluctant to do so. It comes naturally to vampires to fly."

"I don't know," I shrugged as he released me from his embrace, "I guess part of me just wanted to hold on to some of what I once was. People don't fly, well, not without a machine or contraption, so maybe I wanted to stay grounded unless I was with someone else doing the actual flying."

"You are home now, and you are safe," Amon sobered as he turned to address Winter. "Thank you for escorting Her Ladyship and seeing her safely home. You may return to your patrol duties now."

Winter bowed slightly then turned and silently crossed the Great Hall to disappear into the labyrinthine lower levels of the mansion. I really had only a vague notion of what the security teams on the estate actually did, especially the vampire members. The two mortal members, Bear and Dodge, functioned as any security guard would, manning the gate house and patrolling the perimeter of the grounds, but the others? I had no clue and any notion to ask Amon was quickly squashed by my little inner voice. It insisted that was just someplace I did not need to go, so I mostly listened. I wondered of course, but I did not ask.

"So your journey proved successful," my mate slipped his arm around my shoulders and turned us to walk deeper into the mansion.

"It did," I did my best impression of him, though he didn't notice or if he did he made no comment. "And the Grimoire is safely tucked away and protected. I'm glad to have that off my mind."

"I imagine so," he nodded thoughtfully, "and what is next for you?"

"Now that things are settling down again," I took a deep sigh and plunged forward, "I'd like to get back to performing. I don't know what Estella was told about my going AWOL, but I hope the story was convincing enough that she'll take pity on me and let me return."

"The manager was told that you were having physical issues," Amon explained, "but only in the vaguest terms. She assured Lily, who called her on your behalf, that you would be welcomed back. She said that she would work you back into the schedule whenever you were ready to return."

"Whew, that's a relief," I shook my head slightly. "Things were so crazy when I returned to the estate with one thing after another. It just hit me that I'd simply disappeared from performing. I was hoping I wouldn't have to change my public identity again and find somewhere else to perform."

"You need not," he offered as he opened the door to the downstairs corridor, "but you may wish to reconsider returning to the stage so soon."

"Why?" I stopped dead in my tracks, turning to face my beloved, "Why should I reconsider?"

"My love, precious," he took my hands in his and kissed my fingers gently, "you were hit by dragon fire.

578

It is amazing that you are still with us. No one knows how this energy will affect you, your body as well as your powers. As far as anyone knows, you are the only vampire to have ever survived such an experience."

"Yeah, I know," I admitted, as the scenes of the battle field rose in my mind with startling vividness. "So, how long are you suggesting I delay my return to performing?"

"I would suggest you wait until after the next full moon," he slipped one slim hand along the side of my neck, pulling me closer to him. "If all goes well and you experience no unusual affectations, then it would likely be safe." He placed his mouth on mine, effectively cutting off any comment or complaint. I'd lost the argument, but as his tongue parted my lips and found its way into my mouth, I realized I didn't care. I was home, safely in the arms of my beloved once more.

As we rounded the corner and approached Amon's coffin room, a sudden hush fell over the place, startling me.

"Sun's up!" I gasped at the sensation. I'd been sensing the sun's arrival as anathema since becoming vampire, but this sensation was different. It felt like someone had flipped a switch, OFF and not ON. The mortal world was stirring, coming to life again, and it suddenly felt to me like my world had just shut down. *'Fascinating!'*

"You should feed, my love," Amon remarked, "for you look exhausted."

"Gee, thanks," I tried to laugh, but lacked the energy to do so. "And I think you're right. It took me three tries to cast the spell on the Grimoire. I think it drained my batteries!"

"I have a surprise for you," my mate said simply enough, but there was something in his comment that gave me pause.

"Surprise?" I looked at him doubtfully.

"For you," he opened the door to the coffin room. Inside, besides his own large coffin, which we often shared, and my coffin, in which I rested when he was away, a third coffin stood with its lid open. Surrounded by the tufts of white satin lining, a young man lay motionless with his head propped on the satin pillow, hands folded neatly across his middle. His skin was tanned and his face had nary a wrinkle. Dark hair was smoothed back from his forehead and a tiny scruff of beard fringed his strong jaw.

"I don't understand," I looked at the man in the coffin then back to Amon. "What do you mean this is for me?"

"To feed, my love," he explained. "Until you have fully recovered you need to feed on fresh blood. So until that time, this coffin will hold those who will sustain you."

"He's not dead?" I looked skeptically at my love. "So why's he in a coffin?"

"It is just simpler to contain him thusly," he nodded, "and the 'sleep' he is in is easier to maintain in its confines."

"Sleep," I muttered, my mind awhirl with questions.

"It is a sleep," Amon insisted. "You will feed and when you have had your fill he will be awakened. He will return to his world with no memory and no evidence to indicate that anything unusual has happened."

"You're sure?" I couldn't help but ask. Something felt wonky and I couldn't put my finger on what it was.

"I assure you, Pet," my mate sighed, "I have no desire to harvest humans or affect the population. You feed and he shall be returned to the place from which he was taken."

"Okay," I shrugged, noticing the blush of good health on the man's cheeks. When I saw the corner of his mouth twitch then noticed the subtle throbbing of his jugular vein, barely visible above the collar of his shirt, all doubts fled. I was famished and satisfaction was just steps away.

"I know you prefer your privacy when you feed, Beloved," Amon offered as he moved toward the door, "so I shall leave you for a time."

"Thanks," I responded then added, "and Amon?"

"Yes, love?" He stopped and turned back to me, eyebrows raised,

"Why this?" I gestured toward the man in the coffin, "In all the time we've been together, since I became vampire, you've never had a human over for dinner. Why now?"

My mate favored me with a perfectly wicked grin, his eyes shining with delight at my twisted sense of humor.

"To be honest," he bowed slightly, "it was Ulrich's idea. Your mentor suggested that by feeding on a mortal such as this you would be able to practice your new ability and become more proficient wielding it."

"And how will this help me practice my new power?" My mate was not being very forthcoming with information and I couldn't help but wonder why. "I've had at least one connection with someone that did not prove to be factual, either his mind suffered dyslexia or it was imagination and not memory. How will you or Ulrich determine what's what?"

"This man is known to me," Amon explained, "and I know some of the details of his history. What you get from touching him will be compared to what is known. In that manner we can tell if what you are receiving is memory or something else."

"So, am I to just avail myself of his blood as he is in this sleep state," I looked doubtfully at the sleeping man in the coffin, "or am I to wake him? I've never tried to 'read' someone asleep or spellbound."

"Follow your instincts, Passion," Amon replied. "I look forward to hearing what your ability offers you."

"Great!" I sighed deeply and considered the matter before approaching the coffin. "Okay, I'm going to do this MY way!"

The man was beautiful and appeared quite robust and healthy; I had to give Amon credit for his taste. His brow was wide and clear, eyebrows dark and not too heavy, eyelashes long and lovely. Gently, I reached out and touched the side of his face and his eyes fluttered open. Dark eyes regarded me calmly and did not look away from my own. Quickly, before he had a chance to recover his wits and startle, I trapped him with my gaze and he smiled slightly.

"Yes," he murmured as my intentions made their way into his thoughts, "please!" He sat up, moved the mane of his hair that was long enough to brush the top of his shoulders aside, and offered me his throat.

As enticing as the view was, and it was, I couldn't restrain myself and moved his head further aside before sinking my teeth into his jugular vein. His blood was rich, hot, and very powerful. I could feel it singing through my body as I fed. Once the initial rush of feeding was passed and I could think complete thoughts again, I opened my mind, my new power, to this man and was almost instantly sorry I'd done so. Dusty heat bore down on me, grit filled my eyes and nose, the scent of carnage and gunpowder smoke was heavy all around me. Body parts lay strewn here and there across the village center and half-starved stray dogs wandered around looking for sustenance. I saw my weapon in my hand, my fingers deftly cleaning and loading it as I'd been trained. Flashbacks of writing my girlfriend back home by the light of a battery powered lamp inside a tent that offered little protection from the elements of this harsh land swam into view. Saying good-bye to family and friends at a small airport and walking across the tarmac to board a small plane flickered in my mind's eye, just before the satisfaction of accepting the challenge to serve rode over me.

At length I pulled my mouth from Ory Broussard's throat and stood back, blinking at the intensity of what I'd seen.

"So," I sighed, "you were a soldier in Afghanistan, huh? And you witnessed more than enough bloodshed to last you a lifetime. I'm sorry, Ory." I licked the tip of my left index finger and smoothed it over the puncture wounds I'd left. They disappeared immediately leaving clear, unblemished skin. Placing the palm of my right hand across his brow and closed eyes I simply said, "Sleep!" and pulled my hand away. Ory did not stir at his release but seemed to sleep deeply and peacefully.

My mate's motive in choosing this particular specimen for me to feed on became crystal clear. Not only was his blood powerful and that of a warrior, the images still fresh in his memory were easily accessible and the emotions they invoked were still intense, even raw. There was no doubt in my mind that what I'd received was clearly this man's memories and his blood now strengthened and empowered me. I might have been upset with Amon for his obvious manipulations, but I truly grasped his reasoning and intentions, so I felt nothing but love and gratitude for my mate and pity for Ory Broussard. He would never again be the man he once was, a darkness now lived deep inside him and it ate at him more than I ever could or would.

Amon was waiting for me when I stepped into the hallway. He slipped his arm around my shoulders, drew me to his body, and kissed the top of my head. Though he started to escort me forward, I refused to move until he turned to face me. Wrapping my arms around his neck I stood on tiptoes and kissed his mouth deeply. He embraced me around the ribs and lifted my feet from the ground to hold me.

"Thank you," I murmured as I pulled my lips from his reluctantly.

"You are most welcome," he looked into my eyes with a new intensity, as if trying to read my mind.

"I needed that," I explained, "in more ways than one. Ory's blood has refreshed me as I've not known other blood to do and I'm wondering if that doesn't have something to do with my new ability and the fact that I was able to exercise it while feeding."

"So you could tap into his memories," my mate marveled, "and you were able to ascertain his name?"

"Yes," I nodded, kissing his lips again quickly, "I saw his memories and the details of his life. Well, at least for as long as it took me to feed. It seemed I was going in reverse chronological order, but that may not actually be the case, it just felt that way."

"Wonderful," he smiled gently and set my feet back on the floor. "Ulrich would like you to start a file on your computer and journal each encounter you have experienced with this new power."

"All of them," I grimaced at the thought, "or just Ory and any others after this?"

"I believe he wants you to describe them all, beginning with the first time you noticed this power."

"Great!" I huffed, thinking back and mentally counting the number of entries I'd have to type out in this file. "And what's he going to do with this file?"

"I expect he will check your memories and your accounts for accuracy," Amon shrugged slightly, slipped his arm once more around my shoulder and guided me forward.

"This is suddenly less than fun," I fumed.

"Patience, precious," my beloved grinned, knowing full well how I hated the 'p' word…patience, that is.

"I guess it might keep me mildly entertained while I'm killing time waiting to go back to Lamey's."

"That time will be short, I have no doubt," Amon assured me, though I wasn't sure I was buying it. "And there will be another surprise for you soon!"

"Another surprise," I feigned delight, "yippee skippy!" As we made our way along the corridors I slipped my fingers into the waistband of his trousers, wiggling them against his skin.

"Beloved," he peered down at me with a look of surprise, "you have just fed."

"Amon, my darling," I stifled a laugh, "it's not like I'm going swimming after eating! I'm not likely to get a cramp and drown while we're making love, am I?"

"Of course not," he hugged me more tightly, "and there is nothing I would rather do than make mad passionate love to you, however…"

"However," I threw up my hands in mock despair, "here it comes! However!"

"However," he insisted, taking my chin in his hand and kissing me firmly, "I will see that the estate is secure first. You may get started on your accounts and I shall meet you in my bedroom shortly."

"Woohoo!" I giggled and patted his derriere, "we get to see Dave the Dragon!"

"Yes," he sighed dramatically, "you shall see Dave." Shaking his head slowly, but wearing a grin despite himself, my mate released me in the Great Hall. I turned to the left and went up the stone stairs while he crossed the wide hall to the French doors. Though I didn't hang around to witness it, I knew he'd be contacting the gate house, the stables, and the mansion security team before joining me. I suspected he was also in contact with his pack, the vampires and wolves he held dominion over, but that was merely a hunch, or maybe I figured he was doing so because I would do so.

"Oh well," I spoke aloud, though softly, "Dave, here I come!"

Chapter 32

The days following my successfully dispatching the Grimoire after recovering from the dragon fire blast were exceedingly slow for me, despite Amon's assurances to the contrary. Time moved glacially, it seemed. Ulrich and I talked often and he did offer me some books to read. The texts offered various rituals and spells, mostly dealing with sympathetic magic, but they were light diversions at best. I think my mentor and I both missed Siri more than we were willing to admit and it felt like there was an elephant in the room when we were together. The elephant was the black German shepherd's absence and we couldn't bring ourselves to discuss it. Rufus came out of Ulrich's beard from time to time, nibbling a cracker or morsel of cheese, and he'd sometimes run down the witch's arm, perch in his palm and do a little mouse dance, hopping and playing with his tail. It truly did lift my spirits to see the wee creature and how he obviously loved Ulrich.

As my need for nourishment was slight, I certainly wasn't exerting myself, I only fed on two other humans after Ory Broussard. One was an older man, William P.

Davis, still in his prime but likely a decade older than Ory, and the other, Danny Vernier, was probably in his late teens or early 20s. Besides feeding I was challenged to 'read' them as I touched them and then directed to type up what I'd perceived in a file on my computer. It took me a few days, but I did eventually get accounts of all the 'reading' experiences into a file and emailed it to Ulrich's computer.

Winter took me out shooting from time to time and I mentally checked in with Max to make sure my spell making the Grimoire invisible remained intact, but other than that, my time was my own. I practiced my fiddle incessantly, so anticipating my return to performing on stage. Though she didn't say anything, of course, I got the impression that my playing 'The Lady of Shallot' over and over was starting to wear on Lily's nerves, but there was a short passage in the song that I couldn't quite get smooth enough to suit me. To my delight, Elspeth came by one night with her brother lugging her cello along. She joined me on the veranda and we played for quite some time, each enjoying the other's talent. Her training was a bit more classical than mine and I found the challenge of keeping up with her most enjoyable. I'd missed sharing music with others. Amon, Winter, and other members of the Montjean estate were always kind and encouraging about my fiddle playing, but they didn't speak the same language, as it were, and Elspeth certainly did. Bastiaan and Amon joined us on the veranda for a bit before excusing themselves and disappearing through the French doors.

"I wanted to tell you that I took your advice," Elspeth spoke quietly and conspiratorially. "I went out on my own while my brother was away."

"Elspeth," I heaved a sigh, "were you at least armed? Are you comfortable defending yourself if needs be?"

"I've got this," she hiked her long skirt up and pulled a very sharp looking stiletto from her boot, "and I think I'm capable of tearing someone's throat out if I'm threatened."

"But, thinking and doing are two different things," I explained, "so please, from now on if you feel like going out contact me, or even Winter for that matter, so that someone can go with you until you're a bit more experienced in the 'real world'." I made quotation marks in the air with my fingers.

"Oh," she giggled brightly, "okay. I hadn't thought of that. I was just so excited and proud of myself for doing something without Bastiaan."

"I understand," I nodded, "and I know how that freedom feels. I'm happy that you're stepping out, but please...next time?"

"Got it, Cat," she smiled, "I'll call you or borrow one of your guards. I just don't want my brother to find out."

"Your secret's safe," I patted her hand, "and now, a little more music?"

"Please!"

We played and enjoyed ourselves until the wee hours. A blush of pink was just creeping into the sky when we entered the mansion, instruments in their cases. Amon and Bastiaan were discussing some matter, and when we entered the Great Hall and approached them, they clammed up like guilty children.

"What's going on?" I grinned first at my mate then Elspeth's brother. It was almost dizzying to be so close to such incredibly attractive males and I wondered if Elspeth felt it too.

"Just discussing Council matters, my love," Amon replied, relieving me of my violin case. Bastiaan took two steps toward his sister and took the heavy cello case from her.

"Ah, boring stuff," I huffed. "Elspeth, it was great playing music with you. I'd love it if you'd come again."

"I'd be happy to," my new friend bowed slightly. "I'm sure we'll see each other soon."

"Bastiaan," I smiled at her brother then found myself dropping my eyes from his gaze. Curious as to what that meant, I shook it off and muttered something about having a good day or a pleasant morning or something before turning back to Amon.

"I'll excuse myself," I looked into my mate's blood red eyes, pulling my dark glasses down my nose slightly to favor him with a bawdy wink.

"I shall see to our guests and join you soon, my love," he replied succinctly and I dashed up the stairs with confusion filling my head and a blush rising up my neck.

'*Ca-at,*' came the childlike voice again and dread washed over me. If it was the Grimoire again that meant the spell wasn't working, or something had happened to break it. '*Ca-at,*' the voice repeated my name.

"*Max!*" I silently called to the librarian and was pleased and relieved when he instantly answered. When I turned the corner and moved into the corridor I knew it would be safe to speak without risking being overheard.

"Yes, Cat," his voice sounded clearly around me. "How may I help you?"

"I think I heard the Grimoire call my name," I spoke aloud and at a normal volume. "Is it okay? Is it still there and safe?"

"Of course it is," he assured me, "and I'm looking at its spot right now."

"That's odd, isn't it?"

"You never mentioned that the book had spoken to you before," Max offered. "That may change the situation."

"How so, Max?" I queried, feeling Arathia's tentacles wrapping around my world and squeezing ever so gently but insistently.

"Talk to your mentor, Cat," he suggested. "Tell him about the Grimoire and see if you can find a way to separate yourself from it. Obviously putting it here and making it invisible is enough to keep it safe, but not enough to keep it from you."

"Oh, crap," I sighed, wondering if I'd ever be free of the sorceress. "Okay, I'll let you know what I find out. Thanks Max!"

"Blessings to you, Cat," the librarian called gently, his voice dissipating as he severed the connection on our weird form of communication.

My libido had taken a direct hit when the Grimoire's voice echoed in my head, and I decided then and there that I'd not be able to rest or focus until I'd dealt with the blasted book. Disappointed that my carnal workout had to be postponed, I turned around and retraced my steps down the stairs and into the Great Hall. Though the lights still burned brightly the place was empty. Bastiaan and Elspeth had apparently departed and Amon was somewhere seeing to security, I assumed. I had a vague idea of where Ulrich's room was downstairs so I turned to the right and went through the arched doorway to the lower level.

'*Ca-at,*' the voice called again, laughing and this time I just ignored it, intent on finding my mentor.

"Ulrich?" I called as I approached the area along the hallway where the guestrooms were situated. There were actually five guest bedrooms in that area, which was at the opposite end of the hall from the coffin room. "Ulrich, are you there?"

"Mmph," came from behind the second door on the left moments before it swung open and my mentor poked his head out, blinking and rubbing one eye with his fist. "Cat? Is that you? Is something wrong?"

"Yes, Ulrich," I sighed, "and I'm sorry to disturb you, but I have a problem that apparently only you can help me with."

"Oh," he seemed genuinely surprised, "Oh, please. Let me grab my robe. Come in, come in!" He disappeared into the darkness and I heard the rustle of fabric then the overhead lights snapped on. He extended his right arm in a gesture of invitation as he finished tying the belt on his robe with his left hand.

"Again, I do apologize," I offered as I stepped into the small but tidy bedroom. The bed clothes were a bit rumpled, but other than that the room was surprisingly neat. There were matching leather wingback chairs adjacent to the bed and a small table between the two held a black ceramic based lamp. My mentor indicated I take the chair on the left and then lowered himself into the other chair, holding his robe closed as he did so.

"How can I help you, Cat?" He began as he clicked on the lamp between us.

"Well, I think I forgot to mention to you that the Grimoire spoke to me," I smiled at the understatement. "I mean, it called my name and laughed at me. It didn't really speak to me."

"I see," he nodded, running his hand down his beard in contemplation, "and this is a problem?"

"I wouldn't have thought so, but even though I've put the book somewhere safe and put a spell on it to make it invisible, it's still calling my name," I explained. "Is there some way to shut it up?"

"You have to remember that the Grimoire is a living, breathing thing," he smiled gently.

"So I can suffocate and kill it?" I asked in jest.

"You probably could," he responded with a chuckle, "but that might not be a good idea. If you were unsuccessful you'd have one seriously pissed off book of power angry with you!"

"Ah," I nodded, "agreed. So what can I do?"

"Think of it this way," he spread his hands, "that Grimoire was asleep before the Council gave it to you. When it changed hands it sensed the difference in energies and woke up, so to speak. Now it's awake and like anyone who has just awakened, it's hungry."

"Hungry, for what?" I gaped.

"For your blood, now that you're its mistress," he explained. "Look at it as if the Grimoire were a thousand year old toddler who has been disturbed from its nap. It's cranky, it's hungry, and it's in need of distraction."

"Really?" I shook my head in wonder, "A thousand year old toddler, oh my! So, how do I entertain it and get it to go back to sleep? It's not like I can sing it a lullaby, it's a book!"

"You're correct, Cat," he nodded, "it is a book. How better to entertain a book than with a book?"

"So, I'm supposed to read it 'War and Peace' or something? Bore it back to sleep?"

"No," he laughed, "nothing like that. You don't have to read it anything."

"I just slide a book onto the shelf beside it and let it do its own reading?"

"Well," he smiled brightly at me, "you could possibly do that and hope that it would work. But I suspect there's a better way."

"I'm all ears!"

"How do you lull a toddler to sleep?"

"Rock it to sleep with a real rock?" I offered hopefully.

"No, Cat," he huffed in exasperation, "you sing it to sleep."

"So now I have to sing the Grimoire a lullaby?" I wasn't trying to be obtuse but my mentor was not cutting a clear path through the jungle of my confusion.

"No, no," he shook his head. "You feed it some of your blood to satisfy its hunger. Like anything it will grow comfortable once that hunger's gone and it will be easy to lull it to sleep, not by singing it a lullaby but by putting a book of music, with a few ancient lullabies in it, beside it."

"A book of music?"

"Yes, music is mathematical," Ulrich offered, "and the Grimoire will be intrigued to try to understand it. If you put a book of just lullabies beside it the Grimoire might smell a trap and refuse to investigate, but if the book you put beside it has but a few ancient and powerful lullabies scattered through it the Grimoire should be curious and will be trapped once it delves into it."

"Wow, really?" I couldn't help but show my surprise.

"Really," my mentor responded. "It will go back to sleep."

"And Max, the librarian, probably has many books of music," I snapped my fingers, "and he would know where to get copies of ancient powerful lullabies too!"

"Most likely, yes!"

"Thank you, thank you, thank you," I almost squealed in delight, "thank you so much!"

Leaping from my chair in joy, I offered him my hand. We shook hands like we'd just concluded a business deal, and perhaps we had.

"Though I'd prefer to be completely rid of the Grimoire," I admitted, "I guess having it sleeping is better than nothing. Max suggested I try to separate myself from the thing."

"You cannot separate yourself from it now that you're the Grimoire's mistress," he responded, "but by lulling it back to sleep you'll be mostly free of its influences."

"Speaking of which," I smiled brightly, glancing at the rumpled bed, "I'll let you get back to sleep,"

"Thank you, Cat," Ulrich sighed and rose from his chair, "I believe I shall do just that."

Intentionally ignoring Ulrich's qualification of 'mostly' regarding being free of the Grimoire's influences, I exited his room and made my way upstairs, heartened that I now had a plan of attack. I'd reach out to Max again as soon as possible and hopefully we'd put the matter, and the Grimoire, to bed.

For three nights after Elspeth and Bastiaan's visit, I watched Amon suspiciously. When I asked what he was up to he sidestepped my questions or simply denied that there was anything afoot. Realizing there were only so many times I could beat my head against that particular brick wall, I gave up asking questions and just let the matter drop. Max had not responded to my call since Ulrich and I had our conversation and my unease at being unable to silence the Grimoire was growing. It called my name two or three times a night, and once it had awakened me from sleep during the day.

A week later, as I arose from my coffin stretching, yawning, and scratching myself in a rather unladylike manner, I found a large white box with a red ribbon around it atop the now empty 'feeder's' coffin. No one else was around and when I called out I got no answer, so I shuffled my bare feet across the smooth earthen floor and approached the package. A little white note was attached to the red ribbon and it read simply 'For Passion' in Amon's highly recognizable handwriting. Though I couldn't imagine what might be in the box or even why my mate had given it to me, I took little time to consider the possibilities before ripping the ribbon off and removing the lid. Crisp white tissue paper lay carefully folded over the dark fabric beneath and when I hurriedly pulled it away I discovered an elegant, black satin and taffeta ball gown folded perfectly. Pulling it from the box by the delicate satin spaghetti straps, I fell in love with the fitted bustier type bodice and marveled at the voluminous black taffeta skirt. Unable to imagine what occasion this lovely garment might be for, I held it up before me, shook out the length of skirt, and danced around the room in delight.

When I spied my violin case on the shelf next to my clothes my surprise stopped me dead in my tracks.

"I've never brought you down here," I murmured as I ran my hand across the leather case and spoke to the much loved instrument within, "so who did? And just as importantly, why are you here?" My confusion gave way to curiosity and I could stand it no longer, so I draped the ball gown over my left forearm and picked up the violin case in my right hand. True, I'd no contacts in, no dark glasses covering my eyes, my hair probably looked like a rat's nest, and my sleep shirt and lounging pants weren't exactly designed for public, but I had no patience to deal with any of that. Barefoot, I threw open the coffin room door and padded down the hallways and up the stairs. In my excitement I was tempted to call out for Amon and let my cry reverberate through the entire mansion, but there was something too pristine, too elegantly proper about the place to shatter its quiet in that manner. After all, the Montjean estate was no high school gymnasium.

Across the Great Hall and into the study, I skidded to a halt on the Persian rug before the leather sofa. To my relief, Amon and Ulrich were standing near the fire place and ceased their discussion when I made my spectacular, if not exactly graceful, entrance.

"Would you care to explain this?" I looked at my mate, lifting my left arm so he could see that I was referring to the ball gown. "And this? What was it doing downstairs?" I hefted the violin case for dramatic effect.

"Ah," he smiled, "I was awaiting this."

"And?" Patience was not my strong suit and I was already planning what I might have to do to pry the information from him.

"There will be a performance tomorrow night, Beloved," he took the violin from me and placed it carefully on the glass table behind the sofa. "It is customary to have a ceremony when a Master Vampire's sirelings are accepted into another's fold. Those of Sabre's line who are pledging themselves to you and to me will attend as well as the Council of Five and any others of our kind who are so inclined. You and Elspeth shall entertain us after the formalities have concluded but before the celebration begins."

"There's a celebration too?" I paused to allow the image of several hundred vampires and the Council dancing and drinking and partying hearty in the garden, but I just couldn't maintain the image. I couldn't really imagine vampires partying!

"Something of a celebration, yes," Amon insisted, "and that you shall see for yourself in good time. In the meantime, might I suggest you contact Elspeth, who is even now being gifted with a similar garment by her brother, and decide what you two would like to perform?"

"I, um," I shook my head trying to take in what I was being told. "Sure! I guess that would make sense. Wait. Tomorrow night? You're giving us less than 24 hours to pull this together?"

"My love," my mate offered a look of forbearance, "you are not being asked to perform an entire opera. You and Elspeth will simply play two or three pieces, those of your choice, and then everyone will mingle. The ceremony will be formal, but once that is complete everyone may relax and enjoy the rest of the night."

"And then?"

"And then, the following night the moon will be full," he replied. "Once that is passed, assuming you experience no anomalous side effects from the dragon fire, you may contact Ms. Green and have her reinstate you on the performance schedule at Lamey's."

"Woohoo!" I squealed in delight and relief, "A return to normalcy! I love it! Thank you, my love. Now, I'm going upstairs to try this on and get myself cleaned up and dressed. Then I'll call Elspeth. I assume you have her contact number?"

"I do, of course," Amon nodded slightly. "It is on the desk blotter in my office. The note has Bastiaan's name on it."

"Naturally," I rolled my eyes then kissed my love on the cheek before turning to go. "And howdy, Ulrich," I threw my mentor a smile and a brief salute, "didn't mean to ignore you, this is just too…"

"Understood, Cat," Ulrich smiled and toasted me with what I assumed was a mug of coffee, "much excitement. Don't let me keep you. We'll do some work later."

"Sure!" I laughed at the notion of doing any studying or spell working with this ceremony and performance on my mind. "I'll be back down when I have things taken care of for tomorrow."

"I'll await you on the veranda," he bowed, politely dismissing me.

Excited, I took the steps two at a time and raced down the corridor. I was pulling my sleep shirt over my head even as I entered the Sapphire room and, tossing the ball gown across the bed, raked the lounge pants down my legs. The bodice of the garment laced up the front but that was just decoration, I realized as I found the hidden zipper at the back. Forcing myself to be calm and open the zipper carefully, I then took a deep breath before working my way through the crisp crinoline underskirt to the soft lining beneath. A thrill rushed through me as I slipped my arms up the skirt and through the bodice, sliding the delicate straps up my arms and snuggling the garment into place. It felt wonderful and I knew it was perfect for the performance. I coaxed the zipper up and smoothed down the skirt then straightened the black satin ribbon that laced up the front. Being vampire, I couldn't really see myself in a mirror, but I could see the garment and a bit of my outline so that would have to suffice. Opening the armoire that sat against the far wall, I admired the gown in the full length mirror and, oddly enough, didn't even miss my own image.

"I'll have to get Lily to do something with this mop," I shoved one hand into my unruly mane, "but all in all, I think I look pretty good!" Spinning around the room a few times, pretending to waltz in some fairy tale castle, I realized that I was happy, anticipating the performance, and just as importantly, looking forward to getting back to Lamey's.

"Back to reality, Cat," I sighed as I ceased my dance and returned to the side of the bed. "Time to get busy!" Removing the ball gown carefully, I found an empty hanger in the closet and put it neatly away before pulling a pair of jeans out and grabbing a t-shirt from the chest of drawers. Showering and washing my hair quickly, I dressed and donned contacts and glasses, then pulled a blue chambray shirt on, folding the long sleeves up to my elbows. Blades in their holsters securely fastened to my forearms, I pulled on socks and boots, fluffed my air-drying locks and left the room.

In Amon's office, I phoned the number on the note on his desk blotter and Elspeth answered on the first ring. She was as excited as I and we quickly compiled a list of possible pieces we'd play then agreed to meet an hour before the performance to warm up and go over our options. None of the pieces we were contemplating was especially complicated but we did want to do well. She giggled a bit as she described the gown Bastiaan had given her and I couldn't help join in her delight as I described my gown to her. We were both giddy with anticipation.

"*Ca-at,*" the Grimoire called as I ended the call.

"Hush, Grimoire!" I called out in the empty room, only barely restraining myself from shortening the name to Grim. "I'm trying to reach Max and as soon as I do I'll come see you."

Laughter was the response. I tried once more to reach Max, but there was still no answer from the librarian. Realizing that I was going to have to take the matter to Amon, I rose from the leather desk chair, turned off the light, and exited the office.

Later, as my excitement ebbed a bit and I had time to think, my mind returned to the island, the Agathodemon and the bolt of dragon fire I'd received. Something was niggling at my mind, something overlooked or forgotten, and I couldn't figure out what it might be. I played and replayed the image of vampires turning to ash and crumbling to dust. Then the thought of the dragon demon who gave her life to save me, of course, darkened my thoughts and I realized I was doing myself no good. I shook myself from my funk and made my way to the veranda where, true to his word, Ulrich was waiting for me. He was relaxed and sitting with his legs stretched out and crossed at the ankles, a large book spread open on his lap. He closed it and started to rise as I approached.

"No, no," I waved my hand at him, "don't get up. Relax."

"Thank you, My Lady," he smiled warmly, "please, sit. Join me."

"Thanks," I sighed, lowering myself into one of the teakwood chairs.

"I sense you are not interested in studying?"

"I just feel like I have so much going on in my head," I shrugged. "Can we just chat and enjoy the night? I promise I'll study and work twice as hard after tomorrow's festivities!"

"Of course," he agreed readily, "that sounds fine."

We shared coffee, which Lily presented to us on a silver tray along with various sweet and savory morsels, and talked or merely relaxed in companionable silence. I had questions I could ask my mentor, but they were almost too numerous and too overwhelming so I pushed them to the back of my mind and drank coffee. From time to time we shared sporadic conversation, but the silence seemed to roll back in like a tide to the shore and eventually we gave up. We were comfortable, but we could both feel Siri's absence and I wondered if that was what kept silencing us.

"I take it you've had no luck dealing with the Grimoire?" He raised his eyebrows and looked at me as he took a sip of coffee.

"No," I sighed, "and I'm getting a little worried. I can't seem to reach Max."

"So, a trip to the library is likely in order?"

"It is," I admitted, "but first I'm going to see if His Lordship can contact the librarian so I'll know the trip is not a waste of time."

"That seems logical," he nodded in understanding.

"*Max!*" I silently called out on a whim.

"Cat!" the librarian's response was quick and clear. "Can I help you?"

Turning to my mentor I raised one eyebrow. "Can you hear that?"

"I can," Ulrich replied. "It seems your librarian is no longer missing."

"Excuse me, Ulrich," I smiled, "I have a call to finish."

"Of course," he stood and bowed politely as I moved from the veranda, through the French doors and into the Great Hall.

"Max," I envisioned the ink-smudged, slightly disheveled, little librarian behind the expansive desk in the library's main room, "we need to talk!"

Chapter 33

The garden was crowded with newly dedicated sire-lings and otherworldly entities. The ceremony itself was over, having been very formal and quite succinct. I now had the responsibility of some of Sabre's sirelings and Amon had many more. To my surprise, Bastiaan had also accepted some of Sabre's offspring, but none of the other Council members were involved. It was actually a lovely ceremony with those attaching themselves to each of us standing and solemnly oathing themselves to their chosen protector. Elspeth and I quickly got set up on the veranda and began to play Bach's 'Duet in A Minor' as the crowd quieted and turned toward us. Strands of twinkling lights illuminated the trees, outlined the garden beds, and decorated the balustrade that edged the veranda. Wrought iron lanterns hung from arched hooks near the top of the stone wall and splashed the grass with disks of soft golden light. Stars in the night sky overhead danced brightly until the near full moon rose first red, then orange, then yellow and finally white once it was well above the horizon. The light was soft, but the shadows were long and deep.

From where I sat, violin tucked beneath my chin, I could see a few audience members clearly, though others were hidden in shadow or shrouded in cloaks. As Elspeth and I played, I scanned the crowd, looking for faces I recognized. Amon stood with Thammuz and Bastiaan, and Snarl, in his human form, stood alone near the wall. I caught sight of a couple of other Council members, and found Ulrich chatting with Lucius near the edge of the garden. As we neared the final notes of our last movement, I caught sight of a familiar and most unwelcome face in the crowd and it was all I could do to focus on the music and not leap to my feet in alarm.

Ian, to my surprise and dismay, stood silently staring at me, glaring even, from beyond the corner of the veranda. Apparently I had not dealt him a mortal blow in my attempt to escape the island after all! Part of me was relieved that I'd not killed him, while another part of me wished vehemently to do so now. Before the would-be vampire stood Nene and Carly Jo, their faces frozen in terror, eyes wide and unblinking. Ian had one hand on each girl's shoulder and it was clear that he was holding them against their will.

When we finished playing, Elspeth and I stood and took our bows as the crowd applauded politely. There were a few half-hearted calls for encores but not enough of a consensus to convince my partner and me to continue, so we both set about putting our instruments away before joining our escorts. It was all I could do to remain calm and act as if nothing unusual was happening. Just as I opened my case to put my violin away, a heavy blast rocketed through the garden, the earth shuddered, and a bright flash blinded me momentarily. The crowd erupted into a screaming, stampeding herd and began racing for the gates or taking to the skies in their panic. Elspeth grabbed my arm and screamed "What's happening?" to me over the noise. It was impossible to answer and before I could try, Bastiaan, was at his sister's side, grabbing her elbow and hustling her into the mansion. Amon came up behind me, placing a hand on either of my arms, but he did not rush to move me. Instead he lowered his lips to my ear and simply offered "I see them!" so I knew he'd seen the young girls and the man who now held them.

Ian made no move, nor did he allow Nene and Carly Jo to flee with the rest of the crowd. By the time the explosive light burned away to smoke and ash, there were only a handful of attendees left behind. The Council members, except for Bastiaan, stood together looking around, seemingly unconcerned. Amon's security team had appeared in the chaos and guided the crowd safely off the grounds and they were now standing at attention, looking at Amon and me, as well as the stranger holding the two teens.

"Surprised to see me?" Ian smiled maniacally, shoving first Carly Jo, then Nene, ahead of him, attempting to use them as human shields.

"I thought you were dead," I let my words drip venom. "Sure am sorry I was wrong."

"We didn't do nothin'," Nene blurted out. "We just heard the music and were peekin' in at the gate. We didn't mean to come in. This guy made us!"

"Nene, shut up!" Carly Jo growled at her companion.

"It's okay, girls," I nodded and gave them a meaningful look, "I understand. You're not in any trouble. It's okay."

"Talk to me!" Ian yelled, his face turning red. "You owe me! Sabre and Cesare promised to make me one of you and you destroyed them! Someone owes me."

"Relax, Ian," I tried to focus his attention on me and away from the girls.

"Don't tell me to relax, Witch!"

"Cat," Amon spoke in a voice of warning, "please."

"You're right, Ian," I took a hesitant step toward the man, "I do owe you. And when you let the girls go I'll give you what you're owed. Just release them."

"No!" he screamed. "You're trying to trick me. I don't trust any of you. The girls stay with me."

Winter and Chimaera were both holding guns on the man, I could feel Amon's anger building and his Hand of Destruction itching to do its thing. As my gown was sleeveless and it would be awkward, I'd left my throwing blades in their holsters upstairs, but I did have a blade strapped to my thigh. Not exactly practical to reach the weapon beneath all the taffeta and crinoline without drawing attention, I just kept speaking to Ian in a calming voice. Though I was consciously unsure of why I was doing so, I kept slowly moving toward him as well. When there was a span of maybe five yards between us, I extended my right arm behind me, willed Wicked Little Thing into my hand, grasped it firmly and, in a forward and slightly upward swing, threw it right between the girls' heads. It thwacked solidly into Ian's left shoulder, spinning him around backwards and forcing him to release his captives. The wound wouldn't kill him, I realized, but was enough to startle him and give me an advantage.

Rushing forward, I grabbed Nene and Carly Jo by their hands and pulled them away to where Winter and Chimaera stood. The guards accepted them silently and placed the girls behind them, effectively shielding the terrified teens. Ian was screaming and holding his shoulder, blood pouring from the wound. I returned to him just as Amon reached the man, grabbing him by the scruff of his neck.

"You do not intend to make this human one of us!" My mate growled with undisguised fury.

"Put him down, please," I sighed and looked at my love. "I have a plan." And even as I said it, I realized my words were true. I did have a plan. Ian had never told me why he wanted to become a vampire, neither Sabre nor Cesare had confided the reason for their agreement with the man, but I needed to know. I knew he coveted power, but there was something else, something he was trying to hide, perhaps even from himself, and before I made a decision one way or the other I would know the truth.

"Your Lordship," Ulrich interjected, stepping near Amon, "I believe Her Ladyship's plan is a good one and worth exploring."

My Master Vampire cocked his head and looked at Ian. I could see he was weighing his options and then finally he dropped the bleeding man to the ground.

"Proceed with caution," my mate growled at me and took two steps back.

Ian's legs gave way and he crumpled to the ground, still holding his bleeding shoulder. I moved forward and bent down to talk to him.

"I can make you vampire," I looked deeply into his eyes, "or I can heal you, but first I must touch you for a moment."

"I found this," he pulled a familiar vial of blood from his shirt pocket, "but I can't make it work myself. Make me one of you!" He barked, eyes wild with fear, "I want to be what you are. Now!"

"Yes," I took the vial from his bloodstained fingers, "your body must be drained nearly to the point of death before you ingest this." An 'Ah-hah' gong went off in my head when I realized it was the vial of my blood I'd overlooked and forgotten. The battle on the island had happened so suddenly and I'd been so distracted by all that since occurred, I'd completely forgotten the vial sailing through the air and Sabre catching it easily. Relieved to have reclaimed what had been stolen from me, I tucked the vial into my bodice and turned my attention to the wounded man before me.

"First," I insisted, showing him my empty palm before placing it on the left side of his face. The moment I opened my thoughts to his there was a rush of confusion and contention. I could catch brief snatches of memories, his childhood, family, friends, important moments, but something kept breaking in, interfering. Finally I found an image of Ian deep in the earth, though I couldn't ascertain why or what he was doing there.

What I could 'see' is that when he returned from below something came with him. He'd picked up a parasite and it was very strong and very determined. It was the parasite that wanted Ian to be made vampire. It knew that if its host became immortal it would be free to wreak what havoc it intended in this world and would always have a safe haven to which it could return. Though I couldn't figure out precisely what the parasite was, I could feel that it was malicious and that the only reason Ian, the man, remained alive and functioning at all was because he had once been spiritually strong and emotionally determined. Ian had held this thing at an impasse, but now that would be impossible to maintain.

Healing hand itching profusely, I pulled my right hand away from his face and looked into his eyes. For a brief moment I saw Ian, the real human one, in those eyes, then something asserted itself and everything about him shifted. Now, in those cold eyes, I saw the entity that sought to control the man and enter this world for its own destructive pleasures.

For a moment I considered my options. I could heal Ian, of his shoulder wound anyway, and then try to reason and bargain with him, but I had the feeling that the darkness inside him would not be stalled for long. Sinking my fangs into his throat and draining him of what blood remained in his body was also an option, but then I'd have to feed him my blood in order to transform him into a vampire and I'd not done that yet. Something told me that even if I had created sirelings before, I would not want this one as one of my own. Still, it might be interesting to see what....

'NO!' A voice, very masculine and very insistent, echoed through my mind, startling me out of my reverie. Peering around the softly lit garden, looking at each of the attendees that remained, I could not find the origin of the voice, but I was pretty sure I was supposed to heed its message. The only reasonable solution finally surfaced through the maelstrom of my thoughts.

'My love,' I called to Amon with my mind, *'this is not just a man. There is something evil inside him and it will not let him go. I cannot heal him and I cannot make him vampire.'*

'And,' my mate responded immediately, *'you need...'*

'Yes, my warrior,' I answered silently, *'I need your Hand of Destruction.'*

My mate did not question me or my intentions, he simply stepped beside me, offered his right hand to help me stand, then gently moved me away. Without a word he bent down and placed his left hand on Ian's head. The man was silent but the entity inside his body was screaming so loud I thought my head might explode. I tried to cover my ears to quiet the noise, but that had

618

no effect. Though I stood several feet away from the wounded man the force that was expelled from his body as the Hand of Destruction did its work was enough to knock me off my feet and blessed silence and darkness swam over me.

When my eyes fluttered open I found that I was on the ground with Amon cradling my upper body in his arms. Bishop was crouched down nearby, digging through his medicine bag. I could see my mate's lips moving and I could tell that he was speaking to me but I could hear nothing. When I tried to communicate with my beloved via our telepathic connection I found it too was dead. The memory of Ian and the evil darkness inside him swam up from the depths of my thoughts and I looked at the place near the wall where he'd lain prone and bleeding. Only a dark patch on the ground where he'd bled remained. When my eyes met Amon's I felt an instant connection and I was drawn back completely into my body.

"Ian is no more," my beloved assured me. "How do you feel? Are you well?"

"I'm fine," I responded, even then marveling at the truth of my words. "I really am fine! How are the girls? Are they okay?"

Struggling to stand and find the terrified Nene and Carly Jo, I rose as Amon pulled me up.

"The girls are well," he answered. "Their memories have been properly adjusted so none of this trauma will follow them. They are being escorted to their homes."

"Thank Goddess and God," I sighed, straightening my gown. Some smudges darkened the taffeta skirt, likely just dirt, but all things considered the garment still looked good. "I'm glad this night is done!"

"Well," Amon offered hesitantly.

"Wait, it IS done, isn't it?" Looking around the garden I realized it was empty of the night's celebrants. Only my mate, Bishop, and my mentor Ulrich remained.

"There is the matter of your report," my mentor interjected, index finger raised in the 'wait a minute' gesture.

"Trust me, Witch Master," I laughed in relief at the jest, "I'll remember the details quite well tomorrow and I'll be happy to file a report for you then."

"Very well," he bowed deeply and I noticed that he'd gathered his lengthy beard and secured it in two places with leather thongs. In fact, for the first time tonight, I noticed that he looked quite elegant in a black jacket and white shirt and red tie. A tiny silver earring caught the soft lights of the garden and gave him a roguish air.

"Good night, Ulrich," I smiled, thinking myself fortunate to have such a wonderful teacher in addition to my beloved warrior and all the others in my world.

"My Lady," he nodded and touched his forehead, "I shall see you on the morrow."

"Indeed you will," I responded as he turned and walked into the mansion. Bishop closed his leather bag and followed my mentor without a word.

A light breeze bounced the strings of lights in the trees and rustled the rose bushes nearby. My warrior took me in his arms and kissed me deeply. Time stood still briefly.

'Come, Passion,' his thoughts rang clearly through my mind. Our telepathic connection was once more functioning, to my great relief.

"Yes, my love," I laughed as I slipped my arm around his waist and we moved to the veranda. Someone, I noticed, had cleared the equipment Elspeth and I had used in our performance and the garden itself looked tidy, as if nothing had just happened there. I could see no evidence of the explosion and made a mental note to ask Amon about that matter another time. As we neared the French doors I suddenly realized how tired I was, how much I truly needed rest, and how I was looking forward to sleeping in my love's arms.

"Amon," I paused and turned to my mate, "did you happen to notice what happened to my blade, the athame? I didn't notice it on the ground and I didn't actually see Ian pull it from his shoulder."

"I was really rather more curious as to how you came to have it," he responded lightly. "But I saw no evidence of it after you wounded the man."

"It was Wicked Little Thing," I explained. "Arathia's athame that apparently now belongs to me and appears when I will it to do so. It does seem to have a will of its own and disappears when it desires."

"So, perhaps the weapon knew its job was complete," my beloved reasoned aloud. "If it is indeed yours now I should think that no one else could touch it."

"Really?" I smiled, thinking how cool it would be to have such a weapon that would do my bidding and could disappear before anyone else could lay a hand on it.

"You might try to summon, what was it you called it, Wicked Little Thing?"

"I might," I chuckled, "if I weren't so exhausted perhaps I would. But that's for another time.

"So we go to the library tomorrow and see Max?" My mate easily changed the subject.

"We do," I nodded. "Max said it would take him a little time to collect the right book and copy the powerful ancient lullabies we'll need to put the Grimoire back to sleep. He suggested it might be best to do the work at Full Moon and he thinks we may be able to see the Grimoire by that light and not have to disturb the spell of invisibility. I'll give it a taste of my blood and slide the lullabies beside it and hopefully that will be the end of the matter."

"I hope you are correct," Amon squeezed my shoulder and pulled me in close to his body.

"Right now, I want you and our bed," I turned and placed my hands on his chest, rising on my tiptoes to place a kiss on his lips.

"That would be my pleasure, Beloved!" He bent down, wrapped his arms around me, and met my tender kiss with a more hungry and powerful one of his own.

Chapter 34

"Where exactly is Max's library?" I asked Amon as I shrugged into a long black duster, having carefully slid my blade holster adorned arms through the sleeves.

"I could show you where it lies on a map," he smiled, "but of course it would not show on any map."

"Just an idea, my love," I insisted. "You know that I fly with my eyes closed so I have only the vaguest ideas of where it is. The landscape, when we landed, did look hot, dusty, and dry. Was it Italy?"

"If you recall, Max was asked politely to make himself absent from that country," Amon helped straighten my collar.

"I know, I know," I grinned, "but I thought maybe you two had figured a way to remain unnoticed. That seems like something you might do."

"You may be correct," he nodded, "but no. The library is not in Italy. It is actually near Thorn Canyon, Utah, which is why we can easily reach the place."

"Utah, really?" I gaped, "That would have never occurred to me. How cool!"

"It is indeed," he nodded, "as you say, cool. Are you ready to go?"

"I am," I replied, grabbing the vial of my blood from the bedside table and holding it up for him to see before securing it in my pocket.

"You have need of that?" My beloved asked as he straightened his own long black coat and took my elbow.

"Gotta feed the Grimoire," I laughed as we exited the Sapphire room and made our way along the marble floored hall.

The full moon was rising in the night sky as we stepped out onto the veranda. Ulrich sat smoking a pipe in one of the teak chairs near the far end of the patio and had it not been for the scent of tobacco wafting through the air I might not have even noticed him.

"Greetings, Ulrich!"

"Good evening, Cat," my mentor responded, "and good evening Your Lordship."

"Ulrich," Amon nodded succinctly.

"Off to take care of your Grimoire, are you Cat?" He stood and took a long slow draught on his pipe.

"We are," I replied, feeling relief at the mere idea of having the matter done and over with.

"I'll not detain you then," Ulrich tapped the bowl of his pipe on the edge of his hand, emptying the contents into the grass beside the terrace, and bowed slightly before turning to make his way into the mansion.

"Now, ready?" Amon turned me to face him.

"I am," I smiled, "and do I get to go in my usual style or are you going to make me fly on my own?"

"We can fly as you have been," my mate offered, "but I suggest that this time you keep your eyes open. I know that seeing the energy rather than matter, when we fly as we do, bothers you, but the only way to get past that is to practice, tu saisis?"

"Yes," I sighed, "I understand. Okay, I'll try to keep my eyes open, but if I whoops my cookies it's all your fault!"

"Whoops your cookies?" Amon raised his eyebrows as he wrapped his arms around me.

"You know what I mean," I admonished as I wrapped my arms around his neck and kissed his lips firmly.

Power stirred in my gut and rose to meet my beloved's power as we rose in the darkness. I closed my eyes briefly to clear my mind and prepare myself for the dizzying vision I knew was coming. After a few moments, when I felt the air rushing past us and my hair stirring in the wind, I opened my eyes. It took me a few minutes to grasp what my eyes were telling me, but eventually I realized I was looking at the world on a cellular level, everything was energy and nothing was solid. A wave of nausea rolled through me then disappeared. Tightening my arms around Amon's neck, I moved my mouth close to his left ear and murmured that I was watching. He tightened his arms around me briefly in acknowledgement and we flew on.

When we landed at the base of the canyon wall, the wind whistled around us and I noticed roiling clouds in the sky. I had no idea of the weather in Utah or what was common and meant little, but my first thought was that a storm was imminent and we'd best hurry up the path to the library.

"Come," my mate took my hand and led the way along the zig-zagging trail. The urge to keep looking up at the sky or over my shoulder kept stealing over me and more than once I stumbled lightly over a stone or uneven patch of ground.

When at last we reached the library doors a light rain was falling, and though I wanted to ask what the odds of rain coming down when we happened to be there were, I had to put that matter aside to focus on dealing with the Grimoire.

Max greeted us warmly, offering handshakes and smiles. He was obviously happy to see us. The diminutive Tuatha De Danann looked younger than he did when I'd seen him before. Of course, this may have been due to the 'Rolling Stones' concert t-shirt he was wearing or it may have been the super-sized giant Guzzler drink he had in his hand, red straw at the ready. Where in the world one might get such a drink in this area did cross my mind, and if I remembered later I'd be sure to ask, but I told myself 'First things first' and held my tongue as he set the giant drink glass on what appeared to be a Union Jack coaster atop his desk.

"So," he clapped his hands gently and rubbed them together in eagerness, "we have work to do, yes?"

"Yes," I nodded as Amon helped me remove my coat and held it before me as I dipped my hand into the pocket. Pulling out the vial of my blood, I turned to the librarian. "Did you manage to find what I asked you for?"

"Indeed I did," he smiled brightly as he reached beneath the desk and brought out an obviously old and worn book. "This book of musical scores should do nicely and I copied three ancient and powerful lullabies to put into it. I had to copy the lullabies by hand in order to tap into their energy. I couldn't very well use the actual lullabies as we'd no longer have access to them if they were busy working on the Grimoire, you know?"

"I hadn't thought about that, Max," I admitted, suddenly feeling a twinge of guilt at how selfish I must seem. "I'm glad you did!"

"No problem, My Lady," he grinned and his dark eyes twinkled, "I've been doing this job a long time."

"Please," I reminded him, "call me Cat."

"Yes, yes," he bobbed his head up and down, "of course. I'm sorry. Cat, I'll remember."

"So what do we do first?" I asked, leaning one hip against the desk to gain a closer look at the book he'd found to use in the spell.

"Well," he began, "first Amon, my dear friend, is going to set up the chessboard for a game so that the two of us can enjoy ourselves and stay out of your way at the same time."

"Of course, Max," my mate bowed slightly in a mock salute, "I would be delighted." Having taken his long black coat off and hanging it on a hook on the wall beside the door next to mine, Amon looked relaxed and comfortable in a simple white linen dress shirt buttoned down the front, its tail hanging loose over his fitted black jeans. His pant legs were tucked into mid-calf height black leather boots and his hair lay loose on his shoulders. Distracted for a moment, I imagined unbuttoning that shirt and running my hands up his smooth chest then shook my head to focus. Amon set about putting the chess pieces on the board as I turned back to Max.

"And while he does that?"

"You feed the Grimoire first," Max picked up a few sheets of parchment paper upon which I could see musical staffs dotted here and there with various notes. I couldn't see the titles of the lullabies, but realized that's what they were as he neatly tucked them between the pages of the aged book he'd obtained.

"Okay, cool!" I smiled and proudly displayed the vial of my blood Sabre and Cesare had stolen from Zador.

"Very well," he nodded and took the vial from my hand. Opening it carefully, he peered into the glass tube. "Um, My Lady, I mean Cat, um, how old is this blood?"

"I don't really know," I admitted. "I guess it's not exactly fresh. Does that matter?"

"It wouldn't," he replied, turning the vial upside down, "if the blood was still liquid. It appears that this has dried to dust!"

"Oh," I laughed at my own foolishness. How in the world had I expected the blood in that vial to still be useable? "I guess I'll have to open a vein."

"I believe pricking your finger will be sufficient, Cat," he suggested, tucking the book of lullabies in his left elbow, he moved around the desk, opened a drawer, and produced an elongated thumb tack.

"Ah, much better idea," I smiled, accepting the sharp little gizmo from him. "So, how do I do this?"

"First," he rifled through the book and took the three sheets of parchment out again, "I'd like you to put a drop of your blood on each of these. Not a lot, just a drop to kinda entice your Grimoire."

"Okay," I stabbed the pad of my left middle finger with the tack and squeezed it until a drop of black blood appeared, "do I just drop it or smear it?"

"A drop will be fine," he nodded, spreading the music sheets out and holding the first one down. I dropped a splat of blood on it and he moved it carefully aside and placed the second sheet before me. Again, I let a drop of my blood fall to the page and Max moved it out of the way for the third page. When it too had been decorated with my blood, the librarian moved it back and looked at me. "Now, all you have to do is go put a few drops on the Grimoire."

"What? Do I just aim at the empty space and hope I hit it?" I shrugged. "You said something about the full moon's light."

"I did," he raised his right index finger in the air, "I did indeed. You just go stand by the book shelf and I'll show you what I meant."

As I moved to the bookcase adjacent to the desk and leaned over to peer at the empty spot on the shelf just above the bottom shelf, the lights in the library went off and darkness enveloped everything. About to call out and ask what was going on, I glanced up and noticed, for the first time, a skylight overhead. At just that moment the clouds in the sky parted and the full moon appeared casting a very bright beam of light right down around me. To my amazement and delight, the Grimoire appeared shimmering and ghost-like. My initial reaction was to clap my hands and dance up and down, but remembering that my index finger was bleeding for a purpose, I restrained my joy and let my hand hover above the tome. Three drops of black blood disappeared into the shimmering light that surrounded the Grimoire and as the lights in the library came back on something remarkable happened. An orb appeared where the book of power had been and, though it first appeared milky white, it turned scarlet and black, the colors swirling and mingling like an old fashioned lava lamp. In the blink of an eye the orb was gone and the empty space on the shelf returned.

"Now," Max appeared beside me, apparently having returned from turning the lights first off and then on again, "I'm going to go play chess with His Lordship. When the parchments are dry enough you can slip them between the pages of the music book there on the desk and finish up the spell. I know that this seems all rather straight forward and simple, but trust me, I think it's going to take some concentration and some time. We'll be here when you're done, Cat."

"Oh, um, okay," I muttered, glancing at the pages and book on the desk then back at the librarian. "Okay."

How in the world slipping one book next to another could take concentration and time was beyond my kenning, but I figured Max knew what he was talking about and watched him walk to the far side of the room where Amon sat at a small table with the chessboard set up before him.

Once the two men were seated and intent on their game, I turned back to the desk. The blood drops on the parchment paper were drying but not completely dried. I lowered myself and blew on them hoping to speed up the process. Surely it wouldn't matter if they were just a wee smidgen damp, I reasoned silently, as they were going into a book that would be closed and untouched for a very long time, maybe even forever. Opening the worn fabric-covered book, I let the pages fall open naturally and tucked one parchment in before flipping the pages and repeating the process two more times. Feeling satisfied that I'd done everything just right, I picked up the book and turned back to the shelf where the invisible Grimoire was stored.

"Ca-at," the lyrical voice slid around me like a snake and made me shudder.

"Be quiet," I whispered at the seemingly empty shelf. "You've been fed, now hush!"

"*Ca-at, Ca-at, Ca-at, Ca-at, Ca-at,*" the voice sing-songed, sounding strangely inebriated.

"Here you go," I offered, carefully slipping the book of music onto the shelf near where the tome should be.

"*Ca-at, Ca-at,*" the Grimoire taunted. "*Kitty Ca-at!*"

The book of music landed with a thud beside my feet. That annoying and infuriating musical laughter rang out all around me and I sighed. Picking up the book, I had a suspicion that this might be the difficulty Max mentioned. Obviously just slipping the book onto the shelf beside the Grimoire wasn't going to work so I had to come up with another plan. Crossing my legs, I sat on the floor of the library, glaring at the empty space on the shelf and wondering what I could do to be done with Arathia's book. As I flipped through the book of musical scores, I noticed one piece of work that felt familiar so I paused to look at the notes more carefully. Yes, I definitely recognized the melody, and the lyrics were written at the bottom of the four pages across which the piece was spread.

"Would this work?" I whispered to myself, considering trying to sing the Grimoire to sleep even though Ulrich had assured me that wouldn't be necessary.

Perhaps if I actually had a clue of what I was doing I'd not need to sing, but these were desperate times and I was becoming one seriously desperate witch. Verbalizing intentions had long been a way of releasing the energy of a spell, effectively casting it even, and witches around the world chanted and sang. Actually, as I sat there considering the matter further I realized that liturgy often included prayers spoken aloud, verbal invocations, and utterances of magical words and phrases. Maybe my idea wasn't so bad after all!

Though I wasn't keen on anyone else hearing me croon to the Grimoire, I softly began singing as sweetly and gently as I could, taking my time to enunciate each word and keeping the tones as pure and clear as possible. At first there seemed no response, and then, just barely audible, I could hear a voice joining mine. The Grimoire was singing with me! As exciting as that idea was, it was also a bit disconcerting and I bobbled a note before refocusing. Briefly I was singing alone again, but in time the Grimoire chimed in once more. Though I was very intent on my work, I couldn't help but sense Amon and Max moving up to stand behind me. At least they were silent and did nothing to distract me. I sang, and I sang, and when I'd reach the end of the song I'd start again as if the song were never-ending. The Grimoire sang with me, sometimes in tune, sometimes in harmony, and we just kept singing. When my throat began to feel dry and I grew afraid that my voice would crack and ruin the effect, I closed the book on my lap and oh so slowly, oh so gently, slipped it onto the shelf beside the Grimoire. Pulling my hands away from the music book, I scooted myself back from the bookcase, again, gently and quietly. Mentally crossing my fingers, I sang one last chorus of the melody and then fell silent. Nothing moved around me. There was no sound. The Grimoire was silent.

Amon took my left elbow and Max took my right, gently helping me unfold my legs and stand. I looked from my mate to the librarian and said nothing. Too afraid to speak, I turned around and moved to the desk on stiff, shaky legs.

"You did well, Cat!" Max broke the silence and for a moment I was sure I'd hear the music book thunk to the floor as the Grimoire singsonged my name again, but nothing happened.

"I guess maybe I did," I whispered, as my throat was so tired and worn I could barely speak.

"I told you that it would take a while, didn't I?" the librarian smiled.

"A while?" I strained to speak.

"Beloved, Max and I have enjoyed three games of chess while you were working," Amon explained, wrapping one arm around my shoulders, "and then we came to watch and have been standing here for almost an hour."

"You watched?" I cleared my throat.

"We did," he confessed as Max released my elbow and disappeared into another room.

"What did you see?" I wondered aloud, "I mean, besides me sitting on the floor singing to an invisible book, what was there to see?"

"It was beautiful, my darling," my mate said, tenderly touching my chin with one finger. "We could see your energy, and the power and control you wielded, it was most impressive. You had the Grimoire completely enchanted."

"I did?" I knew I'd followed my instincts, but my expectations had been quite low.

"You did, Cat," Max reappeared with a tall crystal goblet of water and handed it to me carefully.

"Wow!" I managed before putting my mouth on the glass and drinking slowly and deeply. The cool fluid soothed my throat and blessed relief followed after just a few swallows.

"Thank you so much," I smiled at Max. "I really needed that!"

"You're quite welcome," he nodded enthusiastically, "and rest assured that should there be any change or development with the Grimoire I will notify you immediately."

"Speaking of which," a sudden thought surfaced, "I tried several times to contact you and you didn't answer."

"Oh, my," he grinned sheepishly and accepted the nearly empty glass that I handed back to him, "that, well, yes. I must apologize. You see, there are labyrinthine tunnels beneath this building and sometimes, well, sometimes I simply must go exploring. I've found some amazing artifacts down there and sometimes the urge just gets the better of me. Again, I do apologize."

"So, when you're down in the tunnels…" I let the thought assemble in silence. At first Max looked expectant, then his expression shifted to one of confusion. A smile lit his face when he understood.

"Oh! The library is sealed tight and entirely safe while I'm away," he assured me. "There are books and other things here that are priceless and irreplaceable. I keep it very well protected, don't I Your Lordship?" He turned to Amon with appealing eyes.

"You do, Max," my mate agreed. "He does indeed, my darling. You need not be concerned."

"Fine," I nodded, still not entirely convinced, "then I guess we're done here. If you two are finished with your chess games?"

"Yes, of course," the librarian beamed, "it was so lovely to be able to serve you both. I do hope you'll drop by from time to time, and don't hesitate to contact me if I can be of further service." Retrieving our coats from the hooks on the wall, Max handed them to Amon and he helped me slip my duster up my arms and onto my shoulders.

"Farewell, Max," my beloved nodded to his Tuatha De Danann friend, "thank you for the games and your assistance. We shall meet again soon."

"Yes, thanks Max," I smiled, heading for the door and feeling suddenly very carefree and happy.

"Bright blessings to you both," Max called as Amon and I stepped into the dark night. The sky was clearing but there were a few wispy clouds left from the storm that had passed. The smell of rain still hung heavy in the air and small puddles of rainwater decorated the usually parched ground. As we made our way to the trail that wound down the canyon wall Amon held my hand and I drew him to a halt when an important matter arose in my mind.

"My love," I started, not entirely sure how to approach the issue, "um, I have a question. Or, there's something I need to know."

"Yes, Darling," he turned toward me and I could see his blood red eyes glowing beneath his dark contact lenses. "You have a question?"

"Well," I paused to gather the appropriate words, "you have told me on more than one occasion that you'd always keep me safe."

"I have indeed," he nodded succinctly.

"But, yet, well," dancing on a delicate thread I continued, "I was kidnapped. I was actually kidnapped twice. And you weren't there!" There. I'd said it. I'd ripped the band aid off as quickly as I could and now could only wait for what was coming.

"Ah," he smiled as if he'd been waiting for me to bring the matter up. "I understand your concern. Let me ask you, were you ever afraid while you were held captive?"

"Afraid?" I had to take a moment to think about it before answering, "Well, no. I was annoyed at being separated from you and I missed everyone at the estate. I was worried about Siri, but mostly for myself? I was curious!"

"Indeed you were," he replied. "You see, beloved, you still have the reactions and memories of a human, a mortal actually. Any human female would have felt threatened, in peril of harm or destruction, but you are no longer a human female. You are vampire and my blood courses through your veins."

"So I was never really in any danger?" I reasoned aloud, kind of almost starting to understand.

"You were not," he raised one eyebrow to regard me candidly. "Your power, your energy, stirs deeply within you when you need it. It responds to stimuli that it perceives without the emotional filter that you experience."

"So…" clarity was so close, so very close.

"You were never without me," he smiled, "and you never will be without me. We share power, but thus far you have not learned to wield it, as thus far you have had no need."

"Ah," I nodded as the cartoon lightbulb above my head finally lit up, "so, I'm not just more than I was, I'm much more than I was!"

"You are indeed," my mate embraced me in delight, "and I have been waiting for you to come to this understanding."

"Why couldn't you have just told me this stuff?"

"How would I have explained it?" A tiny smile played around his lips, "You had no foundation of understanding upon which I could have built this explanation."

"Well, yes," I admitted begrudgingly, "I see that. But, you and I are going to have to discuss this again, and probably many, many more times!"

"I assure you that we shall, my love," Amon hugged me tightly then released me and took my hand once more, "but right now we should return to the estate. You must be weary and I have business to attend."

Following him down the trail, holding his hand, and this time paying attention to the path beneath my feet, I replayed snippets of what had happened at the library as well as the conversation my mate and I had just had. The little voice in my head kept screaming *"There's something missing here!"* but I had every intention of being satisfied with my understanding as it was and put the little voice on 'ignore'.

As we reached the canyon floor I yanked my hand from my mate's and stood stock still.

"What would have happened if the blast of dragon fire had turned me to ashes like it did all the others?" What I'd felt missing had been suddenly found and I couldn't help but blurt out the question.

"I would have moved Heaven and Earth to bring you back," Amon said simply and took my hands in his, "or I would have waited for you as I did before."

"Ah," I smiled, "you're such a romantic!"

Chapter 35

W hen my eyes fluttered open I found myself staring at the ceiling of the coffin room. I yawned and stretched as I sat upright and peered around the room. Before the shelves on the wall beside the door, Amon stood with his back to me, an exquisitely tailored coat stretched across his broad shoulders and his jet black hair gathered in a black leather thong.

"My darling," I called gently to let him know that I was awake.

"Sweetie!" Chimaera smiled broadly as he turned around.

"You!" I snarled, feeling not only disappointed but dismayed, "What are you doing here?"

"His Lordship sent me to watch over you until you awakened," he offered, diamond stud in his left earlobe gleaming in the light, "and to fetch you."

"Fetch me," I grumbled, making my way out of the coffin, trying to decide just how angry I wanted to be. "What am I, a stick?"

"Fine," the dark haired vamp with impossibly pale blue eyes replied, "then he sent me to escort you upstairs, as you have guests."

"Guests are people you invite," I offered, padding barefoot across the room to gather my clothes. "I didn't invite anyone."

"Perhaps His Lordship invited them," Chimaera suggested.

"Where's Winter?"

"I'm sure I don't know," he shrugged.

"So why did Amon send you?" I glared at him.

"I do not question His Lordship's directives," he shrugged, "or his reasons for them. Perhaps that's why one of us in this room does not bear a Mark of Obedience."

"I don't bear a Mark of Obedience," I retorted, "and turn around while I dress!"

"You bear two-thirds of a Mark of Obedience," he grinned and turned his back to me, "and that's two-thirds more than I have."

"Chimaera," I sighed, "I've had a really rough few nights of late and I really don't need your attitude before I've had my first cup of coffee. So, who are these visitors?"

"Agathodemon," Chimaera said succinctly.

"Oh great," I huffed as I stepped out of my gray lounging pants and camisole and donned blue jeans, lace bra, and white silk tunic.

"Help me with these," I tried not to sound pushy, "please, Chimaera." I gathered my forearm holsters and blades and turned around. "I can put them on by myself but it will be faster if you do it."

"What am I now," he sighed dramatically, "your lady in waiting?"

"You would make one seriously ugly lady in waiting," I laughed, imagining him in feminine court attire

"And now I'm ugly?" he feigned being insulted, but he accepted the leather holsters and pushed my sleeves up to strap them on me,

"You know darn well that you're too pretty," I admitted, "and scary as hell!"

"Aw," he grinned wickedly, "I'm flattered!" He secured the blade holster on my right arm and then turned to do the same on my left arm. "There, all done."

"Thank you," I pulled my blouson sleeves down over the weapons and buttoned the cuffs. "Come on." I headed toward the door as Chimaera turned to follow. As we made our way along the corridor I glanced over my shoulder at the gorgeous and obviously very pleased with himself vampire. "And I'll need to stop up here and put my contacts in and brush my hair," I indicated a guest restroom a few doors ahead.

"Fine," he positioned himself beside the door and crossed his arms over his chest, "I'll wait here."

Quickly, anxious to get the meeting with the Agathodemon over with, I smoothed my mane down with a brush, put dark green colored contact lenses in my eyes, and slipped a pair of dark glasses up my nose. When I stepped out into the hall I found Chimaera leaning against the wall, hands crossed over his chest, chin down and eyes closed.

"Sleepy?" I snapped, in an effort to both startle and insult him.

"I am not," he dropped his arms to his side and slowly opened those long-lashed impossibly blue eyes to regard me evenly. "I was listening."

"To what?"

"That is none of your concern," he rebuffed me.

"Fine," I huffed, "then let's go." Not bothering to wait for him, I shook my hair out, smoothed my shirt and started quickly down the hall. I could hear by the sound his boots made that he was hurrying to keep pace with me.

The scene that greeted me in the Great Hall brought me abruptly to a halt. Snarl stood just inside the large double doors wearing a beautiful black suit. His deep gray hair had been smoothed back into a ponytail and the vivid green shirt he wore beneath his jacket enhanced the green aura that was so pronounced when he was in his dragon form. The two Agathodemon beside him were both in their natural state and their shiny scales shimmered the same or very similar green. It crossed my mind that we were likely meeting in the Great Hall so the two creatures could appear as they did, as they'd surely not fit comfortably into the study. My mate stood speaking with the trio until he sensed my arrival, then he nodded to the guests and turned to smile at me. Unable to imagine the cause for such a visit, I moved hesitantly to take Amon's out-stretched hand.

"My love," he greeted me warmly.

"Darling," I nodded and kissed him briefly, "I see we have guests!"

"Indeed," he smiled slightly, and turned to the trio of Agathodemon, "you remember Snarl, and Gristbite."

"I do," I responded politely and succinctly.

"And this is Sear," he introduced the second dragon demon, whom I'd not seen before.

"Sear," I nodded, not quite sure what was proper when being introduced to an Agathodemon in dragon form. Did one offer one's hand? Did one curtsey? Did one bow?

"My Lady," Snarl stepped forward and smiled, his golden eyes glittering, "we are sorry to disturb you, but a matter of some importance has arisen, and well, it involves you."

"What matter?" I asked quickly, hoping to inspire the dragon demon to get to the point.

"Well," he replied, "this!" From Sear he took what I first thought was a white fur-covered pillow with a pale hairless cat curled up asleep on it, but when he presented it to me and I realized he meant me to accept it, I physically took a step back.

"Um," I mumbled, "what is it?"

"It's Ravage's offspring," he explained, "and she wished for you to have it."

"Who's Ravage?" I blinked in surprise.

"The Agathodemon who sacrificed herself to save you," Snarl said proudly.

"So, this is a baby Agathodemon?" I marveled, "And the dragon demon who saved me wants me to, what, raise her offspring? What was she doing on the battlefield anyway if she had a baby? Why wasn't she home tending to her child?"

"Ravage was a warrior, Cat," Snarl offered, "and it was not her place to raise her child, daughter in fact. That task would have fallen to nurse maids and tutors."

"So why don't these nurse maids and tutors have," I pointed to the creature curled up on the pillow, "her?"

"Ravage also had the gift of 'sight'," Gristbite interjected, "and knew what would happen. It was her wish that you raise her daughter."

"What did she see?" I couldn't help but wonder aloud.

"We do not know," Snarl seemed to reclaim the conversation. "Her vision was recorded but it was secreted until the time for us to know is right. She did make it clear that her daughter was to be given to you."

Three imaginary mes were busy in my mind, one was whining "Oh, crap!" and the second was doing her impression of Scarlett O'Hara's maid Prissy wringing her hands on her apron and crying "I don't know nuthin' 'bout raisin' no dragons!". The third me was designing a business card that read "Catherine Alexander-Blair du Montjean, Dragon Master." All imaginary mes were in agreement that Master was better than Mistress.

"What's her name?" I struggled to erase the various images from my mind and focus on the matter at hand.

"The child has no name yet," Gristbite offered.

"Um, well," I shook my head slowly, "don't get me wrong. I'm truly flattered by the gesture, but I don't know how to raise an Agathodemon! I wouldn't know where to begin."

"Rest assured that infant Agathodemon need nowhere near the time or care that human infants do," Sear spoke for the first time and I realized she was female, though she was about the same size as Gristbite so perhaps she was small for a female dragon. "Agathodemon young sleep for months at a time and only awaken when they need to eat or drink. They eat only two or three times a year and grow quite slowly."

"So at what age is an infant considered a child?" I struggled to imagine, "And for that matter when are they considered adult? When can they take care of themselves, leave the nest, as it were?"

"She will mostly sleep and eat for three of your years," Sear blinked ruby eyes at me, "and after that she will develop her own abilities and be able to interact with you as we do."

"So do I have to teach her to speak and to speak English?" I knew the questions were coming fast and furious but there was just so much to consider. I couldn't help but ask one question after another.

"You need teach her nothing like that, but she will learn from you," Snarl offered, "and of course, if you have questions we are at your disposal."

"Does this all have something to do with me seeing those three Elder Agathodemon?"

"It may," he nodded, heavy lids blinking over those golden eyes. "We do not know Ravage's reasoning. We are just doing her bidding to honor her sacrifice."

"Erm," I stepped forward and accepted the pillow, peering closely at the infant Agathodemon curled there sleeping silently, "will she sleep on this pillow? Does she need a bed or a den or something?"

"Beloved," Amon stepped closer to me, "I was contacted previously and have appointed a room deep beneath us adjacent to the wine cellar. Its walls are mostly stone and earth, the floor is earthen, and it is cool and dark. The young one will sleep and not be disturbed."

"You're okay with all this?" I gaped at my mate, surprised at his response.

"I am," he nodded, "and Ulrich agrees that it will be a good experience."

"Ulrich agrees," I wondered aloud. "So, what do we call her?"

"You will know when she does," Sear bowed slightly, "and in the meantime you may refer to her by whatever name you choose."

"Is that it?" I looked up at Snarl, then Sear, then Gristbite, whose eyes I noticed were so deep a green they looked black, "Is there anything else I should know? Is there anything she should not be allowed to do or eat or have? What does an infant Agathodemon eat?"

"A couple of goats or a steer," Snarl shrugged. "Just put it in her den and she'll do the rest. As for anything to avoid? There is nothing we fear, no substance or element is a threat."

"Are you sure about this?" I held the sleeping dragon in my arms, feeling her weight and the warmth of her body. Her skin, and I noticed that it was skin and not scales like her adult counterparts, was pale pink tinged with gray and I wondered when her scales would begin appearing. I wondered about a lot in truth!

"Ravage was sure," Sear offered, "and we trust her judgment, so yes, we are sure."

"Be aware that this is an extremely rare occurrence," Gristbite chimed in. "There has not been an infant Agathodemon raised by another species in many, many centuries. We will be watching, of course, but the child is yours."

"Um," I was suddenly speechless.

"We shall take care of her," Amon offered, sensing that I was overwhelmed. "Thank you for the honor."

"Yes," I managed to utter, "thank you."

"We'll leave you now," Snarl bowed dramatically, "but we still hope to be able to speak with you regarding your experience with the Elders, perhaps someday soon?"

"Of course," I sighed in relief, happy to be thinking about something other than how we were going to deal with raising an Agathodemon. "Perhaps in a few weeks when we've gotten the wee one settled."

"Yes," the golden-eyed dragon demon hissed his s's slightly, I noticed, "soon!"

With that the trio let themselves out the double doors and Amon and I stood blinking in wonder, well, me more than him, I'm sure. Chimaera cleared his throat and I startled, almost dropping the sleeping infant, pillow and all, to the floor. I think my mate and I both glared at the guard before he spoke.

"Would you like me to take the Agathodemon to its den?"

"Thanks, Chimaera," I replied, recovering the precious bundle nicely, "but I want to do it myself. I want to see her quarters and make sure she's okay."

"Of course," he nodded, "then if you've no further need?"

"Go," Amon commanded, "see to your duties."

Offering no further comment, Chimaera made his way past us and exited the front doors, ostensibly to return to his security detail.

My mate took the sleeping bundle on her pillow and I shook my arms, relieved to be free of the weight. I had to admit, from what I could see, and it wasn't much as she was curled up so tightly I could recognize only one tiny ear, the curve of a brow and part of one closed eyelid, the infant Agathodemon was cute. Well, I considered, maybe cute wasn't the proper term, but she was certainly something wonderful!

"Come, my darling," my mate suggested, "I'll show you where she will be staying."

"Yes," I couldn't help but reach out and touch the top of her head ever so gently with one finger, "let's get her settled."

As we made our way to the lower level of the estate, Amon carried the pillow upon which the infant slept almost ceremoniously. He was strong enough that he could hold her away from his body, though I knew it would be impossible for me. I'd be cradling her like a football. I'd known there was a wine cellar in the mansion, but I'd never been there or been curious enough to ask where it was so I was only slightly surprised when we passed Ulrich's quarters and turned abruptly around a corner then started down another flight of stairs.

"So, this is what?" I asked Amon as we continued going deeper, "A sub-basement?"

"Yes," he replied, "that is what it would be considered. Just to the right here and the room beneath the stairs. This is the wine cellar and the infant's room is just to the left."

Stepping before him, I opened the door and let Amon go past me, flipping a light switch on the wall beside the door. The small cave-like room appeared almost magically as the overhead lights came on. It actually did look a bit like a dragon's den, with a rounded stone ceiling and earthen floor. It was cool but not cold and seemed quite dry and comfortable.

"This looks perfect!" I clapped my hands softly, "I had no idea this place existed, and here I thought I'd seen the whole place!"

"There are still some parts of the estate you have yet to see," my mate explained as he crossed the room and gently placed the pillow on the floor in the corner. "But the infant should be safe and undisturbed here."

"Wow!" I gasped, holding Amon's arm as we both looked down at the sleeping dragon demon. "I have a dragon! Or, well, WE have a dragon!"

"So it would seem," he turned and regarded me with an inscrutable expression. "And now we should probably leave her be."

"Yes," I sighed, unable to take my eyes from the child, "I'm sure you're right. We should leave her be."

I meant what I said, but I was enchanted and wanted nothing more than to stand there and stare at her. Amon took my hand and gently pulled me toward the door, turning off the light as we left the room.

"She sleeps so quietly," I gushed, "did you notice that? She doesn't even snore! I think I always expected that dragons would snore. Maybe she'll snore when she gets older. Do you think she'll snore? I wonder if she'll be able to breathe fire. Wonder what her wings look like, she was curled so tightly I couldn't even see them. Did you notice her wings?"

"Catherine," my beloved stopped and turned me to face him, lifting my chin with one curled index finger, "I understand your excitement, but you really must calm down. I am sure your questions will be answered in time."

"Sure," I sighed in defeat, "I know, I know. But, but, this is like getting a puppy for Christmas! We have a dragon! I mean, how cool is that? We have a dragon!"

"We do," he agreed, wrapping his arms around me and silencing me with a long, luscious kiss, "and we have the rest of the night to ourselves."

"Mmmm," was the only response I could offer as his tongue found its way into my mouth and his hands moved gently up my back.

"Now," he spoke calmly when finally the kiss was ended and he took one step back, "you have some training to do with Ulrich, but when you are done I would very much like you to ride the property with me, if you would care to join me?"

"That would be great!" I beamed, then glanced back in the direction of the Agathodemon's den, "You think she'll be alright? Maybe we should watch her for tonight? What if something disturbs her sleep? How would we know?"

"My darling," he sighed deeply, possibly losing patience with me, "Gristbite told me that an infant dragon demon can sleep through an artillery barrage and turn around and be awakened by a feather falling to the floor."

"So how will…" I started to whine. I could feel myself doing it, but was powerless to stop.

"He also told me that we will know it when the infant wakes," Amon insisted. "Apparently long before they awaken their body heat increases to the point where the very air that surrounds them is almost unbearable to a human. I have a climate control monitor on every room on the estate, and the one in the wine cellar is especially sophisticated, so I will be alerted if and when her room begins to warm."

"But," I really wanted to stay close to our newcomer.

657

"Catherine," Amon lowered his voice into a reprimand and I knew I'd lost the struggle. "You have studies with Ulrich, and then we will ride, yes?"

"Fine," I huffed and found myself crossing my arms tightly. I did manage to refrain from pouting, only just.

Ulrich was waiting for me in the study and we spoke at length over what had just transpired and how exciting it was to have such a creature on the estate. We did a bit of work on the computer, mostly discussing the details of my accounts of my new abilities and how I experienced what I experienced. I successfully made myself invisible, walked around the downstairs of the mansion and returned, only to find my mentor yawning hugely. I knew that though he'd been trying to adjust his sleep patterns to match those of us nocturnal he'd not be especially effective. Often after midnight he began growing tired and was sometimes drowsy long before sunrise. When he rested his head on the back of the sofa and closed his eyes, probably intending only to rest for a moment, I sat silently for a few moments and was then rewarded with the sound of his breathing growing deep and regular. I could see his chest rise and fall as sleep took him so I tiptoed out of the room and went upstairs to put on my riding gear.

My beloved awaited me at the doors to the veranda, handing me a pair of riding gloves and donning his own.

He wore his black riding coat, dark trousers, white linen shirt and black riding boots. My riding coat was similarly styled but was rich deep brown and there was leather piping along the edge of the collar. As we headed out to the stables, he held my arm in his and I wasn't sure if he was being gallant or was in fear that I'd bolt back to the house to watch the Agathodemon sleeping in her den. And though that thought had crossed my mind I made no mention of the matter. Lucius had Belladonna and Abraxis saddled and waiting, tied to the posts before the stable and I easily swung myself up into the saddle and took the reins from Amon when he handed them up to me. He followed suit, turned Abraxis and headed him to the security code protected gate. Beyond the estate wall we rode easily taking in the night. The gibbous moon rode high in the sky as mid-summer was approaching and it felt like autumn would soon arrive. We spoke very little on our ride, likely we were both thinking about what had happened and what might soon happen, and returned to the estate relaxed and possibly relieved.

Later, toward the wee hours before dawn, I lay in Amon's embrace in our shared coffin.

"My love," I started, "did you notice that though the Agathodemon all seem to look alike in their dragon forms, their eyes differ in color from one to the next?"

"I did notice that, yes," he replied. "And what made you think of that?"

"I was trying to come up with a name for the little one," I explained, "and thought there might be some inspiration there. I mean, I didn't even see Ravage, so I don't have a clue what color her eyes were. Did you see them that day on the battlefield?"

"I did," he nodded slowly, "however briefly, yes I did!"

"What color were her eyes?"

"I should think they would be considered emerald green," he smiled gently and kissed my forehead.

"Emerald green," I mused aloud. "Okay, I'll call her Emmy then, until she's old enough to tell us otherwise."

"Very well," he squeezed my shoulders, "Emmy she shall be."

When I awoke the following evening I was so confused. I knew where I was, of course, but my thoughts and memories were scrambled.

"Amon," I rubbed my eyes with one hand and looked into the blood red eyes of my mate, "I had the weirdest dream! I dreamed we had a baby dragon and were going to raise her, and she spoke to me in my dreams. Isn't that hysterical?"

"That my darling," he kissed the corner of my eye and whispered into my left ear, "was no dream."

"We have a dragon?" I sat bolt upright in the coffin, trying to put the images in my mind into some semblance of order. "And we're calling her Emmy?"

"We do," he said simply and sat upright beside me, "and we are."

"Wow!" I gaped, still amazed that what I'd thought a dream was real, well, what passed for real in my world. "Can I go see her?"

"Of course you may," he smiled and stepped easily from the coffin. "In fact, the infant should be checked on nightly. I will monitor the temperature of her room from the security office."

"Cool!" I laughed and climbed out of the coffin to dress. I couldn't wait to go see Emmy, to see if she'd moved in her sleep, to see if she was making any sound, to see if anything had changed.

To my dismay and disappointment I found the baby Agathodemon had not moved at all. When I turned on the light in her room, her den, I found her in the exact same position she'd been when we turned off the light the night before. She didn't snore. She didn't move. She didn't open her eyes.

"Wow," I sighed, "this isn't like getting a puppy for Christmas anymore! It's like getting a dead puppy for Christmas!"

Sure, I realized that dragon demons grew slowly, aged very slowly, and lived for centuries, but what fun was it having a baby dragon if all it did was sleep? At least Siri came to see me, licked my face, wagged her tail and burped wicked dog breath at me. The excitement of being a 'Dragon Master' was quickly wearing off.

Chapter 36

As I stepped out the back door of Lamey's, the night wind grabbed my hair and whipped it into my face. With one hand holding my violin case and the other holding a cup of steaming black coffee, my purse dangling from its strap on my shoulder, I had no choice but to bear the annoying tendril obstructing my vision until I reached my car. Resting the violin case atop the Miata's roof, I fished my keys out of my jeans pocket and pressed the 'unlock' button before opening the driver's side door. I slung my purse inside, grabbed the case, and folded myself into the leather bucket seat keeping one eye on the coffee cup, even though it had a lid on it. After slipping the violin into its custom harness near the passenger seat I shoved the key into the ignition and started the car. Once I'd put my coffee into the cup holder on the console, I released the brake and shifted the car into reverse. Finally hands-free, I pulled the hair from my face and raked the little dark glasses from my nose before depositing them on the dash. I was tired, I realized, though it was a happy tired.

Estella, Lamey's manager, had changed the schedule for bands and performers and, to my delight, she'd scheduled us to play from eleven to one, the much coveted 'center' spot between the early and the late bands. From nine to eleven was when the younger crowd swarmed in, dressed to the nines, reeking of cologne, soap, and hair product, and from one to three in the morning, when the night club closed on Saturdays, the hearty partiers, too smashed to make it home but not ready to give up, danced and sang to southern rock bands or heavy metal noise. Our slot, thankfully, was perfect for 'Unseelie' music. It was an older crowd and they were polite, relaxed in their drinks, but not yet inebriated enough to start being rowdy and loud.

The performance had gone well and we had even gotten an ovation, which we graciously accepted, and played two more tunes before saying good night. I was pleased. I was relieved. And I was delighted to be heading home. The night sky was clear, the waning moon not yet visible, and the traffic was light for the wee hours of Saturday morning so I swung the Miata out of the parking lot and into the northbound lane of Holland street. Interstate 10 lay just a few miles up the way and I looked forward to pointing my vehicle east and standing on the gas pedal. When a traffic light turned red I pressed on the brakes and felt the violin case shift in its holder as my purse slid off the passenger seat into the floor.

"Crap!" I fumed as I realized I'd forgotten my stage clothes bag behind. Of course Estella or one of the other employees would no doubt find it and keep it safe for me, and had I been farther away from the night club, even out on the interstate, I might not have bothered to go back for it. But here I was, still fairly near, and it would be no huge inconvenience to go back, so I swung into the church parking lot to turn the car around. As I bounced over the low curb from the street to the paved lot, my headlights briefly illuminated someone standing there. I pulled hard on the steering wheel and brought the car to a halt. There had been no impact; I was sure that I'd not actually hit anyone, but I had to see for myself who, if anyone, had been standing in the church parking lot at such an hour and why. I popped the button on my seat belt, let the strap retract itself, opened the door, and stepped out of the car.

At first I saw no one as I scanned the area only slightly illuminated by distant street lamps and a security light over the side door of the church. Then, as I turned to get back into the car, I noticed the wizened woman I'd seen here before standing impossibly in front of my head-lights. Siri, or an identical dog, sat stoically beside the aged, disheveled looking old lady and my first thought was 'She's got my dog!'

"Siri," I smiled, half greeting and half calling the black German shepherd. I was so relieved to see her again.

"You have no idea how difficult it is to reach you," the old woman croaked in an unsteady voice, raising one gnarled index finger to point accusingly at me.

"Reach me," I shook my head in confusion, "why would you want to reach…" My question dried up in my mind and on my tongue as the woman's image began to shift, to straighten, and to grow in height and width. Her curly, frizzy looking gray hair smoothed, relaxed and even grew longer as her facial features became sharper, more angular, and most surprisingly, more masculine. Even as I watched, fascinated and somewhat repulsed, the slumped and wrinkled old lady straightened, rose, and morphed into a tall, broad, distinguished looking man. Oddly enough, one eye was covered with a black patch, and I thought it amusing that such a detail should appear.

"The beast's name is not Siri," he spoke clearly with a deep, resonant voice. "How it was that you could not hear the name clearly, I don't know, unless that too was part of the shield that kept me from reaching you."

"I," I muttered, completely confused now, "um."

"The dog's name is Geri," the man stepped closer and I felt a twinge of recognition. His one visible blue eye was clear and bright, his cheeks had a healthy glow and his brow was unwrinkled and wide. His gray beard was only slightly darker than his hair, at least it appeared so to me, and his lips were full and fringed by a thick mustache. His clothes were mostly hidden by an oversized garment that might have, at one time, been a stylish trench coat, but there was something in his demeanor that made me believe his appearance was a facade.

"Who are you?" I managed to utter before my thoughts took to the wind and left me speechless once more.

"Do you know me not, Child?" He spread his hands in an inviting gesture and smiled, and as he did so the dog began to dance, wag its tail, and jump up and down.

"I, um," I shook my head then his words sank in and I recognized the voice. "You! It was your voice I heard in the garden. You told me not to keep the promise made to Ian!"

"It was my voice, yes," he nodded, "and I did tell you not to turn the creature you had before you into what you now are."

"Why?" I gaped, "I mean, how, and why, and..."

"My child," he smiled and the light surrounding him made me take a step backwards, bringing my right hip into painful contact with the doorframe of the car. "I am Odin."

"Odin," I mouthed the name as I tried to plug what I knew about the Norse God into my functioning brain. Two thoughts raced towards one another in my mind. 'Holy Crow, it's the All-father!' was only slightly ahead of 'Oh Helsa! It's another freakin' deity and that's NEVER a good thing for me!' and the resulting crash effectively ceased all thought for a few moments. I think I blinked a few times, but I wouldn't swear to it.

"I am also known as Woden or Wotan," he continued speaking slowly as if he knew my mind wasn't functioning at its maximum.

"Woden," I echoed, "or Wotan." Independent speech had not yet been recovered.

"I have been trying to insinuate myself into your world for some time, my dear," the All-father explained. "When first we met I was sure you would sense who I was, but you did not so I sent you a portal that you might join me and we could get to know one another."

"Portal," I mumbled, my mind grasping for purchase.

"And when you failed to come to me I had no choice but to send you Arathia's athame," he continued explaining the fantastic as if he was reciting a grocery list. "You see, when Amon, your warrior, destroyed Arathia it fell to me to hold her things until a worthy replacement could be found. We've been watching you these few short years and it's been decided unanimously that you are that worthy replacement."

"Unanimously," I murmured, wondering if that was an avenue I really wanted to explore further.

"Yes," he nodded curtly.

"So, you sent Wicked Little Thing?" I gaped at the powerful Norse God.

"As that is what you now call it, yes," he smiled broadly.

"So why insinuate yourself?" I mimed quotation marks in the air. "Why not just drop by the house for a beer or a cup of tea?"

"My child," he beamed with amusement, "as addled as your mind is at the moment, as scattered as your thoughts are, as close to being overwhelmed as you now stand in my presence, can you imagine how you might have reacted had I come at you directly? By feeding you subtle hints as to my proximity to you, I've been opening your mind to accepting me."

"So you mean that had you just dropped by the mansion, knocked on the door and introduced yourself out of the blue," I reasoned, "this confusion I'm experiencing would have been so much worse?"

"Most assuredly," he agreed, "and you might have even been unable to grasp it."

"And what," I laughed, "my brain would have exploded?"

"Let's just say I would prefer to avoid that possibility," he joined in the laughter.

"So wait," I waved both hands in the air as if to erase all previous conversation, "why are you here again?"

"There are many reasons," he replied, "but first and foremost is to greet you as a child of mine and to ask you to serve me."

"Child of yours?" Saying it aloud didn't clarify the concept in my mind, "And...serve you?"

"Yes, Catherine, you are indeed a Child of Odin," he nodded emphatically, "and when I say 'serve me' I do not mean that you need bend knee or offer sacrifices. None of that nonsense!"

"So, okay, fine, let's say I am your child," I tried coming at the issue at hand from another direction, "and let's say I'm good with serving you. What exactly does that mean? How do I serve you?"

"It's really rather simple," he smiled mischievously, "you see, I would just work in this world through you."

"And, how exactly would that happen?"

"Just as it did in the garden and in your dreams," he brightened even more as if that was helpful. "You

670

would just hear my words in your mind from time to time as I guide you towards certain ends."

"That doesn't sound so bad," I shrugged, relieved that I'd not have to perform some task to prove my worthiness or some such other nonsense.

"It will not be bad at all," he agreed, "and in fact I have been guiding you, in various small ways, for some time now. But, as the stakes are becoming higher, you need to take a more active role in matters, which is why I am here now with this offer."

"Guiding me in various small ways?" Curiosity was struggling to surface amidst my confusion.

"Well, as I said, I sent the portal to you that you might join me, but as that didn't work out as I'd expected," the All-Father offered, "I adjusted the portal's energy that you might use it to learn the truth of your foes."

"Zador and Naomi?" Suddenly clarity dawned as I recalled my journey through times via the portal.

"Just so, my child," nodding succinctly, he continued, "and it's this and similar guidance I now offer you."

"I can refuse this guidance?"

"You may refuse," he nodded. "When you hear my words or receive guidance from me in any form, you have the choice to accept it or deny it."

"Okay, fine," I heaved a sigh, "I accept your guidance and agree to serve you, so to speak. Thank you for

Wicked Little Thing, and for allowing me the company of your beast, Geri, for a while. Is there more I need to know?"

"Perhaps we could relax in your coach for a bit," he suggested, "as this last bit I'm about to explain make take some concentration and we might as well be comfortable."

"Sure," I walked around the nose of the Miata and opened the passenger side door, removed my violin from its holder, and stepped back out of the way, "please, do have a seat."

Now, when I'd first pulled into the parking lot, the gnarled old hag I'd seen standing with the black German shepherd was maybe 5'5" or so, but when she'd transformed she'd grown both taller and wider. The Norse god I'd been speaking with had probably been 6'8" or more and his chest was wide enough to make two of me so I found it amusing that he'd suggest we sit in my car, as the little sports job had been known to make pretzels of shorter men. I was only able to fit comfortably in it because the driver's seat slid back far enough that my knees didn't smack the steering wheel. Still, to my surprise, and yes, I was still surprised, Odin slipped easily into the passenger seat and his body seemed to naturally adjust to the size of the space. He closed the door and looked around the interior of the car, then picked my cup of coffee up out of the cup holder. Sniffing the brew through the small hole in the lid, his eyebrows lifted and he smiled.

"May I?" He asked politely and I could see that he was anxious for a taste.

"Please," I nodded, wondering at the notion that I was sitting in my car sharing my coffee with the All-father, "help yourself!"

Taking a tentative sip, Odin savored the now cooling brew and swallowed it with a smile.

"Wonderful stuff," he put the cup to his lips and drank again, "wonderful!"

"Yes, the coffee's good," I agreed, trying not to be impatient when I was. I waited as the All-father drank what was left in my cup, secretly relieved that it had been far from full when I'd left the nightclub.

"Now," Odin wiped his mouth on the back of his hand and replaced the empty cup in the cup holder, "as to how you will serve me."

"Yes, that," I murmured, part of me curious and another part full of dread.

"I shall put you at the center of Arathia's energy," he heaved a satisfied sigh.

"Say what?"

"Let me explain," he began patiently. "First of all, nothing is truly ever destroyed. Energy transforms, it changes, but it never ceases to be. When Arathia's form was destroyed her energy was scattered, oh, granted not very far at first though over time her essences drifted farther and farther apart. For a time she was so expanded that she had no consciousness and almost no will. But, as like attracts like, eventually her essences were drawn back to one another and her conscious mind returned, her will roared back into focus and she began to re-manifest herself."

"Wait, what?" I struggled to make sense of what Odin was saying. Yes, I had some general understanding of physics, but this was a bit beyond me. "Arathia can re-will herself back into existence?"

"Not entirely," he held up one index finger and paused. "She had imbued parts of her energy into physical objects, the athame being the primary one and the Grimoire being the secondary. Those objects must be drawn together for her will to focus enough for her to manifest once more in this world. This is why I have orchestrated things so that you, and you alone, will be in the center of her energy, so you can keep it from coalescing."

"Why me?" Okay, yes, there was a tiny pity party going on in the back of my mind and it threatened to overflow.

"Because, my child," he smiled softly, "your energy is the polar opposite of hers. You need do nothing but be, as it is your nature to be creative and generous. It is Arathia's nature to be cruel and avaricious."

"So, I don't actually have to do anything to keep Arathia from returning to this world?"

"You have already thwarted her," Odin replied. "For it was her energy you felt inside that young man in the garden. It was she who wanted you to transform him into a vampire so she could use his physical form to continue to gain strength through that immortality. By having your warrior destroy the human, you released his energy and scattered hers once more."

"That was Arathia I felt in Ian?" I marveled, though it seemed reasonable. "Wait! I used Arathia's athame to kill her?"

"You used YOUR athame to injure her host," he offered by way of explanation, "but your mate destroyed her once again with his Hand of Destruction."

"But she had no connection or control over Wicked Little Thing?" I insisted.

"Not in the state she was in," he shrugged, "and by then the athame had claimed you as its own. So now you know everything. The athame is at your beckon call, I understand you've secreted the Grimoire safely away, and for now, Arathia remains not in this world. You, and you alone, stand against her."

"Well, not totally alone, right?" I grinned, "I mean, you've got my back, so to speak."

"I do," he laughed and it seemed to echo around the small car. "So, do you have questions?"

"I'm sure I do," I confessed with a weak laugh, "but at the moment I've no clue what they are."

"You may always just ask," he assured me as he opened the car door and put one foot on the pavement. "I am at your service."

"Wait," I had a sudden thought, "did you orchestrate things with the Agathodemon? I mean, did you set it up so I'd take a hit of dragon fire and survive? Did you arrange things so I'd end up raising a dragon?"

"I did not," he laughed and the air around us seemed to shimmer with his delight, "but I'm most pleased with how that happened. And I love that you have a dragon!"

"Ah, cool," I opened my door and got out of the car, thinking it was the polite thing to do to stand when a God leaves one's company. "I, um…"

"Catherine," he walked around the nose of the Miata and by the time he reached my side he was once more tall and wide, a powerful presence. "I know that you are still a bit overwhelmed, despite your previous experience with Nemesis, but just know that you have pleased me greatly by accepting my offer. It brings me great joy to know that one such as you, in this world, in this time, is willing to serve me." He spread his arms and actually folded me into an embrace.

My confusion ceased. My thoughts were like crystals. I felt such a deep, powerful sense of peace wash over me and through me.

"May I ask a question now?" I looked up into one brilliant blue eye.

"Ask, child," he looked down at me.

"Vampires don't normally dream, I'm told," I offered by way of introduction, "and I get that I'm witch also, which may be the cause, but I do still dream. You mentioned contacting me in dreams and I now recall hearing you. So, I guess my question is…will I ever cease to dream? Amon thought my dreams might disappear over time. Will they?"

"Ah, yes," he smiled kindly, "I understand your query, and the answer is no, you shall never cease to dream."

"But," I stammered, "why? Is it because I'm a witch?"

"Cat, my darling," the All-father favored me with the most incredible smile, "it's not because you're a witch. You are a child of mine and we do our best work together when you are sleeping. That is when your resistance is, shall we say, least resistant? And, might I add that your resistance is quite formidable. Getting you to the forest meeting with the gnomes nearly wore me out!"

"Wait, the dream with the gnomes?" I gasped at the sudden appearance of the memory of what I'd thought was a dream, "You mean to tell me that actually happened? I was really there?"

"You were," he nodded, "and that was no mean feat, I can tell you! I had to bombard your mind with a good number of fantastic images to get my foot in the door."

"So," I puzzled aloud, "was that a dream or wasn't it? Was I really there or not? Now I'm confused!"

"You were there," Odin assured me, "though not in your physical form. The gnomes do not exist on this physical plane. Had I not gotten you to the elementals that created that charm, it would have eventually taken over your will. After you returned it to them, which I knew you would do, and they gave it back to you, they gave you control over it."

"So, what does that mean?" I was starting to almost put things together.

"It means that you control the tiny sword," he explained patiently, "and that means that you now can control the elements."

"Huh?" I gaped in utter surprise.

The All-father released a peel of laughter unlike anything I'd ever heard before. It was an amazing, musical, laugh of delight and it nearly lifted me off my feet.

"Relax, Cat," he grinned, "you CAN control the elements, but that doesn't mean you have to do so. Think of the ability as just another weapon in your arsenal."

"Good heavens!" Unable to restrain my amazement, I blurted out, "Just how many weapons do I need?"

"You may have no need," he admitted, "but then again, one never knows!"

When the All-father released me and turned to go, he uttered the dog's name and Geri appeared out of nowhere, happily scampering beside him. Another, almost identical, black German shepherd appeared at his other side and as he disappeared across the tarmac I thought I saw two dark birds swoop down from the sky and land on his shoulders, but that might have been my imagination as my mind started swirling again. The All-father and his two canines walked across the parking lot when suddenly a wind blew his hair and his cloak. He and the beasts scattered into a flock of birds that rose into the night sky.

"What did you expect, Cat?" I chided myself, "It's not like a Norse god, no, the Big Cheese of all Norse gods, would grab a taxi or jump on a Vespa to depart. Gotta admit, that was one pretty cool exit though!"

Climbing back into the car, I considered returning to Lamey's for my bag and had just replaced the violin in its mesh harness when something beneath the passenger seat caught my eye. Reaching down with one hand, I caught the corner of my canvas performing gear bag. It had been there all along!

"No, no, no," I murmured, shaking my head, "that's impossible. There's not even enough room beneath that seat for this bag! I know it wasn't there when I left the club."

Had Odin made the thing appear in my car? Had he made it disappear so that I'd be forced to turn into the parking lot to turn around and go back for it? Had it been my imagination?

As I slid the seat belt across my chest and snapped it into place a sudden thought appeared and I slapped my hand against the steering wheel.

"Dang!" I fumed, "I didn't even think to ask if I could have the dog back!"

Starting the engine, I flipped on the headlights, jammed the gear shift on the console into reverse, backed around to point the Miata at the street once more, and wheeled out of the parking lot. Once more northbound on Holland, I relaxed, looking for the exit to I-10.

Part of me was anxious to get back to the estate and check on Emmy, though the temperature in her den had not changed according to my mate. Another part of me wanted to write a wicked expose book and rub it in the Council of Five's collective schnoz. Still another part of me wanted nothing more than to relax and disappear into the arms of my mate and forget what had happened in the past few weeks.

'Beloved, you are flying home to me?' Amon's voice clearly rang through my mind. For a change, it sounded like security, calm, a familiar anchor. Just feeling him with me helped my chaotic thoughts slow and settle. I knew I'd have plenty of thinking, remembering, and much considering to do in the near future, but for now I could happily put that all aside.

'I'm driving home to you, my love,' I responded in kind, *'and since the traffic's light I'll drive fast enough to almost fly!'* Laughing at the expression of consternation I knew Amon would have on his face at my response.

"But, you said that you would fly now," he reasoned.

"No, I said that I'd consider flying," I replied, *"and I did consider it. And then I reconsidered and decided to drive. I like to drive!"*

"But," he began.

"But me no buts, Warrior," I chuckled and cut him off succinctly. *"You know what they say when you've got a tiger by the tail."*

"*I,*" he paused to consider then continued, "*do not know what they say.*"

"*When you've got a tiger by the tail, don't let go!*"

"*Catherine,*" his confusion was edged with humor, "*I do not know…*"

"*Relax, my love,*" I turned the car onto the interstate and accelerated into the night, "*I'm coming home.*"

FURTHERMORE...
(An excerpt from "Cat's First")

The heady scent of blood brought me to my senses. The coppery, salty taste lingered on my tongue. Brittle leaves crunched beneath me as I stirred. My body felt stiff, sore, and strangely unfamiliar. With a sense of dread I opened one bleary eye, the other apparently not yet responding to commands.

Darkness filled the small clearing in the forest, but my nocturnal vision, even with one eye, was enough for me to see that I was not alone. Lifting my head slightly, I spied a body twenty feet or so from me. It appeared half-naked, battered and bruised, though I couldn't see if it was male or female. When I sat up, slowly and with great effort, I noticed another body beyond the first.

"What in the name of Heaven and Hell happened?" I croaked, my voice shaky and raspy.

No answer came.

Peering around the clearing I noticed that I was being watched. Pairs of strangely glowing eyes blinked, appearing and disappearing, between the trees. I recognized Amon's pack wolves. In the darkness, they stood silent and unmoving. It felt reassuring to have them with me.

As I pulled a twig from my tangled hair I noticed that my hands were stained with blood and dirt, and there was some sort of soft tissue matted with fur under my nails.

"What have I done?" I wondered aloud.

The line between my waking world and that of my dreams had blurred when I was made vampire. Surely this was some strange nightmare and I'd awaken any moment. Or perhaps I'd been drawn through another energy portal only to find myself deposited in a strange and foreign realm.

"This has got to be a dream!"

At the sound of leaves crunching, I looked up to see my beloved Amon striding quickly and purposefully into the clearing. He carried a long black garment which I realized could only be my cloak.

"Amon," I almost wept, so relieved was I to see him, "where am I? How did I get here? What's going on?"

"You have no memory, Little One?" He stood before me, one eyebrow raised, a look of concern on his face.

"I, um," I stammered, struggling for the right answer, "well, I…"

He extended one long, elegant hand to me and I put my hand in his. Gently, he drew me to my feet and wrapped the long, black velvet cloak around my naked body.

"This is a dream, isn't it?"

Amon simply regarded me silently.

Looking at the bodies on the ground, clearly battered and unmoving, the enormity of the possibility that I'd been the aggressor, that I might have caused the carnage before me, nearly brought me to my knees.

"Tell me this is a dream," I whispered, "and that I'll wake up. Wake me up, Amon. Please, wake me up!"

My beloved shook his head slightly before looking away.

"Garde rejetèe!" He commanded. The wolves surrounding the clearing turned, and in unison, silently disappeared into the forest.

"Wake me up now, my love," I wept into the velvet brocade vest he was wearing. He wrapped strong arms around me. "Wake me up."

Made in the USA
Middletown, DE
29 April 2019